GUARD OF HONOR

GUARD
OF
HONOR

A Novel by

WILLIAM P. KENNEDY

ST. MARTIN'S PRESS

New York

Design by Susan Hood

Library of Congress Cataloging-in-Publication Data

Kennedy, William P.
    Guard of honor / William P. Kennedy.
      p. cm.
    ISBN 0-312-09292-X
    I. Title.
    PS3561.E429G8   1993
    813'.54—dc20   93-7440
                                                  CIP

First Edition: July 1993
10 9 8 7 6 5 4 3 2 1

In Memory

Joaquin Lopez y Lopez
Ignacio Martin Baro
Ignacio Ellacuria
Juan Ramon Morino Pardo
Amando Lopez Quintana
Segundo Montes

Jesuit Priests
murdered
by officers of
The Salvadoran Army

THE
ATTACK

★ ★ ★

Dave Baldinger lifted his blackened face out of the grass, and listened carefully.

There were sounds. A gurgle from his right where the pool of swampy water seeped over a fallen tree and dropped into a near-dead stream. Screeches from the birds that skipped across the canopy of the rain forest. A rattling of leaves.

He pushed the brush aside so that he could see down the slope of the hill.

There was movement. A stirring in the undergrowth as a rat scampered after a fleeing lizard. A swaying at the edges of the marsh grass. The darting of light beams as they broke through the waving branches above.

But there was no sign of human life around the hut. Baldinger studied it through the steaming foliage; its walls of ill-fitting boards were topped by a rotted thatched roof. It waited, perfectly still, its face in an uneven clearing at the edge of the stream, its sides disappearing into the wall of vegetation that was slowly swallowing it back into the jungle.

He snaked his long, thin frame ahead another few inches, careful not to move the brush that shielded him. Then he waited, alert for any sign of guards who would be watching for him. Maybe his attack plan had worked. Maybe, by cutting through the swamp instead of following the high dry ground, he had gotten to them before they were ready for him.

He pushed back from the hill line, and slid noiselessly down the slope to where Luther Brown was waiting, nearly invisible in a tangle of dead branches.

"You got the attack," Baldinger whispered.

"Thanks," Brown sneered.

"Circle west, around the hill. Stay in the trees until you're behind it and then go in from the back." Baldinger used a stick to draw the route in the mud as he talked.

"What if there ain't no windows?" Brown asked.

"Make some! We'll get close. But we're not going in until you start shooting. Now move. Maybe we can surprise these mothers."

Brown pushed up onto his hands and knees and waved his arm toward Mex Cortines, Bobby Long, and Art Walters. They moved quickly, following Luther into the thicket.

Baldinger crawled further down the slope, around the edge of the dead pond. He pushed through the marsh grass until he reached the dry ground on the other side.

"Bang, bang! You're dead!" Willie Derry was sitting against a rotted log, pointing his index finger into Dave Baldinger's face. His assault rifle was resting across his lap.

"It looks deserted, Willie. If they're here, they're all inside."

"Probably took our flyboy and left," Derry said. "Why don't we just call it a day."

Baldinger ignored his banter. "Luther's going around through the cover and hit it from the back. You take your guys down the stream and cover the front. If they come out, they'll be comin' right at you."

"Who's covering my ass?" Derry asked casually.

"No one. So rig a couple of grenade mines on the path behind you."

"Where you gonna be?"

"Up on the hill with Dickie. If this thing turns into a gunfight, we're your cover on the way out."

"If this turns into a gunfight, our flyboy gets to ride in a body bag," Willie said. He rolled onto one knee, and lifted his hand to the top of his floppy-brimmed jungle hat. Darkened faces rose out of the deep grass behind him.

"Jim Ray, Tony, you stick with me. Cavitt, set a grenade mine, here, and then follow us down to the point." Cavitt turned to offer Baldinger a thumbs-up. But Dave had already turned back into the swamp.

Baldinger had been given his mission in the early morning, before the sun had even begun to lighten the blackness of the night. He had counted his men into the back of a truck, and then jumped up behind them. They rode the truck from the fort back up into the hills, the road turning into an uneven footpath just when the daylight would have made them a dangerously exposed target. Then they had disappeared into the forest with nothing more than a magnetic compass to guide them, an "X" on a grid map to fix their destination, and a small field radio in case they got into trouble.

"Eight miles through this shit could take all day," Sergeant Major Thompson had told them. "But you gotta do better than that. The VCs are probably hanging this poor son of a bitch by his balls. Keep that in mind if you're thinking about takin' a coffee break."

If they stuck to the dry ground, and moved cautiously behind a point patrol, they should make it in five hours. But more than likely they wouldn't make it at all. The VCs knew that the Americans favored the open paths where they could move quickly, so that's where they set their ambushes. No problem, if you were infantry, on a search-and-destroy mission. Let Charlie spring his ambush, and then call in the gunships. But they were Special Operations, on an escape-and-evasion mission. Their job was to find a downed flyer who knew where the search-and-destroy guys were heading. They had to find him quickly before he spilled his guts and put all the patrols in danger. And once they found him, they had to get him out alive. The last thing they needed was a firefight, so they had to avoid contact with the enemy at any cost.

Baldinger had decided to move down through the swamp. The footing was slower, and the risk of getting lost much greater. But in the cover of the dense swamp, he could eliminate the point patrol and just keep moving. And he'd cut the eight miles down to six.

"The swamp?" Willie Derry had protested, lifting the jungle hat from his bright red hair. "I didn't bring my bug spray."

"Ain't no bugs," Luther Brown had answered, flashing an ivory smile across his ebony black features. "The snakes eat 'em."

"Oh, snakes!" Willie said. "Well, that's a different story. As long as there's snakes then I guess we don't have to worry about mosquitos."

Art Walters had held back as Willie turned off the path and bounded into the jungle. "Hey, I ain't big on snakes. Damn things scare the shit out of me."

Willie had laughed. "For chrissake, Art, don't pay any attention to Luther. There ain't no snakes."

"You sure?" Art had asked when he caught up to Willie.

"Sure I'm sure. If there was any snakes, the gators would have gotten 'em."

It was a standard Special Operations "A" unit, operating without its two commissioned officers. Each man had a specialty, with all of them cross-trained in everyone else's specialty. Baldinger was the communications guy. Art Walters had more medical training, right through basic surgery, than most hospital interns. Dickie Morgan was the mechanic and a small arms expert. Tom Cavitt had learned enough about explosives and demolition to drop a good-sized building into its basement. Among the ten of them, they had a speaking knowledge of five different languages.

Baldinger kept his patrol together. It was another risky call. He should have spread them out into an arrow, or at least assigned men to the point and to each flank. In a tight column, they would move across an enemy machine gun like the mindless ducks in a shooting gallery. But he was betting that the VCs would be watching the trails that followed the spine of high, dry ground. His real enemy was the dense undergrowth and the treacherous footing that could swallow up a lone soldier.

At first they moved quickly, the shallow water opening a clear path through the heavy foliage. Dickie Morgan, who was the biggest man in the patrol, had room to carry the machine gun across his shoulders. Mex Cortines had no trouble with the bulky ammunition bags that he wore around his neck, like a scarf. They found a dry streambed that moved in nearly a straight line under the canopy, and Dave Baldinger ordered them into double time. Good call, he thought, remembering his doubts about abandoning the high ground. He figured they had put the first mile behind them in less than twenty minutes. Even when the bed began to puddle up with dark water, there was still a narrow clearing along the bank that they could follow.

The bed emptied into a marsh, with pale grass breaking through the water, and Baldinger started his squad straight through the center. But Cortines suddenly plunged in up to his waist, lost his footing, and was nearly pulled under by the weight of the ammo bags. Bobby Long went after him, and dropped beneath the surface, his arms thrashing wildly as he disappeared. Mex Cortines righted himself, then reached under and pulled Bobby up by the straps of his rucksack. Dave Baldinger and Luther Brown waded up close and helped drag them out.

Baldinger gave up trying to cross the marsh and decided to circle it, but it flooded into the forest on both sides, blocking their path. He had no choice but to order the squad into the dense growth, hoping to move around the water.

The further they went, the closer the sticklike trunks of the trees were packed together. They had to move one careful step at a time, passing the branches from hand to hand to keep them from snapping like whips. The assault rifles kept getting caught in the clawing vines. Dickie had to pass his machine gun through the spaces between the brush and the trees before he could squeeze through himself. It took them half an hour to work their way to the other side of the marsh, and then they could see the place where Mex and Bobby had nearly gone under. They were only fifty yards closer to their destination.

"I need a break," Art Walters panted. He looked down at his blood-streaked arms and hands. "Fuckin' jungle tore me to pieces." He started to lift the pack off his back.

"Keep moving," Baldinger ordered. "We've got half an hour to make up." He started down the streambed before anyone could protest, and the others fell into line.

"This thing weighs as much as an engine block," Dickie Morgan groaned as he hoisted the machine gun back onto his shoulders. Then he staggered into a trot as he tried to catch up with Baldinger.

They had been moving for only another ten minutes when the bed disappeared into another dense marsh. Faced with another agonizing detour into the jungle, Baldinger led the squad into the water. He moved cautiously, feeling with each footstep, as the murky surface rose over his boots and then up to his belt. He shifted his oversized rucksack up onto his shoulder and raised the assault rifle above his head. By the time he was halfway across the marsh, the water was up to his chest.

"Try not to wake any of the gators," Willie Derry whispered to Art Walters.

"Jesus, Willie. Don't spook me, okay?" Art's eyes darted to the edges of the marsh. "There ain't no gators."

"Then watch out for the snakes," Derry answered.

"Knock it off," Baldinger ordered over his shoulder. He saw Mex, who was third in line, struggling with the machine-gun belts that he held high over his head. Mex was as strong as an ox, but he was the shortest man in the patrol, and the water was already touching the bottom of his raised chin.

"You okay, Mex?"

The Latino nodded. "Keep going. Let's just get out of this shit."

When they had climbed out of the swamp, they smashed into another dense rain forest. Again they were passing the branches from hand to hand. Each step of the advance was time-consuming, and Baldinger had to stop every fifty yards to be sure of their direction.

Dumb move, Baldinger now thought. He should have taken the dry paths. He was losing more time to the land than he would have lost to an ambush. And he was beginning to worry that they might be moving in circles, getting no closer to the hut and the downed flyer.

"If this guy is hangin' by his balls, he's already a soprano," Cavitt called from the back of the line.

"We'll be hangin' right next to him if Dave screws this up," Tony added.

A branch slipped through Art's fingers and lashed across Dickie's face. He screamed in pain and crashed to the ground, the machine gun clattering down on top of him. Blood seeped between the fingers that he pressed over his eyes. Art dropped to his knees next to Dickie.

"Jesus, I'm sorry. It just got away from me."

Dickie groaned.

"Honest, Dickie," Art pleaded. "I thought I had a grip on it."

Baldinger doubled back. "Don't start crying, Art. Take care of it. You're the medic. And make it fast. We can't stop." Dave pulled Morgan's hands away from his face. There was a gash across one cheek and blood was gushing from his nose. Art dropped his rucksack and found the medical bag. As he began working on Morgan's face, Derry slumped to the ground.

"Don't get comfortable," Dave snapped. "We're not stopping."

"Comfortable? Here?" Derry laughed, gesturing at the under-growth that filled every square inch. "A cockroach couldn't get comfortable here."

Art smeared an antibiotic jelly over Dickie's cheek. "Can't do much about the nose," he apologized. "It isn't broken. The bleeding will stop by itself.

Mex picked up the machine gun and put it across his shoulders on top of the ammo belts. "I'll take this for a while," he said, giving Dickie his assault rifle in exchange. They closed up their line and followed Dave Baldinger as he pressed further into the rain forest. The second hour was ticking away and they hadn't yet covered the second mile.

They broke out at the edge of another marsh, but this one ran parallel to their line of march. They could move in ankle-deep water and keep clear of the trees. As they picked up speed, their spirits lifted.

"Thanks, Mex," Dickie said, lifting the machine gun back onto his shoulders.

"You okay?" Mex asked.

"Yeah. I got my second wind."

They moved for another hour, keeping the thicket to their left and the swamp to their right. Baldinger kept checking the compass. The needle never wavered. They were closing on their target.

But then there was still another enemy. The sun had climbed high in the sky above the leafy canopy. A layer of steam was beginning to rise over the green water as the rain forest started to boil. Their breathing began to shorten.

"We gotta take a break," Bobby Long whispered toward Dave.

"No time," Luther Brown answered without turning his head.

"Who the fuck asked you?" Bobby Long challenged. "Baldinger is in charge."

Luther pushed past Bobby. "This ain't nothin'. It's hotter than this on Amsterdam Avenue."

"Yeah? Well when you get your patrol, we'll go rescue someone on Amsterdam Avenue," Bobby Long shot back. "But I'm about to drop."

"Three minutes," Baldinger announced. He unslung his rifle, staggered out of the water, and dropped down on the bank. The others collapsed next to him. Dave checked the grid map and then looked at his watch. Dickie checked his face and noticed that his nose had stopped bleeding.

"Three minutes?" Willie Derry complained. "I ain't gonna catch my breath in three lousy minutes." He was sprawled out flat on his back, his boots still in the water.

"Three minutes is a long time if you're hanging by your balls," Mex said. "Or if they're pouring a can of turpentine down your throat."

Willie sat up. "He's right," he said to Dave.

"Yeah!" It was Dickie who was climbing back to his feet.

Baldinger stood and found the squad already waiting for him.

"From here on, we're silent. Nobody talks. And step carefully. We don't want a lot of splashing. Willie, you take the point. And keep a sharp eye. We don't want to find ourselves standing on their front porch."

They moved on, now with much more caution. Willie moved fifty yards ahead, searched carefully, and then waved the others to catch up with him. Then Luther stepped out. They kept alternating the point as they eased forward. The swamp narrowed to a trickle, creating a bed that was as easy to follow as a trail. Dave dropped back in the line until he was with Tom Cavitt.

"Set grenade mines on both sides of the stream," Baldinger ordered. "If someone is coming up behind us we want to know about it."

Cavitt dropped behind and took two grenades from his belt. It was a sidebar in their ordnance training. You could make a mine out of a hand grenade by pulling the pin and blocking the release handle with any of the debris you found on the trail. If someone accidentally disturbed the covering, the handle popped free and the grenade went off. It was a simple way to keep someone from sneaking up behind you.

Luther Brown was on the point when they reached still another marsh formed by a hill that rose to the north. They all crouched by the water's edge while Luther waded across and then crawled to the top of the hill. He signaled them to stay put, and then eased down the slope.

"It's down the other side. Maybe a hundred yards," he reported to Baldinger.

"Any guards?" Dave asked.

"Nothin'. Just the shack."

Baldinger sent Derry with half the squad to swing around to the east side of the marsh. He moved Luther with three of the troops to the west slope of the hill. Then he took Dickie with him across the water, and left him at the base of the hill while he crawled to the top. Luther was right. They had reached their target, and without being discovered, as nearly as he could tell. Maybe the VCs who had picked up the flyer hadn't gotten here yet. Or if they had, they certainly didn't have the time to set a perimeter guard.

Now they were moving to the attack, with Luther Brown swinging around to the west, through the jungle, and coming in from behind, while Willie Derry moved along the east side of the marsh to cover the front. Dave took Dickie with him as he climbed the slope. They would position the machine gun just behind the skyline.

Brown would get the closest, so it was his call as to when they should attack. If the shed seemed empty, then they would just sit and wait. Their best chance would be if they caught the enemy out in the open, bringing in their prisoner. But if there was any activity inside the shed, then Luther would attack immediately. Maybe they would catch the VCs before their officers arrived, with just one or two men guarding the flyer. If that were the case, they wanted to get the prisoner out, and put as much space between themselves and the shed as they could. It might be nice to ambush a VC commander, but those weren't their orders. Get the flyer and get him out. It was a standard escape-and-evasion mission.

Baldinger eased his face over the hilltop and looked through the bramble of ground covering. The door of the shed, which had been closed, was now wide open. Someone was moving inside. A black-clad figure stepped out, a stubby automatic weapon cradled casually in the bend of his arm. He glanced around at the edge of the jungle that framed the small clearing, and then his eyes, blinking at the sudden brightness, panned across the top of the hill. He seemed casual, more a sightseer than a searcher. He wandered across the front of the shed with the indifference of a guard who thought there was no danger of attack.

Bullshit, Baldinger thought. These guys know we're coming. Take their sentry down, and all we'd be doing was giving the bastards inside an invitation to blow away their prisoner. He checked his watch. Derry was probably already in position on the other side of the stream, with his sights locked on the guy in his pajama costume. But Willie knew the score. He wasn't going to risk the flyer just to make the first kill.

Luther Brown was still circling through the bush, coming up behind the shed. He wouldn't see the sentry until he reached the edge of the clearing. That was dangerous, Dave figured, because if his guys even crushed a twig, the guard would hear them. But if they moved silently, then the presence of the VC guard would tell them that the others were inside. Luther would attack immediately.

The guard slipped the sling off his shoulder and leaned the assault gun against the side of the hut. He stepped down to the bank of the stream, fumbled with his pants and then began urinating into the trickle of the stream. His eyes wandered absently along the face of the jungle on the other side.

Baldinger held his breath. The sentry was only ten feet from the thick forest where Willie Derry and his troops were hiding. He was looking right at them. How in hell could he not see them? And where was Willie getting the cool to hold his fire with the enemy so close? The bastard was practically pissing on his boots.

The guard turned away from the stream, stretched in satisfaction, and sauntered back toward his rifle. He stopped abruptly when he heard the soft popping sound, almost like a penny firecracker. Then he leaped toward his rifle just as the shed was enveloped in cloud of gray smoke.

Before he could get the rifle off the ground, Luther Brown and Art Walters were on top of him. Luther dropped him with a single shot. At the same instant, Mex Cortines and Bobby Long charged around the other side of the hut, racing toward the open front door. It was all happening in an instant, just the way they had rehearsed it.

The jungle wall across the stream suddenly broke open. It's Derry, Dave thought, expecting to see Willie's group rushing out into the clear to give fire cover to Luther's guys. But it wasn't Willie. Six of the pajama-clad VCs were leaping the stream's narrow gully, racing up behind Brown and Walters, who didn't have a chance. They went down from the first blast of gunfire, Mex Cortines and Bobby Long dove back around the corner of the shed, driven off their line to the open door.

"Get 'em, Dickie!" Dave screamed. But Dickie Morgan was firing before he heard the order. He had pushed the muzzle of the machine gun over the crest of the hill as soon as he heard the gas grenades. The VCs were startled by the chattering growl of the powerful weapon. They looked up the hill, and spun back toward the cover of the bush. But none of them made it across the stream. They fell in a line by the edge of the water.

"Where's Willie?" Baldinger screamed in rage. The VCs had moved right through Derry's position. Their attack had killed Brown and Walters, and cost Cortines and Long precious seconds in their rush toward the door.

Mex Cortines and Bobby Long tried again. The instant the machine gun had silenced the VC attack, they raced back around the corner of the hut. But they were greeted by gunfire from a new source. The gas grenades drove the three VC inside the shed out through the open door. They came out with their guns at the ready, firing point-blank at the two attackers. Cortines and Long dove back around the door. On the hilltop, Dickie swung his gun across the front of the shed. The VCs fired wildly in confusion, and then dropped at the doorway.

At that same instant, three more pajama-clad VCs broke out of the jungle to the west of the hut, directly behind the two American attackers. They were firing the moment they appeared in the clearing. Morgan turned his machine gun in their direction, but it was already too late. The first rounds they fired had found Cortines and Long before they even knew they were under attack. The chattering machine gun caught one of the VCs, but the other two disappeared back into the dense foliage. Dickie kept firing at the jungle until Dave waved his hand to signal cease-fire.

The gunfire echoed for a fraction of a second. And then the air went still. Once again, Baldinger could hear the trickling of the stream, and the squawking of the birds who had exploded out of the treetops.

Luther Brown's force was gone. The four men were spread-eagled at both sides of the open door. Derry's group was lost too. They had probably walked right into the VCs who had rushed out from the position Willie was supposed to take. There were just the two of them, Dickie Morgan and himself. And maybe the flyer still alive inside the shed. He knew that there were at least two of the VCs, probably waiting behind the curtain of the jungle.

"Keep trained over there," Baldinger ordered Dickie Morgan, pointing to the spot where the VCs had disappeared. "I'm going down and try to get behind those two."

"Give it up, Dave," Morgan answered. "It's lost."

"We still got a flyer in there." Baldinger began crawling away from the hilltop.

"He's dead," Dickie hissed. "If the VCs didn't get him, I sure did. I shot the hell out of that shed when I got the gooks at the door. It's over."

"Not yet," Baldinger answered. He got to his feet and stumbled down the hill, disappearing into the thicket at the point where Luther had taken his men. He kept moving, hunched beneath the branches, his face brushing against the top of the undergrowth.

He could hear the rustle of each leaf that he touched, the snap of every blade of grass that he crushed. He seemed to be setting up a deafening rumble as he rushed forward. Slow down, he reminded himself. The VCs couldn't get back into the shed. The machine gun controlled the clearing. They were waiting, hopefully looking out towards the silent battlefield, expecting that the attack would come down the slope of the hill. He could surprise them from behind if only the noise didn't give him away. Slow down, he kept telling himself. Silence was more important than speed.

He began to measure each footstep, carefully shifting his weight once the step was planted. He pushed the branches aside gently, and held them delicately as they closed behind him. But he kept the muzzle of the rifle aimed ahead, and his finger tight against the metal curve of the trigger. He couldn't see where he was going. The growth was so dense that it blocked everything beyond the next tree, and the light danced around him in blinding streaks. He felt like a swimmer moving beneath the surface of a green sea. Baldinger had thought it would be easy to circle around behind his prey, but now he realized that they would be invisible until he was right on top of them. He could walk into their gun barrels as easily as up against their backs.

He froze at the sound of birds screeching overhead, sounding a warning that he was passing beneath. Or were they warning him? Were the VCs stirring the branches a few steps ahead? For a few seconds, he listened to the deathlike stillness. Then he took his next step.

A black form flashed by the corner of his eye, and his body snapped like a whip. He felt the rifle being ripped out of his hand, and his bush hat spinning from the top of his head. He hurtled sideways and smashed against a tree, then bounced off into the jaws of a vise that wrestled him to the ground. For an instant, he was aware of a grinning face, but the mocking image faded into a sick nausea.

The next moment, he was on his feet, stumbling to keep ahead of the force that was propelling him from behind. Branches were smashing against his chest and whipping at his face. He tried to raise his arms for protection but they wouldn't move. And then he was falling, out into an open space that was blazing with hot light. He slammed against the ground, and found himself writhing in the dirt as he gasped for air. Hands locked onto his shoulders and pulled him back up to his feet. And then he flung toward a circle of bowed forms that were hunched on the ground ahead. He fell into them and rolled over onto his back.

"Try to get comfortable," Willie Derry whispered from the corner of his mouth. Dave saw Willie's face above him. He was sitting with his legs crossed and his hands folded across the top of his bare head. Tony LaRocca was sitting next to him, and then Tom Cavitt and Jim Ray Talbert, all with bowed heads and raised hands. Dickie Morgan was at the end of the line, with fresh blood flowing from his nose.

"Where the hell were you?" Baldinger mouthed at Derry.

"Walked right into their trap," Derry whispered. "They had a ball."

Dave sat up slowly and crossed his legs like the other prisoners. He

14

tried to raise his hands but realized that they were bound behind his back by thin cords that were cutting into his wrists. Ahead of him, he saw Luther and Art, their shapes sprawled out on the ground beside the hut. Two of the black-uniformed figures were crumpled in front of the doorway. Mex's face and arms were sprawled around the far corner of the building.

Half his patrol was dead, the other half were cowered prisoners, and the flyer he was sent to rescue had been cut to pieces by his own machine gun.

"Jeesus Kay-ryst."

The voice boomed from inside the shed. Then two climbing boots, with polished silver eyelets, stepped into the column of light that flowed through the doorway into the darkness inside. Trousers appeared, with razorlike creases down the legs, and then the belt buckle flashed as it caught the sun. The shirt was freshly pressed, almost square at its edges, with tight pleats folded into the web belt. Two rows of colored ribbons topped the flat breast pocket. A square chin. Thin, emotionless mouth. And then the wire-framed sunglasses that were Sergeant Major Elvis Thompson's trademark. The last thing to appear was his forest-green beret.

He stepped like an apparition into the clearing and looked with disgust at the carnage that surrounded him.

"Jesus Christ." This time the voice was soft and mournful rather than booming. "If I wanted mass destruction, I could have given this mission to the Air Force. They would've defoliated the whole fucking forest."

He touched the toe of his boot to the Vietcong soldiers who were sprawled at his feet. "Okay, dead men, the game's over." The dead enemy troops rolled onto their hunches and stood wearily. One of them began peeling off the black pajama top that covered his khaki T-shirt.

"Everyone up!" Thompson yelled.

Luther Brown raised his head and sprang to his feet. Art Walters climbed up slowly, and then Mex Cortines and Bobby Long walked around the corner of the hut. The dead VCs rose from the bed of the stream, and the enemy soldier who had been caught by Dickie's machine gun as he fled into the jungle came back to life. Willie Derry lowered his hands from his head and untied the cords from Baldinger's wrists.

"Special Forces," Sergeant Thompson mused. "Silent! Cunning! Deadly!" He shook his head sadly and then, as he stepped toward the prisoners who were still sitting in a subdued line, he carefully removed his sunglasses so that they could see the despair in his eyes. "You dumb bastards might as well have been playing bagpipes. We heard you coming half an hour before you got here."

Willie Derry chuckled, causing Thompson to stop in mid-stride. Derry's mischievous grin vanished instantly, but Thompson kept him fixed with a steely stare.

"You find incompetence funny, Corporal Derry?"

Derry leaped to his feet and braced at attention. "No, Sergeant Major!"

The sergeant major nodded. "Good. I'm happy to hear that, Corporal. Because incompetence will get you killed. You and the poor bastards who have to follow you. You just got four men captured because you got a louder voice than Tarzan! Exactly what in God's name is it going to take to get you to keep your mouth shut in the jungle?"

He walked in a slow circle around his trainees. "How in hell am I ever going to keep you assholes alive?" When he was back in front of them, he extended his open hand towards Sergeant Bill Campbell, who had led the Vietcong impostors. Campbell reached into his pocket, took out two hand grenades, and placed them in Thompson's hand.

"Which one of you killers planted the grenade mines back on the trail?"

Tom Cavitt leaped to attention.

"Lousy job," Thompson said. "We found them. Here, you can have them back." He tossed the grenades casually at Cavitt's feet. The handles flew off as they landed, and the fuses began to hiss. For a split second, the squad members stared at the wisps of smoke. Then they ran for their lives.

Bobby Long took three strides, racing past Sergeant Major Thompson, and then dove face first into the ground. Willie Derry broke from his frozen position of attention, turned on his heels, and flew into the brush at the edge of the clearing. Dave Baldinger sprang from his haunches onto his hands and knees, and scampered on all fours until the fuse had burned its length. Then he flattened into the ground. Cavitt was still running when the small fuse ignited. But the charge of cordite never exploded.

"Must have been duds," Elvis Thompson said. He turned the jagged casings over with his toe, bringing a roar of laughter from the men in his training cadre. Sheepishly, the soldiers picked themselves up and returned to their circle around the dead grenades.

"Who was leading this fiasco?"

Baldinger rose to attention.

Thompson nodded. "Well, I'll tell you, Baldinger, I really don't know what score to give you on this exercise, because you did a couple of things right. Like cutting through the swamp. Risky! But smart. If you'd taken one of the high-ground trails you wouldn't have gotten this far. We had a couple of traps waiting for you up there."

Dave didn't let his expression show any hint of satisfaction. Thompson always backed a compliment with a barrage of criticism.

"Then there was the machine gun," the sergeant major continued. "I like where you put it. Up on the hill where it commanded the whole clearing. That's where I would've put it."

Baldinger stayed stone-faced.

"But you used the machine gun like a Chicago mobster," Thompson said, returning to character. "You can't just close your eyes and spray the whole area with bullets when your own men are in there. And when your mission is to rescue a prisoner, why in hell would you shoot up the hut were you think he's being held?"

It wasn't a question that Thompson wanted answered.

"Well, maybe you wouldn't have killed him," the sergeant allowed. "But you sure as hell wounded him. So that means he can't walk. You dumb bastards are going to have to carry him back."

The squad members eyes widened.

"What's the average flyer weigh, Sergeant?" Thompson asked his second in command. Sergeant Bill Campbell smirked at the opportunity. "About one eighty," he answered as smartly as if he had researched the figure.

"Derry," Thompson snapped. Willie jumped to attention. "Grab a duffle bag. You got one minute to fill it with a hundred eighty pounds of rocks."

"Yes, Sergeant Major," Derry barked. He picked up the ammo sack that had been brought down the hill along with the captured machine gun. "Brown. Long. Give me a hand with this." Luther and Bobby followed him to the streambed and began firing rocks into the bag."

Thompson checked his wristwatch. "I want you losers back in camp by eighteen hundred. When you get there, you better have this flyer with you. And for your sake, he damn well better be alive."

He turned to Campbell. "Take charge, Sergeant," he said. Then he turned abruptly and marched into the jungle, disappearing into the thicket as calmly as if he had been disappearing through the doors of a grand hotel.

17

"We'll need a litter," Baldinger said. Mex Cortines and Dickie Morgan drew their parrish knives as they ran into the forest to cut a pair of poles for a stretcher. Art Walters pulled a nylon ground cover from the medical bag.

Sergeant Campbell watched as Willie, Luther, and Bobby dumped stones into the duffle. They started dragging it out of the bed of the stream.

"Stop right there," Campbell hissed. He pushed the bag with his foot. "That don't feel like no hundred-and-eighty pound flyer to me. It feels like a fuckin' hundred-pound midget. Put some more rocks in there."

"He bled a lot," Willie Derry tried.

"Fill the fuckin' bag!" Campbell screamed.

By the time the three soldiers dragged the duffle back into the clearing, Walters had the nylon linked around the two poles. They loaded the flyer onto the makeshift stretcher.

"Willie, Mex, take the first shift with the litter," Baldinger said. "Dickie, Luther, take the flanks. Bobby, you have the point."

They formed into a diamond with the downed flyer being carried in the middle. Dave started his men across the stream where they could pick up the high-ground trail.

"Where the fuck are you going, Baldinger?" Sergeant Campbell screamed. "You ain't taking no easy trail."

"We got a wounded man, here," Baldinger shot back. "We'll never get him through the jungle."

"He's bleedin'," Campbell snapped. "You gotta get 'em back fast." He pointed up stream. "Take 'em through the swamp." The sergeant's lips twisted into a smile. "Unless you pussies wanna wash outta here and forget about ever bein' Green Berets."

Willie Derry and Mex Cortines hoisted the litter. Bobby Long stepped into the edge of the marsh, taking up the point position, while Dickie Morgan and Luther Brown fanned out into the flanks. The squad began moving, like a religious procession, back into the swamp that lay between them and the fort.

Fort Francis Marion had been built because of the swamp. It was set into the foothills of the Appalachian chain, along the South Carolina–Georgia border, where tumbling streams merged into the tributaries of the Savannah River. The land was thick with scrub trees, and in the spring, when the streams overflowed their banks, the forest floor turned into a quagmire. To the east, where the land flattened, the low brush and crisscrossing streams were a replica of the Vietnam Delta. To the west, on the slopes of the Piedmont Plateau, the country was a thick, rocky forest, just like the mountain slopes of El Salvador. It was the perfect place to train Special Operations Force units.

At first it had been just an outpost of the major Army bases, Fort Benning and Fort Bragg. It was called Camp Viper because the marshes had bred their own armies of copperheads and water moccasins, and for most soldiers the camp was the scene of their first encounters with deadly snakes. The Army used it for brief training sessions to give its soldiers a small taste of the new kind of warfare that was being fought in unknown places with unpronounceable names.

But then, with the Vietnam advisory mission growing into a full-scale war, and with people's uprisings beginning to dot the map of Central America, a small taste of jungle tactics wasn't enough. Unconventional warfare became conventional. The Army switched its interest from division tactics, designed for the north German plain, to search-and-destroy patrols that could operate anywhere. Special Forces became a more promising career path than artillery and engineering. A Green Beret became a more important symbol than scrambled eggs on the peak of an officer's cap.

Camp Marion was expanded, first with the addition of permanent barracks to house the trainees, and then with communities of tract housing for the instructors and their families. Schools were opened, with classrooms and blackboards, to teach the new tactics of behind-the-lines warfare. Obstacle courses and sand pits were built to rehearse the arts of hand-to-hand combat. And, when a permanent body of instructors and administrators had been assembled, an architect was brought in to design a suitable officers' club, with a bar that reached outside to the swimming pool and inside to the edge of the raised dance floor.

It was named Fort Francis Marion after the backwoodsman of the Revolutionary War. Attacking from the cover of the swampy foothills that were his home, he had destroyed every westward excursion of the redcoats, and earned the tribute "Swamp Fox" from his enemies. They had learned to fear Marion's attacks from the cover of the thick, impenetrable marsh lands, and had too much sense to try to follow him into his lair.

Fort Francis Marion had not only become the focal point of Army training, but had won an international following for its coursework.

Popular insurgencies had suddenly become a threat to half the capitalist governments that the United States regarded as allies. Army officers and national guardsmen, from the Pacific Rim and Latin America, from Caribbean islands and West Africa, suddenly found the tanks and howitzers that they had received under military aid pacts to be useless. They were fighting a new kind of war against armies of their own people; people who lived as tradesmen in their cities and farmers in their countrysides by day, but who turned into revolutionaries with the darkness of night. They needed to learn a new kind of warfare.

They came to Fort Francis Marion to learn. In the surrounding swamps they practiced jungle tracking and the skills of silent killing. In the classrooms of the fort's Special Operations School, they took courses with names like population control, infiltration of civic movements, land denial, and internal intelligence. They learned how to defoliate forests to deny their enemies coverage, how to poison water supplies to eliminate safe havens, how to interrogate those who supported insurgents to learn the identities of the leaders of the insurgents. It was at Fort Francis Marion that the dirty necessities of safeguarding national institutions from the people they were intended to serve was raised to the status of a university major. It became the global resource for all the strategies and tactics of counterinsurgency warfare. Soldiers, guardsmen, and policemen from Thailand, Burma, Singapore, Chile, Peru, El Salvador, Guatemala, Santa Domingo, Morocco, South Africa, and even Iraq, made their pilgrimages to the new shrine of military education, where they learned to fight enemies who won battles by ambush instead of by combat, and who won wars by wearing down their opponents instead of confronting them. When they returned to their native countries, they carried diplomas bearing the seal of Fort Francis Marion.

But to the soldiers who trained there in its early days, it would always be Camp Viper. When it grew to the size of a small city, they reluctantly admitted that it was too big to be called a camp, so they began calling it Fort Viper. And the name was honored throughout the military, even in the halls of the Pentagon. An assignment officer might write a set of orders to Fort Francis Marion. But if he got the assigned officer on the telephone, he would tell him that he was going to Fort Viper.

"Dickie, Luther, you get the litter. Willie, Mex, take the flanks. Art, you relieve Bobby on the point."

They had stopped because Derry and Cortines couldn't keep up. The makeshift litter was unstable, making it difficult to maneuver through the brush. And the weight of the wounded flyer was growing heavier with each step. The crudely cut poles had already sliced through Willie's hands, bonding his fingers in a crust of dried blood. With his arms straining under the poles, Mex had been unable to protect his face from the snapping branches. He had a fresh slash across his forehead, and his cheeks had swollen until his eyes were nearly closed.

"I'll be riding on that fuckin' stretcher if we stay in this jungle much longer," Derry said.

"Knock it off," Baldinger hissed, remembering Thompson's remark that they had made more noise than Tarzan's scream as they moved through the jungle.

They rotated their assignments. "Keep a sharp eye," Dave warned as his men moved out to the points and flanks. "The bastards might be waiting for us."

Baldinger doubted that the exercise was over. Sergeant Major Thompson's exercises were never over. They were all based on his experiences during three tours in 'Nam, where he had learned painfully that the enemy never takes a day off. They were all frighteningly realistic, even to the point of costuming his training cadre in the peasant garb of the enemy.

They had been sent in to rescue a downed flyer because Thompson had once led a patrol to rescue a downed flyer. They were carrying a bag of stones on a stretcher because Thompson's flyer had parachuted into dense jungle and impaled himself on the tree branches. He had to be carried fifteen miles through VC-held jungle to safety.

They didn't wear bug spray because the smell of insecticide had once alerted the VCs to one of Thompson's snipers. The man, and one of his companions, had been hacked to death. They didn't carry food rations because Thompson had learned to trade food for information. "A word of warning can keep you alive a lot longer than a tin of dehydrated beef," the sergeant major preached. So he trained his students to get their food and water off the land. They couldn't even sleep easily in their barracks. The VCs had overrun a safe hamlet during Thompson's second tour, and gone from bed to bed shooting the unsuspecting troops. So Thompson had sent his cadre through the windows of the barracks during their second night at Fort Viper. His message was simple. Relax and you're dead. Take something for granted, and you won't wake up to find out that your assumptions were wrong.

Baldinger wasn't taking it for granted that all they had to do was find their way back to the fort, with the bag of rocks still in one piece on top of the litter. Thompson preached that the enemy was everywhere, and that probably meant that the training cadre was staked out in ambush somewhere between here and the fort. Probably wearing the black pajamas of the Vietcong. Or maybe this time in the straw sombreros of Guatemalan Indians. Don't assume that just because the war game is in Vietnam, that Thompson won't hit us with force of African tribesmen. Assume, and you're dead.

They reached the deep marsh that they had waded through several hours earlier. Dave sent his point man and his flanker around the swamp, through the jungle on the east side. His other flanker circled to the west. He left the stretcher behind and pushed into the water himself. He listened to the stillness, and realized that Thompson's lecture had sunk in. None of the men in the patrol were even stirring the leaves as they moved. The stretcher followed him through the swamp, Dickie Morgan and Luther Brown holding it high above their heads. They were staggering when they waded ashore.

"We shoulda shot this son of a bitch instead of rescuin' him," Brown whispered when they set it down. The squad assembled, and Baldinger rotated the assignments again, bringing fresh hands to the stretcher poles. Now they were moving down the streambed, waiting as their points and flanks spread out, then moving ahead when they saw the "all clear" signal. Their progress was slow, but they were reducing the chances of being taken by surprise.

They were moving in a column along the edge of a marsh when Baldinger suddenly raised his hand to order a halt. He had heard a rustling in the brush across the flat, gray water. Someone had moved across the bank to the water's edge. Baldinger motioned his men to get down, and they dropped to their bellies, setting the litter under an overhang of trees. Their assault weapons raised slowly and swung out over the marsh.

Bobby Long saw it first. A snake had slithered down to the water's edge and was gliding over the boundary debris. Baldinger saw where he was pointing, nodded, and then got back to his feet to resume the march. The others followed, except Art Walters, whose eyes stayed fixed on the snake.

"Let's go," Luther Brown prodded quietly.

Art Walters shook his head.

"What?" Luther asked.

"I ain't goin' into the water with snakes," Walters whispered.

"Just stare 'em down. They won't bother you if you let 'em know you ain't afraid."

"They know I'm afraid."

"Just stare 'em down," Luther repeated. "They ain't no worse than rats, and that's what you do with a rat. Just stare it down."

They reached the end of the marsh and were faced with another tangle of jungle. Baldinger posted two more men, one in front of the litter and one behind. They would handle the branches to keep them from whipping the litter-bearers, and would be on hand to take the poles when the wounded flyer had to be passed through tight breaks in the trees. He pulled the point and the flanks in close to keep them from getting separated. That increased the danger of stumbling into an enemy ambush, but reduced the chances of his men getting separated and lost. The sky was beginning to darken. If one of the squad got turned around in the night jungle, they might not find him. There were stories about trainees who had gotten lost from a patrol and had gone mad, wandering for days in the forest.

Their progress was painfully slow. Each yard of advance demanded hundreds of motions, to set aside the tree limbs, pass weapons through awkward spaces, and open a path for the stretcher.

"We ain't gettin' nowhere," Bobby Long warned Baldinger.

"Just keep moving, Bobby. And keep buttoned up."

They broke out at the edge of another marsh, exhausted from the ordeal and tortured by the slashes across their arms and legs. Tony LaRocca and Jim Ray Talbert, who had taken over the stretcher, started to set it down.

"We're not stopping," Baldinger said, pointing up toward the dimming sky. "We can't lose the daylight." He ordered the flankers out around the edges of swamp. Once again, he took the lead into the middle of the water.

"He's catching Thompson's disease," Willie Derry whispered.

"Let's go," Cortines said, stepping in behind Baldinger.

They were in the middle of the water when the mosquitos hit, moving in dark swarms from the edges of the marsh. Baldinger felt them on his face and neck, and blinked as they flew into his eyes. He waved his hands in a useless attempt to keep them off, then ground his teeth at the pain of their bites. But he kept advancing, trying to keep his attention focused on the surrounding foliage. This was the kind of place where an enemy would set a trap. A place where they could stay hidden in the rain forest while his men would be out in the clear. It was like a duck blind.

"Christ!" It was Tony LaRocca. The insects had torn into his face. He was gyrating in waist-deep water, thrashing at the air.

A few feet behind, Jim Ray Talbert was snapping his head from side to side. With the stretcher tying his hands, it was the only thing he could do to stop the mosquitos that were crawling under his collar. Then, suddenly, he was screaming in pain.

Dave rushed back toward him, ignoring the splashing ripples that he was sending across the marsh. He had to get to Jim Ray and stop his screaming. In the stillness, his pained voice was probably carrying all the way back to Fort Viper.

LaRocca let go of one of the poles so that he could slap at his own face. The stretcher tipped. Talbert tried to right it, but he was fighting his own battle with the swarming insects. The bag of stones rolled into the water. In reaching for it, Mex stepped on the end of pole that Tony was still holding. The branch cracked as it was driven under the surface. Jim Ray spun around and clawed at the sinking duffle bag. Together with Mex, he lifted it out of the marsh. But now the mosquitos were thick across the back of his hands, like bees in the combs of their hive. He screamed again when he saw them, dropped the bag, and began slapping at his hands.

Baldinger arrived just in time to grab Talbert's end of the sinking duffle. Together with Mex, he lifted it back up out of the water. Derry retrieved the half-submerged stretcher. While Baldinger supported the bag, Mex and Willie positioned the poles with their nylon bed. Dave lowered the flyer back into position.

The instant it took weight, the fractured stretcher pole snapped. The nylon folded, and the sack of stones rolled off the other side. Tony LaRocca tossed the useless litter aside, and joined Baldinger and Talbert in their struggle with the weighted bag.

"You guys hold it," Dave said in a stage whisper. "I'll cut us another pole."

"Fuck it," Mex snapped. He pushed his assault rifle toward Baldinger. "Boost it up on my back," he ordered Derry. He dropped down until the water was up to his chin. When he rose up again, he had the wounded flyer across his shoulder in a fireman's carry.

"Let's get out of here," Mex said.

Baldinger shook his head. "You can't handle it alone."

Mex didn't answer. He steadied the load across his back and started wading toward the far shore, ignoring the insects that were circling his face.

Tony LaRocca splashed water over his bitten face, took Mex's assault rifle from Dave, and tried to catch up with Mex. As he ran, his boot slipped off a slimy stone. His knee buckled under his weight and he felt an agonizing tear. He was screaming in pain as he sank into the water.

Christ, Baldinger thought when he stepped back onto dry land. One VC out there in the brush could have taken us all. We were out there in the open, doing a comic dance and screaming our fool heads off.

"Do you suppose those fuckin' bugs work for Sergeant Thompson?" Willie Derry asked.

"Why don't you shut up, Tarzan," Baldinger told him.

★   ★   ★

Captain Henry Roy braked his five-liter Mustang at the first bugle note of evening colors.

"Damn it! I knew this would happen."

He struggled with the seat belt, which always seemed to bind when he was in a hurry, then fired the door open and jumped to attention. His right hand shot up in a rigid salute, touching the fold of the beret which was tipped on his closely shaved, white head. He stood like a statue, nearly six feet tall, broad shoulders tapering down to an athletic waist.

Carol Roy smoothed her dress as she stepped out on the other side. Like Henry, she was tall. But her complexion was darker, and she was shapelessly thin. Her hand went up to hold her long, black hair against the gusty wind.

"Stop fidgeting," the captain whispered from the corner of his mouth. Carol sighed in despair, and dropped her hand to her heart.

Fort Francis Marion had come to a standstill. At the sound of colors, every vehicle had pulled to the side, its occupants scrambling out to render their salutes. Marching formations screamed to a halt, and turned toward the flag. In offices, conversations broke off in midsentence. Work details rose from their assignments. At the officers' club, the waiters stood frozen, the drinks rattling on their trays.

The bugle rushed expertly into its ceremonial fanfare, and the flag began its descent from the top of the tall, white pole. It moved steadily, its fall timed so that it would disappear from view just as the last note of evening colors was sounding. There was a long, anticipatory pause. Then a fieldpiece fired, its sharp crack echoing over the fort, and bouncing back from the slopes of the nearby mountains.

Captain Roy snapped his hand back to his side. When he glanced across the top of the car, Carol was gone. She was already sliding back into the passenger seat.

"Jesus," he said as he buckled his seat belt. "Is it too much for you to stand still for a lousy thirty seconds?"

"My hair was blowing, and you asked me to look my best."

"Colors is the only military ceremony on the whole damn base. For God's sake, Carol, you ought to be able to handle one lousy ceremony."

"What do you want?" she asked casually. "Good discipline, or good looks? I can either salute the flag or hold my hair."

"I didn't want to be late for the colonel's party," he answered. "You could have tried to be ready on time."

"Didn't I lose half an hour looking for your combat ribbons?"

The captain bit off each word. "They're supposed to be in my jewelry box, not tossed into the corner of my damn sock drawer."

"I'm sorry," Carol admitted.

They drove in silence until they reached the driveway of the officers' club. Then Henry tried to put everything in perspective.

"Look, honey, I'm sorry for snapping at you. It's just that Grigg likes his staff to be on time. He likes to come in last. Hell, it's his privilege."

"And I'm sorry if I made us late," Carol admitted. "I don't want to spoil Colonel Grigg's entrance."

She waited until the duty private reached for the door handle. "What's he going to do tonight? Swing through the window from a parachute?"

The club was built on a bluff, at the edge of a curved lake that separated it from the often-dreary activities of the fort. The high ground thrust it well above the tree line, with its main rooms looking toward the west. The glass walls of the dining room, and the broad deck they overlooked, offered a spectacular view of the distant mountains and, at this time of day, of a fiery red sunset. The staff officers of the Special Operations School had assembled on the deck about the time when Henry Roy realized he had misplaced his campaign ribbons. They had been sipping steadily, with the exception of the few moments when they had paid tribute to their flag.

Major Eugene Daks, tall, a bit stoop-shouldered, and with a fleck of gray at the edges of his dark hair, was the senior officer and, therefore, the center of attention. At any social occasion, the junior officers were expected to gather around him and join in the topic of his choice. Since he had come to Special Operations from artillery, the topic was generally explosives. He had learned his craft as a young captain, mining the trails of Morazan and Cabanas in El Salvador, and picked up a Silver Star in the process. Now he taught the school's course in mine warfare, which covered everything from hand-fabricated grenade mines, capable of killing a few men, to large fixed charges which could bring down a railroad bridge.

Henry and Carol Roy parted as soon as they reached the deck. Henry walked to the party surrounding Daks, gave his greetings, and began turning his head in search of a waiter. Carol joined the women gathered around Marilyn Daks, and stood at the edge of a discussion on the problems of the base kindergarten. Marilyn was head of the Fort Francis Marion Parent Teachers Association and, because of her husband's rank, was allowed to pick her subject of conversation as well.

Daks was in the middle of a story that held the men's attention. They had been training a group of Venezuelan officers who were faced with revolution in some of their cities. "Standard village mop-up exercise," he explained. "They're all down low, under the windows, reaching up and pitching the grenades through, then dropping flat to the ground. Really enjoying themselves. Big grins every time the blast comes through the windows over their heads. So there's this one guy, with black wavy hair and a curved mustache. He's a real big deal. I think he's a colonel. Anyhow, he comes creeping up under a window."

Daks bent low beneath the height of the deck railing and began acting out his story. "He pulls the pin with his teeth." Laughter from the surrounding officers interrupted his story. "Honest to God, with his teeth, like he's been watching old Steve McQueen movies. Then he reaches up"—Daks's hand reached over the rail—"and tosses the grenade over the windowsill. Then he sticks a finger in each ear, hunches down, and closes his eyes."

Daks was hunched down with his eyes closed and his fingers in his ears. "He waits, counting off the seconds. You could see his eyes squeezing tighter with each second. But nothing happens. There's no explosion." Daks opened his eyes suspiciously. "So he opens his eyes and slowly pulls his fingers out of his ears. He waits some more. Still no explosion. You can just see him thinking that the grenade must have been a dud.''

Henry Roy began to chuckle, guessing where the story was going.

"So he stands up, right in front of the open window. I scream, 'Get down!' He smiled at me. 'No need, Senior Major. It's a dud!' Then the dumb son of a bitch turns and sticks his head through the window to see if he can find the grenade.''

"Jesus, no," said Captain Brian O'Leary.

"I swear to God," Daks answered. "He leaned way in. All I could see was his ass draped over the windowsill. And then the grenade went off.'' Daks could hardly get the words out over his own laughter. "This greaser comes flying ass first out the window like a champagne cork out of a bottle. He runs backward for about twenty feet and falls flat on his back. When I get to him, he's staring at the sky with this shit-eating grin, pounding his ears with his fists to try and make the ringing stop.''

The officers were convulsed.

"His hair is singed right to his scalp, and the mustache is smoking.''

"Ten-hut!''

It was O'Leary who saw Colonel Barry Grigg striding across the dining room, and called the others to attention. They were all facing the glass doors when their commanding officer stepped out on the wooden deck.

"At ease, gentlemen," he said. He turned toward the wives and bowed slightly. "A pleasure to find such lovely company.''

A chorus of "good evenings" was returned.

Grigg turned back to the men. "Someone get me a drink.''

Henry Roy darted after the waiter without asking for Grigg's order. The colonel's taste for sour mash was nearly as legendary as the man himself.

Barry Grigg had rescued Special Operations from the dark days following Vietnam, and given it a personality that mirrored his own—physical, bright, confident. He was West Point's all-time wrestling champion, and at one time NCAA champion in two different weight classes. He held the obstacle course time records at both Fort Bragg and Fort Benning, and the one-handed push-up record at half the Army's officer clubs, and at least one of the Navy's. He regularly ran Fort Viper's obstacle course with new trainees, always demonstrating just how deficient they were in physical readiness.

Grigg's academic credentials were just as impressive. He had finished second in his class at West Point, missing first by a digit that came three places after the decimal point. He held masters degrees in mathematics and psychotherapy, the first so he could plot his own mortar trajectories and the second to help him break prisoners during interrogation. He had a fluency in Vietnamese and Spanish, and a reasonable competence in Farsi.

In one way or another, Grigg had been part of every behind-the-lines and covert mission that the Army had undertaken. As a spanking-fresh lieutenant, he had driven an airboat into Vietnam, been smuggled into Cambodia, and flown a light plane into Zimbabwe. As a captain, he had led forces on a dozen illegal crossings in and out of Nicaragua. Soon after being promoted to colonel, he had commanded the team of advisers that arrived by commercial flight in El Salvador.

When he was given command of the Army's Special Operations training center and appointed dean of the school, Colonel Grigg had assembled a staff that matched his experience. Vietnamese mines, some as simple as sharpened sticks driven into the ground, had taken a great toll on American forces, and so Grigg determined to make the school expert in the art of mining. Major Daks had impressed him with his work in helping the Salvadoran army salt its countryside with mines, denying the rebels access to even the most meager footpaths. Grigg brought him to the fort as its antipersonnel mine instructor.

Captain Brian O'Leary was working at the Pentagon, interpreting reconnaissance photos beamed down from spy satellites, when he came to the colonel's attention. More than once, Grigg had been victimized by erroneous intelligence based on faulty surveillance. He had O'Leary transferred to Fort Francis Marion to bring profession-alism to the courses on intelligence gathering.

Captain Henry Roy had been working in chemical warfare at the Rocky Mountain Arsenal. Grigg brought him to El Salvador to teach the National Guard how to use defoliants and poison water supplies. He was impressed with Roy's knowledge of chemical agents and, instead of returning him to the arsenal at the end of the tour, had him transferred to Special Operations, and then to the faculty of the Special Operations school.

Major Victor Jordan was a psychiatrist, educated by the Army, and assigned to study the reaction of American prisoners to physical deprivation and abusive interrogation. Grigg read his reports and found them accurate descriptions of prisoners he had rescued from the

Vietcong. He brought Jordan to Fort Francis Marion to work both sides of the street; a course in the art of interrogation, and a course in resisting interrogation.

They all found Colonel Grigg a most demanding superior. He felt that the men he trained were the last barrier between the American way of life and the onslaught of the barbarian hordes, and he insisted that all his people measure up to the responsibility. He worked them long hours for endless days, and was totally intolerant of even minor failures. But he matched them hour for hour, and was even less tolerant of his own failures. And, on occasions such as this, he brought them together with their wives to pay tribute to their dedication, and apologize for the inconveniences he had caused their families. He had ordered that the cost of the evening's banquet be put on his personal bill, and even though he was single and had never learned to dance, he had handed an envelope of cash to the band leader to assure that there would be spirited music well into the night.

*　*　*

As they dragged toward the camp, Baldinger's patrol became aware of the music, the even tempo of a drum and occasional flights of a trumpet.

"Name that tune?" Willie Derry tried for the drama of a game show host. No one picked up on the humor. They were in too much pain to find anything humorous.

Tony LaRocca's torn knee had stiffened to the point where he couldn't bend it. For a while, he had kept up by combining a step with a skip, but the awkward motion had raised blisters on his good foot. Now, he had one arm over Dickie Morgan's shoulder, and the other over Art Walters's. Art was the only one who could give direction to the group because Dickie's eyes were swollen shut.

Derry's hands were still oozing from the cuts caused by the litter pole. Bobby Long had staggered against a broken branch and sliced open his thigh. Now his whole leg ached. Luther Brown had one bad hand from the litter, and a cut face from a snapping branch. Tom Cavitt was sliced across the neck and chest, and Jim Ray Talbert had gotten some leeches under his trouser leg.

Mex Cortines had carried the bag of stones through the resistance of the marshes and over the uneven floor of the rain forest. Long after he had given it to Dave, he still had no feeling in his arms and shoulders.

Dave hadn't come even close to matching Mex's endurance. Within half a mile, he let the wounded flyer slip over his shoulder and crash to the ground.

Derry and Brown had tried sharing it for a while, each twisting corners of the duffle into handgrips so that they could carry it between them. But Willie couldn't keep his grip with his battered hands. Each time a corner slipped through his fingers, the sudden change in weight pulled the sack out of Luther's grasp.

Baldinger had hoisted it to his shoulder again. But with the whole weight on his back he had been unable to keep pace with the others. Finally, Mex had taken it up again, and carried it for the last mile. Sergeant Campbell was waiting for them in front of the barracks.

"Fall in," Campbell ordered. He stepped to the end of their rank and plumbed along their chests. "Straighten up this formation, or we'll do two hours of close order drill right now."

They struggled to toe an imaginary line.

The sergeant marched down the rank, and stopped where Mex had placed the duffle bag on the ground. "What's that?" he demanded.

"A wounded flyer, Sergeant," Mex snapped back.

Campbell bent down and touched the bag. "This man is wet," he announced with feigned shock. "He's a wounded hero. Which one of your cowardly mothers let this great American fall in the stream?"

Baldinger spoke before any of them could confess. "Sergeant, he didn't fall in a stream. He's soaked through with fever. Probably malaria from the mosquitos in the swamp."

Campbell rose slowly and moved menacingly until he was in Dave Baldinger's face. "You trying to be funny, Corporal?"

"No, Sergeant."

"You're ordered to go in and bring out a man. You fuck up the attack and shoot the poor bastard full of holes. And then you fuck up the rescue and drop the guy in a swamp. You know what I think, Corporal Baldinger?"

Dave stayed at attention with his eyes aimed straight ahead. He knew Campbell wouldn't wait for an answer.

"I think you dumb bastards let this man die. I think he's dead." Campbell wheeled to the squad. "Who's your medic?"

"I am, Sergeant," Art Walters shouted.

"Okay, Medic, step out and tend to this man," Campbell snarled. "I want you to tell me whether you feel any pulse."

Art put his hand on the duffle. "No, Sergeant."

Campbell's eyes turned back to Baldinger. He screamed, "You killed him, you dumb bastard. You killed him with your stupidity!"

Baldinger was still looking straight through the sergeant's face.

"Well, since you killed him," Campbell screamed, "it's up to you to see that he gets a decent burial. So I want you, Baldinger, to dig a grave right now. And I want all you assholes out here ten minutes after reveille, in dress greens for burial services."

Campbell wheeled and marched away from the battered squad.

"Fall out," Baldinger said more as a gasp than an order. He told Art Walters to get a ride for Tony LaRocca and Dickie Morgan over to the infirmary. He set up a watch schedule so that the cadre couldn't pull a surprise attack, and then he went to find a shovel.

"I'll help you dig, my friend," Mex Cortines offered.

Baldinger shook his head. "No way, amigo. You already carried more than your share."

"About the same as carrying a sack of coffee down from the mountains," Mex answered. "No big deal."

★　★　★

Colonel Grigg had been patient throughout the meal. From his place at the head of the table, he had looked down on eight couples, and presided over conversation that was suitable for both men and women. His officers had hung on Marilyn Daks's every word as she continued her discussion about the PTA fund-raiser. When she mentioned the need for a giant thermometer so that the success of the drive could be publicly recorded on the grade school lawn, Brian O'Leary had offered to build it. And the wives were equally attentive to the men's concerns. When Lieutenant Fran Keller, a small arms specialist, and Major Jordan, both Little League baseball coaches, complained about the need to practice through midday, two of the women offered to bring lunches for the kids.

But after dinner, the table gradually segregated and conversations found their gender. As couples returned from the dance floor, the women tended to sit together while their husbands stood in a casual circle. It was easy for Grigg to raise the questions that had occurred to him during the evening, while leaving the wives to chat about whatever in hell women liked to chat about. With each tune that band played, he might lose an officer who would lead his wife to the dance floor. But he always had the attention of enough of his faculty to float a conversation about school business.

He asked Daks about the plastic-cased, high-explosive mines that had been buried all over the desert by the Iraqis. Had anyone figured out a way to detect them? How in hell were they ever going to be able to remove them? Daks talked about sensors that could detect the plastic explosive rather than searching for metal cases.

He got Henry Roy aside to discuss a new chemical agent that could make the water in a stream undrinkable. Roy told him that it worked exactly like the bacteria they had used in the past, causing diarrhea and dehydration, making guerrillas too sick to fight, and the people too sick to help them. "The problem with the old stuff," Roy allowed, "is that they may be too dumb to realize it's the water. They get dehydrated, so they drink more and more of it, and then it could become fatal." The new chemical, Roy explained, wouldn't kill people, even if ingested in great quantities. Grigg liked the concept. He wasn't interested in mass murder; just in disabling the guerrillas and the populations that supported them.

Brian O'Leary found himself drawn into a conversation on interpreting surveillance photos. He felt that they were getting too sophisticated for most of the foreign officers they were training. "If we could just convince these guys to fly over insurgent sanctuaries and tell them what they ought to be looking for," he said. "But most of them are scared stiff of being brought down in enemy country. Hell, there's probably someone they've killed in half the families." Grigg nodded his agreement. Even when we gave friendlies photos from our satellites they didn't know what they were looking at.

As the evening wore on, the separated groups that had formed during the cocktail hour were re-created. The officers gathered around Grigg to talk shop, while the wives were left to fend for themselves. The bribed musicians, who had found a following among some of the other officers, were ignored by the officers of Special Operations.

*   *   *

Baldinger left Mex to finish their freshly dug grave, and pulled himself up the steps of the barracks. It was time to relieve Derry, who had been posted as a sentry just in case Sergeant Major Thompson decided to have his cadre of VCs pull a sneak attack on the Americans. It had been a day of failures, and the squad didn't want to finish it off by allowing themselves to be murdered in their beds.

"Halt! Who goes there?" Derry was collapsed onto the battered couch in the recreation room. His bush hat was on a lamp table, and his assault rifle was on the floor next to his feet.

"Turn in, Willie," Dave said, settling into one of the soft chairs. "I'll take the guard."

Derry sat up straight. "I'm okay. I got my second wind. I was thinking that maybe we ought to treat ourselves to a little fun."

Baldinger smiled. Willie had been threatening that he was going to die of exhaustion when they were out in the swamp. Now he was looking for a party.

"We've got an early funeral detail. I don't think any of the guys are going to want to head into town."

"Who said anything about town," Willie answered. "We've got the music from the officers' club. All we need to do is order up a few drinks."

"You're crazy," Baldinger told him. "The guys have had it. We're all too beat . . ."

The screen door at the bottom of the stairs squeaked. Derry jumped up, grabbed his hat and picked up his rifle. He took up a sentry's position at the rec room door. They heard heavy footsteps on the stairs.

"It's Mex," Dave said. Willie tossed his hat across the room and onto the sofa.

"Grave's all ready," Cortines said as he lumbered into the room. "Only thing it needs is a cross."

Dave touched his forehead in a salute of thanks. Mex dropped into a chair.

"Hey, Mex. What say we take a run over to the officers' club and bring back some champagne?" Derry suggested.

Mex looked at Willie in disbelief.

"You know something," Derry said, changing the subject. "We weren't using our heads. We shoulda dumped the rocks into the swamp and just carried the empty bag. We could have refilled it just before we got back into camp. Who'd ever know?"

"Sergeant Major Elvis Thompson would know," Baldinger answered. "I bet he had guys watching us every step of the way."

A car squeaked to a stop outside the door. Willie ran to retrieve his assault rifle while Dave edged over to the window. "It's Art," he announced. "He's got Dickie with him."

Dickie Morgan had a bandage across his face, but the swelling was down. His eyes were wide open.

"They're keeping Tony," Art Walters said.

"Overnight?" Willie Derry asked.

The two newcomers dropped into the sofa. "Longer than overnight," Art explained. "They think he tore up some knee ligaments. They're probably going to operate."

Baldinger winced. If it was that serious, Tony would wash out of training. With a bad knee, he'd never get back into the program.

"Ball-buster," Derry said. They all nodded their sympathy for Tony. He'd been doing pretty well. Another four weeks and he would have earned his Green Beret and the unit flash patch of a Special Operations command.

Willie jumped up. "I'm gonna get us something to drink. Anyone want to come with me?"

"Where?" Art Walters asked.

Baldinger answered, "Willie thinks they run a take-out service over at the O Club."

"What do you think I been training for?" Derry demanded indignantly. "I'm silent! Resourceful! Deadly! Maybe I don't know enough to rescue a flyer from enemy forces. But I sure as hell ought to be able to rescue a few bottles of hootch from those bozos over at the officers' club."

Dickie Morgan began to laugh.

"Whatta ya say, Dickie. You comin' with me?"

"Jesus, Willie," Baldinger cut in, "the poor guy can hardly see."

Derry persisted. "How about you, Art?"

Walters smiled. "I'm not sure that's such a good idea."

"Oh, yeah," Derry smirked. "We'll see whether it's a good idea when I get back. I'll bet all you ladies will help me drink it."

He started towards the hallway.

"Where you going?" Baldinger demanded.

"To freshen up my blackface," Derry said. "Then I'm goin' behind enemy lines. I'm going to make old Elvis Thompson proud of his troops."

★   ★   ★

"What in God's name are you people talking about?" Carol Roy demanded as soon as she had managed to get her husband onto the dance floor.

He put his arm around her and drew her close. "Just shoptalk," he said. "The colonel is always working."

"Shoptalk?" Carol ridiculed. "Planting bombs. Poisoning water. Do you have any idea how terrible all that sounds?"

Henry Roy smiled. "It's just coursework." But the smile disappeared instantly. He could tell that she was furious.

"At one end of the table, we're talking about bake sales to buy more crayons for the kindergarten. At the other end, you're talking about poisoning people. It's completely insane. It's sick!"

He pulled her closer until their bodies were rubbing together. "Do you want to fight, or do you want to dance?" he asked, trying to sound lecherous.

Carol pushed back a bit. "It's hard to get horny over the grim reaper. Can't you guys leave it behind you for just one evening? Do you have to spend every minute being professional assassins?"

The captain relaxed his hold on her. "Not now, Carol. We're not going to go into this now."

"When?" she demanded. "When would you like to sit down and decide whether you want to teach kids how to play baseball, or teach generals how to poison the kids' water?"

He pulled her close, not to romance her but to silence her. She had taken a few drinks, and her voice was rising above a whisper.

"For chrissake, cut it out. We're in the Army. This is what we do."

Marilyn Daks, who was dancing with her husband, leaned close to them. "Could I bother you two for a ride. No rush. Just whenever you're going."

Major Daks rolled his eyes toward the table where Colonel Grigg was sitting. "The boss wants to try some ideas out on me. Looks like I'm in for a long night."

Carol answered, "Be happy to, Marilyn. Whenever you say. To tell the truth, I'm fighting a bit of a headache. I wouldn't mind leaving right now."

★　★　★

Willie Derry waded along the edge of the lake until he was at the foot of the bluff, directly under the officers' club deck. The cement basement of the building, with its steel loading door and screened-over windows, was just thirty feet above him. He leaned into the hill, grabbed a tree branch, and took a deep breath. Then he began to climb.

How did he get himself into these things? If he had half a brain, he would have taken Baldinger's suggestion and dragged himself off to bed. But that wasn't Willie Derry's style, he chided himself. Willie always has to make one more smartass remark, or think up one more really dumb idea. Exactly what in hell was he doing scaling the hill under the goddamn officers' club? Christ, he didn't even want a drink. All he was doing was showing that he didn't give a damn about the Army, with its castes of rank and privileges. But if he didn't give a damn, then what was he doing here. Nobody had drafted him. And, sure as hell, nobody had twisted his arm to get him to volunteer for Special Operations. He had spent a couple of months sucking up to a sergeant and a lieutenant just to get the appointment. So why was he playing the wise guy? The cuts on the palms of his hands were bleeding again, and his legs were throbbing with the pain he had felt in the marshes. So why didn't he just turn around and go back to the barracks?

He was halfway up the hill, keeping himself close to the ground, when the music suddenly stopped. He heard footsteps on the deck above him, and realized that he was crawling right under the noses of maybe half the brass at Fort Viper. All one of them had to do was look down and he'd be on his way to the stockade. What was he supposed to tell them? That he was on a training mission?

Willie held perfectly still, careful not to even breathe on a leaf. He raised his eyes slowly, and then blinked in disbelief. He was directly under two women, with an unobstructed view up their dresses all the way to their panties. Terrific, he thought. Now they can get me for perversion. "You were taking lewd advantage of officers' wives," the court officer would charge. "God, no," he would answer. "I was just stealing liquor." Some defense. He'd be lucky to get off with ten years of hard labor.

The orchestra roared into a fanfare. There was excited laughter above, and then the ladies and their officers clumped across the deck and into the club. Under cover of a near-deafening rock beat, Willie scampered up the hill and pressed himself against the basement wall. Keep going, he prodded himself. You'll never have a better chance. With the din of the orchestra and the hilarious shouts of the dancers, he could dynamite the door off its hinges without attracting any attention.

He reached into his belt, pulled out the wire cutters, and began cutting through the window screening. Halfway up one side, the cutters slipped from his fingers. When he reached to pick them up, he saw that both his hands were flowing blood.

He cut across the bottom, and then up the other side, until the protective screening was hanging like a shade in front of the window. He bent the screen out, and then searched the glass to be sure there were no alarm contacts or conductive taping. He waited until the singer was screaming his imitation of a doped-up rocker, and then smashed one of the panes. He reached in, raised the window, and pulled himself over the sill. Three minutes later, he rolled out through the window, reached back, and carefully lifted a light canvas bag from inside, taking great pains not to rattle its contents. He was pressing the screening back into place when the ruckus from the dance floor stopped. Derry froze against the wall as the exhausted dancers burst out onto the deck gasping for air. Once again, he was looking up at a lingerie catalog, probably the last ladies' undies he would ever see before he was dragged off to Fort Leavenworth. He wanted desperately to get out of there, but all he could do was remain perfectly still until the music gave him cover. He reached carefully into the bag and twisted off the top of one of the bottles. Now he needed a drink.

Baldinger still had guard duty at the top of the barracks stairs when Derry slipped open the screen door. Dickie Morgan, Art Walters, and Bobby Long were scattered like rag dolls on the rec room furniture. Jim Ray Talbert was lying on the floor, trying to stretch his back. Mex Cortines was dozing in one of the soft chairs.

"Everybody up," Derry said. He posed in the center of the room, holding up the canvas bag.

"Christ, you're bleeding to death," Walters said. Derry's hands were still oozing, and there were dark red smears along the sides of his trousers.

"I got me some medicine," Derry answered, lifting the bottles dramatically out of the bag. He had two bottles of bourbon, a bottle of gin and another of rum. "Something for whatever ails you."

"You didn't get any mixers," Bobby Long complained as he reached for the rum."

"No ice?" Baldinger asked with a grin.

Derry feigned shock. "Mixers? Ice? I thought we were jungle fighters. We're supposed to eat the moss off rocks and the bark off trees. Next thing you sissies are going to want to send out for orange slices and paper umbrellas." They poured straight drinks into the paper cups from the water fountain.

"Here's to our dead flyer," Derry toasted.

Dickie Morgan hesitated. "I sure shot the poor son of a bitch full of holes."

"You did him a favor," Mex consoled, sipping at his rum.

"I killed him," Morgan reminded Cortines.

"He was in prison," Mex answered. "They never woulda let him out. He's better off dead."

Baldinger chuckled. "Maybe you can sell that idea to Sergeant Thompson. He likes his prisoners alive."

Cortines thought for a second. "If it's my choice, I'd rather be dead. There's no way I'd live inside a prison cell."

Derry was reaching for his second drink. "Glad to hear that, Mex. I'll never have to waste my time trying to rescue you."

"I wouldn't wait for you, my friend," Cortines answered. "First guy tries to put me in a cell, I go right for his throat."

"They'd put a bullet right through your head," Tom Cavitt said.

Cortines nodded. "Yeah, but that's okay. I'd rather be dead."

He tossed off the rum. "I'm half dead right now. I think I'm gonna turn in."

Cortines dragged out of the rec room toward the sleeping quarters.

Dickie Morgan stood up. "Mex has the right idea. I think I'll pack it in. This course is a killer."

"Screw the course," Art cursed. He felt the sudden quiet and looked around at the curious faces. "Well just look at us, for chrissake. Dickie's face looks like he did ten rounds with Mike Tyson. Willie's hands are cut to pieces. Tony's gonna need surgery."

The paper cup slipped through Willie's fingers and splashed corn whiskey across his lap. The squad began laughing at his accident. Willie nodded, acknowledging his foolishness. "My hands are such a bloody mess, I can't even hold a drink. Jesus, guys, we're letting them beat the hell out of us. And for what? So that we can get ready to fight the Vietcong. Christ, the last Vietcong put in his retirement papers when I was two years old. I mean, is this Special Operations pure bullshit, or what?"

"We're gonna get some desert training," Bobby Long reminded him.

"Oh, great," Willie Derry mocked. "You figure there's gonna be another raghead who needs his harem rescued?"

Luther Brown smirked. "Maybe they should be teaching us house-to-house fighting in case we have to rescue Detroit."

"That would make a lot more sense than learning to stare down snakes," Derry answered.

They all laughed at their sorry situation. They were identical:

close-cropped, cleanly shaven, superbly physical, dressed in matched uniforms. And yet they were all different. Baldinger was a sandy-haired Iowan, the high school graduate and easily successful athlete who had joined the Army as a way to earn college. He had taken to the military challenge exactly as he had taken to the challenges of school football and baseball, with a quiet determination to be the best he could be. Willie was the perpetual wise guy, a Boston Irish kid who had been humiliated by the nuns and beaten by the brothers until he was big enough to fight back. He had decked the Reverend Brother Timothy, headmaster of a Christian Brothers high school, on the night of his senior prom when he was caught pouring rum into the fruit punch. He hadn't been asked to come back for graduation. Luther was as street kid from a section of Harlem that was an open-air flea market for drugs. He had wandered away from grammar school because there was no father at home to make him go, and become a lookout for one of the crack lords by the time he was fourteen. A civil liberties lawyer had recommended the Army as an alternative to jail sentence when he had been caught doing one hundred ten miles an hour on the East River Drive in a stolen Porsche.

Jim Ray Talbert and Bobby Long were mountain boys, one from West Virginia and the other from Tennessee. Jim Ray had gotten bored with changing tires and pumping gas, and had enlisted in the Army to find some excitement. Bobby had run away from a rocky, uneven patch of farm land, and then been unable to make a living. He had chosen the Army in preference to returning to the backbreaking work, and to a sneering father who had always told him that "you ain't never goin' to amount to nothin'."

Dickie Morgan was from Kentucky, destined to follow three generations of men into the coal mines. He had been left idle in an empty town when the coal company shut down. Tom Cavitt had picked the military in preference to clerking in his uncle's hardware store in Toledo, Ohio, a job that had waited for him to finish high school. Tony LaRocca was an army brat, son of a warrant officer who had risen through the enlisted ranks. Army life was all he had ever known and he had never even considered an alternative career. Mex was an immigrant and apparently an orphan, although none of them knew for sure. He was secretive about his family, but there were enough references to hard times to give the others the impression that he had joined the Army to escape a life as as migrant farmer. Art Walters had been a burden to two maiden aunts after his parents had died. He was quiet and studious. A doctor, or maybe a lawyer, his aunts had predicted. He had dayhopped to an extension of the University of Wisconsin for a year, and then decided that the most important step he had to take was getting out of the two ladies' household. He hoped to go back to school when he finished his hitch.

The Army had meant something different to each of them. A career. An escape. A temporary retreat. A source of funds. But right now it meant exactly the same things to all of them. Pain. Exhaustion. Frustration.

"If I had half a brain, I'd sign out of this dump in the morning," Willie Derry mumbled through his gathering stupor. "Plenty of cushy jobs in the Army."

"Good thing you don't have half a brain," Tom Cavitt consoled, setting them all laughing in Willie's direction.

Then Art Walters got serious. "I don't know. I guess it doesn't make a hell of a lot of sense puttin' ourselves through all this." He looked at Baldinger, who was the one they all turned to in a crisis. "What do you think, Dave?"

Dave glanced up at Derry. "I think Willie had a bad day."

"A real ball-buster," Willie agreed.

"But Willie likes bad days," Baldinger continue. "If they had a course that was tougher than this, that's where Willie would be."

"Bullshit," Derry answered. His voice was getting loud, and his speech was beginning to slur.

"Hey, think about it," Dave persisted. "We all volunteered for the Army when we could have stayed at home with our feet up."

Luther Brown interrupted. "Not at my home."

Dave nodded to acknowledge the remark, but he plowed ahead with his thought. "So we're in the Army doing nothing in particular, and then we hear about a school where they teach you to parachute out of airplanes. Why the hell did any of us volunteer for that? I mean, it isn't natural to jump out of an airplane."

"It was somethin' special," Brown said, as if his answer was perfectly logical.

"Right," Baldinger acknowledged. "We've all bought into this Army, and we're not satisfied to just be good soldiers. We all want to be something special."

"Just because we took jump training," Tom Cavitt argued.

"It wasn't just jump training," Dave continued. "Didn't we all sign up to jump in on top of the Iraqis? Someone want to tell me what was so appealing about that?"

Jim Ray joined the conversation. "I didn't volunteer," he offered. Baldinger narrowed his eyes and looked at him skeptically. "Well," Talbert defended, "I guess I volunteered, if you wanna get technical about it. The captain stood up in front of the company and said, 'We're volunteering to jump into Kuwait. Anybody who wants out, raise your hand.' What was I supposed to do? Fink out on the rest of the guys?"

"And then," Baldinger concluded, "we heard about a school where they drop you behind enemy lines and forget about you. So what did we do? Put in our papers and head home to our girlfriends? No. We all volunteer to come here." He thought for a moment about what he had just said. "Volunteer, nothing. I bet we all kissed some officer's ass to get the appointment."

Luther Brown tossed off the rest of his drink. "So what are you saying Dave? That we're all crazy?"

"Well, we're all gettin up at the crack of dawn tomorrow to say prayers over a bag of rocks," Dickie Morgan admitted. "I guess we have to be a little bit nuts!"

"Not nuts," Baldinger answered. "It's just that all of us are trying to prove something."

"Prove what?" Art Walters asked.

Dave held up his palms. "I don't know. Maybe that we're tough guys."

"Who do we have to prove it to?" Luther demanded.

Baldinger shook his head slowly. "Damned if I know. But I'll tell you one thing. When they come up with a program that's tougher than this, one so tough that they only take one guy a year, each of us will be running over the others to be that one guy."

"That's a crock," Derry pronounced. He refilled his cup, spilling some of the whiskey over the edge. Then he looked at Dave. "You're kidding, right? There ain't no school that's tougher than this."

★ ★ ★

Marilyn Daks carried the conversation on the ride home from the club. Squeezed into the Mustang's backseat, she leaned forward, her face between Henry and Carol. Looking from one to the other, she reviewed the events of the evening, praising every detail of Colonel Grigg's hospitality. She seemed unaware that Grigg had barely spared her a word, or that her husband, who had danced with her only twice all evening, was still giving all his attention to the colonel.

Henry turned into a residential street that was curbed with white-washed bricks, and braked in front of a small, cement-block and stucco ranch with a tile roof. It was identical to the other senior officers' houses, set on matched lots along both sides of the street. Captain Roy's house, on the next street, shared the same simple floor-plan, lacking only the carport on one side and the screened porch to the other. Junior officers could only look forward to these amenities.

Carol had to get out of the car so that Marilyn Daks could squeeze from behind her seat. Henry helped her out, and escorted her to the front door while Carol meandered aimlessly in the driveway. As Marilyn searched for her key, she said, "I don't think Carol had a very good time." Her tone suggested that there was purpose to her comment.

"Of course she did," Henry Roy lied. "She enjoys getting together with the staff."

Marilyn smiled as the captain took her key and fitted it into the lock. "I doubt that she enjoys having the colonel monopolize her husband on her evening out. I know I don't. But you might suggest that she at least try to pretend. Particularly if you're planning on a career."

"I thought she had a wonderful time," Henry protested.

"I hope so," Marilyn answered. "I like Carol very much. And I like you, Henry. I hope the two of you see the future in the same way. I know, for several years, I didn't see myself living on Army bases for the rest of my life. I wasn't having a wonderful time."

She closed the door behind her before the captain could answer.

Henry didn't look at Carol when they walked back to the car. He started the engine, bumped over the curb as he hurried his U-turn, and drove home in stony silence. As soon as they were in the house, he walked straight to the liquor cabinet. When Carol came out of the bedroom, wearing her robe, he was still in his uniform jacket, sitting with his feet on the coffee table, a tall drink cupped in his hands.

"Did you have to make it so damn obvious?" he demanded.

She looked genuinely bewildered.

"Christ, you might just as well have told them that you didn't like them."

"Who?" Carol asked.

"Everyone, damn it! The colonel. The whole staff. Their wives. Everyone. It was obvious you couldn't stand being with them."

"I thought I covered it pretty well."

He tossed off a swallow of the liquor. "Not well enough. Marilyn knew that you hated being there."

Carol laughed. "That's funny, because I know that Marilyn hated being there, too. Hell, she's a bright lady. How could she enjoy being ignored by her husband?"

"Maybe she has a little respect for her husband's work," Henry Roy challenged.

She looked at him in disbelief. "Respect for his work? For the love of God, Henry, Major Daks's work is blowing people up. He teaches foreigners how to mine their own countries. And is Grace Jordan supposed to respect Major Jordan? Isn't he the one who teaches the course in torture?"

"We teach special warfare," he snapped, jumping up and starting back to the liquor cabinet.

She followed at his heels. "That's what you call it. But tonight it sounded like bombing, and poisoning, and murdering. Jesus, it's like we're married to the four horsemen of the apocalypse. You're all sitting at the end of the table in your hoods, holding your scythes. And you think we're having a good time?"

He wheeled in rage, and the back of his hand flashed across her cheek. Her face turned under the force of the blow, but she didn't let herself back up even a step. She stared back at him in shock. Roy blinked his eyes in disbelief at what he had just done.

"Carol . . ." he said dumbly.

She shook her head in disgust, turned, and marched into their bedroom, closing the door behind her.

It was an hour later before Henry dared to turn the door handle and follow the beam of light that pointed toward the bed. Carol was covered up to her eyes by the blanket. Her back was turned toward his side of the bed. He sat on the edge, looking down at her.

"Carol," he whispered. She didn't answer, but he hadn't expected an answer, even though he knew she was awake. "God, I'm sorry. I don't know what got into me. I'd never hurt you. You know that."

There was no response. Not even a change in her breathing.

"It's just that this is what I do. I'm an Army officer. I want to get to the top. And this is my chance. It's a hot command. Colonel Grigg is going to wear a lot of stars, and he can take me with him. When he asked Daks to stick around, I felt like I was being passed over. I got scared. And then when you didn't seem to care, I guess I got mad. You know I didn't mean it.

She sighed, and turned her face into the pillow.

"I know it's a game," he continued. "I know you hate all this formality. All this rank stuff. But if you could just try not to show it. That's what Marilyn was trying to tell me. That it shows, and that it's hurting our chances.''

It was a game, and they had talked about it many times before. Carol had said that she had no intention of spending her life picking up after the wives of senior officers. She didn't want to jump to her feet every time Mrs. Colonel-something-or-other entered a room, or have to get involved in flower arranging just because it was the hobby of the current commanding officer's wife.

Henry had argued that it was no different in other careers. "You think when the senior partner's wife speaks, all the junior partners' wives don't pretend to be interested?''

"Sure they do," Carol had argued. "But they don't live together the way Army families do. They don't have to pretend every day of their lives.''

But tonight Carol wasn't taking up the argument. She was lying perfectly still, her face buried in the pillow and the blankets.

He stood and began undressing, folding his trousers and buttoning his jacket carefully over a heavy wooden hanger. He removed his service ribbons from the jacket and set them into one of the sections of his jewelry case. He slipped wooden trees into his shoes, and buffed them with his socks before he set them on the closet floor. Then he took a fresh pair of pajamas from the bottom drawer of his dresser and tucked the top into the pants before he slipped into the bed.

Henry leaned across and kissed Carol's hair. "I'm really sorry," he said. "Please don't hate me." He waited a moment, then turned away from her and stared toward the wall. A minute went by before he heard her voice, a muffled whisper buried in the bed covers.

"I don't hate you, Henry. What I hate is what's happening to you.''

★　★　★

Major Daks waved toward the waiter as he listened to Colonel Grigg. It had been a long monologue, and Grigg's pace wasn't showing any signs of faltering. They would need another drink.

Grigg had begun nearly two hours ago with some general comments about the need to update the curriculum. The world was changing, and the work of Special Forces would have to change with it.

"I don't see us going back into Southeast Asia," he had mused, "and there isn't going to be much support for revolutions in Latin

America.'' Daks had nodded his agreement. "So," the colonel had continued, "maybe we've got to take our courses out of the jungle. I mean, where are *today's* hot spots. The Middle East. Southern Europe. Maybe even the old Soviet republics. Hell, there isn't a rain forest in any of them."

"True, Colonel," Daks had said thoughtfully. "But we have to be ready for *tomorrow's* hot spots. We might find ourselves in South America. Or Africa."

"Of course," Grigg had agreed. "And I'm not suggesting that we drop any of the present training. But I think we have to add on to it. We have to pay just as much attention to desert fighting. Or even door-to-door fighting in some damn city in the Balkans. That's my point. We have to make sure that Special Forces is totally relevant for anything that might come up. And we have to be ready to train friendlies from any kind of country."

Grigg had taken the courses one at a time, and plunged into the details, explaining exactly what he had in mind. He was in the middle of O'Leary's work in surveillance when the waiter set two more bourbons on the table.

"Christ, how many of these things have we had?" Grigg demanded, suddenly breaking his train of thought. He looked from the drinks down to his plastic, multifunction watch. "Oh, will you look at this. It's after one. I'm sorry, Major. Mrs. Daks will be after my head."

Daks laughed. "No sweat, Colonel. Marilyn knows this is important.

Grigg sighed the check without even looking, and tossed off the last drink as he was pushing away from his chair. "Please tell her I'm sorry. Tell her when I get talking about the school I lose all track of time."

"I'm the same way," Daks said as he followed his commanding officer toward the door.

The colonel's Corvette was waiting at the foot of the steps. The instant he had cleared his chair, hand signals from the waiter to the front door had sent one of the parking attendants scurrying after it. Grigg was out of the circular driveway and accelerating back toward the parade grounds before Daks's off-road Bronco came into sight.

The major had no reason to fear his late arrival at home. But that wasn't because Marilyn understood the importance of his work. It was because she had stopped caring years earlier, when he had volunteered as an adviser for the Salvadoran Army. Given the choice between a staff assignment in Germany, and another tour in a remote, god-forsaken mountain range, he had chosen the mountains. Instead of taking a cushy billet that would have allowed her to share Europe with him, he had decided to leave her behind. "This is where it's happening," he had explained. "If we don't stop them here, our next defense line is going to be the Rio Grande. And, hell, it's only twenty-two months," which, she guessed, was his way to avoid saying "two years." She had pushed the travel brochures back into the drawer, gone to the airport to wave at his plane, and then returned to an empty house. The Daks's house had been empty ever since.

He was thinking of the evening's conversation as he steered the gentle curve that bordered the parade grounds, and feeling fortunate that he worked with the colonel. Grigg, he realized, was already preparing for the next era of Special Operations.

The guerrilla talents required to operate behind enemy lines had never been popular with the military's top brass. In the Pentagon, status was bestowed by the size of the budget you commanded, which made an arsenal of tanks, bombers, and supercarriers far more relevant than a cache of parrish knives and lightweight assault rifles. Careers were built by marching to the sound of the cannons. Allegiance to an army that tried not to make any noise at all was considered a career-limiting assignment.

But then, in Vietnam, tanks and howitzers had proven of limited value. The enemy never massed across a front line that tanks could attack, and never owned anything that was worth the cost of an artillery shell. In a war of ambush, intimidation, and political intrigue, a special kind of army was needed. And President Kennedy had ordered one built, authorizing the green beret as a legitimate append-age to the Army uniform.

President Johnson had been much more conventional. In his view, brute force was the key to victory. Bomb tonnage and body counts were easier to measure than the contentment of peasant farmers. Hearts and minds of the civilian population were simply an appendage to their balls. Polished brass came back into vogue, and Green Berets were hidden away in ambitious officers' closets.

But world affairs had taken still another unexpected turn. The staff of the American embassy was taken hostage, leaving the regular Armed Forces fuming in hopelessness. And when President Carter had called for his special forces, there were none to answer. The team assembled by the Joint Chiefs to conduct a stealthy raid into the desert had failed miserably. Later, the titanic task force they launched against a minor annoyance on the island of Grenada had given a Keystone Kop demonstration of incompetence. It became painfully obvious that a scrupulously trained force capable of special operations was needed. Congressmen even called for a new branch of the Armed Forces, politically the equal of the Army, Navy, and Air Force. The Joint Chiefs had cringed in terror. But over their objections, the Green Berets came back out of the closet.

Grigg recognized the opportunity. His dark army of counterinsurgency specialists were regaining popularity, and the funding for their activities was growing. But, as he had spent the evening explaining, they couldn't keep the spigot open if they continued to dress as jungle fighters. Some senator or congressman was bound to ask what jungle he had in mind. "If we're talking about the Middle East," a representative with an aircraft engine factory in his district was bound to ask, "wouldn't we have greater need for the light helicopter?" And the appointed marshals of the conventional military would be only too eager to answer, yes.

Grigg was expanding the scope of his operations so that the Special Operations Force would be the right response for any future threat to America. In the process, he was creating a future for his associates. When they gave Grigg his three stars, there might even be one left over for Major Daks. No doubt about it. Grigg was a true visionary.

As he turned the corner into his street, Daks killed his headlights. The master bedroom was at the front of the house, and he didn't want the lights to disturb Marilyn. He never considered that she might be waiting up for him. He shut off the engine as he turned into the driveway, letting the car coast toward the carport. Then he pumped the brake, pulled up on the hand-brake, and twisted the key out of the ignition.

His hand was on the car door handle when he was blinded by a white flash, and heard the concussion, so sudden and loud that the noise was painful. He was hurled backward and sideways, ripping the seat belt from its anchor as he flew through the door. Major Daks smashed against the side of his house as the hood of his off-road truck ripped through the roof of the carport. The right fender tore off, and cut like an ax through the supporting stanchion.

Daks started to scream as the rafters came tumbling down on top of him. But his voice was suddenly silenced.

THE
INVESTIGATION

★   ★   ★

Ten-hut! Pree-sent Ahms!''

The ranks on each side of the open grave snapped their salutes. With great reverence, Bobby Long and Tom Cavitt began lowering the duffle bag to its final resting place.

They were wearing their dress greens, with pressed trousers tucked into glistening jump boots. The Green Berets that had been awarded at the end of the first phase of their training were precisely angled on their heads. But there were no badges on the berets. The uniforms had no flash patches indicating unit assignment. The "Special Operations" arc was missing from the edges of their shoulders. Those wouldn't be awarded until the class completed the final phase of the qualification course. Some of those participating in the burying of the downed flyer might not get them at all.

They had arrived at Fort Francis Marion fourteen weeks earlier, coming from Army units around the world. All were qualified paratroopers. Five of them had already been through Ranger training, where they had mastered the physical and weapons skills necessary for the elite combat units. But none had been even remotely prepared for the demands of Special Operations.

For the first four weeks they had lived on the obstacle courses and mountain trails, meeting physical challenges that would have broken the bodies and the spirits of even the best-trained college athletes. That was the easy part of the program, and among men who had already survived jump school and Ranger training, the dropouts were few.

During the second phase, they had been in specialty training, taking classroom courses in medicine, communications, demolition, engineering, language. For two weeks, they had moved from course to course, gaining an overview of all the subjects. Then each of them had concentrated on a single subject. Special Operations units could be behind enemy lines for months, operating without friendly human contact. So to assure them the services of a doctor, a year-long medical internship, taught by physicians, was squeezed into six weeks. The graduates could handle almost any medical emergency up to and including the amputation of a limb. Special Forces might have to cross rivers, build fortifications, or help shelter friendly natives. The field engineering specialists learned to construct bridges, aerial tramways, water systems, and even housing, using whatever materials might be available. They would certainly be called on to destroy enemy facilities; buildings, roads, runways. The demolition graduates could paralyze an entire fortress with a handful of plastic explosives. Because the success of a mission and the lives of all the men might depend on any one of these specialists, the coursework was taken seriously. Only half the candidates who had entered the program emerged successfully from the second phase.

Now, in the final five weeks, it was all coming together. Physical strength, moral courage, and technical skill were being fused together by the enormous pressure of realistic combat missions. Less than half the men still in the running would be graduated to Special Operations units.

Bobby Long and Tom Cavitt stepped back from the grave's edge and fell into line with their saluting comrades. Then Baldinger called, "Order Ahms!" In unison, their hands snapped back down to their sides.

Sergeant Major Thompson walked solemnly to the head of the grave, removed his beret, and folded his hands across his belt buckle. His face tipped skyward.

"Heavenly Father," he prayed, "may this fallen hero be the last victim of our stupidity. Because that's what killed him. Stupidity. It wasn't that these fine young men weren't trying. You saw how hard they worked cutting their way through the jungle. And it wasn't that they lacked courage. Why they walked bravely into the same stream with your deadliest snakes. It's just that they haven't figured out how to use the brains you gave them. So they made mistakes. And in our business of fighting wars, mistakes usually kill someone." His face dropped back to the men who were still locked in attention. "I pray they learn before they get themselves killed."

He put the beret on his head, and the material fell into the proper jaunty shape. "Baldinger!" he yelled.

"Yes, Sergeant Major!"

"Lead these men in humming taps!"

He turned and marched off toward the noncommissioned officers' quarters. Behind him, off-key voices struggled to find a common cadence for the mournful dirge.

"Okay, you assholes!" Sergeant Campbell's voice came instantly after the last hummed note. "I want this grave filled and then covered so that I won't be able to find it. If I do find it, you're gonna have dig 'im up and move 'im someplace where I won't find 'im. And then I want all of you out in the pits in exactly ten minutes. Last one to get there is the first one I fight."

Campbell looked up and down the ranks, flaunting his disgust.

"Dismissed!" he snarled.

They raced into the barracks, stumbled through a uniform change, and were back out at the grave in just over a minute. Four of them began tossing the piled earth back into the hole. The others raced to the back of the barracks and cut a six-foot strip of sod from the lawn. They carried the sod around to the front and fit it into place over the fresh dirt.

"We ain't gonna make it," Luther said, glancing at his watch, "unless we run our asses off."

"We'll run," Dave answered, "but in formation. We're all going to get there at the same time. Nobody's gonna be last."

The pits were large rectangles, bordered by railroad ties, and filled with sawdust. They were used as the rings for training in hand-to-hand combat. Sergeant Campbell stood in the center pit, leaning casually on a pugil stick, a long pole, padded on each end so that it looked like a kayak paddle. He watched as the formation double-timed toward him, and then assembled along one of the ties.

"You're late!" he yelled from his position in the center of the sawdust. "You're all last! So I'll just pick my opponent. Unless one of you pussies wants to volunteer for the first lesson."

He twirled the stick like a drum major's baton and let it fall across his shoulder. "What's the matter? Nobody feeling vicious today? I thought you were supposed to be tough guys." Campbell stared at every face, looking for eyes that would dare to challenge his own gaze. There were none.

"Okay," the sergeant concluded, "then I guess I'll pick my own fight. Derry, get out here."

Willie stepped out of the rank, but stopped short of crossing the railroad tie. "I'm out of action, Sergeant. Medical problem!" He held up two bandaged hands."

"There ain't no medical problems, here," Campbell answered.

The smile that had been playing at the corners of Willie's mouth vanished. "I can't hold the stick, Sergeant," he tried.

Campbell sneered. "Too bad, 'cause without a stick, you're gonna get your ass kicked." He nodded to one of the cadre. A pugil stick came sailing through the air and landed at the edge of the sawdust, just across the tie from Willy's feet.

"You'd be surprised at what you can do with cut-up hands," the sergeant taunted. "Last night some guy with bloody hands broke into the officers' club and stole some liquor. Bet that guy would be able to hold onto a stick."

Willie bent slowly, keeping his eyes on the sergeant. He lifted the stick and squeezed it with his fingertips.

"You need helmets," one of the training cadre called out. He picked up two of the lacrosse helmets that were worn during the combat and started into the pit.

"No we don't," Campbell snapped.

Baldinger sucked in a breath. Campbell had never found Willie's humor amusing.

"He's gonna nail 'em," Luther whispered under his breath.

The whole squad tensed.

Willie stepped across the line and into the sawdust, holding the pugil stick parallel to the ground, feinting with the padded ends. He crouched forward, moving his weight to his toes. Campbell smiled and casually lifted his stick off his shoulder. "Whenever you're ready, Derry."

Willie moved in, faked with the left end of his stick, then swung the right end at Campbell's leg. Campbell ignored the fake, then dropped the left end of his stick to block the blow. "Too predictable," he screamed at Willie. "C'mon. Show me somethin' different."

Derry danced back and reset his balance. He lunged forward, swinging the right end high into a decending blow. As soon as Campbell moved his stick up in defense, Willie pivoted and thrust the left end forward in a spearing jab. Campbell danced a step to his left as the padded end of Willie's stick flashed by. "Better," Campbell said. "But you didn't get through Rangers with that shit. Give me your best attack."

Willie tried to tighten his grip. His hands stung, and when he glanced down he could see the blood soaking through the bandages.

"C'mon," the sergeant mocked. "We ain't got all day. All the other pussies are waitin' for their turn."

Willie rushed straight toward Campbell, leading with the right end of the stick. As Campbell dodged to his right, Willie slashed with the left end of his stick. Campbell caught the blow between his hands, just as Derry had expected. As the two poles clattered together, Willie ducked under the high end of Campbell's pugil and drove his padded right end into the sergeant's side. It was a clean hit that knocked Campbell back, but Willie's follow-up with the left end of the stick missed its mark. He knew that he had left his whole left side open even before he saw the right end of Campbell's stick flashing toward him. It lashed across his ribs and dropped him to one knee.

Campbell instantly followed up on his advantage, swinging the other end of his stick like a scythe. It took Willie's legs out from under him and dropped him on his back. The sergeant jumped forward, slamming his foot onto Willie's pole, and pinning his hands to the sawdust.

"You're dead, pussy," he sneered, and he drove the left end of his pole into Willy's gut. Derry's eyes widened as he gasped frantically for air.

The sergeant stood over his victim for only a second, then danced away to the edge of the pit and set the pugil stick for another attack. "On your feet, you gutless mother," Campbell screamed. "We're just gettin' started."

Derry dragged himself to his knees. He tried to pick up his stick, but it kept slipping through his fingers. Sawdust was sticking to the bloody bandages. He wiped his hands on his shirt leaving stains of red grime. Then he wrestled the stick back into his grip. The instant he turned, Campbell was on him.

Campbell fired the right pad at Derry's leg. Willie blocked it and moved away. They circled. The sergeant's next assault was a series of blows delivered in a staccato from both ends of his pole. Willie blocked them all as he backed across the pit, and then dodged to his right before he reached the railroad tie.

Campbell's eyes narrowed. He didn't like to be shown up by his trainees, and Willie had just blocked his best combinations. He launched another furious assault, feinting and then striking in lightning combinations. Willie parried them all as he retreated, and then closed on the sergeant. Their pugil sticks locked together in front of their faces, crossed in an "X" and bending under the strain as the two men tried to force one another back. For an instant, Derry seemed to be gaining the advantage, moving Campbell back toward the boundary defined by the railroad tie. But then the sergeant jumped back, shifting his weight to his left leg. His right leg fired out in a vicious kick that landed with a dull thud right into Derry's groin.

He dropped as suddenly as if he had been shot through the head, first to his knees and then onto his face. He gagged, struggling for breath, and then vomited up the night's drinking.

The sergeant circled with his pugil stick at the ready. "C'mon, you pussy. You haven't shown me anything yet." Derry rolled onto his shoulder. There was blood-red sawdust all over his hands, and yellow sawdust clotted on his lips. He forced himself to his knees, fumbled with the stick, and then fell forward on top of it.

Baldinger broke from the rank and rushed into the pit, dropping to his knees next to Derry.

"Get your ass out of here, Baldinger. This exercise isn't over."

Dave was kneeling beside Derry, holding his friend's face out of the dust. "It's over, Sergeant," he said without ever looking toward Campbell. "He's had it."

"Then you pick up the stick," Campbell screamed. "Let's see what you're made of, you yellow mother."

Baldinger took Derry's arm over his shoulder and began lifting him gently.

"You hear me, pussy," the sergeant hissed, moving across the pit toward his victims. "I told you to pick up the pugil stick."

Baldinger ignored him as he started walking Derry across the sawdust toward the railroad tie. Campbell charged forward, swinging the right pad in a tight arc. It smashed against the side of Baldinger's jaw, dropping him like a cut tree. When Dave fell, Willie Derry staggered and then toppled down on top of him. Sergeant Campbell leaned over the two bodies. "Pussies," he screamed. "What in hell is goin' to take to make fighters out of you!"

Art Walters stepped over the railroad tie and walked across the sawdust toward Dave and Willie.

"Don't touch 'em," Campbell snapped.

Walters strode past the two sprawled forms, bent down, and picked up the pugil stick. Then he turned, as calmly as if he had taken a book from a shelf, and walked back to the edge of the pit.

"You goin' to take me on?" the sergeant laughed derisively.

Walters set the stick across the edge of the tie. Then he slammed his boot down on it, breaking it in half. Campbell's eyes widened. "You little mother—" he started.

Art stepped out of the pit. "Luther, Mex. Get Dave and Willie." The two trainees jumped out of rank and ran to their companions. Campbell took a step toward them, brandishing the stick that he still held in his hands.

"We're takin' them out," Luther told his sergeant. He helped Willie to his feet. Mex took Dave's arm, pulled him to a sitting position, and then lifted the limp body onto his shoulders. Campbell watched speechless as they walked out of the pit.

"Let's get out of here," Walters told the squad. They formed a casual double column, with Luther Brown supporting Willie Derry in the front rank. Mex Cortines, helping Dave Baldinger keep his footing, fell in at the rear.

"I didn't dismiss this class!" Sergeant Campbell screamed.

"Detail, for-ward, march," Walters ordered. The squad turned its back to the pits and stepped off toward the barracks.

"You're finished, Walters," Campbell screamed. "You just washed out." He took a furious step after them but stopped at the railroad tie as if it were an electric fence.

"That man is out of here," he yelled, "and if you mothers don't want to wash out with him, you'll get back here now."

They fell into step. Art Walters began to count the cadence.

"You're headin' for the stockade, Walters." Campbell's voice cracked from the strain he was putting on it.

"Ter-up. Ter-up. Ter-up, two, three, four," Art intoned as the squad marched off.

★   ★   ★

Major Daks stepped out of the staff car, and nodded toward the corporal who was holding the door. He raised the plaster-encased arm out of the sling, and shook his head to explain why he hadn't opened the door himself.

"You'll get used to it, Major," the corporal said sympathetically. He nodded toward Daks's house. "From the look of it, sir, you're damn lucky it was only your arm.

Daks waited until the staff car had pulled away before he turned his attention to the house and assessed the damage. The carport was gone. The demolition instructors who reported to him had gone over the area carefully, and removed even the smallest fragments of wood and concrete. They planned to reassemble the structure back in their classrooms so that they could assess the type and location of the explosive charge. The gravel driveway terminated in a deep, round pit. A large section of stucco siding was missing from the wall of the house, leaving the cement blocks exposed, and the bathroom window that opened onto the carport area was boarded over. His eyes wandered absently over the house, but they focused sharply when they reached the peach tree that grew next to the carport. Its branches were singed, and stripped of every leaf and every piece of fruit. It was an ugly tangle of twigs instead of a tree.

Daks shook his head in amazement. By all rights, he ought to be dead. The shrapnel of gravel that had stripped away the stucco and sawed through the carport supports should have cut him in half. It was the heavy, four-wheel-drive truck that had saved him, blocking the direct blast and deflecting the bulletlike stones.

The door flew open and Marilyn charged across the lawn toward him. Behind her, Captain Martin Johnson stepped into the sunlight. Daks raised his good arm, draped it on his wife's shoulder, and accepted her kiss. "I was so worried," she said. But he was walking toward Johnson before she could finish her greeting.

"What the fuck was it?" the major demanded as he passed the captain and continued on inside. Johnson followed at his heels, turning his back to Daks's wife.

"A fragmentation grenade," the captain said.

Daks dropped into a soft living room chair. "I'd really like a bourbon on the rocks," he said toward his wife. Then he looked at Johnson. "Captain?"

"Bourbon would be great, ma'am," Johnson told Marilyn.

As soon as she left the room, Daks turned on his captain.

"You sure?"

Johnson nodded. "No doubt about it. There were chunks of the casing all over the place. Standard Mark, and as near as we can tell, no special firing device."

"You telling me someone just pulled the pin and rolled a grenade under my car?"

Johnson was still standing. "No, I think it was planted as a mine. It was buried under the gravel, maybe a couple of inches into the soil. It was the gravel that did most of the damage. Stripped the tree. Tore the stucco off the house. You have about two pounds of gravel in the oil pan of your car."

"Where's the car?" Daks asked, suddenly remembering that it hadn't been in front of the house.

"In the lab. I'm sorry, Major, but I think it's totaled. The engine is pulled right out of the transmission and the frame is bent. We'll put it together for evidence, but I don't think anyone's ever going to drive it."

Marilyn came back into the room holding the drinks, each one wrapped in a cocktail napkin. "Please sit down, Captain," she told Johnson as she handed him the bourbon. She asked her husband whether she should prepare snacks, or perhaps sandwiches. He shook his head. In response, she began listing all the things in the refrigerator that might go nicely with their drinks. The major said no to each of them, the edge of his impatience beginning to show.

"Could we be alone for a few minutes," he finally told her. She smiled at the captain, handed each of them a second napkin, and left the room.

The instant she disappeared, Daks leaned toward the younger officer. "You know what you're saying? You're telling me that someone is trying to kill me."

Johnson considered. "Sure looks that way."

"A lunatic," the major snapped, jumping up from the chair. "My wife might have driven the car home. Or Captain Roy and his wife could have pulled into the driveway when they were dropping Marilyn off. Any of them could have been killed."

The captain nodded in agreement. "Mines aren't terribly precise weapons."

"Jesus," Daks said. "I was just thinking. Marilyn always backs the car into the carport at night so that she doesn't have to back into the street traffic in the morning. If she hit that thing with her back wheels it would have blown the gas tank." He shook his head in gratitude.

"I hadn't thought of that," Johnson admitted. The heavy construction of the off-road vehicle had saved the major. But if the gasoline had ignited, there would have been no escape.

The major finished his drink, and disappeared into his kitchen for a refill. He was already talking when he came back through the door with a fresh drink in his hand.

"Whoever he is, this guy is sick. I mean, what kind of weirdo puts a mine in a residential area where it could kill innocent woman or children? For chrissake, there are kids on this street and they play all over the place. Just think, if I didn't hit that thing last night, then it's still sitting there. Waiting for my wife to back in. Maybe waiting for the paper boy."

It was two hours later when Colonel Grigg's Corvette squealed into the driveway and braked with its front bumper hanging over the crater. The colonel knocked politely, paid his respects to Marilyn, and followed her out onto the screen porch where Daks was stretched out on a chaise.

"Stay right there," he insisted as the major tried to rise. He pulled one of the chairs up against the chaise. He said no to the offered drink, and then yes to his favorite bourbon when it was offered a second time.

"You don't look bad. Not bad at all."

Daks lifted the plaster cast. "This is it. If the roof hadn't come down on top of me, I probably would have gotten away without a scratch."

They spent a few minutes analyzing his extraordinary luck. The force of the explosion had tossed him far out of the car, like a round being popped out of a mortar. But the oversized engine, the transmission, and the front end differential had blocked the blast of iron fragments and hot gravel, and had dampened the initial surge of heat. By the time he slammed against the wall of his house, the damage had already been done. Daks was right. If the roof hadn't come down on top of him, dropping a two-by-four joist across his arm, he could have simply dusted himself off and gone to bed.

"The guys are pretty sure someone set it," Daks offered.

"That's just speculation," Grigg answered immediately. "They're not sure how it was detonated. Even when they finish the investigation, they still might not be sure." He paused for another sip of his drink. Then he volunteered, "Hell, it might even be an accident."

Daks looked shocked. "It was a live grenade, in my driveway."

"Oh, I'm not saying it was an accident," Grigg corrected. "I just don't want any speculation until we have some good solid evidence. First we get all the facts, then we see what we can prove. In the meantime, I don't want to fuel any rumors. A lot of loose talk won't help the reputation we're trying to build for Special Operations."

The colonel declined the offered second drink and then ordered the major to stay home the next day. "No rush getting back." He smiled. "The important thing is to make sure you're over this and feeling better.'' He thanked Marilyin profusely for her hospitality, complimented her on the color scheme of the living room, and told Daks once more how well he was looking.

But the major wasn't following the small talk. His mind was racing, trying to get ahead of the colonel's thinking. Grigg was hinting that perhaps the explosion was just an accident, and it was easy to figure out why that was the verdict he would prefer. An accident wouldn't be controversial. Nobody was killed. The injuries were minimal. There was very little damage to his house, which was the only piece of government property involved. It would be just a routine report that would attract little attention as it passed from an in-box to an out-box on some Pentagon bureaucrat's desk.

But the attempted murder of a Green Beret officer? That was the kind of easily sensationalized crime that had nearly put Special Forces out of business many years ago, when a Vietcong double agent had been mysteriously murdered. The top Army brass would seize it as further proof that a corps of stealthy killers, operating outside the rules of normal military discipline, couldn't be trusted. Generals would leak it to their favored congressman as evidence that scarce funds were better spent on tanks and fieldpieces than on throwing knives and Green Berets. It was just the kind of news that the parade ground officers could use to shut down the Special Operations School, and turn Fort Francis Marion back into Camp Viper. At the least, it could cut the head off all Grigg's plans for expansion of the Special Operations role, and change a tour of duty with Special Operations from a smart career move to a ticket to oblivion.

Daks could admire the direction that Grigg's thinking was heading. Except that even a harmless accident had to have a cause. "A grenade carried about as a training aid by the demolition instructor." Or "an antipersonnel mine, left in or on the vehicle belonging to the instructor." There were lots of ways to explain how a grenade had been accidentally detonated in his driveway. The problem was that all of them made him look like an idiot. What kind of demolitions expert leaves live explosives lying around?

If Grigg were going to pass it off as an accident, then he was going to turn Major Daks from a victim into a fool. Daks's career was going to be the sacrifice that had to be paid to maintain the rising reputation of Special Operations. Fair enough, for everyone except Eugene Daks.

He remembered that Grigg had encouraged him to take the next day off, and decided that he'd better make sure to be at his desk in the morning, probably a half hour early.

★ ★ ★

The rec room could have been a funeral parlor, heavy with a sad silence. Dave Baldinger, Willie Derry, and Luther Brown were pacing, ignoring one another as they passed. Dickie Morgan was on the sofa, thumbing through a magazine without even glancing at the photos. Jim Ray Talbert, Mex Cortines, and Tom Cavitt had claimed the soft chairs, but they were all sitting uncomfortably on the edges of the cushions. Bobby Long and Art Walters were missing, Bobby because he had gone to the hospital to visit Tony, and Art Walters, because he was over at the training unit headquarters, hearing the verdict on his insubordination to Sergeant Campbell.

Jim Ray was the first to break. He looked at his watch for the third time in the past three minutes, bounded out of his chair, and walked to the window. "What the fuck are they doing? Holding a jury trial?"

"It ain't a trial," Tom Cavitt said. "It's a hangin'."

Derry broke off his pacing. "If he's out, then I'm out!" he declared. No one responded so he added what was eating at his guts. "The whole damn thing was my fault."

"That's not true," Baldinger answered instantly.

But Derry wouldn't be consoled. "Then whose fault is it?"

Baldinger shrugged his shoulders. "I don't know, Willie. Does it have to be someone's fault?"

"Yeah," Dickie Morgan snapped, throwing aside the magazine. "When someone gets fucked, it has to be someone's fault. And this is that asshole Campbell's fault. He damn near beat Willie to death. And then he tried to knock your brains out." His last remark was directed to Baldinger.

"Maybe my fault," Baldinger said, confessing what he had been thinking. "If I'd stayed outside the pit, then maybe he would have just cursed Willie some more. Maybe it all would have been over. I've been thinking that my going inside the pit was the turning point."

Jim Ray Talbert turned from the window. "That's bullshit, Dave. The guy was completely out of control. He went apeshit!"

Baldinger nodded. It was certainly true.

Tom Cavitt said, "He musta found out that Willie was in the officers' club. He really wanted to make an example out of him."

62

"What the hell do you guys think I've been saying!" Derry shouted. "It all started with me. And it ain't fair that Art has to take the rap."

"It all started with that bastard, Campbell," Luther Brown reminded them. The guy is completely crazy."

"He's not crazy," Mex Cortines corrected, speaking softly to himself. He was surprised when every face snapped in his direction.

"You defending him?" Cavitt asked suspiciously.

"He ain't crazy," Mex repeated. "He's just Army. He gotta be the winner, and he don't care much what happens to anyone who ain't on his side. He knows how to fight, and he don't give a damn about the guy he's fightin'."

The screen door at the foot of the stairs banged. The squad dove toward the sofa and chairs, rushing to look as if they had been sitting comfortably. They listened to the climbing footsteps.

"Oh, for God's sake," Dickie Morgan snarled when Bobby Long poked his head into the recreation room.

"Ya hear anythin'?" Bobby asked. Their expressions told him they hadn't. "Hey, they ain't going' to wash him out. Hell, they spend eight weeks teachin' him to do brain surgery. He's the smartest guy they got."

Baldinger asked about Tony LaRocca. Bobby responded by drawing a finger across his throat. "Gone. It's gonna take him six months of therapy after the operation. And then he probably won't be able to requalify as a jumper."

They stiffened when the screen door banged again. This time they made no pretense of being relaxed. They were all staring at the top of the steps when Art Walters appeared.

"How'd it . . . ?" Willie Derry began. But he stopped when he saw there was no need for the question. Art was carrying a fat manila envelope. They all recognized it as his service record, and the mandatory six copies of his new orders.

"Back to Fort Bragg," Art said, brandishing the envelope. "I'm now part of the Eighteenth Airborne Corps."

"Ah, Jesus," Baldinger sighed. He turned away from Art and found himself looking at a blank wall.

Derry looked for something to punch. "Bullshit," he snapped.

"We gotta do somethin'," Luther said.

"No way," Art told them. "I'm outta here, and I'm glad to be going. I'm a medic, not a goddamn jungle fighter. When you guys are out staring down snakes tomorrow, I'll be staring up some young lovely's skivies. I'm gonna have a lot of free time on my hands."

"Son of a bitch, Thompson," Jim Ray Talbert said. "You'd think he'd give you a break."

"He did," Art answered. "Told me he'd let me off with ten hours' punishment duty. He wanted to make it disrespect instead of disobedience, insubordination, disruption of an exercise, and all the other crap that Campbell gave him."

They looked at each other in amazement. You could get ten hours for leaving a pocket unbuttoned. For what Art had done, Thompson could have sent him to the stockade.

"Ten hours?" Derry asked. He had been averaging ten hours of disciplinary duty a week. "And you didn't take it?"

Art Walters stood in the doorway to the sleeping quarters, where he could look back and see all the men in the recreation room. "Hey, listen up, and listen good. I wanted out. Coming back on the march yesterday, when we were wading with the snakes, I said to myself, 'What the hell are you doing here?' And I didn't have a good answer. Then last night, Dave says we're all trying to prove something. Well, I'm not trying to prove anything."

Baldinger stuffed his hands into his pockets. "I thought we were just talking, Art. I wasn't saying anyone should get out of this place."

"I know," Walters answered. "But it got me thinkin'. This morning, I knew when we were burying the rocks that I was going to ask for my ticket back. That's why I went into the pit. Someone had to stop that asshole, and I was the one with nothing to lose."

Luther Brown's hands tightened into fists. "That bastard Campbell! Somebody ought to get that mother."

"You know what I think?" Art continued. "I think the sergeant major knows that Campbell went too far. I think that's why he wanted to let me off with just ten hours."

"Take the ten hours, for chrissake," Derry said. He was begging more than ordering.

"That's what Thompson told me. 'It's only ten hours, Walters. You can do push-ups for ten hours!' But I told him I'd take my medical training to the Airborne. It'll be good for me and good for the Army."

"What'd he say?" Dickie Morgan asked.

"Nothing. He just nodded, and then he helped me fill out the papers."

Art waved to the group. "I got a bus to catch, and I gotta be packing." He turned out of the recreation room, leaving the rest of the squad to resume their mournful silence.

It was nearly an hour later when Baldinger walked into Walters's room and closed the door behind him. Art was almost ready, wearing his uniform greens. He was stuffing the last few things from his top drawer into his duffle.

"You want this?" he said to Baldinger, and tossed him the green beret he had folded and was about to stuff into the bag. "I don't think I'll want to wear it around the Airborne guys."

Baldinger tried to laugh at the joke. Airborne was the elite of the spit-and-polish Army, and they didn't enjoy being reminded of the Green Beret's special status. But the laugh died on his lips. He settled on the edge of the bare mattress, rested the beret on his knee, and began to smooth it flat. "You shouldn't be leaving, Art. You already made it through the worst of this. You're a sure bet to graduate."

"I don't think this is for me," Walters answered. He pulled on the drawstring that tightened the duffle over his things.

"Cut the crap," Baldinger said. "You're not leaving because you don't like being in a pond with snakes. You're being tossed out because you tried to help me. And that makes it my fault."

"Dave . . ." Art tried to interrupt. But Dave kept talking.

"We can go to Thompson together and tell him what happened. Jesus, Willie was a bloody mess and I was out cold. Campbell had gone nuts. He could have killed one of us. You're the medic. You had to do something."

'Dave . . ."

"No, damn it! Listen to me. They have fourteen weeks invested in you. Eight weeks of medical training. Half the guys who started medical training flunked out, and you finished at the top of the class. Thompson doesn't want to lose you. He'll listen."

"Dave, I already talked to Thompson. And you're right. He doesn't want to lose me. But I don't want to stay. I want out of here. This isn't something that just happened. This is my decision. I'm quitting."

Baldinger still didn't believe him. He looked at him with his face squinted. Walters pushed the duffle aside and sat on the other end of the blue-striped mattress.

"Look, this place is great for the rest of you guys. You're a soldier, Dave. You're a leader. The top guy in the squad. This is the Army's top training, and you're the top guy in the unit. You can probably get into officer school and get a commission if you want."

"Bullshit," Dave snapped. But Art kept talking.

"In a different way, it's right for Luther, too. Hell, he grows up in a ghetto with five kids in one room and a toilet. The Army is giving him a chance he never would have had on the outside. And Mex. He doesn't talk about it, but you can guess what it's been like for him. He can have a real career in the Army instead of living on his hands and knees picking beans. But you pay a price when you buy into this stuff. A big price.''

''What the hell are you talking about?''

''I'm talking about violence. That's what the Army is all about. And this place is the best that the Army has to offer. This place makes violence an art.''

Dave shook his head. ''That's just Campbell. Mex was just saying that Campbell doesn't give a damn who he hurts.''

''It ain't just Campbell,'' Art interrupted. ''Look at the courses we've been taking. How to kill without making any noise. How to plant high explosives. How to start fires. How to poison wells. Campbell didn't write those books. And look at the training exercises. They don't just teach you to kill someone. They teach you to hate him. To despise him. To curse him while you're pulling a wire around his neck.''

Walters stood up, grabbed the heavy bag, and dragged it across the bed. He let it bounce onto the floor.

''You know what finally got to me this morning?'' he asked. Dave looked up blankly. ''It wasn't just that Campbell was beating the hell out of Willie. And it wasn't just that the bastard seemed to be enjoying it. It was the things he kept calling him while he was hitting him. 'Pussy. Motherfucker.' Like he wasn't a man. Like he was some kind of garbage. Before they can make you think you're a killer, they have to make you forget you're a person. Before they can make you violent, they have to get you used to violence. That's what this whole place is about Dave—making you forget you're a person and getting you so used to violence that you don't care who gets hurt.''

He started to lift the duffle, but the bag was so stuffed that he couldn't get a grip on it. Dave wrapped his arms around it and lifted it up onto his shoulder. ''It ain't all violence, Art. They taught you to be a medic.''

Art Walters struggled to get the duffle into balance. ''I know. There's lots of good things. I've learned how to save people's lives. I guess that's the problem. I like saving 'em better than shooting 'em.''

He held out his hand, and Baldinger took it and shook it. ''Good luck, Medic,'' he said.

"Crazy, ain't it," Art said as he shook Dave's hand. "You blow 'em up, and I try to put 'em back together again. And we're both in the same Army."

Walters left the room. Baldinger looked around at the empty closet, the open dresser drawers, the stripped bed with the bare mattress turned up to show the wire springs. His friend hadn't left even a trace of himself behind. He had made his decision, and then he had followed through on it.

And Baldinger had made his decision, hadn't he? Certainly he had decided that Sergeant Campbell wasn't going to drive him out. Maybe Campbell didn't care what happened to his enemies, but Campbell wasn't what the Army was all about. Baldinger had embraced the Army, welcomed its challenges, and signed up for its most demanding training. The Army, he believed, would make him a better man, not tear away his humanity, as Art Walters believed. The Army stood for justice, not victory at any price, as Mex Cortines claimed. He believed that, didn't he? Because if he didn't, what was the point in all the discipline? What good was the training if, in the end, he was nothing more than an efficient killer?

He looked down, and realized that he had been tossing Art Walters's green beret back and forth, from hand to hand. He folded it carefully, and slipped it into his pocket.

*   *   *

Major Daks was at his desk when the corporal tapped on his open door and told him that Colonel Grigg wanted to see him. He jumped up eagerly. He knew that Grigg had been secreted in his office with a captain from the base commander's staff, and he was anxious to find out exactly what was going on. If they were talking about the explosion, then they were talking about him.

He had gotten up early after a restless night, managed to assemble the coffee pot with the one hand that he could use, and tried to dress himself without disturbing Marilyn. He was able to get the shirt on over the cast on his left arm, and fit the buttons with the fingers of his right hand. But he was helpless with the necktie.

Marilyn had been annoyed that he was going to the school. Grigg had practically ordered him to take the day off, and she knew he wasn't completely recovered from the trauma of the explosion. She had felt him tossing and turning all night long, unable to rest or to find a comfortable position for his rigid arm. A day spent between the chaise on the porch and the soft chair in the living room was exactly what he needed. And besides, the workmen would be coming to repair the driveway and start reconstructing the carport. She knew they would have questions that she couldn't answer.

She had tried to delay him with the promise of an elaborate breakfast, his favorite thick bacon and soft fried eggs. But he had gulped down the coffee and kept reminding her of the time. Wearily, she had dressed and driven him over to the school.

Daks had been doing paperwork when Grigg had charged into the building promptly at 0800 hours. The colonel had looked into the office, told Daks that he should be home in bed, and then added that a legal officer from command staff was due at 0830. "As long as you're here, you probably ought to join us."

He had heard the officer arrive and announce himself as Captain Robert Gordon. Daks peeked through the open door as the corporal lead Gordon to the colonel's office. He never remembered seeing the man before, either at any of the military ceremonies or at any of the events at the officers' club. Gordon was young, probably not over thirty, with horn-rimmed glasses that made him look more like a clerk than a soldier. He was almost six foot and reasonably well built. But his dark hair was cut, not shaved like the Airborne and Special Operations officers who populated the base. There was a softness to his physique that made it very unlikely he had ever run the obstacle course.

Daks had waited impatiently, shuffling through the papers, weighing them down with the cast on his left arm whenever he had to write something with his good right hand. But his eyes had kept darting into the corridor, waiting for the colonel's door to open so that he could be summoned inside.

When the corporal came for him, he was ready. He knocked on Grigg's door and then opened it without waiting for an invitation. Grigg was at his desk, in pressed shirtsleeves with his tie pulled up tight. Captain Gordon was sitting opposite him, still wearing his jacket. There were mugs of coffee on the desk. Grigg introduced the officer, and gestured Daks toward the remaining side chair. "Captain Gordon," he said when the major was settled, "is judge advocate on General Wheeler's staff. He's going to be working with the military police on the investigation."

"Investigation?" Daks was pleasantly surprised. He had convinced himself that the colonel would try to sweep the entire incident under the carpet. But his pleasure was short-lived.

"There has to be a report," Gordon said. "Pretty much routine. Even though it's probably just an accident, we have to decide what caused the explosion. Colonel Grigg was explaining that you're the explosives expert, and that your people are already trying to put everything together. I guess you'll be able to tell me what blew up and where it was located."

Daks looked across the desk at Grigg. "Is that how we're handling it, Colonel? As an accident?"

"For the time being," Grigg answered immediately. "Unless something comes up, there's not much else we can call it. But I've told the captain I want a thorough investigation. I want to find out exactly what happened."

Daks turned his attention to Gordon. The guy was a pencil pusher who probably couldn't tell a hand grenade from an atomic artillery round. The captain could pull all the paperwork together. But if General Wheeler and Colonel Grigg really wanted to get to the bottom of things, they wouldn't be turning the investigation over to someone like Gordon.

"We'll help in any way we can," Daks told him. "Our guys should be able to tell you what kind of grenade it was, how the fuse was set, and exactly where it was when it detonated."

Gordon smiled gratefully. "That should make it pretty simple for me, Major."

"What we'll be counting on you for, Captain," Daks continued, "is telling us how it got there."

The captain seemed suddenly confused. He turned toward the colonel for help. "You don't know how it got there?" he asked. "I just assumed that with the major handling weapons all the time—"

"That I keep hand grenades in my garage," Daks said, completing the thought sarcastically.

"We don't know how it got there," Grigg stated. "That's one of the things we have to find out."

Gordon looked from one officer to the other. He slipped the yellow legal pad off his lap and rested it on Grigg's desk. Then he took off his glasses.

"Colonel, I'm not sure I'm the right man for this job. I'm a lawyer. I've been to law school and to the Judge Advocate General course. When I head up an investigation, it's usually into the legal aspects of a case against a soldier who's gone AWOL, or who broke up a saloon in town. It's all pretty simple stuff, where the guilty guy is standing in front of you with the evidence in his hand. But what you're suggesting is detective work, and I'm not a detective. I have no experience in police investigation. And I don't know the first thing about explosives."

Daks was beginning to like the captain. He might not be a soldier, but the guy was certainly honest.

Gordon shifted his attention to Major Daks. "You talked about how the grenade might have gotten into your driveway. Were you implying that someone might have put it there intentionally?"

Daks shrugged and turned his palms up. Captain Gordon nodded that he understood, and turned back to Grigg.

"If someone intentionally mined Major Daks's driveway, Colonel, then we're not investigating an accident. At a minimum, it's reckless endangerment. Most likely, it's intent to commit murder. In any case, I'd be in way over my head. It would be a police matter. Army Special Investigations, or maybe the FBI since it occurred on a federal facility."

Grigg tried not to smile at the innocence of the young captain. The commanding officer of a military post had authority and power unrivaled since the death of the last Russian czar. General James Wheeler would prefer to surrender Fort Francis Marion to the Cuban Army rather than allow even a single representative of any other branch of government to intrude on his post. "I think it's a bit early to be talking about the FBI," he said to Gordon. "And frankly, I doubt very much that we're talking about attempted murder or reckless anything."

"But, Colonel—" Gordon was about to explain the legalities of even threatening someone with a deadly weapon, but Grigg wasn't interested in a discussion.

"I told General Wheeler that we had to investigate an accident," Grigg said, "and you're the general's answer to my request. So you've got the ball, Captain, until you present me with something that proves we need to involve outside agencies. Until then, this is a base matter."

He looked from Gordon to Daks. "I think that about covers it, Major. I'll need a few more minutes with Captain Gordon. On another matter." Daks rose immediately to attention, wheeled, and headed toward the door. Another matter, my ass, he thought to himself. He closed the door behind him. He guessed that that his patron colonel was about to prompt Captain Gordon toward a complete cover-up.

"What's your starting point?" Grigg asked as soon as Daks's footsteps moved away from his door.

"Armory records," Gordon guessed. "Maybe the military police can find a grenade that's not accounted for."

Grigg nodded. "Probably worth checking, just for the record. But you won't find anything. There's a lot of ammunition used here at Fort Marion. No one could account for it all. I'm sure you'll find all the records have been juggled to come out even."

Gordon felt properly corrected. "As I said, Colonel, I'm a little out of my league. Perhaps you can point me."

"My guess is that Major Daks brought that grenade home in his own car. Maybe caught up under a fender, or bouncing around on a bumper."

"From the officers' club?"

Grigg's eyes rolled. "Captain, he could have carried that grenade in and buried it under a tire any time in the past six months without ever knowing it. He may have driven over it a couple of dozen times since then. Only this time, his car hit it just right to break off the pin."

Captain Gordon jotted the notion onto his legal pad.

"Of course, there's always a possibility," Grigg allowed, leaning back in his chair, "that someone could have set it."

The captain wondered, "Who would do such a thing?"

"Captain, the training on this base is extremely demanding. People crack under it. A trainee who's been pushed to the limit. Maybe one who got a lousy grade in Major Daks's course. Or one of the noncoms in the training cadre. Daks writes fitness reports on most of them. It could be that the major cost one of the noncoms an advancement in grade. Then there's the Airborne officers. They really don't have much of a stomach for their counterparts in the Special Operations. Or it might even be a Special Operations officer who figures Daks got a promotion or a commendation that he was entitled to."

Robert Gordon looked up from his notes. "That just about covers everyone on the base."

"You can see what I'm getting at, Captain. But that's not even the half of it. Just to add more possibilities, you ought to know that Major Daks's wife runs the PTA for the base school. I think she also chairs the flower club. The major isn't interested in the base school, and he doesn't give a damn about flowers. I don't think they spend a great deal of time together."

Gordon waited for Grigg to finish the thought. As the seconds passed he looked more and more lost. "You're not suggesting that Mrs. Daks . . ."

"What I'm suggesting is that if you find out who Major Daks does spend his time with, you might find a husband who has a damn good motive, or maybe even a wife who's been loved and left. The possibilities go on and on, Captain, and your chances of running them all down are virtually nil. Which is why I don't want to hear a lot of loose talk about attempted murder or reckless endangerment. I think you can use your time better by trying to find out how an accident might have occurred than by looking for phantom assassins."

★   ★   ★

It was Luther Brown's patrol, another of the training missions designed to create the terror of Special Operations behind enemy lines. They had been marching all day, climbing the slopes of the Appalachians that rose to the west of Fort Viper. Late in the afternoon, they would reach Sector Foxtrot, a dense forest growing at impossible angles out of sheer rock cliffs. Exactly at sunset, when the light dropped suddenly behind the mountains, and darkness struck like death, the exercise would begin.

An Airborne unit from Fort Bragg was scheduled to drop into Foxtrot at first light. Luther's unit was to assure them a safe landing zone. The opposing forces, this time assumed to be Latin American guerrillas, would once again be played by the training cadre.

"Reconnoiter the area," Sergeant Major Thompson had instructed in his briefing, as casually as if he were telling them to take a stroll around the parade grounds. In the jagged terrain, a single step forward could require scaling a thirty-foot rock wall. "Determine the presence, if any, of hostile forces." They could count on hostiles who would know the direction from which they entered the sector, and had been better briefed on their mission than they had. "Find a suitable landing area for assault helicopters." That meant flat ground, clear of heavy foliage, and away from any cliffs that could create downdrafts. It also meant a location that provided the assault troops with numerous routes for quick movement away from the landing area. "Deliver the precise coordinates of the area chosen to the approaching force." He was telling them that they had to be absolutely certain of their position. That they had to set up a field radio, and get a coded message back to the helicopters waiting on their pads, fully loaded, with their rotors already spinning. "Mark the area." With electronic homing beacons that the helicopters' navigation systems could lock onto. "And defend it from hostile fire." That meant patrolling a perimeter at least a thousand yards from the landing point. If the guerrillas were inside that perimeter, they could catch the copters at their most vulnerable point, when they were hovering above the treetops, and destroy them with small arms fire. Thompson had been clear that the ultimate failure of their mission would be to bring the helicopters into an enemy ambush. "You'll fail this exercise if the Airborne force isn't able to put down. You'll be out on the highway with your termination papers if the pilots even hear a gunshot."

All this was to be accomplished in a period of less than eight hours, over dangerous terrain, in blinding darkness. And, because this is the way it would be in a real incursion, the hostiles of the cadre were familiar with Sector Foxtrot, just like native insurgents. To the squad members, Foxtrot could just as well be a foreign country.

"So how do you think they're gonna fuck us this time?" Luther Brown asked.

"Any way they can," Baldinger answered. "They don't like to lose."

"There's probably only one piece of open ground in the whole sector," Cavitt guessed. "And they're probably sitting on it waiting for us to walk in."

"That's not in the game rules," Brown protested.

Dickie Morgan laughed. "This is war, you dumb bastard," he howled in his best imitation of Sergeant Campbell. "There ain't no fucking rules in war."

"Hold it down!" Baldinger suddenly interrupted. He stretched out a hand, palm downward, and listened to the silence of the evening forest. "Anyone hear something?"

They looked inquisitively from one to another.

"I don't hear nothin'," Jim Ray Talbert volunteered.

Mex Cortines shook his head. "Me neither." But as he said it, he was aware of a distant rumble.

"Yeah, I hear it," Brown said to Baldinger. "Sounds like an engine. Probably the trucks bringing the enemy to the exercise."

"Maybe we can hitch a ride," Willie proposed.

"No way," Brown sneered. "If they found us out in the road with our thumbs up, they'd stick a machine gun in our faces and take us prisoner. Can't you hear Thompson asking what kind of an infiltrator hitches a ride with the enemy? We'd all be washed out!"

Derry looked at Luther in disgust. "They can't take us prisoner until the exercise starts," he argued. "And the exercise doesn't start until sundown. That's the rule."

"This is war, you dumb bastard!" It was Dickie Morgan, repeating his impression of Campbell. "There ain't no fucking rules in war."

They were all laughing at Morgan when Luther Brown suddenly ordered, "Shut up!" They all listened as the engine noise ground through a gear shift. The truck was coming up behind them, along the road that they were walking. "If there ain't no rules, then we better get our asses out of here," Brown said. He made a hand signal toward the woods. "Let's go."

They scampered off the two-track road, down a slope and into the trees. Brown told them to take cover. Then he ordered Baldinger into some heavy cover that was on higher ground, closer to the road. "See if it's them, and get a count if you can." Baldinger moved away in a crouch, dodging through the clumps of trees.

The distant rumble grew into a roar, interrupted by pauses as the truck shifted speed. It was only a few moments before they could hear the banging of the clutch. Luther glanced up without raising his head, and saw the line of exhaust smoke as the truck labored by them. The engine noise died quickly, and within a minute, the forest fell back into silence.

Baldinger ran down the hill to the squad. "It's them," he told Luther Brown. "I counted fourteen. They looked like a truckload of migrant workers. Panchos. Sombreros. I wonder where the hell Thompson gets his costumes."

Brown gave a hand signal and they climbed back up toward the road.

"Who's the commander? Campbell?" he asked Baldinger.

Dave responded with a blank look. "No. I didn't see any of the top sergeants. Whoever is in charge must be coming up later."

"We should ambush the bastard," said Derry. "See how smart those guys are when they don't have a copy of our battle plan."

Luther Brown snarled, "That's not in the game rules."

He was treated to a singsong chorus of the whole squad imitating Campbell. "This is war, you dumb bastard. There ain't no fucking rules in war."

Brown formed them up as soon as they were back on the road. "If there's no rule, then they could've stopped the truck further up the road. We could be marching into an ambush."

Bobby Long rolled his eyes. "C'mon, Luther. Don't be so dumb. They wouldn't do that."

"Let's form a diamond," Brown ordered without bothering to notice Bobby. "Baldinger, take the point. Derry and Talbert, you guys got the flanks."

They hesitated for an instant, wondering if he was serious.

"Move it!" Luther snapped. Baldinger turned and dashed up the road to the point position. The squad stepped out.

In the point position, Baldinger was a sacrificial pawn, assigned to walk alone into whatever ambush an enemy might set. The Army training manuals described him as a lookout, responsible for sighting hidden dangers, and giving the rest of the patrol a timely warning. In theory, he would see the lurking enemy before they could see him, turn and rush back to the squad leader, and tell him to stop the squad before they all walked into a trap. In fact, it was assumed that an enemy, with time to disguise its position, would see him first. The hope was that one of the enemy gunners would get trigger happy, and blow his head off. The sound of the gunfire would be the timely warning.

As he moved forward, his eyes searching the vacant edges of the forest, he thought about his true role as an exposed target. He was a combat casualty, even before the combat was started. It was insane. First they had been taught not to trust anything during a combat exercise. Assume, and you're dead, as Thompson like to remind them. Now they were learning not to trust anyone or anything, even outside the confines of the training exercise. "There ain't no rules!" Nothing you could trust except your own survival instincts, like an animal that lives every second of its life in fear of the predator. It was like Art Walters had told him: "First they have to make you forget you're a person."

He reached a bridge that crossed the shallow channel of a small stream. "Stay off the bridges," he remembered Thompson screaming. "Be suspicious of anything man-made." A shed that offered a few minutes of relief from the scalding sun was the perfect setting for an ambush. Give it a wide berth. A bridge was the perfect ploy for splitting a force in half. Don't cross it. Don't ever put half your force on each end, because if they blow the bridge, they've reduced you to two small forces.

Baldinger left the path and slid down into the culvert. He stepped into the stream that barely washed over the toes of his boots, and crouched down under the bridge. There were no charges, no wires, no indications of tampering. He pulled himself up the opposite bank and began moving ahead along the road. But he stopped suddenly, and looked back at the bridge. Then he raced across, back toward the patrol. Brown ordered a halt as soon as he realized that Baldinger was coming back toward him.

"We gotta conference, Luther. I got an idea."

Luther pulled away from him. "What's the problem? We gotta keep goin'. We got a schedule to meet."

"You're thinking about the rules, Luther," Baldinger answered. "And that's a mistake. Like Campbell's been telling us 'there ain't no rules.'"

Luther turned back to him. "What are you talking about?"

"I'm talking about Sergeant Campbell, or whoever's in charge. He's coming up this road in a jeep to lead his peasant revolutionary army. Which means he knows where the enemy is, Luther. He's got to rendezvous with them. And I bet he's got a great briefing map of the area right in his pocket."

"Yeah?" Brown already knew what Baldinger was telling him. "So what?"

"So he has to drive across this bridge. They've been telling us for weeks to stay away from the bridges. But they just drove their whole force over this bridge, and now their brilliant leader is going to be driving over it."

Luther's white grin was already broadening. "And you're thinkin'—"

"The same thing you're thinking," Baldinger answered.

Luther chuckled. "It's crazy, Dave. But I love it." He turned to the squad, which was waiting for his order. "Hey, guys. Get back here. We got somethin' cookin'." They assembled in the brush by the roadside and Brown began to explain their tactics.

"You're gonna do what?" Tom Cavitt couldn't believe what he was hearing.

"We ain't gonna get away with this," Jim Ray Talbert said through his laughter. "But I'd sure like to give it a try."

"They'll wash us out," Dickie Morgan counseled. "Sure as hell, we'll all be back in Airborne in the morning."

"For what?" Willie Derry demanded. "All we're doing is what they been doin' to us. Ain't this the kind of thing they been teachin' us?"

Tom Cavitt looked shocked at the idea. Dickie Morgan seemed frightened. But Luther had already made up his mind.

"Okay, I'll go on ahead with the patrol. Baldinger, Derry, you two hang back and see what you can do with that bridge." He pulled the field map out of the baggy pocket of his fatigues, studied it, and found a point near the entrance to Foxtrot. "We'll hole up and wait for you right here." Dave and Willie checked their maps to be certain of the rendezvous point.

"Fix a time," Dave suggested. "Let's say you wait one hour and ten minutes. If nothing happens here, we'll come after you in exactly one hour."

"One hour and ten minutes," Luther Brown agreed. "Then you're on your own." He turned away from the bridge. "Long, take the point. Okay, guys, let's get moving."

Mex Cortines stepped directly in front of Luther. "Let me stay with the bridge," he offered. Luther shook his head. Leaving two behind already thinned out his patrol. If they didn't catch up with him, he'd be undermanned for almost any action.

"If it's Campbell, this could turn into one hell of a street fight." He nodded toward Baldinger and Derry. "Neither of 'em has done much time on the streets. It's gotta be either you or me."

Brown glanced back to the bridge and watched Dave and Willie disappear into the culvert. Mex was right. They might not be ready for all the things that could happen once there were no rules. But he had to keep a fighting force together. "I can't afford to leave three of you," he said.

Mex patted him on the shoulder. "Don't worry, my friend. I'll find you." He looked up at the mountainous forest. "I'm used to this kind of country."

"Okay, Mex. But bring 'em back to me. I'm gonna need 'em."

Mex broke from the patrol and raced back toward the bridge. He jumped into the culvert and chased after Dave and Willie who had already started dismantling the span.

It was a simple log bridge. Two straight trees had been cut down and stripped into long poles. They were stretched parallel across the culvert, their ends deeply embedded in the high ground on either side. Then shorter, thinner logs had been cut into eight-foot lengths, and tied edge to edge across the two poles to create a bridge fifteen feet long and eight feet wide.

Baldinger and Derry were underneath, digging furiously with small shovels. They had each taken one of the foundation poles, and they were working side by side to dig away the supporting earth. Mex jumped in next to Willie, whose hands were still bandaged. He moved like a machine, firing the point of the shovel into the rocky soil, and tossing the earth into the bed of the stream. Dave's pace picked up as he tried to keep up with Mex.

"How much time you figure we got?" Derry panted.

"No way of knowing," Baldinger said. "But if we hear a jeep coming, we'll stick a grenade under each of these and blow the damn thing."

Cortines dropped his shovel, planted his feet and set his shoulder under one of the spanning poles. He strained upward, grunting under the effort. It suddenly broke free. Dave scampered around Mex and began backhoeing dirt from under it.

Derry's eyes were wide. "Holy shit," he said. Mex Cortines was holding up a corner of the bridge. When Baldinger finished shoveling, Mex crouched down to lower the pole. It was hanging in midair.

They dug furiously under the other pole, and then Cortines braced under it and lifted it off its footing. This time Willie Derry tore the supporting earth away.

"Leave some of it, Willie," Dave reminded him. "We have to leave enough to hold it. It has to look like a bridge."

Mex set it down gently. The end of the pole caught just enough of the bank to keep the whole structure from dropping into the culvert.

Baldinger checked his watch as they climbed out of the culvert. They had been working for over twenty minutes. They couldn't wait long for Sergeant Campbell to arrive.

Derry studied the top side of the bridge, which looked just as sturdy as when they had walked across it. "You don't suppose this sucker might hold up?" He asked Cortines. Mex turned and looked at Baldinger.

"There's nothing holding it up now. We're okay."

They picked their hiding places. Baldinger went down through the riverbed and crouched into bushes on the other side of the bridge. Cortines and Derry separated and found cover on either side of the road, at the end of the bridge from which the car would approach. The waiting began with each minute dragging by like an hour.

There wasn't any time to waste. If they didn't leave an hour before their rendezvous with Luther Brown and the patrol, then Luther would start off into Sector Foxtrot without them. Any information they were bringing him would be useless. They would both be pursuing separate missions with neither force strong enough to carry it out.

Five minutes slipped by with no sign of Campbell's jeep. The only sounds were the wind in the tips of the branches, the splashing of the anemic brook, and the birdcalls from overhead.

Baldinger began feeling uneasy when ten minutes had passed. He checked his watch and found that they had less than half an hour to make their move. There was no reason in hell why Campbell should fit into their time schedule. He was driving. He could make it from the bridge to Foxtrot in five minutes. He had all day to drive past.

Another five minutes. Now the whole plan seemed harebrained. It wasn't even a plan, Baldinger admitted to himself. It was an act of vengeance. He was going outside the rules to get Campbell, because Campbell had gone outside the rules and washed Art Walters out of Special Forces. It was an act of defiance. You bastards want to cheat? Well I can cheat too. Except that he wasn't sure he could. He didn't even know whether he should. Maybe it was like Art Walters had told him. First they have to teach you to hate. They have to make you forget you're a person.

He broke from his cover and started out into the road, intending to call the whole scam off. He was going to get Willie and Mex, and race up the road to overtake Luther Brown and the others. But then he heard a mechanical sound, out of place against the backdrop of natural noise. It was an engine roar, low and throaty, that occasionally soared up into a high-pitched whine. Baldinger slipped back into the woods.

Cortines and Derry tensed, involuntarily leaning forward ready to spring. But just as they were sure it was coming closer, it dimmed and went silent. They listened carefully, confident that it would reappear. But as empty seconds ticked by, they began to believe that they had never heard it at all.

Then it leaped at them. The gurgle of the engine down-shifting seemed to blast in their ears, and the car appeared around a wall of green foliage that masked a turn in the road. They all crouched lower and then froze as if they were posing for a time exposure. The engine found its rhythm as the jeep straightened its wheels and began accelerating toward the bridge.

Campbell was driving, already costumed for the exercise in a colorful shirt over olive drab fatigues. A broad-brimmed straw hat was in the passenger seat. His only personal touch was the mirrored sunglasses with the wire frames. He touched the brakes to slow the car as it neared the wooden bridge.

Willie winced when the front wheels began vibrating over the logs.

The damn bridge was holding! Then the back wheels jumped off the dirt road and onto the wooden roadway. Baldinger cursed under his breath.

The jeep vanished. At one instant it was rolling cautiously over the timbered roadway. The next instant it was gone. There was a dull thump. Not the screeching of metal or the shattering of glass that they expected, but more the sound of a giant fist slamming down on a wooden table. Baldinger broke out onto the road and rushed toward the culvert. He saw Cortines and Derry coming at full speed from the other side. When they reached the fallen bridge, they had Sergeant Campbell surrounded.

He was sitting in the shallow run of the stream, his head turning in disbelief, the sunglasses cocked to a ridiculous angle. The bridge, still perfectly intact, was sloped down into the ditch at a steep angle, one end up on its foundation, the other end nearly in the water. The jeep was still on the bridge, its left front wheel hanging off and spinning in space, its rear end resting against the steep slope of the culvert.

"Son of a bitch!" Campbell roared. He picked himself slowly out of the water, and wiped the mud from his hands on the legs of his pants. He walked cautiously to the jeep, and began inspecting its hopeless predicament. "Son of a bitch!" he screamed again, and he pounded the hood with his fist.

"Hey, take it easy! That's government property!"

Campbell looked up to see Willie Derry smiling down at him. The assault rifle that Willie carried on his hip was pointed straight into the sergeant's face. Cortines was standing a few paces to Willie's left, aiming another assault rifle toward his head. In faltering Spanish, Derry ordered him to put his hands on the top of his head and to climb up out of the chasm. "You're our prisoner," Willie informed him. The sergeant seemed confused, so Cortines repeated the order in perfect Spanish.

Campbell hesitated a moment, looking wide-eyed from Derry to Cortines. Then he screamed, "You guys lost your fuckin' minds or somethin'?" He began climbing up toward them, his hands swinging free at his sides, and his fists clenched. "Prisoner, your ass," he cursed. He nearly jumped out of his boots at the deafening blast of the assault rifle behind him. He spun quickly, lost his balance, and fell against the slope. Baldinger was standing on the other side of the stream, his rifle at his shoulder. "You're not dead," Baldinger yelled in better Spanish than Willie's. "That was a warning shot. You're our prisoner. Now put your hands on top of your head and climb out."

The sergeant leaned back and looked straight above his head. Derry and Cortines had stepped to the edge, and had their guns pointing down on him. Derry was laughing. "Climb up," he ordered.

Campbell turned in rage and began clawing his way up the side of the slope. "You're goddamn right, I'll climb out. And then I'm gonna show you a real war."

His hand went under the floppy peasant shirt and pulled his automatic pistol out of its holster.

"You wanna play for real, you mother? I'll show you somethin' real."

Willie backed away from the edge as Campbell neared the top. "Get your hands on your head," Derry ordered, but his tone had lost a measure of its certainty. When he told Campbell, "You're our prisoner," it sounded more like a question than an order.

Campbell walked straight toward the muzzle of Derry's rifle. "Go ahead, ya dumb pussy. Fire all your blanks. Then I'll fire what I got." As he walked, he raised the pistol until it was aimed straight into Derry's face. With his thumb, he cocked the hammer.

From across the culvert, Baldinger could see the pistol. He watched helplessly, his rifle loaded with training blanks, as Campbell closed on his friend. Derry's rifle dropped down toward his side as he stared down the barrel that was pointing right between his eyes. He's going to kill him, Baldinger realized. He had called the training game off when he decided to capture Campbell outside the zone. It wasn't a game anymore. It was real. And Willie Derry was about to pay with his life.

Mex took a lightning step toward Campbell. The sergeant was too involved in his charge toward Willie to see him coming. Mex's fist looped down low and smashed into Campbell's gut, stopping him dead in his tracks. His body bent forward, the gun dropped out of his hand, and his head fell towards his belt buckle. Mex grabbed Campbell's hair in his fist, jerked his face upward, and then smashed it down on the point of his rising knee. Campbell staggered backward, his face a starburst of crimson.

"Jesus Christ, Mex," Willie whispered in horror. But he was too stunned to move. Mex moved right into Campbell's face, and snapped a flashing right fist across his jaw. The sergeant fell backward over the edge of the culvert and rolled down the slope into the stream.

Cortines charged down the hill after him, and Baldinger rushed down from the other side. Campbell started to push himself up out of the mud, but Mex's boot landed in the center of his back. Baldinger had already passed around Mex and was at Campbell's feet, pulling the laces out of his climbing boots. He twisted the boots off and tossed them up to Willie. "Get rid of these," he yelled toward Derry. They had been taught that, in rough country, a prisoner wasn't going anywhere without his boots. But Willie made no move toward the boots. He was standing frozen, staring down at Campbell's automatic pistol.

Mex bent Campbell's hands behind his back, and Baldinger quickly bound them with the shoe laces. He pulled the knots tight and then used the ends of the string to tie the thumbs together. Mex then grabbed the sergeant's hair and pulled him up to his knees.

Baldinger quickly searched through the shirt pockets, then found the exercise training map in the buttoned pocket of Campbell's fatigues. He studied it for a moment and found the markers for the only two possible helicopter landing points within Foxtrot.

Campbell was gagging on the blood that was running from his shattered nose back into his throat. "You fuckers are goin' to pay for this," he managed.

Dave stuck the map in front of his clouded eyes. "Where are your forces?" he demanded, using the Spanish that had been specified for the the exercise.

"Fuck you," said Campbell in his gutter English.

Mex pulled back on his hair. "Answer the man."

Campbell managed a cocky smile. "You wanna real war. Okay. All you get is my name, rank, and serial number." He spat in Dave's face.

"Where's the cadre?" Baldinger screamed at him. He pushed the map nearly against Campbell's nose.

"Fuck you," the sergeant repeated.

Baldinger and Cortines looked at each other. They hadn't thought it through. They didn't know how far they should go.

"It's loaded," Willie Derry's voice said. They looked up the slope and found Willie standing at the edge, holding Campbell's pistol in the palm of his hand. "They're real bullets."

Mex switched his grip to the collar of Campbell's shirt and dragged him into the stream. Then he threw him face first down into the water. "You get one chance to tell me," Cortines said. "Then I drown you." He nodded toward Baldinger.

Dave dropped to his knees so that Campbell could see the map.

"Where's your force?" he asked.

Campbell shook his head. "You pussies don't scare me."

Mex put his hand on the back of the sergeant's head and pushed his face into the muddy water.

They had all been taught how to resist interrogation. In their first week of field training, each of them had dropped into the open country and then were hunted down and taken prisoner by the training force. They hadn't resisted their capture. After all, it was only a training exercise. But their cockiness had disappeared the moment they found themselves alone with the enemy, the first time they had felt a fist crash into their ribs and realized that their captors weren't pulling their punches.

Willie had cursed at the cadre team until they stripped him and staked him out over an ant hill. They sat in the shade, sipping ice tea while the ants gathered around his belly and began biting at his flesh. Within minutes he had been begging them to listen to his confession, and then screaming information at them while they pretended to ignore him.

Within two hours of his capture, Dickie Morgan had been completely convinced that he had fallen into the hands of real terrorists. They made him straddle a bamboo pole, his toes dangling inches above the ground. The pain quickly became unbearable, but each time he toppled off, they beat him with rubber hoses, and then lifted him back up onto his perch. This can't be happening, he kept telling himself, these guys are Americans. But then their identity changed in his blur of agony. Somehow, he reasoned, he had gotten lost and wandered into a band of outlaws. He told them everything he knew about Special Operations training.

Dave Baldinger had been bent backward over a barrel. They tied a cloth over his face and poured water on it until he was taking in water with every breath. He gagged, and then choked, but they kept pouring the water until he was sure he was drowning. They'll have to stop, he reasoned. This is just training, They won't want to hurt me. But soon his body was racked with his coughing. His chest was on fire from lack of air. He could feel the life draining out of his arms and legs. He began to think that his torturers didn't realize how far they were going. They would kill him accidentally if he didn't make them stop. So he answered all their questions about the best ways to break into Fort Viper and murder all his fellow trainees.

Mex Cortines had been stuffed into a tiny hut, made of sheets of corrugated metal. It was too small for him to stand or even sit, and the sun beating down on it made the metal almost too hot to touch. He spent twelve hours on his hands and knees locked into the darkness. Each time he passed out from the heat, he fell against one of the sides, which burned him back to consciousness. When they dragged him out, he still refused to talk. His interrogator had shrugged his lack of concern and then ordered him back into the box for another day. Mex kept his silence until they took him outside and he saw the box again. Then he fell crying to his knees and babbled the answers to every question they asked.

What they were teaching them, through painful experience, was that any one of them could be broken. It was just a matter of time; a few minutes for some of them, a few days for others. The old Geneva rule of just name, rank and serial number simply didn't work. You had to talk. But if they found you were lying to them, you were surely dead.

The squad members had been trained to appear cooperative right from the start. To reveal anything that wouldn't pose a direct danger to their unit or its mission. To pretend not to know the critical information, but to reason along with their captives as to what the essentials of the mission might be. They were taught to think while they were being interrogated, not about their chances of survival, but how they might stall revealing further information. If they could hold out for a few hours, the things they knew might not prove fatal to their companions. If they could hold out for a few days, nothing they said would do any real harm.

But the key to holding back information was the appearance of giving information. The key to survival was the appearance of cooperation. Campbell had violated his own lessons. He had spit in the faces of his captors, confident that this was just a war game. And they would break him exactly as they had been broken themselves. By convincing him that the game had gotten out of control. That they were indifferent to whether he lived or he died.

Mex snapped Campbell's face out of the water and the sergeant was immediately convulsed with coughing. He tried to gulp down air to fill his lungs, but each breath was cut short by a spasm. He tried to twist his face away from the stream, but Mex had a knee planted firmly in his back.

"No more," Campbell finally managed between pants. "Jesus, no more."

"Where's the cadre?" Baldinger demanded. "Call out the coordinates." The map was covered with a grid, with numbers along one edge and the letters along the other. All Campbell had to do was give them a number and a letter.

"There!" Campbell gasped. "Right above the landing zone."

"Which landing zone? There are two of them."

"On the right. The one on the right." It was hard for the sergeant to talk. He still hadn't caught his breath.

Baldinger studied the map. It didn't make sense. If they staked out one of the landing zones, they were leaving the other unprotected.

He looked at Cortines. "He's lying, Mex. He isn't going to tell us anything."

Mex grabbed the back of Campbell's head, like a bowling ball. With slow, steady strength, he pressed his face back into the muddy water. Campbell fought back for a moment, hunching his shoulders and trying to twist his head out of Mex's grasp. Then, after a few seconds, his body went limp. Baldinger studied the water around his face. It was perfectly still. The sergeant wasn't struggling yet. He had inhaled deeply when he felt his face being pushed down towards the surface. Now he was holding his breath.

From the top of the culvert, Willie Derry looked down with satisfaction. Campbell's pistol still rested in the palm of his hand.

Dave watched carefully. After about thirty seconds, an explosion of bubbles broke the surface next to Campbell's face. An instant later, the sergeant's shoulders hunched. His head began snapping from side to side. But Mex's grip kept his face buried in the water. Baldinger waited another few seconds. Campbell began arching his back, trying to throw Mex off. But Mex was as firm as a rock. He was raised up on the knee that he kept fixed between Campbell's shoulders. His weight leaned effortlessly on the back of his victim's head.

Baldinger nodded. It was obvious that Campbell was desperate for air. "Okay, let's try him again."

But Mex's position never changed. Campbell's feet kicked furiously, but he was pinned helplessly.

"Let him up," Baldinger said.

Mex answered with a sneer.

"Hey, Mex! Let him talk before you kill him," Willie called from the top of the hill. He wasn't really concerned. He was more involved in ejecting the clip from the handle of Campbell's automatic, and stripping the round from the chamber.

The bubbles had stopped. Baldinger saw a stain of red diluting in the water around Campbell's head.

"Let him up! He's had it." He looked into Cortines's face. "That's enough, Mex. He'll tell us."

Cortines shook his head. "He ain't gonna tell no one nothin'."

"Mex, stop! For chrissake, stop!" It was Derry screaming from the top of the hill. He suddenly jumped onto the slope and came running, stumbling, toward the men grouped in the stream.

Baldinger grabbed Mex's arm and tried to tear it away from the sergeant's head. He went cold when he felt the steely muscles through his friend's shirt. Mex was much stronger than he was, and had a leveraged position on top of his victim.

"Mex, you're killing him! Let go!"

Dave sprang from his knees, throwing his weight against his comrade. He bounced off uselessly. He wrapped his arm under Mex's chin, and tried to twist him backward. It was like wrestling with the trunk of a tree.

"Let go, Mex! Let go!"

Cortines didn't waver, his weight driving the bloody face further into the silt of the riverbed. Baldinger realized that Campbell had stopped struggling. His legs were splayed out as if they were paralyzed. His torso, which had been pumping furiously only a second before, had suddenly gone still.

Willie dropped his assault rifle and raced at full speed into the river. "Meeexxx . . ."

He was screaming when he hurled all his weight and momentum against Mex's shoulder. The impact drove his friend sideways, and toppled him into the river next to his victim. Baldinger scrambled past the two sprawling forms, grabbed Campbell by the shoulders, and lifted his face out of the stream. Water poured out of the sergeant's mouth and nose. He dragged the leaden body, and threw his face and shoulders up onto the dry bank. Then he pressed the flats of his hands under Campbell's shoulder blades and began pumping with a steady, rocking motion. "Breathe, you fucker. Breathe!"

Derry and Cortines were sitting in the stream a few feet away. Mex was staring dumbly at Derry.

"What the hell's the matter with you?" Willie demanded.

"He was gonna kill you," Mex said. "He was gonna shot you in the head."

"I'm okay," Willie told him. Then he asked cautiously, "Are you okay?"

Mex nodded. "Yeah. I guess so."

They turned together toward the explosion of coughing. Campbell had vomited up a flow of water. He was sucking in air, and then choking on it. Baldinger rolled him over and lifted him to a sitting position. The sergeant's head bounced up and down with each cough. His eyes opened and began to focus. Willie crawled through the stream toward Dave. Cortines stood slowly, wobbled for an instant before he found his balance, and then walked toward the others.

Campbell's eyes drifted over Derry and then locked onto Mex. He pulled back, nearly breaking the supporting grasp that Dave had on his shoulders.

"Keep him away! Don't let him near me!" There was genuine terror in Campbell's expression. "Please, I'll show you. Let me show you."

Derry looked around quickly. He saw the crumpled map on the bank, across the stream, and splashed through the water to retrieve it. "We'll ask him once more, Mex!" he yelled as he started back. "Any more lies, and he's yours!"

Dave could feel Campbell trembling in his arms. "I'll show you. I swear. Don't let him kill me." Baldinger understood. The sergeant was broken, just as he had been broken. He held out his arm as if to keep Mex away.

"No more lies," Dave threatened. Willie shoved the map under the sergeant's face. "Where's the cadre?" Dave demanded.

"C three," Campbell blurted. "C three."

Baldinger studied the coordinates. "That's a ridge," he said suspiciously. "A rock wall." The hand that was holding Mex away began to lower.

"They're on top of it," Campbell pleaded. "They got one guy posted near each landing area to call 'em in. When you guys make your pick, they'll be able to fire down on you from the top."

It made sense. The ridge was curved like a horseshoe, with one of the landing areas to either side. The landing areas were halfway up the rise of the land. Even if the choppers made it in, the men they landed would come under fire as soon as they left the area.

"Get his boots, Willie," Baldinger said. "I think we'll take our prisoner with us." He lifted Campbell to his feet. As soon as the sergeant found himself face to face with Mex, he took a quick step backward.

Mex now understood what had happened. He reached out and grabbed the soaked shirt, twisting it slowly in his fist. "You think of anything else, my friend, you better tell us. If this goes bad, I'm going to find another river.''

They moved quickly along the road, with Baldinger out ahead and Willie and Mex flanking their prisoner thirty yards behind. At first, Campbell was unsteady, still wobbly from his ordeal and robbed of his balance by having his hands tied behind his back. But gradually, his military bearing took hold and he began setting a march pace that his escorts had difficulty matching.

Before they reached Foxtrot, Baldinger decided that they should abandon the open road and cut into the dense woods. They tightened up their formation in order to keep one another in sight. Dave kept checking his watch. Leaving the road meant that the cadre wouldn't pick them up the second they entered the exercise area and be able to shadow them throughout the night. But it also meant that they were moving more slowly than Luther had when he had gone ahead. They had to be sure to reach the rendezvous on time.

They broke out of the forest at the edge of a stream. Baldinger lead them along its bank, away from the road, until they came to a distinctive "S" bend in the stream's course that he was able to identify on the map.

"We're inside Foxtrot," he told the others. "Luther should be just over that hill." They were none too early. The sun was growing large at the tops of the mountains to the west and the light was already fading. He walked out onto the sand that had narrowed the stream at one of its turns. "We should be able to cross here."

Campbell hesitated as they started into the water. If he fell, he would be helpless with his hands tied behind his back. Willie pushed him ahead, but he kept a reassuring hand on the sergeant's shoulder. The water rose to their waists, but moments later they were climbing out on the opposite bank. Then they were back into dense forest and headed up a steep, wooded incline, cutting back and forth in switch-back route to lessen the severity of the climb. They were nearly to the top when Bobby Long jumped up from the brush and waved toward Baldinger. Dave follow the signal and walked directly into Luther's camp.

"You got him," Luther Brown said with an ear-to-ear grin as soon as he saw Campbell.

"That ain't all we got," Cortines answered. Baldinger pulled the crumpled map out of his pocket and waved it in the air.

Derry sat the sergeant down in the center of open ground, pulled a nylon bag out of his rucksack and dropped it over Campbell's head as a blindfold. Then he pulled the boots off his prisoner's feet and carried them to the conference that had formed around Brown and Baldinger.

"You think he's levelin' with us?" Tom Cavitt asked once Dave had pointed out the strategy of the cadre.

"Yeah, he's leveling with us." Dave shook his head. "I thought Mex had killed him. It was damn scary."

Luther gave Mex a thumbs-up. "I'm glad you stayed behind, amigo."

Luther mapped out a simple plan of attack. They would cut to the west during the night, circling around the cadre that was positioned on the rocky bluff, their eyes searching to the south. Subdue the cadre first, and then post a guard around the perimeter of the landing area. They would have plenty of time left to prepare for the dawn arrival of the choppers.

Bobby Long was shaking his head before Brown finished. "Ain't gonna work, Luther. You're forgettin' about the bluff. Fuckin' thing is a forty-foot wall of rock. How in hell are you figurin' we're gonna get past it?"

"We're gonna climb it," Brown answered matter-of-factly.

"In the dark?" Long rolled his eyes as if Luther were an idiot.

"It's a tough climb, Luther," Baldinger agreed.

"That's why we're doin' it," Brown said. "'Cause the bastards are never goin' to be expectin' us to come over the rock."

Willie Derry nodded toward the hooded form of Sergeant Campbell, sitting as still as a tree stump in the center of the clearing. "He won't make it to the top with his hands tied. And I don't trust the bastard enough to cut him free."

They all turned toward the sergeant. They had been taught never to let a prisoner out of their sight unless he was dead.

"So let's kill him," Dickie Morgan suggested. Their heads snapped toward Dickie, who was suddenly perplexed by all the attention he had attracted. "I mean, tell him he's dead. As part of the war game he has to stay put. He can't talk to no one."

"I'm afraid we're past playing games, Dickie," Baldinger said. "We're way outside the rules. If Campbell gets free, he'll head straight for the cadre, and I don't feel like racing him up the side of a mountain."

Tom Cavitt pulled a coil of thin climbing rope out of his rucksack. "Won't be any problem. We'll tie him in a harness and leave him at the bottom. When we get to the top, we can hoist him up after us."

Baldinger looked back at the sergeant. "He'll take a hell of a beating pounding against the rocks," he worried out loud.

"Tough," Willie Derry snapped. "Didn't he drag us through a swamp a couple of days ago?" He held up his bandaged hands. "I didn't get these openin' a beer can."

A sudden darkness swept over the treetops and dropped like a shroud on top of them. The sun had fallen behind the mountain range, the first shot in their one-day practice war.

They marched westward for almost an hour, climbing steadily through forest so thick that they were feeling their way in the darkness. Luther had cut Campbell's hands free so that he could take handholds during the steeper parts of the climb. But he was tied around the waist by ropes that connected to Dickie ahead and to Mex, who followed right behind. Cavitt was the first to break out of the cover and find himself at the base of the ridge. They left Bobby behind to guard the trussed-up sergeant as they began their climb.

Mex Cortines took the lead, trailing the long climbing rope behind. It was easier than the rock climbs they had practiced, because the face of the bluff was dotted with small trees and puffs of shrubbery that seemed to grow out of every crevice. They provided sturdy steps, and handholds that were always within an arm's reach. But it was more difficult than their practice sessions because they were working at night. Mex couldn't see far enough ahead to pick a continuous line. For every advance, there was a moment of retreat as he ran out of secure footing and had to drop back to find another path. And at each turn, he had to free and then retie the safety line that kept him from falling and served as a guide for the others.

They climbed for an hour without any certain knowledge of the progress they were making. Below, there was darkness which gave no indication of distance. Above, there was only the blank sky. The bluff was too steep for them to see the top. Each of them could only concentrate on the world within his grasp, moving the length of his arm, finding a foothold, untying and then retying to the safety line. Every error was painful. Even in the short distances that the lines would allow them to fall, they smashed against branches or swung in against the bluff's stone face.

Willie Derry rested with his foot braced in the crook of a tree. His hands were bleeding again, and the point of a branch had torn through his shirt and cut a deep gash into his shoulder. Baldinger pulled up next to him.

"You okay, Willie?" His voice was a soft whisper.

"I don't know," Derry gasped. "Are we having fun yet?"

"It can't be much further," Dave encouraged. He gave Willie a pat on the back. "You can make it."

Cortines suddenly found himself at the top. He pulled on a rock outcrop, lifting his head above his hands, and found he was looking into empty darkness instead of into the face of the bluff. He scampered over the edge and collapsed on flat ground, gasping for his next breath. Jim Ray Talbert lifted over the edge and rolled into a heap beside him.

"We made it, damn it. We made it." He was almost hysterical.

One by one the others toppled over the ridge. Luther Brown, who had taken the last position to keep his patrol ahead of him, finally reached the flat ground. "Okay, guys. Let's get with it," he ordered in a whisper. "We still gotta pick up our luggage."

He snapped the climbing line which they had trailed up the bluff, sending a signal down to Tom Cavitt. Cavitt secured the line onto Sergeant Campbell's harness, and then connected it to his own belt. He cut Campbell's hands free. Then he snapped a signal back up the rope. The men at the top began hauling up on the line, making it easy for Campbell and Cavitt to guide themselves up the face of the cliff.

Brown laid out his attack plan. The patrol would stretch out in a long line and circle around behind the edge of the ridge, surrounding the position where Campbell had told them the cadre would be waiting. Then they would hold until the first hint of light. He didn't want to close on the training force in the darkness, where it would be impossible to coordinate their advance, and where they would run the risk of stumbling blindly into the enemy force. He left Cavitt guarding the prisoner, and led his patrol into the forest.

They were in position for more than two hours, each waiting alone in the empty stillness. The cadre, Baldinger reasoned, was probably no more than a hundred yards away, spread out along the face of the ridge, facing down at the forest top below. They, too, needed the morning light to see the patrol, which they assumed would come marching dumbly under their gun sights.

The birds began chirping even before they were aware that the eastern darkness was lifting. Brown straightened up onto his knee. Dave felt his grip begin to tighten on the stock of his assault rifle. Derry looked around, found that he could make out the shapes of individual trees and bushes. Then he was able to find Dickie Morgan's form hunched thirty yards to his right.

The sky lightened, a thin line of gray silhouetting the tops of the distant trees. Luther raised his hand, sending a signal that was passed down along the line. Then he began to inch forward, taking care not to stir the branches. The patrol rose out of the ground cover and moved forward silently.

The troops of the cadre were dug in along the edge of the ridge, already alert to any movement in the forests below. But they were completely unprepared for the attack from their rear. Baldinger simply slipped up beside a camouflaged soldier who was absorbed in slowly panning his binoculars across the distant trees.

"You're dead, Sergeant," he whispered in the man's ear, trying to make his faltering Spanish sound authentic. "My parrish knife is sticking right through you."

The sergeant lowered the binoculars, turned his face toward Baldinger, and smiled. "Son of a bitch! How did you get here?" He pulled a red tag from his shirt and handed it to Dave, confirming that he was out of the war game.

"Over the ridge," Dave told him, relaxing back into English.

The sergeant looked down the dizzy height of the cliff, and realized that the platoon must have climbed it in the darkness. "Nice job! I guess we'll be buying the beer."

Willie Derry snapped a twig just as he was stepping up behind a soldier who was sitting waist deep in wild grass. The man's head turned right into the barrel of an assault rifle.

"Dead, or prisoner?" Willie demanded.

The man set his weapon down carefully and tore his tag in half. "Prisoner," he decided, answering in the Spanish that Willie had used.

Dickie Morgan wasn't so fortunate. As he moved toward one of the cadre members who was stretched out on the ground, he walked past another who was hidden in nearby bushes. Just as he raised his rifle to claim his kill, he felt the muzzle of a rifle jabbing in his back. "Drop it," a voice demanded in well-accented Spanish.

A quick blast of gunfire shattered the morning stillness, it's echo carrying for seconds across the open country. "Take their tickets," Luther's voice ordered from the edge of the woods. "I just blew you two dudes away." He had circled up behind Dickie and killed the two cadre members. But as he stepped out of the cover, there was another blast of gunfire. The cadre solder on the flank had gone undetected. He was now charging down the line, his assault rifle at the ready. "I got both of you,'' he said. Luther Brown rolled his eyes in despair. Dickie Morgan let his weapon drop idly to his side.

Then the cadre soldier suddenly toppled. Baldinger, who had been crouching next to his prisoner, leaped up and brought the man down with a perfect football tackle. They struggled in the grass for a moment until Dave had his parrish knife pointed at the enemy's gut. "You're dead,'' he announced.

"Guess so,'' the cadre fighter conceded.

The skirmish lasted for only a few seconds. Of the fifteen members of Sergeant Campbell's band of revolutionaries, seven were dead. Campbell and five others were taken prisoner, their tags torn in half. Two, according to the information Campbell had volunteered, were still free in the forest below, patrolling the landing areas. The Special Operations unit had lost two men. But one was Luther, the patrol leader. Dave Baldinger, as squad leader of the last exercise, was now in command.

He moved immediately. Campbell was brought up and put with the other prisoners, with Cavitt left behind to guard them. He sent Mex, Bobby, and Jim Ray down the face of the cliff and into the forest to find the cadre soldier who was between them and the landing area he had selected. Then he and Willie took the radio gear and circled back around the ridge to approach the chosen landing area from the other side.

The sun broke over the horizon while Baldinger and Derry were still moving westward. Dave knew that back at the Airborne base, the troops were already loading into the helicopters. He had to move quickly to secure the landing area. And yet it was risky to call them in while he still had one of the cadre close by. Unless Mex could find the man and neutralize him, he could prove deadly. All he had to do was wait near the landing zone until the first copter was hovering over the treetops. A single blast of small-arms fire could bring the first chopper down, splashing burning aviation fuel all over the clearing. It could turn the mission back in defeat.

He knew that he shouldn't have left Tom Cavitt behind to guard the prisoners. He was already short of manpower, and Cavitt should be with Cortines, giving him a better chance of finding the cadre soldier. In war, where lives were subordinate to the mission, the right call would have been to kill the prisoners. And even though this was only an exercise, he was supposed to be playing it as if it were a real war. He shouldn't leave prisoners unguarded behind his line, but at the same time he couldn't afford to leave a valuable squad member behind just to watch over them. Baldinger understood that he was compromising his assignment.

But even in a war game, he hadn't been able to give the order to execute the men. "First, they've got to make you forget that you're a person," Art Walters had said to him. "Before they can make you a killer, they have to make you forget that you're human." Baldinger figured he hadn't forgotten yet. And even though he wanted to wear the green beret, he wasn't sure that he ever wanted to forget. He was a winner. But not at any price.

Willie secured a climbing line at the top of the bluff. He glanced at his swollen hands. "I hope these things don't give up on me."

"It's easier going down," Dave answered. He grabbed the rope and swung himself out over the edge.

"Yeah," he heard Willie answer. "At least if you fall, you'll be goin' in the right direction."

The sun was well above the trees when they reached the bottom. The heat was already rising, and Dave could feel the sweat soaking into his shirt as he and Willie double-timed through the woods. There was enough light coming through the trees so that they could see the breaks ahead, and they were able to move quickly. Within minutes they broke out into the clearing of the landing area.

Baldinger unpacked the communications gear. First he darted into the center of the clearing, and placed the battery-powered radio beacon that the choppers would home in on. Then he tossed the end of the voice-frequency antenna wire into a tree and stretched it tight. While he worked, Willie prowled the edges of the clearing, looking for any sign of the enemy. It made sense that the man had been warned by the sound of the gunfire. Once he realized that his fellow insurgents were under fire, his best move was to get to the landing area and protect it from attack.

Okay, Baldinger thought when he had powered up his radio. Everything is ready. The Airborne troops are in their planes, and the rotors are turning. All they needed was his signal that the landing area was secure. It was his call. Bring them in on the hope that they would find the cadre soldier who was nearest to them. Or wait until he saw Mex Cortines lead the insurgent out of the woods. Either way, he was risking the troops. The longer they sat on the pad watching the sun climb into the sky, the more they lost the advantage of surprise.

His radio crackled. "Early Bird, this is Eagle. Do you read me?" It was Sergeant Major Thompson's voice.

He lifted the handset and pressed the key. "Eagle, this is Early Bird. Loud and clear."

Thompson's voice answered immediately. "Early Bird, this is Eagle. We're ready to fly. Repeat, ready to fly."

Baldinger decided. "Eagle, this is Early Bird. Your nest is ready."

He left the radio, picked up his assault rifle, and ran into the woods after Derry. Tactics dictated that he should set up a defense line a hundred yards from the clearing. That would put him and Derry in front of the cadre soldier with Mex and the rest of the unit beating the bushes at his heels. But there was the chance that he was already behind them, waiting at the edge of the clearing. In that case, Eagle was as good as dead. Baldinger decided to keep moving, searching the dense woods at the edge of the clearing.

Minutes past with nothing but the sounds of morning, the brush of wind, and the chattering of the birds. He and Willie were moving noiselessly, searching carefully for the one man who could destroy the Airborne attack. Suddenly there was a distant chattering of gunfire. The birds flew out of the treetops overhead. There was an instant of quiet, and then the clatter of answering gunfire. Baldinger and Derry turned and moved cautiously toward the sound. They dropped down as they heard branches smashing in the woods ahead of them, and then a sombrero-topped figure charged out of the brush. Derry popped up and squeezed the trigger of his rifle.

The cadre insurgent staggered to a stop, stunned by sound of the rifle blast. His head snapped around, taking in Derry to one side and Baldinger to the other. "Ah, shit!" he yelled, and reached for the red tag on his shirt.

"Hold fire!" Baldinger screamed out into the woods. "Hold Fire! We've got him."

Mex Cortines broke through the bush at the heels of the cadre soldier, and then Bobby Long appeared. Jim Ray Talbert sauntered into sight a few seconds later. His red tag was missing, which meant that the insurgent had gotten him during their first encounter.

"Set up a defense line right here," Baldinger ordered Cortines. He still had three men in action. He would use Mex, Willie, and Bobby to protect the landing area from attack by the last of the insurgents, who probably would have been alerted by the gunfire, and certainly would hear the incoming helicopters. He turned and ran back toward the landing area.

Almost immediately, he heard the popping sound of the helicopters' rotors, and seconds later the whine of their engines. The mantislike shapes flashed in over the treetops, the first one centering over the landing area. Nylon lines dropped from the open doors and then Airborne troops began sliding down to the ground. As soon as the last soldier touched down, the copter banked and slipped back out over the trees. The next chopper pounded in over the landing zone and tossed out its drop lines.

It took less than three minutes for the six copters to disgorge their troops, along with sacks of equipment and ammunition. In less time than that, the Airborne soldiers had set up their own defensive lines. As the last helicopter banked away from the landing area, the first chopper reappeared over the trees. The pitch of its rotor sound changed abruptly as it settled toward the ground, its downdraft kicking up a cloud of dust. As soon as it had landed, Sergeant Major Thompson stepped through the side door and ducked under the blades, his uniform pressed to razor creases and his boots sparkling like the morning sun that reflected from his dark glasses.

"Where's Brown?" Thompson called to Baldinger.

"Dead, back up on the ridge," Dave answered. He gave his casualty report.

"Any opposition?" Thompson tried to make it a legitimate question even though he knew that there had been opposition from the cadre.

"Eight dead, six prisoners, and one still out there," Baldinger said.

Thompson nodded, and looked around the landing area. He had sent his best Special Operations instructors into Foxtrot to prevent the landing. His trainees had beaten the best.

"Good work," he complimented.

"It was Luther's show," Baldinger answered.

The two groups assembled next to the helicopter. "These guys are in body bags," Luther Brown said as the dead members of a cadre were moved forward. "These are prisoners." He released the five trainers who had been taken prisoner up on the ridge. Then he pushed Sergeant Campbell out into the center, his hands tied behind his back.

"This is bullshit," Campbell shouted. "They cheated. This exercise doesn't count for shit."

Thompson could see the cut across Campbell's face and the trace of swollen purple flesh.

"They captured me outside Foxtrot, before the goddamn exercise even began. They broke the rules."

Baldinger pulled his parrish knife and cut the cords from Campbell's wrists. "This is war, Sergeant. There are no fucking rules. Isn't that the way you taught us to play it?"

Campbell wheeled on him. "I'm bringin' you up on charges, Baldinger. You and the spic and that stupid asshole Derry. You disobeyed direct orders. You assaulted a rankin' noncommissioned officer. You broke every rule in the book."

"What rules?" Luther Brown challenged.

Thompson nodded Campbell into the helicopter.

"What happened out here?" he demanded.

"We won," Brown answered. "We made our mission."

Thompson looked from Luther back at Campbell, who was brushing away the hands that were trying to help him into the chopper. "We'll hold our critique at fifteen hundred hours. You and Baldinger better be there."

"Yes, Sergeant Major," Luther Brown snapped as he saluted. He stepped back so that he and his squad would clear the helicopter for takeoff.

"Get your men aboard, Brown," the sergeant major told Luther. "When you win an exercise, you get to ride home."

Luther turned grinning toward the men in his unit. Willie Derry was already diving through the door of the chopper.

The critique, which followed every training exercise was generally a closed affair. The training officers gathered in Thompson's office, where cold beer was opened behind closed doors. Informally, they discussed every aspect of the exercise and evaluated everyone's performance, their own as well as the trainees. They assigned performance scores to each member of the Special Operations unit, with an additional score for the member who had been the acting commander for the exercise. Some were given points toward the total that they needed to pass the final phase of their training. Others had points deducted. Then the cadre members agreed on the strategy they would follow in order to help the recruits correct the deficiencies that had been noted.

But this critique was a trial. Thompson ordered the men to assemble in one of the classrooms at the school. He took his position behind the instructor's desk, and put the cadre on one side of the aisle. Brown and Baldinger, wearing fresh fatigues, were isolated on the other. They waited in near silence until ten minutes after the appointed starting time, when the jeep pulled up delivering Sergeant Campbell from the hospital. Campbell blasted through the door in his dress greens, squinting over a thick bandage that was taped across his cheek. He hesitated for an instant while he took in the arrangement of the room, and then found a seat in the front row of the cadre.

"Before we begin critiquing the exercise," Thompson started, "I think we have to find out whether we had an exercise." He nodded toward Campbell. "Bill, I think you want this whole day disqualified."

"You're damn right I do," Campbell snapped. "The unit broke the rules. They went way outside the exercise guidelines. They initiated action a fuckin' hour before the starting time and at least a mile outside Foxtrot." He jumped up out of his chair and jammed a pointed finger across the aisle. "And then I want him"—he was pointing at Baldinger—"washed out of here. Him and two of his buddies, Derry and Cortines. For disobeying my order that they get back into line and follow game rules.

Luther Brown was instantly up out of his chair. "Sergeant Major, if anyone gets washed out it has to be me. I was in command of the unit and they were followin' my orders."

"Sit down!" Thompson snapped at Luther. "Sit down and shut up until I tell you different." He watched with blazing eyes while Luther wilted, and settled back into his chair. Then his eyes flashed back to Campbell. "What happened out there, Sergeant?" Baldinger felt his stomach beginning to churn. Thompson was certainly starting out on Campbell's side.

Campbell hit the highlights of his charge. They had undermined the road bridge outside the exercise area, and taken him prisoner a good hour before the sunset starting time. Baldinger, Derry, and Cortines had ignored his order that they rejoin their unit and proceed with the exercise. Then Cortines had assaulted him while he was attempting to enforce his order, and Baldinger and Derry had assisted Cortines in tying him up so that he couldn't lead his unit. They were damning charges and, as Dave listened to them, all completely true, as far as they went.

"It was no training exercise," Campbell said. "It was a fuckin' street fight. Run by a bunch of thugs who don't belong in the Army, much less in Special Operations."

Thompson waited until Campbell sat, then he looked across the aisle. "Corporal Brown?"

Luther didn't get up. "I saw the opportunity to take a prisoner who would have information about the enemy's operations," Luther said. "I ordered my men to get him."

The sergeants of the training cadre looked open-eyed at one another. They had wondered how Luther's force had known exactly where to find them. Now they were beginning to understand.

"And you disobeyed Sergeant Campbell's direct order?" Thompson continued.

Baldinger put his hand on Luther's shoulder to keep his friend from answering. "I was in charge of that part of the operation," he said. "Brown had gone ahead with the rest of the unit."

"Then *you* disobeyed the order of a superior," Thompson challenged.

"No, Sergeant Major. I ignored the threats of an enemy prisoner."

One of the cadre laughed, then caught himself as Thompson's steely glance swung in his direction.

"We were working under our standard training rules," Baldinger continued, "that every minute of our lives is a training exercise. We keep a guard posted in our barracks so that the enemy doesn't come in and get us while we're asleep. The enemy leader should be just as cautious. He wasn't."

Thompson was beginning to get the picture. "You're saying you went around the rules of the exercise because your instructors go around the rules of the exercises?

Baldinger looked across at Campbell. "No, Sergeant Major. What I'm saying is that there are no rules. That's what we've been taught."

Thompson's hands tightened into fists. "No rules about assaulting senior ranks?"

"We didn't assault a senior rank. We interrogated a prisoner, exactly the way we've been taught. And we broke him."

"Fuckin' Mexican tried to kill me!" Campbell yelled, jumping to his feet. "He was going to drown me. The crazy son of a bitch . . ." He broke off abruptly in midsentence, as he realized that all the eyes in the cadre were fixed on him. It was their standard ploy in interrogation. Scare the guy. Make him think that you're going to keep his face under the water until he dies. That was exactly what they had done to him. And he had just admitted that he thought he was going to die. "They weren't followin' the game rules," he said weakly to Thompson. Then he eased back into his chair. Thompson watched him until he was settled. Seconds passed before he turned his attention back to the trainees. His hands were no longer locked into fists.

"Brown, Baldinger, you're dismissed," the sergeant major said softly. "We can handle the rest of the evaluation ourselves." Luther and Dave snapped to attention. "But there's still a charge of disobedience on the table," he added before the two trainees could turn toward the door. "I want Baldinger, Derry, and Cortines confined to barracks. I'll send for them when I'm ready."

Baldinger and Brown marched out of the room.

★　★　★

Captain Robert Gordon braked his car in front of Major Daks's address and leaned over to look through the passenger window. There was no mistaking the house. The new breezeway wall was only half framed out, and the carport roof was raw planking. He backed up to swing into the driveway, but then thought better of it and parked his car at the curb. He checked his watch and decided to wait a few minutes. His appointment was at 1600 hours, and he was five minutes ahead of schedule.

Gordon was already in well over his head, leading an investigation without any idea of where he was leading it to. He was delving into Army records without any appreciation of their significance, and poking into the hidden corners of military life without a clue as to the secret priorities and personal agendas of the people involved. Only a professional soldier would know where to look and what to leave unexamined, and he was anything but a professional soldier.

He had been a decent pre-law student at Penn State, who had joined the Army's Reserve Officer Training Corps as a way to finance his tuition. At graduation, he owed the Army three years of service and had been ready to deliver on his commitment. Then an alternative had been offered. If he pledged five years of service, the government would pay his way through law school. From the front end, five years seemed an eternity. But Robert wasn't in any particular hurry. He had no clear career path in mind, and there were no romantic commitments that he was determined to honor. So he had allowed the Army to pay his tuition and board at the University of Virginia Law School, and then had put on a uniform and walked across the street to the Judge Advocate General School, which shared the Charlottesville, Virginia campus. For the past four years, he had lived on Army posts, serving the legal needs of the commands as staff judge advocate. The position was critically important to the military, but just a job to Gordon. He was already crossing off the days he had left before he would return to civilian life and begin with his legal career in earnest.

As staff judge advocate, he had an unusual relationship with the other officers on the post. He was one of them, sharing their uniform, their social activities, and the amenities of their officers' club. But, at the same time, he was separate from them. Their business was war. His was justice. Their tools were khaki-painted helicopters, tanks, and trucks; oil-coated automatic rifles and carefully weighted throwing knives. His were the leather-bound volumes of the U.S. legal code. Their fraternity was one of physical ordeal and breathless danger. His concerned the latest interpretation of a word or phrase, rendered by an obscure judge in a backwater courthouse. The investigation of the explosion at Major Daks's home was drawing Gordon into the affairs of the real Army. He was finding the landscape unfamiliar, and the signposts difficult to read.

He had been able to make a start with the clerical portions of the investigation. He had read the report of the ordnance experts, who had determined the type of grenade, its exact location, and the manner in which it had been set. He had reviewed the armory records, learning, as Colonel Grigg had promised, that every single hand grenade was meticulously accounted for. Following Grigg's advice, he had pulled all the fitness records that Daks had written over the past year, and had identified all the men who had received a poor grade from the major. The military police were in the process of checking up on each of them. And he had ordered a detailed cross-check of the service records of everyone assigned to the post, isolating individuals who had served with Daks in past commands, and might be harboring a grudge from some long-forgotten incident.

But now, he was starting to investigate the real Army face-to-face. To ask what kind of slight or personal affront could cause a sane man to leave a hand grenade as a calling card? Which flirtations the women considered flattering, and which touched the men's concept of honor so that death was the appropriate penalty. Which training regimens honed physical and mental skills, and which destroyed the mind? An Army man would instinctively know the answers. As an outsider, Gordon might not even understand the vocabulary.

He rang the doorbell, imagining a Marilyn Daks who would explain why the major, in Grigg's words, didn't spend a lot of time at home. He was surprised when she opened the door wearing a tasteful, summery dress over a very presentable figure. She played an excited hostess, greeting him with a generous smile, relieving him of his cap, and taking his drink order as she showed him to the screened porch.

The major was waiting for him, seated at a round patio table, and wearing a sports shirt buttoned over his cast so that one sleeve was empty. Daks was cordial, but businesslike. After a few words of small talk, he dove right into the details of Gordon's investigation.

He took the list of men, stationed on the post, who had served with him during any of his previous assignments. There were eight, six present members of the school staff who had been part of the military assistance group, in El Salvador. "Yeah, I remember where I met them. All except this one. Who the hell is he?" Gordon checked his notes. Their careers had crossed in Nicaragua when the man arrived as an adviser a week before Daks finished his tour. They had, in all probability, never even spoken.

"Did you ever have a confrontation with any of these men?" Gordon asked. Daks was shaking his head before the captain finished the question. "Nothing worth remembering. Oh, hell, in the Army we all live on top of one another. I suppose I could have had words with any one of them. But nothing out of the ordinary."

Next, Daks took the list of subordinates whom he had given less than glowing fitness records, and smirked as he read the names.

"Real bunch of losers," he said, with no great show of concern. Only two names rated a comment. One was Sergeant William Campbell, who had physically beaten a recruit right in front of Daks. "The guy went completely ballistic. He was trying to kill the kid when I stepped in." The other was Captain Martin Johnson, the same man who had led the investigation into the exposion. "Marty's not a bad guy. Just that he thinks too much and doesn't always obey an order."

"Would either of them want to get back at you?" Gordon asked.

"Sure," Daks said casually. "But Campbell doesn't have the brains, and Marty wouldn't have the guts."

Robert Gordon made a note to have the military police run a check on the activities of both men.

Next, Daks read his staff's technical analysis on the explosion, nodding impatiently at each conclusion. "Okay," he said. "Nothing here that they didn't know ten minutes after my guys arrived." He pushed the report back to the captain.

"The military police agreed with your staff," Gordon confirmed, "that the grenade was carefully set into the ground. I believe it's a technique that you use called a grenade mine. Do you agree with that conclusion?"

Daks didn't hesitate. "Of course. What other conclusion is there?"

There was one more possibility. The one that Colonel Grigg favored and the one that would certainly simplify Gordon's investigation. He raised it hopefully.

"Suppose," the captain tried, "that the grenade were on your car. Maybe left on the bumper, or on the running board. You could have carried it right into the carport with you."

"Then how did it get buried?"

"I was thinking," Gordon answered, "that it might have rolled off when you hit your brakes. Then a wheel might have rolled over it and pushed it into the ground. Perhaps even dislodged the pin."

Daks nearly laughed. "Captain, have you ever thrown a hand grenade?"

Gordon looked sheepish. "I'm afraid not."

"Have you ever seen a hand grenade?"

The captain slipped off his glasses. "I had four years of ROTC, Major. Three of them were spent learning how to salute."

Daks laughed. "Do you have a first name, Captain Gordon?"

"Bob."

Daks extended his hand. "Call me Gene."

Marilyn stepped onto the porch with two drinks and tried to be invisible as she set them on the table. The major lifted his glass in a gesture of a toast and the captain responded.

When Marilyn had retreated, Daks picked up the conversation. "The accident is Colonel Grigg's idea. Truth is that the colonel really doesn't want to get to the bottom of this. He just wants the whole thing to go away. So he'd love to have you decide that the grenade rolled off the fender of my car. That makes it an accident, and it makes me the scapegoat for being careless with live ammunition. But the fact is, it just couldn't have happened that way."

Daks reached for Gordon's legal pad and turned it in front of himself. With the captain's pen, he drew a grenade and showed how the safety handle was secured with a pin. The grenade couldn't explode until the handle separated. And the handle couldn't separate until the pin was pulled. Even if his wheel had driven over it and pressed it into the ground, it still wouldn't be armed.

"We could play a baseball game using a grenade for the ball, and we'd be perfectly safe. First, you'd have to pull the pin. But even then, nothing would happen as long as you were holding it with your fingers wrapped around the handle. The handle flies off when you throw it, and then it's armed." His point was well taken. Someone had to deliberately remove the pin. And then the grenade had to be set so that the handle was held in place. A car tire wouldn't be precise enough.

"So it's no accident," Gordon concluded.

"I don't think so," Daks said.

"And you can't think of anyone on this base who would have any reason to harm you?"

The major shook his head. They sat silently for a moment, sipping their drinks, while each tried to think of the next line of inquiry. Gordon finally broke the impasse.

"Well, Gene, you were the only one present at the time of the explosion. And you've had a couple of days to think about it. What should I be looking for?"

Daks smiled. "That's easy," he answered. "You're looking for a madman. Someone who attacks without reason, and doesn't give a damn who he hurts."

Gordon didn't seem to understand.

"Let me tell you something," Daks continued. "Marilyn got a ride home with friends and left me with the car. She could have just as easily taken the car and left me to hitch the ride. And if she had, that grenade would have gone off under her.

"Henry Roy and his wife drove my wife home. They parked in the street and walked her to the door. I asked Henry why he didn't pull into the driveway and he threw up his hands. No particular reason. He just didn't. But if he had, then Henry and Carol get blown up along with Marilyn."

Captain Gordon tried to comment, but Daks waved off his interruption. "There's something else you have to think about. When was the damn grenade planted? Because if it was during the day, then Marilyn had a couple of ladies from the school board in for a meeting. And if it was there in the afternoon, then the paperboy came by. He leaves the paper in the mailbox, just inside the breezeway. Anyone of them could have stepped on it and set it off."

Gordon acknowledged his point with a grim smile. "I was thinking the same thing, when I looked at the technical report, but from the other perspective. What if you didn't drive over it? Suppose you left your car in the street, or didn't pull all the way into the carport. It would still be out there, waiting to kill someone."

Daks was nodding vigorously. "Exactly. That's why this guy is insane. I mean, if he took a shot at me and the bullet blew a hole in my hat, we'd at least know what we were up against. There would be someone out there trying to kill me. A thinking human being who obviously thought he had a reason to get rid of me. But this animal just left a bomb buried in the ground. Maybe it kills me. Maybe it's someone else. Someone he's never even met. But it doesn't matter to him. He doesn't care.''

The major finished his drink. ''So that's the answer to your question. That's what you're looking for. An animal who doesn't care who the fuck he kills.''

Gordon glanced back at the newly framed carport as he walked away from the house. It was easy to visualize the details of the explosion. He could see the point on the ground where the experts' report had placed the grenade. He could imagine the shearing force of the blast as it shot out from under the car, and he could visualize the structures that supported the roof being cut in half. It was a miracle that the man he had just spoken with was still alive.

He had learned quite a bit from their brief conversation. First, that no matter what Colonel Grigg hoped, he was not dealing with an accident. Second, that he could throw logic to the wind. The person he was stalking was someone who wasn't acting logically. Someone who had been squeezed so tightly in the vise of military discipline and violence that he no longer had a balanced regard for life. That meant the assault could have been touched off by anything, from a trivial slight to a brutal assault. It also meant that, having failed once, the person he was looking for would probably strike again. He didn't have a great deal of time to waste.

★　★　★

''You guys ain't takin' the fall alone,'' Luther Brown said solemnly. ''It was my patrol and my call. Anybody washes out on account of this, it has to be me.''

''Just cool it, Luther,'' Willie Derry answered. ''You weren't even there. It ain't your fault.''

''I was the one who came up with the idea,'' Baldinger added.

They were crowded into Dave Baldinger's room, awaiting their summons to Sergeant Major Thompson's verdict. Luther, Mex Cortines, and Bobby Long were leaning on the wall. Willie, Dickie Morgan, and Tom Cavitt were sitting on the edge of the bed. Jim Ray Talbert, who had the guard, was out in the rec room, sitting on the top step with his rifle lying across his knees.

Baldinger sided with Derry. He reminded Luther, "You told us to capture him and search him for maps. Up to then, we didn't have any problems. We should have given up on it when Campbell said he wasn't playing war games. That's when the trouble started, and you had nothing to do with that."

"You were followin' my order," Luther repeated.

Derry laughed. "I don't remember you orderin' Mex to coldcock the son of a bitch," he said.

"And you didn't tell us what to do if the bastard started waving a loaded pistol," Mex added.

Baldinger nodded slowly. "From where I was standing, he looked damn serious. You had to stop him, Mex. You had no choice."

Derry and Baldinger had been discussing their probable fate, with Mex looking on almost disinterestedly. They all shared in the assault on a ranking noncom. It didn't matter that Mex was the one who had hit him. They were all working together. Willie figured they would be washed from the program. "Out on our asses," he had said. Baldinger had advised that they not jump to conclusions. "Thompson's a pretty fair guy. We didn't do anything that they didn't teach us." But secretly he agreed with Derry. They were probably out on their asses. And they'd be lucky to get away with that. Disobeying a ranking noncom could get you a lot of punishment time cleaning out latrines. Hitting one could get you sent to the stockade.

Tom Cavitt and Dickie Morgan had walked in on the conversation, both unaware of how the information had been extracted from Sergeant Campbell. Their worry was that the exercise would be thrown out because the sergeant had been captured before the official starting time. They thought they might have to go through the whole thing again. "We won it fair and square," Dickie was wailing, when Luther and Bobby were passing by the doorway. Luther had gone into a rage.

"Fuck the damn exercise," Luther Brown had yelled into Dickie's face. "We can do that exercise again with our hands behind our backs." Then he told Tom and Dickie what Willie, Dave, and Mex were up against.

"You held his head underwater?" Cavitt had asked in awe. "Holy shit, I don't believe it."

"Standard interrogation procedure," Derry had answered. "Page twenty in our Cub Scout manuals."

And then they had started talking. Tom Cavitt tried to be encouraging, arguing that Campbell had been a prisoner and not a ranking noncom. "They're not supposed to beat on us, but they sure kicked my ass when I was playing prisoner. It's the same thing." Dickie Morgan and Bobby Long were less optimistic but more logical. "He couldn't be a prisoner until the exercise started. Till then, he was a sergeant and the rankin' noncom. The way I see it, you guys are in deep shit."

That was when Luther began arguing that Willie, Mex, and Baldinger weren't at fault. It was his patrol and his call. He had started out the door, announcing that he was going over to Thompson's office and turn himself in. Dave had advised him to wait it out. "No reason to confess until Thompson decides that there's been a crime," he had said.

"I ain't goin' to let you take the rap," Brown had insisted. And then their conversation had started around again in the same circle.

Baldinger stopped listening. He couldn't concentrate on the convoluted theories that his friends were offering to explain why he would be drummed out of the Army, or the arguments that proved he would get off with a few punishment hours. The sergeant major would decide. What held his attention was the image of Sergeant Campbell pointing a loaded pistol into Willy Derry's face, and the memory of his friend, Corporal Miguel Cortines, commiting coldblooded murder.

It was Art Walters's warning coming to life. Accept violence, and you stop being human. Then, when you were no longer a person, violence became an acceptable weapon. Without doubt, the sequence had destroyed Campbell. In teaching the arts of killing, he had lost all respect for life. He had been taken down and humiliated, and his response was to fire into the face of his opponent. And Mex, the gentle giant of the squad—he had pressed Campbell's face into the water as if the sergeant's life were meaningless. He had been trained, when interrogating a prisoner, to act as if it made no difference to him whether the prisoner lived or died. Baldinger had watched him deliver on that training.

Was it touching him as well? Baldinger remembered that he had tried to break Mex's death grip. But he also remembered watching from across the stream as Campbell marched toward Willie, and wishing that the rounds in his automatic weapon had been real instead of blanks. Had he been turned? Had his training been so effective that he could now kill without feeling? That he would follow the wishes of his commanding officer without any regard for the people who came under his fire?

"So what are you goin' to do, Dave?" It was Bobby Long, pressing him for an answer.

"Do? About what?" Baldinger hadn't heard the question.

Tom Cavitt repeated it impatiently. "If they bring you up on charges? What are you going to do if they bring you up on charges?"

"Answer the charges," Baldinger said.

They were still weighing possibilities an hour later when a jeep pulled up outside their barracks. Seconds later, Jim Ray appeared outside the door. Brown, Baldinger, Cortines, and Derry were wanted right away at Sergeant Major Thompson's office in the training school.

"What the hell do you think it means?" Bobby Long demanded as Luther, Dave, Mex, and Willie began filing out of the room.

"It means Thompson has decided whose asses to hang out," Willie Derry told him.

Sergeant Major Thompson was waiting in his office, a small room with two desks jammed against opposite walls, which he shared with another senior noncom. The four trainees filed in and toed a line on the small amount of floor space that was available.

"Stand at ease," Thompson said without looking up from the papers that were spread in front of him. In unison, they took a relaxed pose with their hands hanging loosely behind their backs.

"The exercise counts," he announced, "less a ten-point penalty for starting ahead of time and outside the exercise zone." He paused, flipping the papers as if he were looking for an answer. "Even with the penalty, it's a passing grade for everyone involved." Then he looked up. "Overall, a damn fine performance. Going over the bluff was first rate. Your instructors tell me you took them completely by surprise."

They should have been delighted, but their stony faces never flickered. They knew that the more important questions still hadn't been answered.

"It was a well-conceived operation, Brown. You used your training well. You're dismissed."

Luther Brown hesitated. "Sergeant Major, if you're not done with these guys, I'd like to stick around."

Thompson glared at Luther. "I'm done with you, Brown. Move it!"

Luther snapped to attention, executed his about-face, and marched out of the room. Thompson followed his exit until he heard the door of the outer office close. Then he turned to the others.

"For failure to obey a training officer, each of you assholes gets ten demerits. Derry, that puts you right on the edge. You got no room left. Three more demerits will wash you out, you understand?"

"Yes, Sergeant Major!"

"Anything. A late roll call. A screwup in the field. Even a missing button and you're gone."

"Yes, Sergeant Major!"

Thompson studied Derry, a good soldier but a guy who enjoyed cutting corners. He doubted he would make it, but he hoped he'd find a way. In the field, he wouldn't mind knowing that Derry was covering his back.

"I'm giving you guys the benefit of the doubt. It's hard for me to believe that you're so dumb that you can't tell when a noncom in my training unit is giving you an order or when he's playing the enemy and he's legitimately your prisoner. But just this once, I'm going to believe it. Just make goddamn sure that you get it right the next time, you hear me?"

They sang back like a church choir, "Yes, Sergeant Major!"

The sergeant focused on Mex. "Cortines, assuming you really believed that Sergeant Campbell was a prisoner in the exercise, your interrogation must have been damn convincing."

Mex said nothing.

"And Baldinger," Sergeant Thompson continued, "you did a good job when you took over the patrol. Good decisions. Good execution."

"Thank you, Sergeant Major!"

"One thing, though. You have to be damn careful when you take prisoners. They slow you down, and you tie up needed men guarding them. You keep them long enough, and pretty soon you're their prisoner."

"They surrendered when we overran their position," Baldinger reminded the sergeant.

"That doesn't mean that you have to take them with you. In 'Nam, we had a wounded VC surrender to us. We lost a day on a mission carrying the son of a bitch. And that night he crawled out of his litter and tried to kill one of my guys with his own knife. Slashed his face and took two fingers off his left hand. We never made our rendezvous."

Baldinger knew what the sergeant was suggesting. He had thought of it himself when he gave up a man he desperately needed just to keep a guard on his prisoners. "Are you telling me that I should have killed them? That I should have shot them and left them up on the ridge?"

Sergeant Thompson turned back to his work. "I'm not telling you anything," he answered. "All I'm doing is trying to keep you alive."

109

Thompson listened as the outer door shut behind them and then, a few seconds later, as they closed the front door. He heard the explosion of their voices the instant they were outside the building. They had reason to be overjoyed. He had let them off lightly. Had he sided with his sergeant, the three of them would have been placed under house arrest to await their court-martials. They'd be facing severe penalties. Fines and reduction in rank as a minimum. Time in the stockade if they got tough judgments.

But he had overruled his own sergeant, and acted on the minimum charge. Instead of "assaulting a ranking noncom," he had chosen "disobeying training instructions." It was like charging a machine-gun-toting mass murderer with disturbing the peace. Sergeant Campbell would be furious when he heard the outcome.

But Thompson didn't care about Campbell's reaction. He had already decided to transfer him out of the training operation before he did any more damage to Special Operations. He had cost Special Forces a very promising medic just the day before, and Thompson wasn't going to let him destroy three more candidates. He was out of control, and in their line of work a man who was out of control was a mortal danger to everyone around him.

Campbell had gone over the edge, making the severe discipline a sadistic end instead of a necessary means. Thompson drove his men mercilessly because he knew that combat was merciless. He marched them to the edge of death because that was the surest way of helping them stay alive. But Campbell had lost track of the reason. He was merciless because it demonstrated his boundless authority. He lived on the edge of death because it was a sick display of his own courage. It was bad enough that he had crossed from a training officer to street bully. But now the bully had been called out and shown to be frightened and frail. Under interrogation, he had quickly betrayed his own force. He probably had forfeited the respect of his fellow cadre noncoms. He had been disgraced before the men he was training. In order to regain his stature, he probably would become even more vicious. Special Operations wasn't about viciousness. It was about effectiveness.

What Thompson now understood was that somewhere in the course of his faithful service to his country, Campbell had undergone a fundamental change. He was no longer a man who knew how to kill. He had become a killer who still wore the trappings of a man. It wasn't his fault. In living with the cunning and ruthlessness of an animal, he had become an animal. In waking each morning with the sense of impending death, he had lost all respect for life.

Thompson didn't want Campbell punished. Campbell hadn't created the hot, high-tonnage press that had reshaped him. That had been built by the needs of his country. Nor did he want him disgraced. The Green Beret and the Special Operations shoulder arc were awarded to men who proved they could live beyond the limits of human endurance. You couldn't strip them away because the life they had learned had proven too much for their sanity. But he did want Campbell out of the unit. His madness could prove contagious especially among men who were already living at the very extreme of reason.

★   ★   ★

Captain Gordon felt like an insurance salesman. He had been calling all the training officers' homes, setting up appointments, and then arriving with his briefcase full of papers. He had politely refused the cups of coffee which the wives felt compelled to offer in the morning, or the cooling drinks that they offered in the afternoon. Inevitably, they exchanged a few awkward minutes of small talk, and then sat around the kitchen table and got down to business. The civility of the setting seemed out of place with the topic of murder, much more suited to explaining the benefits of a freezer plan or the details of his company's new twenty-five-year life policy.

He had learned very little during his two days of questioning. Yes, of course, the officers knew Major Eugene Dak. A fine officer and a great guy. Outgoing, with a hell of a sense of humor. And, yes, they had met his wife. Lovely woman. The wives certainly seemed to admire Marilyn Daks. Has a great way with people, one of the women had observed. I don't know where she gets all her energy, another had added.

Everyone had heard about the explosion. "I thought his propane tank had gone off," one lieutenant commented. I was stunned when I heard it was a grenade. I mean, the guy is a weapons expert. You wouldn't expect him to have that kind of accident."

"A hand grenade?" The women were genuinely shocked. They knew that their husbands were working with dangerous weapons every day. But to have a hand grenade explode right next to your house? That was truly frightening.

At about this point, in each of the interviews, the Army husband had suddenly become suspicious. "Hey, are you saying that someone might have put that grenade there intentionally?"

"We have to consider everything," Gordon had answered, trying to keep his questions sounding routine. But as he quickly learned, there was nothing routine about the suspicion he was mentioning. The officers and their wives had all been visibly shaken by the thought of someone attacking their homes with military weapons.

What he had learned had come not so much from the information they provided as from the first instinctive reactions to his questions. When he had offered that Major Daks had been deliberately attacked, Captain Brian O'Leary's wife had dropped her coffee cup, earning a quick rebuke from the captain. They had sat on the edges of their chairs for the rest of the interview, throwing guarded glances at one another when each new question was asked. Officially, they knew of no reason why anyone would want to harm the major, but it was obvious that there was at least one reason that they shared.

Major Jordan, the psychologist who taught the course on interrogation, had smiled when he heard that the grenade might have been set deliberately. "Incomprehensible," he had decided, while Robert Gordon was making notes on his comments. But later, while relighting his pipe for the fifth time, he had allowed that "Daks is something of a fieldpiece. A hot cannon. I suppose it's understandable that he would make a few enemies."

For the record, the major was a model officer, and his wife a Joan of Arc. In reality, his name was a flash point for some of his colleagues and their wives.

Carol Roy struck him immediately as different from the other wives. When he had telephoned for an appointment, she had been unimpressed with his reference to an important Army investigation, and unconcerned that his work had been ordered by General Wheeler. She had made it clear that she didn't welcome military intrusions into her home, and had suggested that he take up his business with Captain Roy. He had been left to plead with the captain for a moment of her time. Now, sitting across from her at her dining room table, the difference was even more pronounced. Unlike the other wives he had met, who were appendages to their husbands' career and rank, Carol was clearly her own person. It was Henry Roy who offered the refreshments, and when he said yes to a cup of coffee, it was Henry who went to fetch it.

Neither of them had been shocked by the suggestion that the explosion had been caused by a grenade. The captain was close to the people on Daks's staff, and had heard the results of their investigation before Gordon had. Carol told him that the news had spread like wildfire as soon as he had begun asking questions. Henry Roy admitted that he knew the grenade had been set like a mine. He wasn't startled by the possibility that someone may have been trying to kill the major. Carol had smiled at the suggestion. "Funny, isn't it?" she commented. "Major Daks teaches people how to set mines. Then someone sets one in his own driveway." She seemed to enjoy the irony.

"There's nothing funny about it," Henry Roy admonished. "Anyone could have set off that grenade. Women, children. There's no telling who could have been killed. Or crippled."

Carol didn't back down an inch. "It's the same kind of mine that Daks teaches his students how to make," she argued. "You said so yourself. When one of Daks's students plants a mine, anyone could set it off. Women, children. There's no telling who might get killed."

Captain Roy was flustered by her attitude. He looked apologetically at Robert Gordon. "Obviously, it's not the same thing."

"Why?" Gordon asked.

Roy was puzzled by the question.

"Why isn't it the same thing?"

Carol looked suddenly pleased to have found an ally. Her husband looked angry.

"You can't be serious," he shot at the attorney.

"No, please, I was being flippant," Gordon apologized. "I've never been trained in these weapons. I was shocked that someone would plant an explosive where it could kill innocent people. How does Major Daks—any of us, for that matter—make certain that the mines we plant can't kill innocent people?"

"By not putting them in innocent people's driveways," Captain Roy shot back. His voice had a finality to it. He didn't want to pursue the question.

Captain Gordon moved on. Could they think of anyone who had any reason to wish harm to Major Daks or his wife? Any rivals? Any disputes? Captain Roy was shaking his head in despair while Gordon was asking his question.

"It doesn't make any sense at all," he answered. "Gene Daks is a terrific guy. He's a fine officer. Jesus, he's a war hero. He's darn near as much of legend around here as Colonel Grigg. I can't believe that anyone would want to see him dead."

Carol didn't volunteer an answer.

"What about Marilyn Daks?" Gordon persisted. "Can you think of any reason why anyone would want to hurt her?"

The captain gave the standard answer that Gordon could almost write from memory. "A wonderful woman. So involved. I don't know where she gets the energy." Again, Carol didn't volunteer an answer. Robert Gordon decided to press for one.

"No one would want to hurt Marilyn Daks," Carol said. "She's been hurt enough."

He waited for her to elaborate on the comment. When she didn't, he decided not to pursue the question any further.

There was one more line of questioning that he had for the Roys. They had driven Marilyn home, and had been the last official visitors prior to the explosion.

"Why didn't you pull into the driveway? That would seem to be the most natural thing to do."

Roy wasn't sure. He sometimes parked in the Daks's driveway. Sometimes it just seemed easier to stop in the street and cut across the lawn to the footpath that led from the driveway to the front door.

Was that what he had done when they brought Marilyn home?

"No," Henry answered, "we walked up the driveway as far as the path, and then took the path to the front door. Marilyn was dressed for the party. She was wearing high heels. I suppose that's why we didn't take the shortcut across the lawn."

"Did all three of you go up to the front door?"

"No," Henry said. "Just Marilyn and myself."

Gordon turned to Carol. "You stayed in the car?"

"Yes," Carol answered. But then she immediately corrected herself. "Well, no, actually, I had to get out to let Marilyn get out from the backseat. Then I think I walked up the driveway and waited until she opened the door and went in. Then I followed Henry back to the car."

"But you never went as far as the carport?" Captain Gordon continued.

"No," Carol said. "I don't think so."

Henry Roy was suddenly angry. "What the hell are you getting at, Gordon? What difference does it make what Carol was doing?"

Robert rushed to apologize. He was just trying to find out where each of them was. "I was wondering if either of you saw anything, or heard anything? Anything out of the ordinary?"

Henry shook his head. Carol answered with a simple "No."

Gordon thanked them profusely as he gathered his papers.

"Do you have any ideas?" Henry Roy asked him as he stood to leave.

Gordon hunched his shoulders. "No. Nothing meaningful."

But, in fact, he was learning a great deal. Carol Roy clearly didn't share the official euphoria for Major Daks and his wonderful work at the school. And far from being in awe of Marilyn Daks and her many accomplishments, she seemed to have a genuine pity for the woman. Gordon didn't think for a moment that she was afraid to confront her husband. But it was obvious that she didn't want to embarrass him. Maybe she could put some names on the uneasiness that seemed to surface each time he probed for information about the major.

He called her the next morning, and asked her when it might be convenient for her to stop by at his office.

"Why?" she demanded.

He was surprised at her abruptness. Army wives usually tested to find which way the political winds were blowing before answering any official request.

"A few answers I'd like to clear up. Just routine," he said trying to make his request sound unimportant and unthreatening.

"What answers?" Carol persisted. "I thought everything was clear last evening."

Gordon knew that there was no evasive way to talk to Carol Roy.

"What was clear," he said, "was that you thought there might be reasons why someone might want to attack Major Daks. I'm at a dead end unless someone familiar with the major gives me a little help." He paused, but there was no response. "I'm hoping that you'll help me before whoever did this tries again."

Still no response. The line was so quiet that he wondered whether she had hung up on him.

"I'll think about it," he finally heard her say.

Captain Gordon wasted most of the morning with Major Topping, commander of the military police unit, reviewing the cross-tabulations of the service records that they had been running on the base computers. Only three of the men posted to Fort Francis Marion had incidents of violent and vengeful attacks in their service records. Aside from Sergeant Campbell, none of them had ever served with Major

Daks. Virtually everyone on the post had extensive small-arms training, and probably had the knowledge and skill to set the grenade mine. It was all accurate data, but there wasn't a shred of useful information. He had turned back to the report of Daks's explosives experts, detailing the facts of the incident. He had already read it several times, but perhaps there was something obvious that he had missed. He was halfway through it when the corporal knocked on his door and announced that Mrs. Carol Roy was waiting to see him.

She wore a simple skirt and man-tailored shirt over a pair of casual sandals. Her long hair was pulled back, but her face was masked in heavy framed sunglasses. She rested a straw handbag on his desk as she sat, took off the glasses, and held them in her fingers. Gordon thanked her profusely for coming to see him, but then fumbled as he tried to introduce his topic. Carol rescued him by going straight to the topics that she had aborted the previous evening.

"You asked my husband what the difference was between the mine set in Major Daks's driveway, and the mining techniques he teaches. Captain Roy evaded the question. The fact is that there is no difference at all."

"That's a simple answer," Gordon commented.

"It's the simple truth," Carol Roy said.

Robert Gordon tried to be diplomatic. "Is there any reason why Captain Roy wouldn't agree with your view?"

"Because he believes in his work," she said without hesitation.

He was plainly puzzled by her answer.

"Captain, how much do you know about my husband's work at the Special Operations school?"

He smiled. "Not very much, I guess."

"Do you know what the school does?"

"Teaches counterinsurgency warfare?" His answer had the intonation of a question.

She nodded. "Army officers, National Guard officers, policemen from friendly nations come here to learn how to put down insurrections in their own countries. They learn how to think like guerrillas and fight like guerrillas. You should get yourself a copy of the school handbook. I think you'd find it quite an eye-opener."

He was still perplexed.

"Major Daks's students learn how to mine roads and paths to make it too dangerous for insurgents to travel. That denies them the mobility that they need to survive. But, of course, peasants use those same roads to bring farm products to market. Putting a mine on a public road doesn't strike me as being very different from putting one in the major's driveway. Either way, you can't really be sure who it might kill.''

''I guess the difference,'' Gordon said defensively, ''is who uses the road. If we know that it's an insurgents' route—''

''My husband's specialty,'' she interrupted, ''is chemicals and bacterial agents. It's a technical term for poisoning wells. I think he would tell you that they only poison the wells that communist revolutionaries drink from. The idea is to deny water to the enemy. If you deny them water, you deny them the use of the surrounding countryside. At least, that's the way he explains it to me.''

Gordon realized that he had tapped a cascade of personal bitterness. ''You've made a study of the school,'' he offered.

''No, at least not intentionally. But you can't get away from it. The work of the school is table conversation in my house. It's the social chatter whenever we go out for an evening with the captain's friends. Which brings me to the other comment I made last night. I said Marilyn Daks had already been hurt enough.''

Gordon nodded, acknowledging that he remembered the comment.

Carol continued, ''Marilyn has been living with her husband's profession for twenty years. Ever since I've known her, she's been trying to do something good to repay his debts. She's a fine lady, but she's had a lot of the life squeezed out of her. No one would want to cause her more pain than she's already suffered.''

Carol raised her sunglasses to her face. She picked up the straw handbag. ''That about covers all the things I left unsaid last night.'' She started to get up.

''Could I ask you one or two more questions?'' Captain Gordon said quickly. The sunglasses came down from her eyes.

''Can you tell me how any of this might relate to the attack on Major Daks? I guess I can see that his work is . . . distasteful. But counterinsurgency warfare is a legitimate military concern. I'm not sure I understand—''

She interrupted him again. ''You asked if there were any reason why anyone would want to harm the major. I guess, among most of the people here at the fort, there wouldn't be anyone. They all share your 'legitimate military concern.' But there are probably thousands of people from dozens of countries who have had their roads mined and their water poisoned. Any one of them could have a score to settle with Major Daks.''

"A foreign national? Here?"

"They come in every month, for training at the school," Carol said. "Maybe one of them has already had some experience with the subjects we teach them."

Once again, she reached for the handbag.

"Mrs. Roy . . ."

"Carol," she told him.

Captain Gordon took a moment to phrase his question.

"Carol, I very much appreciate your help. But why are you telling me this? It doesn't put your husband in a very good light, and you seem to care a great deal for him."

For the first time in the conversation, she hesitated. "I suppose that's why I'm telling you. You're an outsider. Maybe you can throw a little light into the dark corners, and maybe some of these people will take a fresh look at what they're doing. I guess I'm trying to save my marriage. But not at any price. I'm not going to live the way Marilyn Daks has lived."

She had given him an opening for a line of questions he had been afraid to pursue. "You don't think the Daks have a very happy marriage?"

"I think Marilyn has learned to keep up appearances."

"What about the major?"

"I think the major is happy teaching people how to plant mines."

Gordon drew a deep breath. "Mrs. Roy, is the major having an affair with anyone on the base?"

She was instant with her reprimand. "You're out of line, Captain. You don't really expect me to answer that."

He didn't back down. "I was hoping you would. Particularly if there's someone out there who might try again. As you keep saying, 'A mine doesn't care who it kills.'"

Carol thought for a long time, first whether she should answer at all, and then about what answer she should give. "In the military, Captain, we live on top of one another. There are a lot of things that we learn not to notice. I honestly don't know who's bedding down with whom. It's not that I don't care. It's just that it isn't our greatest sin."

He stood with her and walked her through the outer office, thanking her for her help. Then he watched her as she walked down the path to the street and slipped into her car. He gathered that Major Daks may have given several of the husbands on the post reason to dislike him. He couldn't help wondering whether Henry Roy was one of them.

On the way back to his office he stopped at the corporal's desk and asked him to get a copy of the course curriculum at the Special Operations school. Then he began organizing a new search of the base personnel records. This time he wanted the names and backgrounds of the foreign nationals who were students at the school. And, he added, the names of anyone on the post who had lived in any country where Special Forces had operated.

Carol turned into her driveway and, in an act of defiance, rolled all the way to the end. She had heard the other wives discussing the precautions they were taking, and had listened to Henry's concerns over breakfast.

"I don't know what happened at the Daks's house," he had admitted. "Maybe someone has it in for him. Hell, he might know who's after him and just doesn't want to talk about it. But there's always the chance that there really is some lunatic out there who's got a grudge against the school. So, until we get some answers, we ought to be careful."

He had then suggested that she park on the street instead of in the driveway, check the front door carefully before opening it, and not open any mail that she couldn't readily identify. It was when he had suggested that she lift the hood of her car before getting in and starting it that she had lost her patience.

"Jesus, Henry, I really don't want to join the bomb squad." She had jumped up and taken her plate to the sink.

"It's no big deal," he had snapped at her. "It takes you two seconds to lift the hood, and there's only a couple of places you have to look."

But Carol had no intention of lifting the hood, or of leaving her car out in the street. She was battling to keep the school's grim agenda from touching her life. Once she began looking over her shoulder, she would be admitting that the battle was already lost.

She opened the front door quickly, without looking for any signs of forced entry, and started immediately into her preparations for the evening's dinner. There was the poached salmon that Henry said they couldn't afford, but ate with such pleasure; a seasoned wild rice that was the only recipe she had brought to their marriage; and fresh asparagus, which she hated but which was a favorite of his. She broke out the white linen tablecloth that she seldom used because it was such a problem to wash and iron, two of the three place settings of their wedding china that they had been given, two of their four silver settings, and a tall white candle for the center of the table. From the bottom of Henry's closet she took one of the two remaining bottles from the case of California chardonnay they had bought two years ago, and put it into the refrigerator to chill.

Carol picked an outfit that Henry always complimented, white cotton slacks and a sheer dark blue blouse, and laid it out on the bed, then showered and dressed. Her timing was close to perfect. The fish was just about to go into the poacher when Henry pulled up on the street and cut across the lawn to the front door.

He was clearly pleased by her efforts, helped her with the final items for the table, and made a minor ceremony out of opening the wine. Carol supplied most of the conversation while Henry took the lead with the food. She waited until he had taken his second salmon fillet before she told him about her meeting with Captain Robert Gordon.

Henry looked up startled, as if it were the first sound she had uttered all evening. He listened carefully as she recounted the details of the interview, repeating Gordon's questions and her comments nearly word for word. The only thing she omitted was Gordon's question about why she hated the school, and her response about trying to save her marriage. Henry spent just a second weighing the pros and cons of her answers. Gordon had been appointed by Colonel Grigg, so it was important to appear cooperative and helpful in his investigation. But Gordon would also report his findings to the colonel, so it wasn't good to say anything negative about Special Operations or the school. She had pretty much dodged the question about Daks sleeping around, which was good. You never wanted to be quoted negatively when referring to a senior officer. And Carol had given Gordon a whole new line of inquiry. She was absolutely right. The madman that Daks said they should be looking for might well be linked to one of the countries in which Special Forces had operated or whose officers they had trained. But, on the other hand, she was almost making it sound as if the attacker would have every right to seek vengeance.

"I hope you weren't too negative on the school," he said suspiciously. "You know Gordon will be talking directly to Grigg."

"I tried to be honest," she responded. "I told him to get the course catalog and make up his own mind."

Henry picked at his second helping of fish, and then decided that he wasn't hungry. He refilled his wineglass while Carol cleared the dishes and brought dessert.

"Maybe you shouldn't have any more conversations with Captain Gordon until this blows over," he advised casually as he was lifting his dessert fork. She looked at him questioningly. "I think Grigg wants the incident wrapped up quickly. Either he catches the nut who set the grenade and puts him away, or else the whole thing was just a careless accident. There's nothing to be gained by us getting involved. We cooperated. We showed good faith. You even went out of your way to be helpful. That makes us look good. I think we should leave it at that."

It was Carol's opening for the topic she had been hoping to raise all the while she had been planning the dinner. "God, but I hate this pretending. I hate to think about what's best for Colonel Grigg and Special Operations before we decide what's best for us."

"It's the military," he said, as if that were the answer to her anxieties.

"Can we talk about December?" she asked. December was when Henry's tour would be over, when he would have to decide to either commit for another four years or leave the Army.

He rolled his eyes in despair, then looked down at the good china and the linen tablecloth. "Is this what all this is about?"

"I'm not happy living this way, Henry," she said. "I'm not sure I want to sign up for another four years of it. Maybe hand grenades and parrish knives are just what the world needs. But I don't think they're what we need."

He got up from the table and left his wine for the stronger stuff that was in the bar. "I'm an Army officer. You knew what I was going to be when we met at the Point. You knew what I was going to be when you married me. Nothing has changed."

"Then it was uniforms and parades," she said. "Now it's bombs in the driveway. Everything has changed."

He found the bottle of bourbon. "The reason you're not happy is that you don't try to be. The others girls seem to enjoy themselves. They get into the swing of military life and don't let the problems get them down. But all you see are the problems. All you do is find fault."

His voice had grown a bit louder, and her volume rose to keep pace. "And that makes me wrong? I'm not supposed to see problems with dynamite under the hood of my car? Or find fault with table conversation about poisoning people's water?"

He slammed the bottle down on the counter and reached for the jacket he had discarded on the sofa. "I'm going over to the club for a nightcap," he declared.

"For God's sake, Henry, will you please sit down so that we can discuss this? We can make choices about what's best for us. We shouldn't just re-up in December without thinking about what else we might do.''

He was buttoning his jacket as he started for the door. ''There's nothing to discuss. This is my work. This is what I want to do.''

He bolted out without looking back. Carol ran to the door but decided not to follow him outside. She watched helplessly as he marched across the lawn toward his car. ''Son of a bitch,'' she said to herself. Then, as he reached the car, she called out after him, ''Don't open the door until you check under the hood!''

He turned just long enough to glare at her, then slammed the door behind him. The tires squealed as he raced away.

★ ★ ★

''I just wanna practice my Spanish,'' Willie Derry was insisting. But the other guys were too busy laughing to listen to his argument. ''I mean it. The young ladies at Mex's joint are all from fine Latin-American families. It helps you pick up the right accent.''

''I know what you wanna practice,'' Jim Ray Talbert chuckled. He made a loop with the fingers of one hand and pushed the index finger of the other hand through it.

Dave Baldinger put on a despairing look. ''I can think of lots of things you can pick up in that place, Willie. But a Spanish accent isn't one of them.''

''Hey, it ain't a bad place,'' Mex Cortines said, defending his favorite hangout.

''Why don't you work on your Korean?'' Tom Cavitt taunted Derry.

''There's a Korean whorehouse?'' Willie asked, which set them all laughing again.

They flashed their passes as they walked through the security gate.

''Stay the hell away from the Garter,'' the military police sergeant who was in charge of the gate called after them. ''I don't want to be bringin' you assholes back in body bags.'' He was Airborne, and a dance hall called the Diamond Garter was the Airborne hangout, off-limits to prudent Special Operations recruits.

''No sweat,'' Dickie Morgan called back. ''We're trained to live behind enemy lines.''

''To prosper!'' Willie Derry corrected. ''We're gonna bang all the ladies at the Garter, and put it on your tab, Airdale.''

They ambled across the highway to the dirt-field parking lot where Baldinger kept his car. Like everything around the fort, the lot was run down, its sign fading and the paint peeling off the side of the wood-frame office. They climbed into Dave's station wagon, a relic from the hunting and fishing trips that had been the recreation of his pre-military life. Luther Brown and Willie filled in the front seat, and Bobby, Dickie, Tom, and Jim Ray jammed into the back. Mex slid over the tailgate.

"You gotta get a bigger car." Jim Ray grunted as he slammed the door against his shoulder. "This boiler is gettin' too tight."

They had twenty-four-hour passes, not long enough to travel anywhere interesting, but too long to waste inside the post. They had reserved rooms in the Oaks Motel, a line of flat cottages with a sign on the highway that still boasted "Color TVs in every room." The Oaks's clientele were either servicemen from Fort Marion or hookers from the clubs on the strip and, more often than not, a pairing of the two. The cases of beer they would need were already on the back deck of the station wagon. Their female companionship was about fifteen minutes ahead on a street of bars, topless joints, and pawnshops where there had been a single saloon in the days of Camp Viper, and that had grown in step with the Army's investment in Fort Francis Marion.

They had all agreed to crowd into the three rooms they had rented, reasoning that they probably wouldn't do much sleeping.

"Suppose I bring a broad back with me," Bobby Long had questioned. "What am I supposed to do? Let you guys watch?"

"You gotta share," Derry had reasoned. "That's what Special Operations is all about."

They stopped at the Oaks Motel, checked in, and loaded the beer into one of the bathtubs along with bags of ice cubes. Then they drove down to the strip, parked the car, and began making the rounds. Cortines led the parade into Peso Pete's, where the menu was written in Spanish. It didn't matter, because none of them were planning on eating. They ordered tequila and sat through a couple of performances by the topless dancers. But the only hostesses who came near their table pulled up close to Mex. Most of the other girls were busy with Latino customers, and the ones who were free made a point of ignoring the uninvited gringos.

"Maybe we ought to let them know we're friends of Mex," Bobby Long suggested.

"Sure," said Luther. "Just get up on the table and tell 'em that some of your best friends are beaners. They'll all wanna meet you."

Bobby suggested the Garter. "Might as well get it over with."

"Why don't we save it for the end of the night," Baldinger answered. "That way, if someone gets killed, he won't miss out on the whole evening."

When they got up to leave, Cortines stayed snuggled with the hostess.

"Meet us at the Oaks," Baldinger told him.

"Sure," Mex answered. He smiled at the young lady. "But don't wait up for me. If I'm late, you can start without me."

They hit half a dozen places, their early enthusiasm waning in the boring sameness. Sometimes the girls were dancing on the stage and sometimes on the tabletops. In one place the hustlers came to the tables and in another they lounged beckoning on the bar stools. But always the suggested sex was a sales pitch for overpriced drinks. And everywhere the amplifiers were turned up too far.

"I wonder what Mex is doing?" Dickie Morgan asked, glancing at his watch while a naked girl danced a few feet away.

"It's gotta be better than this," Luther Brown agreed. He raised a fresh bottle to his lips and drained it in four gulps.

"Time to look in on the Garter," Bobby Long decided. Willie Derry agreed enthusiastically and stuck the singles that were on the table into the dancer's G-string. She flashed a genuine smile.

"No big deal," Willie told her. "It's deductible."

They were stunned when they walked into the Garter. Three dancers were grinding away out of habit, and the disc jockey was screaming enthusiastically. But the place was nearly empty. There were a couple of Airbornes dozing at the bar, and two more at a table with two of the hostesses.

"You don't suppose they all got shipped back to Iraq," Baldinger mused as he looked around in disbelief.

"Maybe the place has been posted," Brown offered. The Army doctors always asked men who showed up with VD where they had met the girl, and then posted the place as off-limits. The men always blamed the place that was a favorite of a rival unit, making sure their own hangout stayed open.

Dave threw up his hands in despair. "Looks like an early night." They all agreed, even though it was still a few minutes before midnight.

They found the missing Airborne troops when they drove back to the Oaks Motel. All the windows were bright, and the light cascaded out across a crowded parking lot. They could hear music blaring from boom-boxes as they searched for a parking space.

"I guess we picked the wrong motel," Bobby said. "Looks like one of these mothers is having his sweet sixteen party."

"Animals," Willie Derry said, wagging his head in disgust. "Nothing but animals."

When they started toward their rooms they realized that the lights were burning in their windows as well. Then they saw the crowd of shapes behind the window shades.

"The bastards have our rooms," Luther Brown said.

"Screw the rooms," Jim Ray snapped. "Our beer is in the bathtub."

Jim Ray had his key out before he noticed that the lock and doorknob had been ripped out of the door. He pushed it open and was immediately pushed back by the two huge paratroopers who filled the doorway.

"Private party, frog-heads," one of them announced. "We already got all the girls we need inside."

"Hey, thanks for the beer," the other one laughed. There was a roar of amusement from inside the room."

Derry started toward them, but Baldinger caught the back of his shirt. "Don't do something dumb, Willie," he warned.

Derry pulled out of his grasp. "What could be dumber than jerks who fall outta airplanes." He charged toward the door which was quickly filling with more Airbornes. Luther caught him with a strong arm around his neck, and Dave grabbed him in a bear hug.

"You ain't got room for no more demerits," Luther Brown screamed into his face.

"You don't need this, Willie," Dave grunted as he helped wrestle Derry back toward the car. The paratroopers howled at Willie's embarrassment and the retreat of their Special Operations rivals.

"Sit on him," Baldinger told Bobby, Dickie, and Jim Ray. They had Willie stretched out across the backseat, and they piled in on top of him.

"I ain't runnin' away," came a muffled voice from under the pile. "No fuckin' way I'm runnin' away from Airbornes."

"Nobody's running," Baldinger screamed back. He slapped the keys into Luther Brown's hands. "You're driving." Then he ran around the car and jumped into the passenger seat, ignoring the taunts that were being shouted from the motel.

"Let's go," he said to Luther, who burned out of the parking lot. The car had just shifted gears when he told Luther to slow down. "Let me off at the corner. Then drive around to the back street and wait."

"Wait for what?" Luther asked as he slowed the car.

"Our beer. It will be coming out of the bathroom window in about five minutes."

Derry's laughter came from under the bodies in the backseat. "Jesus, Dave, take me with you."

But Baldinger was already out of the car. And a second later Tom Cavitt was out with him.

Baldinger jumped into the brush that lined the road, and began working his way back toward the motel. Cavitt stayed right at his heels.

"What are we doing?" Cavitt asked in a whisper.

"We'll bring them out, and then we'll go in. Standard escape and evasion."

"Didn't we flunk that one?" Cavitt reminded.

"We better not flunk it this time," Baldinger said.

They crouched across the driveway from the motel parking lot. Dave scanned the windshields. Nearly every car had a base sticker.

"First open the door," he told Cavitt. "I'll take the car. Then we'll take the room." Cavitt responded with a thumbs-up sign.

Dave moved close to the ground, keeping the parked cars between him and the motel windows. The soldiers had gone back inside and there was no one in the parking lot. The third car he searched was a small sports sedan with the driver's door unlocked. He saw books of paper matches in the console, and then found cigarette butts in the ashtray. Right on, he told himself as he pulled the hood release latch.

He closed the door gently, slipped around to the front of the car, which faced away from the rooms, and eased the hood open. It took only a few seconds for him to find the gas line, disconnect it, and let the fuel trickle out. Then he lit one of the cigarette butts, folded it into the books of matches, and placed the smoldering matches on an engine support frame, directly under the open fuel line. He eased the hood down and crept back across the driveway.

Cavitt was waiting in the shadow of the building. "Too much light," he told Dave.

"They'll have other things to worry about." Baldinger smiled. He glanced over his shoulder to the road that ran behind the motel. His car, with its headlights extinguished, was rolling silently into view.

They waited nearly a minute. "How long is this going to take?" Cavitt whispered.

Dave shrugged. "How long does it take a cigarette to burn?"

The response was instantaneous. There was a flash under the hood of the car. The cigarette had ignited the book of matches, which burst into flames. A fraction of a second later, there was a hissing sound as the fumes inside the vacated fuel line ignited, and burned like a fuse toward the gas tank. Then came the deafening explosion. The car jumped forward, smashing through the light, wooden fence that separated the parking lot from the road. A ball of flame tossed the trunk lid aside, and rolled fifty feet into the air. A second later, the entire car was ablaze.

"Nicely done," said Cavitt.

"I paid attention in class," Baldinger answered

All the motel-room doors seemed to open at once. The Airborne troops rushed outside, stopped for an instant to take in the burning car, and then raced toward their own cars to save them from what was promising to become an inferno. Burning gasoline was already running underneath the cars parked near the blazing sports sedan. Baldinger and Cavitt broke from their hiding places, ran past open doors until they reached the first room they had rented, and rushed inside.

The room was a shamble of toppled furniture and discarded beer cans. Three women were searching for their clothes, dressing themselves in the process. There was a man passed out in the room's only soft chair, and two others sleeping on the rumpled bed. Dave and Tom walked quickly through the debris and went straight into the bathroom, closing and locking the door behind them. Baldinger lifted a case of beer out of the tub and fired it through the louvered bathroom window. It carried the whole window frame with it as it fell away. At the same time, Cavitt dumped the ice out of the large plastic bags and began filling the bags with the loose cans. As quickly as he filled one, he handed it to Dave who tossed it through the opening where the window had been. They worked quickly and silently until they had emptied the tub.

Cavitt grabbed the shower curtain bar, pulled himself up, and swung his feet through the window. A second later, he dropped down into Luther Brown's waiting arms. Baldinger followed immediately. They gathered up the case and the plastic sacks of beer cans and raced to the car.

"Drive around the block. I wanna cruise right past those suckers." It was Willie Derry, who was still being restrained in the backseat by Jim Ray Talbert and Bobby Long.

"Okay," Baldinger agreed, "as long as you promise to keep your mouth shut. We can look, but we don't want to call attention to ourselves."

Willie agreed enthusiastically. "I just wanna hold up one of the bags of beer so they can see it."

"'Fraid not," Luther Brown said. "That would be blowin' our cover. We're phantoms. We leave no trace."

They were laughing uncontrollably as they passed by the front of the Oaks. The sports sedan was still burning brightly. Around it was an enormous traffic jam of tangled cars trying to make their escapes. Some of them were crashed into others, and the Airborne troops were jumping up and down on interlocked bumpers.

They knew they couldn't leave the beer in Baldinger's car. The paratroopers would spot the evidence and probably torch the station wagon the same way the sports sedan had been torched. And they couldn't bring it onto the post. So they climbed up a hill behind the parking field, found a comfortable clearing, and leisurely worked their way through the stock. At one point, Willie stood unsteadily, and raised his beer can in toast.

"I give you Dave Baldinger, pride of Special Operations, leader of the greatest mission in Green Beret history."

Beer cans raised all around.

"If I'm ever trapped behind enemy lines," Willie continued, "I'll never lose hope. I'll know that Dave Baldinger is out there somewhere, and that somehow he's going to get through and set me free."

A brief cheer, and then they all drank.

"Yeah," said Tom Cavitt, wiping his lips on his sleeve. "He may throw you through a bathroom window, but one way or another Dave'll get you out."

"Wow," Willie Derry interrupted. "Did you see that fuckin' blast? That car musta jumped ten feet. Jesus, it was better than a howitzer round."

"Mex shoulda been there," Luther Brown said. "Ain't no woman who can be this much fun."

Tom Cavitt noticed that Baldinger was the only one who wasn't laughing. "Hey, what's the matter Dave? You wishin' you had stayed with Mex?"

"I'm just thinking," Baldinger answered. "You guys know what I just did?"

"You rescued our beer," Derry said in a genuine admiration.

"And our honor," Brown added. "We showed them jumpers who runs this Army."

"What I did was blow up a car, maybe even a whole parking lot full of cars, for a couple cases of beer," Baldinger remembered out loud. He shook his head in disbelief.

* * *

When Captain Robert Gordon was summoned to Colonel Barry Grigg's office, he had little to report. There were lots of promising leads, but no hard evidence.

He had run down all the men who had received unsatisfactory fitness reports from Major Daks, and zeroed in on Sergeant William Campbell. The sergeant, military police investigators had learned, was indeed given to violent outbursts, and was a man who always answered an affront. In fact, he had been relieved of training duties after a series of scary incidents with his current squad of trainees. Campbell certainly knew how to set a grenade mine, and would probably pull the pin eagerly if he thought he was getting even. He claimed to have been in his barracks the night of the blast, and denied knowing anything about it. "You oughta be questioning the major," he had taunted his interrogators. "Sounds to me like he doesn't know how to count the grenades he checks out."

They had interviewed the men who had shared past service assignments with the major. One, an Airborne captain, was plainly delighted that Daks was being professionally embarrassed. "I guess I wouldn't mind seeing him taken down a peg," he had admitted. "But I'd take him on face to face. Bomb-throwing doesn't appeal to me." The captain had given them a solid alibi explaining why he couldn't have been near the major's house on the day of the explosion. But parts of his story hadn't checked out.

Gordon had followed up on Grigg's idea of a love triangle. The military police had taken the security photos of the school officer's wives to the better hotels and lodges within two hours' drive off the base. He had been secretly relieved when none of them could identify Carol Roy. But Captain O'Leary's wife had indeed checked into a country guest lodge with Major Daks on several occasions, which probably explained why her hands had shaken so much that she couldn't hold a coffee cup. And O'Leary, as best they could tell without calling him in for questioning, had been unaccounted for after he left the faculty party. Robert had proof of infidelity, which he knew was none of his business. But nothing positive that would link Captain O'Leary to the hand grenade.

He had also followed up on Carol Roy's suggestion that the culprit might be from one of the foreign countries where Special Forces had operated. The cross-check of the nationalities of people on the base was still in progress, and the interviews of the foreign students in the present training class were proceeding as quickly as the diplomatic nuances would allow.

He was also looking for a way to pick up his interview with Captain Henry Roy. Like it or not, Henry and Carol were known to have been in Daks's driveway an hour before the explosion. Carol had been vague about the moments when Henry was helping Marilyn Daks with her key and she was alone. She had displayed a rather remarkable knowledge of the specific techniques taught in the school, as well as an obvious contempt for what Daks had done to his wife.

He had lots of irons in the fire, but none of them hot enough to brand a criminal.

"I'm sorry, Colonel. Maybe with a bit more time," he began. He was surprised to see that Grigg was not at all disappointed.

"You looked, you inquired, you studied the situation," Grigg told him almost as a compliment. "And you found nothing."

Gordon had to agree. That was about the sum of it. But he felt obliged to add, "Of course, I have no experience as an investigator. Maybe people trained for this . . ."

The colonel sneered at the suggestion. "You did a thorough job, Captain. No one expected you to be Sherlock Holmes. I think the reason you couldn't find anyone with a strong motive and a ready opportunity is probably that there is no one. You have no hard evidence of a perpetrator because, in all probability, there is no perpetrator. I think we can probably chalk this up as the kind of accident inherent in our training mission."

Gordon could sense that he was being let off the hook. But he was still bothered by some of the evidence he had reviewed. "The problem I have," he suggested cautiously, "is that ordnance experts are unanimous that the grenade couldn't have gone off accidentally. First, there's the pin. It has to be removed. And then, if the grenade isn't to explode right away, the handle has to be held in place."

"I know how hand grenades are armed," Colonel Grigg reminded the legal officer. "And I wish I had a dollar for everything the experts told me couldn't happen that actually did happen." He got up from his chair and walked absently to the window. "I suppose, when we call it an accident, that there is some implication of carelessness on Major Daks's part. And I appreciate that the people who work for the major want to protect him. Hell, he's that kind of an officer. He inspires loyalty in his staff. I still intend to write him one hell of a fitness report. As far as I'm concerned, he's star material. I don't think that calling this incident an accident is going to hurt him one little bit.''

Next, the captain reminded the senior officer of another explosion that had occurred recently. ''The car that blew up in the motel parking lot. I understand that there's some concern that Special Operations people might be involved. Now, if we were able to establish a connection, that would indicate that there may be someone who—''

''Captain, there's no connection. We all know damn well what happened at the motel. There were a couple of dozen Airborne troops there, and there weren't enough young ladies to go around. They were doing a lot of drinking. Obviously, someone felt that someone else had outhustled him for time with one of the women. Someone got angry.''

Gordon's eyes widened in disbelief. ''So he blew up the guy's car? That's a pretty drastic solution, Colonel.''

''These are paratroopers,'' Grigg reminded him. ''Not choirboys.''

As his last hope, Gordon suggested that they might delay another few days. ''All the records on people with foreign origins are being reviewed. And we've found some personnel records with inconsistencies that have been referred back to the Pentagon,'' he said. ''We should have more information in the next day or so.''

Grigg sighed. ''You have more faith in the Pentagon than I do. Besides, I've got your boss, General Wheeler, breathing down my neck. The general likes things in his command kept nice and tidy. I don't see any reason to keep him waiting.''

The captain nodded his agreement, gathered up his papers, saluted, and turned to leave the office. There was no dissuading the colonel from the report he wanted. Gordon could, if he chose, go over the command's head, and appeal to his superiors at the Judge Advocate General staff for more time. But he had nothing concrete on which to base an appeal. And even though staff judge advocates didn't technically belong to the command at the post where they were stationed, they had been encouraged always to give full consideration to the command's priorities.

''How long is it going to take?'' Grigg asked when Gordon had his hand on the doorknob.

''A day or two. Three days at the most.''

Grigg checked his calendar. There was a ceremonial review on the parade grounds the next morning. ''How about tomorrow?'' he suggested. ''Right after the parade.''

Gordon went straight to his office and set to work. Using his index fingers, he pecked out the cover to his investigation report, four pages that detailed the incident and that restated his own assignment to conduct an investigation of potentially criminal activity. It took him two more pages to list the steps he had taken and the reasons why each of the steps were considered prudent.

Next he typed summaries of each line of investigation. There was the technical evaluation that had fixed the type and location of the explosive, and related it to the damage done to the car and the carport. There was the review of fitness reports, and the subsequent interviews. And there were the numerous cross-tabulations of personnel records. He omitted any reference to Daks's extramarital activities, or to the lady most recently involved. Instead, he summarized the numerous personal interviews he had held, which indicated that Daks was well respected and well liked, and that his wife was universally considered an asset to the command.

Finally, late in the evening, he wrote his conclusion. "There appears to be no casual relationship between this incident and any individual assigned to the post, nor any of the activities or missions pursued on the post. In the total absence of any evidence or suggestion to the contrary, we are forced to conclude that the grenade was accidentally carried to the aforementioned residence, by any of the many official and personal vehicles that would have reason to call on Major Daks or his family, and that it was detonated by that action of the major's car as it transited the driveway.''

He reread his words, and then attached the many documents he had gathered. The assembled report was thick and weighty, exactly the kind of response that General Wheeler favored. He liked documents to be imposing enough so that there was at least a chance that no one would bother to read them.

Read it carefully, Gordon realized, and it was shamefully incomplete and filled with holes. But to the casual reader, it was a detailed investigation which could safely be filed beside the incident it described.

An accident, Gordon told himself, as he sealed the report into an envelope for delivery to Colonel Grigg the next day. That would be his verdict. That would be the verdict that Grigg would accept and pass on to General Wheeler. And that would be the verdict that the general would send to Washington as part of the mountain of correspondence that left Fort Francis Marion for the Pentagon every day.

Best of all, the colonel would have his verdict right after the next morning's parade, exactly when he wanted it. Gordon had finally become part of the real Army.

THE
ACCUSED

★ ★ ★

It was a standard military pageant in which the troops formed up into a parade, rendered a salute to dignitaries on the reviewing stand, and then listened to speeches that warned of dire global threats. The occasion was the anniversary of the opening of Fort Francis Marion, a minor event that didn't generally bring the heavy-hitters down from Washington. Only once had it attracted a cabinet member, when President Reagan sent his Secretary of Defense to the Francis Marion anniversary parade in order to launch a trial balloon on a nuclear disarmament treaty. The fort was so obscure that the press hadn't picked up on the speech.

This year there was no one of the cabinet rank. An under-secretary of the Army was on the reviewing stand along with the local congressman, to demonstrate the civilian control over the military. The ranking military representative was a retired three-star general who had once been the United States liaison to NATO. The other seats were taken up by General Wheeler's staff officers and their wives, the mayors and constables of the surrounding towns, and the pastor of a nearby Baptist church, who would invoke the Lord's blessings.

The ranks seemed thin as the troops fell into formation. In the infantry companies, where the soldiers wore the standard dress greens, half the squads were visibly short. Among the paratroopers, where the standard uniform was altered to permit the trousers to be tucked into jump boots, one batallion commander was without staff. And the Green Berets were short an entire Special Operations unit, its members scattered to plug holes in the other units. The marching band's problems were apparent the moment it struck up the first notes of its march. The row of drummers was down to two snare drums, and the bass drum which kept the march tempo was nowhere to be found.

As the ranks wheeled to form the parade, several soldiers darted out of formation. Before the band had marched into line, one of the tubas staggered off the field. Then an infantry company commander wandered out of the line of march and collapsed in clear view of the dignitaries.

General Wheeler's adjutant was horrified. The general was a stickler for military decorum and would expect even a soldier who had been shot through the heart to keep in step until the end of the parade. The adjutant expected to hear the general curse under his breath and order someone to get the names of the dropouts. But when he glanced from the corner of his eye, General Wheeler seemed not to be noticing the losses from his ranks. His sallow face was bathed in sweat, and he seemed to be having difficulty in keeping his balance.

The band marched by, the drum major executing the eyes-right on behalf of all his troops. Wheeler and the retired general responded with snappy salutes. Then the colors passed, Old Glory held high while the regimental colors were dipped in tribute. Everyone on the reviewing stand rose in unison, the officers saluting while the civilians raised hands to their hearts.

It was at that instant that General Wheeler belched, pressed his fist against his mouth, turned abruptly, and rushed to the back of the reviewing stand. He started down the steps, lurched sideways, and bounced off the railing, then regained his footing and made it to the grassy field. He started running toward the nearest building, the base museum, which was located directly behind the colors and the ceremonial cannons. But he had gone only a few steps when he staggered, fell to his knees, and vomited down the front of his dress uniform. The adjutant reached the fallen leader in time to see his unfocused eyes rolling in his head and to hear his voice gurgle that he was dying. Then the general collapsed into his own mess.

Several more troops broke ranks during the blessing, and two of the officers on the reviewing stand left during the brief remarks by the under-secretary. A colonel's wife swooned and fell out of her chair during the address by the retired NATO general. She grabbed the man by his leg as she attempted to break her fall, and dragged him, still clutching the microphone, down to his knees.

The command's remaining ranking officer rushed the ceremonies to a speedy conclusion and dismissed the mustered troops. Several of them fell on the grass as soon as their ranks were broken. One of the Green Berets, who had passed the full course of medical training, immediately called the base hospital and requested assistance. "Send everything you've got," he ordered. "We've got an emergency here."

"We don't have anything to send," came a panicky response. "People are dropping all over the base."

The hospital had been overwhelmed long before the parade had begun. Children seemed to have been the first to fall victim. Dozens of them had awakened in the early-morning hours crying with nausea and vomiting. Parents had administered the standard drug-store cures, but then became concerned as the symptoms worsened. At sunrise, they had begun calling the hospital. Nausea, vomiting, and diarrhea were the universal complaints. Children who had played until they fell asleep the previous evening now seemed to be rushing toward dehydration.

The doctors were just beginning to examine the sick children when queasy parents began to show up. One mother was taken ill in the waiting room while the doctors were tending to her child. Then a lieutenant, who had left for the parade grounds after assuring his wife that their prostrate daughter would be just fine, nearly fell through the emergency room doors. His uniform trousers were soiled and there were yellow stains down the front of his jacket.

The medical staff had looked around at the rapidly filling beds. No disease, even in epidemic proportions, could hit so many people so hard and so quickly. They figured that they had a massive case of food poisoning on their hands, and sent staffers to seize samples of everything on the shelves of the post exchange. At the same time, they began taking histories from all their patients.

By 0900, the starting time of the parade, there had been more adults in their waiting rooms than children. Half the adults were wearing full-dress uniforms. And then came the call from the parade grounds, demanding that they rush ambulances to the scene. Everyone on the base seemed suddenly to be desperately ill.

General Wheeler was driven to the officers' entrance by his aide, and had to be helped out of the car by two nurses. Then the aide suddenly turned his head and got sick, and moments later one of the nurses dashed away from the general toward the ladies' room.

At 0930, the head surgeon, Colonel Richard Liggett, realized that his facilities were simply overwhelmed. There were patients in every room, and new arrivals stacked like cordwood in the hallways. Worse, a third of his medical staff were now showing the same symptoms as the patients. He described his plight to the head of medicine at a major teaching hospital in Atlanta.

"Nothing could be this contagious," he said in a frightened voice. "A healthy visitor walks into the waiting room, sees a patient, and suddenly gets sick. Then a healthy nurse rushes to the sick visitor, and the nurse is sick before she can get her patient to an examining room." Specialists in contagious diseases were aboard helicopters within the hour, on their way to Fort Francis Marion.

Captain Henry Roy came directly home from the parade grounds, and began telling Carol about the anniversary day disaster. "It must be a bug that's going around, because a lot of the troops were absent," he said enthusiastically. "But there's General Wheeler, standing on the center of the reviewing stand, doing his best to look like God. The next second, he's running like a rabbit across the grounds. One hand is clamped over his mouth, and the other hand is clamped over his ass. It was the most humiliating military retreat since Napoleon."

Carol had to laugh despite her usual sympathy for people in distress. Wheeler was a martinet, the personification of many of the things about the military that she resented. Deprived of combat, he tried to raise the most trivial ceremonial activities to the same level of importance as the D-day invasion. Wheeler had once transferred a duty officer off the post, and perhaps crippled his career, because the evening canon had fired several seconds later than sunset. The thought of him being embarrassed at one of his trumped-up historical moments was close to being delicious.

But even while she was laughing, she was aware of a gagging in her throat. The laughter seemed to upset her stomach, and within seconds, she was on her knees in the bathroom. Henry dried the breakfast dishes while he was giving Carol a moment of privacy. It certainly couldn't be anything she ate, he thought as he put the cereal bowl and the coffee cup back on the shelf. Unless the milk she used on her cereal was bad. He went to the refrigerator and smelled the container. But as he was deciding that it was perfectly sweet, he knew it couldn't be the food. He remembered the casualties on the parade grounds, too many of them to have shared a common meal. It must be some sort of flu.

As he helped Carol to her bed, he noticed the clammy sweat on her face and neck. When she pulled away from him and ran back into the bathroom, he realized that she was quickly becoming dehydrated. "Try to drink something," he told her as he left to return to the school. "Water. Ginger ale. Even if you can't keep it down, at least try." She nodded, and then ducked back behind the bathroom door.

Henry was halfway back to the school when he felt the first tidal wave of nausea. A street later, he pulled the car to the curb and barely got the door open before he was racked with vomiting. He was suddenly so sick that he couldn't raise his head. Then, in the depths of his own helplessness, he made the connection. "Sweet Jesus," he mumbled as he dragged himself back into his car. "It's the water supply. They've gotten the water."

He collapsed into his office chair after calling in vain for his absent corporal. It took him three tries to get an answer at the hospital, and ten more minutes to get a Colonel Liggett on the line. "It's the water," he said. "The water is poisoned."

"What water? What are you talking about? Who is this?" Liggett's hospital was in crisis. He had not time for crank calls.

"This is Captain Roy. Captain Henry Roy, from the Special Operations school. The base water supply has been poisoned."

"Poisoned? What poison?"

"It's a bacterial agent. Shigella shigae. Everyone on the base has bacillary dysentery. Replenish fluids and salt. And keep testing the water. The water can kill you if you drink enough of it." Roy threw the phone aside and pushed his face into his wastebasket as he was wracked with another flow of vomiting.

A quick test of the tap water flowing into the hospital proved that Roy was right. Then a test of the main lines flowing from the base pressure tower turned up heavy concentrations of the same bacterial agent. Liggett ordered the water supply to the entire base cut off, and a telephone chain passed the word to every household.

Once they knew they weren't victims of a wildly contagious disease, the doctors were able to attack the symptoms they were confronting. The stream of patients continued well into the afternoon. And volunteers were kept busy answering telephone calls from suddenly stricken people. But by evening, the water shutdown began to reduce the flow of new victims. And the antidehydration treatments began to effect cures. At 2300 hours the medical staff looked around and realized that they were pretty well caught up.

The young children, who were first stricken, were the first to recover. Some were ready to go home during the night, but had to await the recovery of weakened parents. By morning there were children playing loudly in all the hospital corridors. No one asked them to be quiet. There was a sense of thankfulness that they were all alive.

Adults began recovering the next day. Henry Roy was released from the hospital early in the afternoon and went straight home to Carol, who had toughed it out in her own bed. He stopped at the base exchange to pick up some bottled water, but had to settle for club soda. The bottled water shelves were empty. General Wheeler was released during the afternoon, and driven straight home in his staff car. Word spread that he had returned to duty, and then the other stricken officers hastened to follow him out the door. By the second evening, the hospital was pleasantly quiet. The emergency was over.

The military police, with the help of the army engineers, determined that the flow from the surrounding streams was pure, but that the treatment plant, the pressure tank, and the plumbing systems were all contaminated. They were able to reconstruct the chain of events that had brought Fort Francis Marion literally to its knees.

The base tapped several of the streams of pure mountain water that flowed down from the Appalachians. In order to eliminate the sediment it carried and to lessen its mineral taste, the entire supply was treated. The water was batched into settling tanks. Then individual tankfuls were passed through filters into aeration tanks, where each batch was flowed continuously for forty-eight hours. From the aerators, the water was pumped, again in a mass quantity, to a holding tank. And the holding tank was pumped, continuously, up into the water tower to create the required pressure for the entire base's water supply.

The bacterial agent had been added during the aeration process, creating a single batch of heavily contaminated water. The batch had been pumped into a separate holding tank and then, at some point of time, raised into the tower. The agent couldn't disperse into the entire water supply and dilute itself because it was kept separate until it plunged down from the tower into the water mains. It was flowing out of household taps while it was still alive and potent.

Throughout the command structure, fingers began to point. First, General Wheeler landed on Colonel Grigg for "keeping shit like that on my base." Grigg echoed the reprimand to Henry Roy, even though the captain swore that the material had been kept under lock and key. Roy, in turn, raised hell with the MPs who should have been guarding the school building.

But through all the finger pointing, one face was inescapably clear to Colonel Grigg. The grenade in Major Daks's driveway had been no accident. Nor was Daks the only target of the assault. Someone was using Special Operations methods to attack the entire base. Fort Francis Marion was under seige.

He summoned Captain Robert Gordon, and handed back his draft report without even a hint of apology for having pushed him to a premature verdict.

"We're not looking for a pissed-off husband," he analyzed as he paced his office like a caged animal. "And we're not looking for some idiot with a grudge against Major Daks. The grenade . . . the bacteria . . . this has to be someone we trained in Special Operations. And whoever it is, the son of a bitch is taking on the whole base."

"You're sure they're related?" Gordon asked, holding his own report of the attack on Major Daks and the preliminary report on the tampered water supply.

"For chrissake, Captain, they're both right out of our training manuals. You think it's a coincidence?"

"We don't know that it's one person," Gordon pointed out.

Grigg slammed his fist on the desk. "One person. A whole squad. What difference does it make? Whoever is doing this knows Special Operations like a book. If it's more than one person, then they have to be working together, because I just don't believe that two Green Berets have gone nuts at the same time."

Gordon reintroduced the suggestion he had made at their first meeting. "We should have professionals working on this, Colonel. I'd like to bring in some outside help."

Grigg waved away the suggestion. "General Wheeler doesn't like to hang out his dirty laundry. We've got to handle this ourselves."

"With all respects to General Wheeler, sir, we may have a maniac loose on the base. I think our priority should be in finding him, or them, before he attacks again. We've been lucky, so far. No one has been seriously hurt. But our luck may not hold up."

"I know that," Grigg snapped. "If it was my call, we'd have brought the FBI in right at the start. But it's your show. I'll give you anything you need. People. Access to records. Anything. But you're the one who has to find some answers."

The colonel was being less than honest. Had it been his call, he wouldn't have shared his concerns with General Wheeler, much less with the FBI. Special Operations had many enemies throughout the military and its ranks of congressional supporters. There were dark suspicions about his secret army, its methods and its ethics. A crazed Green Beret killer was his worst nightmare, just the kind of incident that could be used to discredit all his hopes. Like Wheeler, he needed to have the man found and neutralized quickly and quietly, and the fewer people that were involved the better it would be. But he couldn't keep the lid on his problem for very long. Rumors were already flying around the post. Not just the infantry and Airborne troops, but even their wives and teenage children understood that their water supply had been deliberately contaminated. They knew they were under attack by someone from Special Operations. And there was no way to keep them from talking.

Grigg's officers maintained a respectful silence. It was unseemly to be talking about their crisis—almost like discussing cancer in front of a cancer victim. But that was only part of their difficulty. There was also an unmentioned mutual suspicion that they were all beginning to harbor. Anyone on the base could have had access to a hand grenade, but the bacterial agent was a different matter. It had been kept at the school, locked into a chemical closet in Captain Roy's small laboratory. The school was a closed facility with access limited to the teaching officers and their immediate staffs. Of course, there were the students—the Special Operations candidates who were in the second phase of their training program, and the foreign military contingent. But the students came, took their lessons, and then left. The run of the building, and the casual after-hours access that a thief would probably need, were limited. It seemed most likely that the person who had invaded Captain Roy's supplies would have to be someone associated with the school. Maybe the officer whom you were meeting for cocktails, or the one who had invited you and your wife over for dinner.

The silence was no problem for Marilyn Daks. She had learned to sense the major's priorities and moods and knew instinctively what subjects were off-limits. Anything derogatory to Special Operations clearly fitted that category, and so she continued to dwell on flower arrangements and PTA events. But it was galling to Carol Roy. "We've all been poisoned, but we're not supposed to talk about it?" she challenged as she and Henry were dressing for dinner at the officers' club. "For God's sake, Henry. You want me to look under the hood of my car, and leave the mail out in the mailbox because someone might be trying to blow me up. Now I guess you want me to try the water on the cat before I drink any of it myself."

"Just don't bring it up at dinner," he asked. "And if someone else mentions it, just don't make a big thing of it. We'll probably have the guy in a couple of days, and then it will all be over."

Henry went out ahead of Carol to start the car, hoping she wouldn't notice him checking it over before he turned the ignition.

"You're sure it's safe?" she taunted before climbing in beside him.

He winced. "That's exactly the kind of remark I hope you'll avoid tonight."

As they were driving, she asked, "What do you think the odds are that one of our dinner companions might be the phantom?"

"Jesus, Carol . . ."

"Maybe Gene set the hand grenade himself, so he wouldn't be suspected when he tried out the bacteria in the water. Or it could be Captain Jordon. Isn't he the one who specializes in torture?"

"Interrogation," he corrected through clenched teeth.

"I'll bet it's Jordon," she thought aloud. "He probably wants to get someone arrested so that he can try out his latest techniques. What's he using these days. Thumbscrews?"

He slammed on the brakes.

"You know what you're doing, don't you? You're making me choose between the Army and you."

She stared dumbly at him for a moment as she realized he was right. She already suspected that she couldn't live in an organization dedicated to the efficient production of violence. She knew that in a violent world it couldn't be avoided, and that some people had to specialize in it. But she had learned that she couldn't be one of those people.

"I guess you're right," she admitted. "And I guess I'm afraid that you've already chosen."

While Henry and Carol Roy were trying to make small talk with their friends over dinner, Captain Gordon was working late into the night. His time was short. The Peruvian officers were finishing up their training courses and would be returning to their country to take up their battle with the Shining Path Maoists. A group of Army officers from El Salvador was scheduled to arrive two days later. Grigg was embarrassed enough that the Peruvians had witnessed the fallibility of his program. He had told Gordon that when the Salvadorans heard stories about mysterious explosions and poisoned water, and raised their first question concerning their safety at the school, he had to be able to tell them the culprit was already behind bars.

To meet the impending deadline, Gordon was working with probability. He agreed with Grigg. Because the weapons chosen for the two attacks both came from Special Operations training, it was probable that they were related. The person or persons he was searching for knew Daks and understood his specialty. He or they also knew how to use bacterial agents, and knew where Captain Roy kept them. Outsiders' knowledge about Special Operations probably wouldn't reach that level of detail. The odds were that their attacker was someone directly connected with the school.

While the first attack was focused on a single individual, the second was directed against the entire base. Assuming the attacker wasn't completely insane, then he had to have been acting on hatred for the entire command, perhaps even for the whole Army. The sum of these suppositions defined a Green Beret who had been wronged in some way by the military.

How many could there be? the captain wondered as he poured through a mountain of printout gathered from the personnel records. He was so deeply involved in the hunt that he didn't hear his office door blast open.

"We've got something, Gordon."

He looked up over the top of his glasses. It was Major Topping. He held out a small plastic bottle, wrapped in a plastic sandwich bag. Its seam was split and the cap was missing.

"We found this in the water aerator," he said.

They called Henry Roy, who left his dinner at the officers' club and rushed over to identify the bottle. The bottle was standing in the middle of Gordon's desk blotter, exactly where Topping had placed it. The two officers had been moving around it and examining it from every angle.

"You're certain that this is the container?" Topping asked.

"Positive," Roy answered. "I can even see the outline where the label used to be."

"Well, at least we know how the stuff got into the water," Topping said. "Someone tossed the whole bottle into the open slats of the aerator. Sooner or later, all that churning had to break it open."

Gordon knew *how* the bacteria had gotten into the water. It was *who* that he was grappling with. "Could there be any fingerprints on it?" he asked.

Topping chuckled. "It's been bouncing around in the aerator for nearly a week. That's pretty much like putting it through a dishwasher a couple of hundred times. We're lucky we can figure out that it's a bottle."

"Damn," Gordon cursed. "I thought we might have something."

Major Topping lifted the bag by its edge, and studied the bottle inside. "I'm not saying it's impossible. The FBI has all sorts of tricks for restoring fingerprints. It's just that it's a long shot."

"We don't want to go to the FBI," Gordon told him. "Can't we check it here on the base?"

"Not a chance. We don't have that kind of equipment. All we have is an ink pad and a roller. You want to get anything off this, it'll have to go to Washington."

Gordon hesitated. Colonel Grigg had told him specifically not to call in outside help. But he wouldn't be bringing anyone in. He was just looking for an expert lab analysis. "How long will it take?" he asked the military police officer.

"A couple a days to know whether there are any prints left on it. Then, if there are, a couple of weeks to try and find a match. Maybe never if the print doesn't have much detail. There's millions and millions of prints that they have to check against."

"We can cut that down," Gordon said. He looked at the personnel summaries stacked on his desk. They could have the FBI check just the prints of his primary suspects; school staff and people trained at the school. "We could give them a list of no more than two hundred names."

"Maybe a week," Major Topping speculated.

The Salvadoran officers were arriving in four days, Gordon remembered. A week seemed impossibly far off. But it was the only clue he had that offered a real chance of positive identification.

"Is there anything we can do to speed it up?" he wondered. "General Wheeler wants this wrapped up in a hurry."

* * *

They called the mission their "walkabout," after the manhood test of the Australian aborigines. Each of the trainees would be flown out to a remote corner of the exercise area, and handed a map that showed his destination at another corner. He could take his parrish knife and field compass. Or, if he chose, he could trade one of them for a canteen of water. Then he had three days to reach his destination. To make the walkabout competitive, the exercise area was under constant patrol by hostile forces. Sometimes they were crack Army Rangers. More often they were the Airborne troops from the base, or the Eighteenth Airborne from Fort Bragg. Occasionally, they were the foreign military contingents training at the Special Operations school.

If the Special Operations candidate got caught, he would be picked up in a chopper and flown back to his starting point. His task was the same, but there was less time to complete it. In case he got lost, there was the one extra item he carried that was called the "cop-out kit." It contained a radio beacon that would send out a homing signal to the patrol helicopters, and a smoke bomb to be set off when the responding copters came into the area. A few men who had failed their walkabout had still made it into Special Operations. But no one who had copped out had ever been flashed into an active unit.

Willie Derry and Tom Cavitt were the first to go into the forest. "Cowboys and Indians," Willie had laughed as he waited with the others on the helicopter pad. "Guess which side I'm on?" He took a long feather and stuck it at a jaunty angle into the band of his soft field hat. Then he ran the edge of his parrish knife over his finger. "Not only am I gonna break their time record, but when I come strolling into my home base, I'm gonna have a couple of Airborne scalps hanging from my belt."

Cavitt was quiet, clearly nervous about his chances. The compass and map weren't his strong points, and there was a good chance that he would lose his way. He had decided to throw away his cop-out kit as soon as he cleared the landing area. No matter what happened, he wasn't going to call for help. "Don't do anything crazy," Baldinger had warned him. "The radio beacon could save your life."

Sergeant Major Thompson was on the chopper when it landed. He held out a canteen of water. "Anyone want to trade?"

"Don't need it," Willie answered. "I can find water under rocks. I can eat the bark off trees."

"I'll trade it for this," Cavitt said, offering the cop-out kit.

"Get aboard," Thompson said, suppressing a smile. He trained his men to be cautious, but he liked to see them a little cocky.

The copter lifted off, then headed over the treetops and out toward the mountains. Good luck, Baldinger thought, as his friends disappeared.

His turn came the next day. It was he and Jim Ray who turned down the canteen and climbed into the helicopter. As soon as they lifted off, Thompson tossed them each a heavy, black blindfold. "Put these on. We don't want you scouting the area."

As soon as Dave found himself lost in the darkness, he felt his mouth go dry. He began to sense the loneliness that would be his only companion for the next few days, and with the loneliness came fear. He tried to postpone it.

"How are Derry and Cavitt doing?" he asked. "Any word?"

His only response was the pounding of the helicopter rotors. It was Thompson's way of telling him that he was already on his own. He tried to keep track of the time. Maybe it would be useful to know how far from the base he was. But then he felt the chopper turning randomly. They were flying around, all over the area. When they took his blindfold off, he would truly be in an unknown world.

The rotor noise changed its pitch and Baldinger felt himself settling lower. There was a crunching as the chopper's skids touched the ground.

"Talbert," the sergeant major barked. Dave could hear Jim Ray and Thompson climbing out through the door.

"Give 'em hell," he shouted toward Jim Ray. There was no answer.

Minutes later, they were pounding back into the air to begin another series of random turns. As they flew, Dave ran through the strategy that he had discussed over and over with the other members of the unit.

First, get away from the landing area. The patrol forces probably knew where the landing areas were, and even if they didn't, they could see a helicopter touching down. They could close in quickly. Next, move out toward the edge of the exercise area. That would most likely be away from the patrols who would be stationed between the landing areas and the finish lines where they could interdict the shortest and most likely routes. Finally, don't take the shortest and most likely routes. Move around the periphery of the exercise, through the most rugged country that you could handle. "Make 'em chase you through the worst shit you can find," Luther Brown had commented. "That's where we got the edge. We're trained for it. They ain't."

"Hole up during the day," Dickie Morgan had advised. "Let the Airborne go play in the heat. We gotta be better at night than them."

They were all good ways to keep from getting captured. But they were also good ways to get yourself helplessly lost. That was the decision he would have to make over and over again during the next few days. Which was more dangerous? The dark, impenetrable mountains that the Airborne and infantry would find impossible? That the foreign troops wouldn't even consider entering? Or the more open areas where you had a much better chance of finding your way?

The rotor noise changed and the chopper began to drop. The engine roared just before the skids touched down.

"Okay, Baldinger."

He blinked at the bright light as soon as Thompson pulled off the blindfold, then stepped out into a rocky clearing.

"Last chance to swap for the canteen," Thompson said.

Baldinger shook his head. He was afraid that his voice would crack if he tried to answer.

The sergeant major handed him a map. "The guy who drew this has never been in the area. It's about as good a map as you'd have if you got dropped into Peru."

He pointed to a small, hand-drawn circle. "This is where you are right now. That's a fact." Then he pointed to a small square. "This is where you have to be by twenty-four hundred hours on Thursday."

Dave nodded and then folded the map into his pocket. Thompson turned and jumped back through the door. The engine sound rose a few notes and the chopper jumped into the air. Baldinger stood perfectly still until it disappeared over the trees. Then he ran out of the clearing and into the curtain of the forest.

He moved as quickly as he could, brushing the branches away from his face and moving into heavier country as if he were being drawn by a magnet. He kept going for almost two hours, trying to ignore the heat that had instantly turned his fatigues into wet rags, and the thirst that was already burning in his throat. When he pulled up, he was in dense brush, shaded from the sun, and probably a mile further away from his destination. It was then that he settled down to study the map.

He was in the northeast corner of the area, much closer to the fort than he would have guessed from his time in the air. His goal was a point on the western perimeter, further south, but not impossibly far-away. He could begin by moving due west, but that would take him up into the rocky bluffs that they had climbed in Sector Foxtrot. It would be a relatively safe route, probably forbidding to the infantry and Airborne troops. But it might prove to be an impossible path without climbing equipment, and even dangerous if he were forced onto the sheer face of one of the cliffs.

Dave decided to move immediately along the safe perimeter, until he was well up into the highlands. Then he would use the cover of night to venture deep inside the exercise area in order to skirt the most difficult country. By dawn, he planned to be back up in the highlands, where he would wait out the daytime hours. He would make the next move at night, hoping to walk into his target area before the following dawn.

He used the compass to keep himself moving in a straight line, although no part of his route was really straight. He was always moving further north or further south than he intended, keeping his priority on the densest cover that he could find. But nowhere in his sector of the map did he see any indication of a stream or a pond. The thirst, which now made him uncomfortable, would become crippling if he didn't find water.

The darkness was welcome because of the cool it brought. But the refreshing cool quickly became cold. The sweat that coated his body and was like glue under the fatigues, suddenly turned icy. He knew he couldn't stop without risking a chill. So he kept driving forward even though the path lines through the trees were fading in front of him.

Dave turned further south, into the more dangerous regions that were probably closely patrolled. If he angled back toward the east, there was a wide stream. But he could almost count on the stream being closely watched, so he decided to push his thirst a little further.

He moved more carefully, and if anything more quietly. Each branch was lifted and then eased back into position. He paused every fifty yards, and spent a minute listening. Only when he was sure of the quiet did he step on ahead. As he moved, he kept checking the compass, trying to estimate how far he was going and what his magnetic direction actually was. And he checked the time. He had to allow himself enough time to get back into the rugged foothills before daybreak.

There was a sound ahead; the snap of a branch and then a muffled curse of pain. Exactly the noises they had been taught to avoid. Baldinger froze. He could hear more branches thrashing up ahead. Slowly, he lowered himself to the ground, and then pressed himself into the dirt.

The sounds grew louder. Carelessly louder. He heard a voice, and then a barked command, "Keep it down." He remembered Thompson's words. They might as well have been carrying bagpipes. A boot crushed into the underbrush no more than ten yards to his left. Then there was the wheeze of labored breathing barely five yards to his right. The patrol was spread out in a dragnet, and he was right in the center.

"There ain't nobody out here," a stage whisper said. "There ain't nobody dumb enough to be out here."

"We're out here," a commanding voice blasted back. "Now keep your goddamn mouths shut."

The patrol passed to both sides of him. Baldinger had to smile at the uproar they were creating. Put that patrol in El Salvador, or in Peru, and they would all be dead before the sun came up. He gave them plenty of time to move away, then rose up to his knees and began moving through the bush.

An hour before sunrise, he began heading back to the west. But he could feel the fatigue in his muscles. It had been about fifteen hours since he had taken any water. The parrish knife suddenly seemed heavy and useless. He found himself wishing that he had traded it for the canteen.

He kept the pressure on himself, turning a bit to the north in order to find steeper rock faces. He worked carefully up one of them, until he found a covered ledge that was perhaps twenty-five feet above ground level. Then he squeezed under the foliage to await the sunrise. He fell asleep before the cherry-colored disc popped over the treetops.

The popping of helicopter rotors woke him. There were a pair of gunships cruising slowly over the forest, only a few hundred yards away. Underneath them, he could see patrols as they passed through the clearings. It was a concentrated search, zeroed in on the territory he would have to cover to reach his assigned destination. Baldinger realized that his decision had been correct. If he had been trying to move now, in the daylight, he'd have no chance at all. The smart move was to make no move at all. But he knew he couldn't last the day without water. His first move once darkness fell would have to be toward one of the streams.

He drifted back into sleep, while the sun climbed to its full height and then began dropping toward the mountains. Again, he awoke to the sound of rotors, and he held perfectly still while the copters zig-zagged across the forest cover. When they turned away, he started down the face of the bluff. But he realized immediately that each movement was more difficult for him. It wasn't just the lack of water. He had now gone more than thirty hours without food. His own weakness was becoming a fatal enemy.

He foraged along the base of the cliff, finding moss and plant roots that he knew he could eat. But the food choked in his throat. He gathered what he could find and stuffed it into his pockets. Then, even before the darkness was fully protective, he headed toward the point where one of the streams emerged from the mountains. In a direct line, it was less than a mile away. But at that point it broke out into open country, a perfect spot for the enemy force to set up an ambush. Dave turned away from his destination, back into the hills he had just left, and tried to find the source of the water in the rugged, mountainous country.

It was dark when he heard its sound, almost a rattling as the water splashed through the gravelly soil. He crept up to it carefully, and waited in the wooded cover for what seemed endless minutes, his thirst agonizing with the water so close. Only when he had detected no motion for nearly an hour did he venture out to the exposed edge of the stream. Then he drank carefully and ate the roots that he had carried with him.

Baldinger used his knife to cut a section from a tree branch, and spent another hour hollowing it out to form a wooden canteen. He filled it with water, then cut one of the pockets from his fatigues and balled it up to use as a stopper. He took a second and longer drink from the stream, then moved back into the woods and began retracing his steps in the darkness.

He was able to keep moving all night. Twice in the dense woods he came across the enemy patrols. One group was resting by the edge of a clearing. He backed away and then gave the area a wide berth, probably losing an hour of time. Later, he walked right up behind one of the flank guards of a patrol that was moving slowly through the forest. These guys had been very quiet and very thorough. Dave had pushed a tree branch aside and seen the back of a soldier no more than ten yards ahead. He froze as the man searched silently through the underbrush and then disappeared into the cover ahead. Baldinger looked to his left. A line of troops was moving slowly on a heading parallel to his own. He dropped slowly, holding the branch so that it wouldn't snap back into position. He stayed perfectly still for several minutes after the last man had disappeared from sight.

He wasn't worried about the time. His forced march during the first night had bought him all the time he needed. And he was in little danger of missing his target. He was probably within a few hours of it, and he had all the next night to find it. His biggest danger was the patrols. He would find a safe cover and stay in hiding throughout the day. To hell with breaking anyone's time record. All Dave wanted to do was stagger in before the deadline and put the exercise behind him.

He used the last hours of darkness to work his way back up into the western rugged country. Then he found a covered crevice and ducked into hiding before the first pale light appeared in the east.

Again, the choppers came with the sun. They beat through the sky overhead, turning back and forth over the forest canopy, and then moved off to the east. Baldinger was tempted to move out behind them. It would be easier to find his way in the daylight. But he resisted the temptation. He had his battle won. All he had to do was stay in hiding until the darkness. Then he could make it home with a day to spare.

He slept for a few hours, and was ravenously hungry when he awoke. He fought back the urge to find more food, and contented himself with a few sips of water from his homemade canteen. He was settling back for a few more hours of rest, when he heard the shouting in the forest ahead of him.

"Over here," a voice screamed.

"Keep him down," came another voice.

"I got him. I got him."

There was a piercing scream. "Son of a bitch!"

"Get the bastard. Get him and sit on him."

Another scream. This one was weaker and more agonized.

"We got him. Goddamn, we got ourselves a Green Beret."

"Fuck off!"

"Hey, look at this son of a bitch. He must think he's Geronimo, or something."

"Maybe we oughta stick that feather up his ass."

And then a defiant voice. "You can kiss my ass, you dumb Airdale."

Baldinger recognized the voice. It was Willie Derry, whose deadline was sunset. And the goddamn Airborne was about to call a helicopter and get him flown back to his starting point.

All he had to do was stay put. He had the exercise whipped. But there was no way he was going to leave Derry in the hands of the Airborne.

He broke out of his hiding place and eased carefully down through the forest. He wanted to rush to Willie's aid, but that would have been a dumb mistake. If he let himself get captured, there was no way he would be of any use to his friend. Instead, he moved slowly toward the uproar, making sure of each footstep. He could still hear the voices, now more efficient than excited.

"Get him back to the landing area. Then we can call the choppers."

"Tie his goddamn hands. We don't want him gettin' no ideas."

Baldinger saw them, a patrol of five men. There was one walking on each side of Willie, a point man out front, and two holding up the rear. They had abandoned the forest cover and were following an open path.

Why the hell not, Baldinger thought. Nobody is hunting for them. He followed at a distance, willing to let them move further away rather than risk the kind of mistake he could make by hurrying. Then he saw the clearing, more than open enough for a helicopter landing. There was a tent canopy pitched to one corner that shaded a table with a radio, a half-dozen pinned-up maps, and a couple of folding chairs.

"We got us one," the point man boasted as he stepped into the clear. Two more soldiers came out from under the tent.

"Great," one of them congratulated. "Three passes for every one of these jungle rats we bag."

"Don't make any plans," Willie told the soldier. "You ain't bagged anything yet."

There was an explosion of laughter. "What are you goin' to do, jungle rat? Take on all seven of us?"

"You're fucking right," Baldinger said to himself. He pressed closer to the edge of the clearing.

"Hummingbird, this is Base Four. We got a Green Beret here who needs to go back to school. Can you come and pick him up?"

They were smiling at one another, glancing at Willie who seemed suddenly helpless, surrounded with his hands fastened behind him.

"This is Hummingbird," the radio crackled. "Nice going Base Four. I'm on my way."

One of the soldiers reached out and snatched the feather from Willie's hat. "Think I'll keep this as a souvenir," he said. "Something to tell my grandchildren about."

Baldinger backed away from the clearing. Then he turned and ran back up the trail. He kept running until he could hear the wash of the approaching helicopter. He pulled the radio beacon out of his cop-out kit, set it, and tossed it into the thicket. "Go fetch, Hummingbird," he called after it. Then he pulled the yellow smoke flare, set the timer to its full thirty seconds, and pulled the safety pin. He rolled it into the bush next to the beacon.

He headed back toward the clearing, but this time avoiding the path. If he had figured it right, half the squad would be charging up that path in about twenty seconds. He looped back into the woods, making a roundabout approach toward the copter landing site.

He could see the chopper approaching, still up about a thousand feet, but already beginning its descent toward the clearing. Suddenly it leveled, lifted a bit, and hovered uncertainly. In the tent, the guy on the radio stepped to the edge of the opening and said something to the rest of the squad. Baldinger looked back down the path. Right on cue a thick yellow cloud of smoke was seeping up through the trees. The moment it appeared, the helicopter's nose swung toward it and the rotors began to roar.

In the clearing, there was shouting and pointing among the troops. Four of them turned and began running back up the path toward the billowing tower of yellow. That left one of them guarding Derry, plus the two who were tending the equipment in the tent.

Baldinger moved quickly, around the edge of the clearing until he was behind the tent. Then he dashed out of the woods, swinging his parrish knife at the tent ropes. The canvas canopy dropped instantly, coming down on the struggling forms of the two men inside.

The whoosh of the tent caught the attention of Derry's guard who had been looking admiringly at the column of smoke that was being blown into swirls by the descending helicopter. He turned just in time to see Dave's fist whistling toward his face, and dropped right into his own shadow.

"Yaahooo!" Willie shouted. He held still for the instant it took Dave to slash the rope that tied his wrists.

"Let's move it," Dave snapped as he started back toward the cover of the woods.

"Right with ya," Derry answered. He grabbed the limp body of the man Dave had knocked out, and searched his pockets until he found the feather. Then he rolled the man over and stuck the feather between his buttocks. "Now ya really got a story for the grandkiddies," he said. He picked up the fallen soldier's rifle and charged off after Dave. But he pulled up abruptly as he passed the tent. There were two forms, half risen to their feet, moving under the canvas as they worked their way to the edge.

"Hey, you guys, can you give Hummingbird a message for me?" The two forms stopped dead. Derry stepped onto the canvas, and crashed the butt of the rifle down on top of each of the heads. "Tell Hummingbird I said 'good night.'"

Willie had to run for nearly ten minutes before he caught up with Baldinger. "Where the fuck we going?" he demanded. "There's four more of 'em back there. Christ, maybe we could get ourselves a helicopter."

"Willie," Dave said. "We're not supposed to capture the whole Airborne. We're supposed to avoid them."

"Yeah," Derry agreed. "I'm runnin' out of time, ain't I?"

He pulled out his map and spread it on his knee in front of Baldinger. "Here's where they dropped me," he said, pointing toward a circle that was in the southwest corner of the exercise area.

"Jesus, Willie, we're going to the same place," Dave nearly shouted. He took his own map from his pocket and laid it next to Willie's. "We have the same finish line."

Derry looked carefully. "Yeah, but look where I started. I had a hell of lot more country to cover than you did." He turned around, took off his hat, and slammed it on the ground in anger. "It ain't fair. Someone really has it in for me."

"What the hell does it matter?" Baldinger demanded. "You're nearly there. All we gotta do is survive until dark."

He grabbed Willie by the shirt and nearly dragged him deeper into the brush.

It was 2340, just twenty minutes before Derry's deadline, when Dave and Willie came walking out of the bush and ambled up to the lighted tent that marked their finish line. One of the training cadre sergeants jumped up and rushed out to meet them.

"You guys okay?"

"Okay," Baldinger answered, "but I could use some water." Now that he had reached the finish line, he felt as if he were going to faint.

"You want water?" Willie asked.

Dave turned to him bleary-eyed.

"Why didn't ya say so?" Willie dug into the pocket of his fatigue pants and pulled out a canteen. "I got plenty of water."

Baldinger's eyes widened.

"I took Thompson's offer when he was turning me loose. I traded him for the parrish knife."

They bunked at the finishing station, then caught a ride on a helicopter back to the fort. Mex and Dickie greeted them with a fusillade of questions. They were due to take off for their walkabout the next morning.

"Take the water," Willie told them.

Dave nodded in agreement. But then he reminded Willie, "Of course, the knife came in handy at one point."

Derry laughed. "I wonder if they ever got back to the guy with the feather sticking out of his ass. Maybe some damn vulture found him and fell in love with him." He was starting to tell Mex and Dickie about the two Airbornes under the tent when the door to the rec room snapped open and Sergeant Major Thompson stepped in.

"Ten-hut!" Baldinger called.

"Take it easy," Thompson said. He looked at Willie and Dave. "Nice going." Then he smiled. "Airborne says somebody cheated. They think they had one of our guys and someone sprung him."

"Airborne's got its head up its ass," Dickie Morgan answered.

Thompson nodded. "I think it was a feather," he said. "You guys know any one who leaves a feather as a calling card?"

They looked innocently at one another.

He turned to Mex and Dickie. "Cortines. Morgan. You two guys are delayed until twelve hundred hours. We got the choppers tied up in the morning on search and rescue.

They looked startled.

"One of our guys?" Baldinger asked.

The sergeant nodded. "Cavitt. He's way overdue, and we haven't heard his cop-out signal."

"Christ, he was talkin' about throwin' it away," Derry remembered.

"I hope he changed his mind," Sergeant Thompson told them. "He didn't take the canteen."

In spite of their exhaustion, Willie and Dave stayed up all night, waiting for word about Tom Cavitt. Dickie Morgan, who needed sleep to prepare for his ordeal, sat with them. "Don't worry about Tom," Willie advised with bravado. "Cavitt is going to come through this just fine."

"I ain't worryin' about him," Dickie kept insisting. "I'm just a little tense, that's all." And he questioned them, asking about their worst moments, and when it was that they knew they had it made.

Mex was the only one who was able to sleep. He seemed fatalistic about Cavitt. "If they wash him, they wash him. It ain't life and death. This ain't the only way to be someone." And he was supremely confident over his chances on the walkabout. "I know what I gotta do," he told them as he walked out of the rec room and headed toward his bed.

"What the hell's with him?" Derry demanded after Cortines had left. "Don't he care about Tom?"

"He cares," Baldinger answered. "We all have different ways of covering our feelings."

In the morning, Dave and Willie walked out to the helicopter pad with Dickie and Mex. The news they received as they waited was mixed. Luther Brown had made it to home base in record time. Bobby

Long was still on the course. Jim Ray Talbert had been captured less than a mile from his finish point. They'd flown him back to his start. With just one day left, he didn't have much of a chance. There was still no word on Tom Cavitt. The training cadre had gone to his start point and were working their way toward his finish line. They had found his cop-out kit, but so far no sign of him. "Unless the guy is hiding from us, he's really got himself lost," was the report that Sergeant Thompson had received. Baldinger didn't figure that Cavitt, without any water, was hiding from anyone. He hoped the cadre would be able to track him down.

The helicopter roared down out of the hot midday sun. Sergeant Major Thompson climbed aboard and then helped Dickie and Mex up. "Either of you men want to trade for a canteen?" he asked.

Mex shook his head. "I'll stay with this." He ran his hand down the side of his parrish knife.

Dickie handed over his knife. "I'll take the water."

Thompson tossed them their blindfolds.

The whirling blades began pounding, and the chopper lifted off toward the forest.

*   *   *

Colonel Grigg felt helpless, trapped between events that he couldn't control. The Salvadoran officers, who were to train at the school, would be landing in just a few hours. There was no way he could delay their arrival. General Wheeler was demanding assurances of their safety. Assurances he couldn't give, until he knew who in hell it was that had put the entire fort under siege. And the base legal officer, Captain Robert Gordon, was explaining to him that, while he had made considerable progress, he was still unable to identify the culprit.

Gordon was detailing the steps he had taken, explaining the multiple cross-checks through which he was filtering all base personnel who had even a remote connection with Special Operations.

"There are the people you've trained, especially those who flunked the course but ended up back in the Airbornes. Any one of them could be bitter about washing out. And then there's the list of people who have any connection with countries that you've operated in." He indicated that they were running checks on every one of them to isolate people who were on the base, but not accounted for, when the two attacks had occurred.

It was a thorough piece of work, executed with all the excruciating detail that Grigg had always associated with lawyers. And, as he had learned to expect from lawyers, the results were ambivalent. Gordon had narrowed his investigation down to about a hundred names. The problem was that he had no clear-cut timetable for getting it down to one.

"What you're telling me, Captain, is that you're at an impasse."

"I'm afraid so, sir, unless we get a break on the fingerprints. Or unless one of the service records turns up someone with a suspicious history."

Grigg's shoulders sagged until his chin came to rest on the fingers that were folded in front of him. "There's one other possibility," he said. "Maybe, when this guy pulls his next stunt, we'll catch him in the act."

He knew he sounded bitter. He didn't intend to be critical of the young captain. Gordon had warned him that he had no experience as an investigator and had advised him to bring in outside help. And the captain had gone along with the wishes of the command, when he could have gone around them and straight to his superiors on the Judge Advocate General's staff. It had been his own decision to keep the investigation in-house, and the failure was probably his fault. But, still, the colonel felt victimized. He had worked for years to rebuild the reputation of Special Forces, and to put to rest the rumors that emanated from the Pentagon, from the military academy, and from the elite Army Ranger and Airborne commands: rumors that his Special Operations units were sanctuaries for social misfits, and that their cutthroat tactics were unworthy of the nation's military tradition. Now one misfit, one cutthroat seemed about to undo his life's work.

"If you had to take a guess, Captain?" He knew it was a question born of desperation. And he wasn't surprised when Gordon wouldn't answer it. Lawyers, he suspected, didn't guess. They dealt in facts, and the captain's problem was that the facts didn't add up.

"We should have the fingerprint report in a day or so," Gordon said. "And I'll keep pressing ahead with the personnel records. Maybe we'll get a break."

Grigg nodded without enthusiasm. All his military training had convinced him that only fools count on breaks. "Thank you, Captain," he said to conclude the meeting.

He would call General Wheeler and put a very different spin on the facts he had just heard. The search had been narrowed down to two small groups. And he expected to have corroborating evidence in the next day or two. He would offer every assurance that the whole matter would be settled quickly, before it could possibly pose any threat to the visiting Salvadorans or embarrass the command in any way. Then he would get out to the airport and offer his greetings to Colonel Pedro Maritin, a coming power in the Salvadoran Army, and protégé of one of the country's three wealthiest families.

Colonel Grigg winced at the shrill whine of engines as the Saberliner pulled up in front of the operations shed and turned to a stop. He waited until the engines were shut down and the door lowered before stepping forward to greet the arriving officers. Colonel Maritin was the first through the door. He hesitated for a moment, posing in his deep blue uniform and the dark sunglasses that seemed to be a badge of authority among Latin-American officers. Then he jaunted down the steps, followed closely by his five staff officers, and greeted Grigg effusively in perfect English.

Maritin was young, certainly younger than two of his outranked staff, and in excellent physical condition. On the ride back to the visiting officers quarters, Grigg commented that the obstacle course would probably not be much of a challenge to him, and the visitor commented that his training regimen included boxing and handball. He also brought up the fact that he was a skilled horseman, a member of the national polo team, and a marksman. Grigg tried to seem impressed, even though he had read all Maritin's credentials in the official biography that preceded him, and doubted very much whether he would make the first lap of the obstacle course. Part of his orientation program, after the first evening's ceremonial dinner, was to demonstrate that in the real world of counterinsurgency warfare, official military biographies counted for very little.

Pedro Maritin had come from a middle-class family of tradesmen, wealthy by the average statistics for his country, but poor when compared to the closely interlocked families that owned ninety percent of the country's wealth. His parents had paid his way into a prestigious boys' school, hoping that he would make the acquaintance of the sons of the landed families, and had spent most of their savings before realizing that the important sons all studied abroad. But his proper deportment, academic achievements, and athletic skills made him a class leader, and won the notice of the Guiterez family. They were always on the lookout for promising young men who could serve their nearly imperial interests.

On the Guiterez recommendation, he was accepted as a cadet into the officer corps, and then sent to the Barrios Military Academy. Upon graduation, he was awarded the rank of lieutenant in the Salvadoran Army, and began apprenticing the task of making El Salvador safe for the interests of those who owned it.

He had risen rapidly during the seventies, when the country was torn with revolution. The urban laborers and agricultural peasants had been reminded of their dignity by a clergy that had tired of blessing the landlords' every prerogative, and had been organized into an effective force by communists. Their demands for land reform and progressive taxation put them into direct confrontation with the ruling families, and with the Army and National Guard forces that the families kept almost as their personal retainers.

At first, the Salvadoran military had little trouble with the unruly peasants. But then skilled leaders, trained in Moscow and Havana, had taken the lead in the people's cause, and made better use of the arms and supplies that communist governments made available. Army officers, like Pedro Maritin, had all they could do to secure the fortresslike estates of the landed families. They rarely ventured out into the guerrilla-controlled countryside.

It was then that communist success attracted the attention of the United States, which felt its borders threatened by any peasant revolution, no matter where in the world it was occurring. One in its own hemisphere seemed already halfway up the row of toppling dominoes. Millions in military aid flowed to the government forces, and a group of U.S. military advisers, called MILGP, arrived to teach them exactly how to deal with the vagaries of insurrection.

Maritin had learned faster than most. He was, as he claimed, a skilled horseman, but he was quick to grasp the superiority of the helicopter over a sturdy mount. He was a crack shot, but he recognized that aircraft-mounted Gatling guns gave him a much greater margin of accuracy. He was a savvy woodsman and pathfinder, but he was impressed with the efficiency of simply defoliatating the forest.

The Americans had a special school, set up at Fort Gulick, in the Canal Zone, for training the leaders of Latin American armies. Pedro was the perfect candidate, and three months later was a leading graduate. He returned to his war-torn country and put his lessons in counter-insurgency warfare to good use. He had taken the lead in depriving the insurrectionists of their supporting villages, and in silencing the clerics who offered them moral support. He had shown expertise in planning the concerted attacks in which his troops were like foxhounds, simply beating the bush to drive the guerrillas out into the open, and under the sights of the dragonfly gunships. The noble families had recognized that, in Pedro Maritin, they had a dedicated disciple, and they saw to it that he was rewarded with more ribbons on his chest and more fringe on his shoulders.

It was when the insurgents mounted their final push for power that Maritin came to the forefront. As they stormed into the cities in a Tet-like offensive, the Army and National Guard units began to crumble. But Pedro understood the true source of the insurgents' strength. He led furious attacks into the residential neighborhoods, and stormed the sanctuary of the college campuses. He inflicted terrible pain on all the communities that favored the insurgents, leaving their streets cluttered with bodies. Soon shutters were closed over windows and stores were shut up tight. He made it obvious to all that the real victims of the guerrilla assault were not the hated landowners, but rather the poor and the landless whom the insurgents were sworn to help. The revolution retreated back into the mountains where it could safely be ignored. And Maritin emerged as the man on horseback, the true defender of the privileged class.

These were the views he expounded over the dinner that Grigg hosted for him and his aides. He leaned back from the table, a brandy in one hand and a Cuban cigar in the other. "We need to sharpen our skills," he assured Colonel Grigg. "Perhaps even establish a school like yours within our own country."

Grigg responded that he would certainly help.

"This peace we now enjoy is artificial," he said while his staff officers nodded in agreement. "The communists have come to the table only because the collapse of their allies has deprived them of the guns and resources that they need. But they'll be back. There are other sources. Perhaps the Maoists who are attacking the government of Peru."

Grigg mentioned the truce that had been signed between the Salvadoran government and Farabundo Martí, the communist national libration front.

"A terrible mistake," Maritin answered through a cloud of cigar smoke. "We had them on their knees. They had no support from outside communists, and little support from their countrymen. We could have finished them off." He pointed the hot end of the cigar toward Grigg. "It was your country that held our hand. A terrible mistake."

Grigg reminded him that he had been on the ground in El Salvador at the time, commanding the Special Operations group. "If you'd killed any more of them," he said, "there would have been no one left to sign a surrender."

As they drank more brandy, their conversation wandered away from politics and the serious business of warfare. Maritin indicated that he hoped to devote one weekend to a shopping spree in Atlanta. He had accumulated a good bit of money, but it was difficult to find real quality to spend it on in El Salvador. He wanted to spend another weekend in New Orleans. "I've always been fascinated by the city," he said.

When he seemed to have lapsed into a carefree bliss, Grigg found his opening for a brief mention of the problems they were experiencing. "It may even be one of our own trainees," he speculated. "Certainly the techniques he's used would indicate that he's familiar with our methods."

"A turncoat?" Maritin seemed genuinely stunned.

"I think *lunatic* is more accurate," Grigg responded, not liking the implication of rational choice that was implied in the notion of a turncoat. "At any rate, we've got him pretty well identified, and we expect to put him out of action within the next few days."

"Without fanfare, I presume." Colonel Maritin smiled. He glanced at his associates. "We would simply have him disappear."

It was after midnight when Colonel Maritin allowed that perhaps a good night's sleep was in order. "I trust you have a busy day in store for us," he said to Grigg as he was rising from the table.

"Busy, indeed," Grigg answered. He smiled at the tipsy officers. "See you all at oh-four-thirty hours. Wear your fatigues." A staff car took the visitors to their quarters, a condominium complex set on a slope that overlooked the mountains. There was an armed guard at the entrance to the complex, and another posted at the door to each building. Maritin returned the stiff salutes that greeted him.

He unlocked the door to his apartment, and smiled appreciatively at the tasteful furnishings. He had a comfortable sitting room, with an efficiently arranged desk equipped with a multiline telephone, a personal computer, and a facsimile. His toiletries were already laid out in the bathroom and, across the hall, his clothes had been hung in the walk-in closet.

Colonel Maritin took off his jacket and slacks, and hung them on a polished wooden hanger. He put shoe trees into his shoes, and slipped his tie over one of the pegs of the tie rack. The shirt and socks went into the waiting laundry hamper. He went into the bathroom, brushed his teeth, and relieved himself. Then he stepped into the bedroom, and groped along the wall looking for the light switch. He was surprised that the lights didn't go on when he flipped the toggle.

He clicked the switch on and off several times, sighed with disappointment, and then began feeling his way into the invisible room, hunting for a lamp. He never recognized the noise that he heard to his right, or saw the tight, hard fist that flashed across his jaw. He felt himself spinning in a dizzy circle, suddenly feeling sick to his stomach. Then darkness fell over him as his body sprawled across the bed.

Maritin had moments of consciousness. At one point, he felt as if he were being shaken awake. He seemed to be bouncing up and down, his head bobbing and his arms flailing uselessly. He had glimpses of the ground rushing past as if he were being carried. But then he lapsed back into his stupor. Later—he had no idea how much later—he felt himself falling. Instinctively, his hands flew up to protect his face, but his head crashed against a hard wood floor. He had an ant's-eye view of a room that seemed to be filled with neat rows of chairs. His mind began to clear. But then strong hands locked across the back of his neck. A pain stabbed down his back. He was grateful when he lapsed back into unconsciousness.

When he woke, he was upright, seated in a hard wooden chair. He raised his chin from his chest, and began to make out faded shapes against a gray background. He tried to wipe his eyes, but his hands and arms seemed to be paralyzed. Maritin blinked, trying to bring his world back into focus. Slowly, he began to see the ropes that fastened his wrists to the arms of the chair. He tried to get up, but felt the cords that were cutting into his ankles.

The colonel shook his head and blinked furiously. He was seated on a raised platform, looking down at rows of empty chairs. It was still night. The room was in darkness except for the red glow that came from the exit light over a distant door. And the building was empty. The only sound was his own labored breathing.

Then he saw the wires.

There were two, one red and the other green, running in tight curls across the floor and climbing up the side of the chair. One ended in a small alligator clip that bit into the soft flesh on the inside of his thigh. The other disappeared under his shorts. He followed the wires off the edge of the platform and into the dark corner of the room. There he could make out a table. He was puzzled until he recognized the transformer on top of the table. It was then that he knew what was about to happen.

He had seen the machine before, in the dark cellars of Army garrisons and police stations throughout his country. He remembered the first occasion when he had seen it used.

A young man, probably still in his teens, had been caught with four automatic weapons hidden under sacks of beans in the back of his rusted truck. Maritin was called because he was pursuing a group of insurgents in the area. It was obvious that the boy was a courier, probably on his way to a rendezvous with the guerrillas the colonel was chasing. Maritin watched as two soldiers held the prisoner and a third fired punch after punch into his stomach. His ribs were broken, and blood was running out of the corner of his mouth, but the young man wouldn't tell where he was bringing the guns. A few more of the thunderous blows to his body, and he would probably die with his secret.

Maritin had stepped in and blocked the soldier's fist. He grabbed the prisoner's hair, raised his face, and looked at the cloudy eyes.

"Tell them, before they beat you to death." The Americans had taught him that dead prisoners were useless.

Somehow, the boy had managed the strength to spit on the colonel. The spittle, clotted with blood, ran down the front of his uniform shirt. A soldier had raised the butt of a rifle.

"No," Maritin ordered. He wasn't sure whether he was trying to keep a potential informer alive, or whether he was struck with the young man's courage.

A police captain, who had been standing on the edge of the beating scene, had tugged on the colonel's sleeve. "Get him to the police station. He'll talk to us," he promised.

"I don't want him killed," Maritin had said. And then he added, "I want information."

The policeman had gestured to two of his colleagues, who threw the prisoner into their police car. Maritin followed them to the station house, a concrete building with barred windows, certainly the most substantial structure in the small mountain village.

They had walked the boy into a back room, thrown him into a chair, and tied his arms and legs. Then they set the machine on a table in front of him, and fastened the wires, one to his thigh, and the other to his genitals. A policeman forced open his mouth and stuffed it with a dirty cloth. "We don't want him to bite his tongue off," he said as he patted the young man's cheek with the palm of his hand. "Then he wouldn't be able to tell us what we want to know." He took a pitcher of water and poured it into the boy's lap. "It seems to work better when they're wet," he explained.

They had all stepped back, away from the machine and away from the prisoner whose eyes were brightening with fear. Then one of the policemen slid the handle of the transformer halfway up the slot.

The boy's body snapped like a whip, shaking the chair until it nearly tipped over. The pain screamed out of his eyes. He pulled so hard against the ropes that held him to the chair that he cut through the flesh of his wrists. Maritin had never seen such violent agony explode through any animal, and the total silence made the suffering seem even more intense.

The policeman had pushed the transformer handle back down to off. The wracked body stopped thrashing and slumped into the chair.

"A little more?" he asked cynically.

The boy's head shook frantically.

"All right," the policeman said, "a little more." He pushed the handle up slowly, enjoying the results which intensified with every inch the handle moved. The young man twisted violently. His face went ashen, and his teeth began to grind the rag to tatters. The policeman kept easing the transformer handle higher, watching the body stiffen and twist until the young man was almost standing out of the chair. He closed it quickly, and the boy's body dropped as if it had been thrown from a window.

One of the policemen stepped forward and ripped the torn cloth out of the boy's mouth. Two of his teeth, broken off at the roots, came out with it.

"Where were you taking the guns?" the police captain asked.

The prisoner hesitated.

The captain nodded toward the policeman who was operating the machine, and the man reached his hand toward the power handle. Before he could touch it, the boy began screaming. He yelled out the name of a village. "Santa Rosa. To Santa Rosa."

"Where in Santa Rosa?" the captain demanded.

"The schoolhouse. To the back of the schoolhouse."

"And who were you going to give them to?"

"I don't know!" the boy screamed.

The officer reached for the handle.

"Manuel. A man named Manuel."

"His family name?"

"Please, Jesus please, I don't know."

The policeman pushed up the handle. The young man screamed and then bit through his tongue.

Maritin had ordered many prisoners connected to the machine. But he had never been able to stay during an interrogation. He had run out of an Army barracks when he saw them connecting the alligator clamps to a young woman's breasts. Her screaming had followed him into the bushes where he had gotten violently sick. At another time, the Army troops had the machine on the back of a jeep, hooked up to a battery. They were connecting it to children in a village, while they interrogated the parents, and the parents were spilling out information as they reached to save their children. He had turned his car around and raced away.

Now, he realized that he was about to be its victim.

The dark form of a man, his face scarcely visible, moved out of the shadowy corner and reached toward the transformer. Maritin screamed in horror, but there was no sound. A rubber wedge had been pressed back into the corners of his mouth.

A voice spoke in his native language.

"We met before, Colonel. Now it's your turn."

★　★　★

Colonel Grigg jogged in place at the beginning of the obstacle course, a two-mile trail that was constantly blocked with obstructions. There was a twelve-foot-high log wall that had to be scaled. A hundred-yard stretch of ropes, crisscrossed like a net, that required each step to be carefully placed. A hundred-foot length of sewer pipe that had to be crawled through. A mud trench that had to be crossed, hand over hand, on a horizontal ladder. A stream that was forded by swinging from ropes. A mesh of barbed wire that had to passed under on knees and elbows. In addition to the individual barriers, there was the trail itself. It wound up steep hills, was interrupted with sheer drops, streams, and marshes, and cut through dense forests where the path was only inches wide. New arrivals at the school were seldom able to complete the course. Generally, they collapsed around the first-mile mark, were helped out to a parallel road, and driven back to their quarters. By the end of the first week most could run it under thirty minutes. During week two, they would cut that time in half. By graduation, they would do it in twenty minutes, carrying an eighty-pound rucksack.

Grigg glanced at his watch. Zero-four-thirty hours, and none of the Salvadoran officers had yet shown. He wasn't surprised. The new arrivals generally didn't take the school terribly seriously. One group he remembered had brought tennis racquets. And at his welcoming dinners, comments like Maritin's about weekend visits to Atlanta, and even Disney World, were fairly common. Military officers were always getting caught up in the perks of rank and in the machinations of advancement. It was easy for them to forget what war was all about.

But the obstacle course would change all that. Within the first half mile, the Salvadorans would vomit up last night's dinner. By the second barrier, their manicured fingers would be torn and bleeding. Somewhere before the first mile was completed, they'd rip muscles in their legs and groins. By the time they collapsed, face-first into the mud, none of them would be thinking about Disney World.

Two of the aides strolled up the path to the starting gate.

"You're late," Grigg barked, with no trace of the cordiality he had effused the evening before. "You'll have to make up the time on the trail."

He looked over their shoulders and saw the third member of Colonel Maritin's staff running to catch up. But Maritin was nowhere in sight. The son of a bitch thinks he can sleep in, Grigg thought. But he didn't want to embarrass the senior officer in front of his subordinates. "You gentlemen can start now," he said. "I have a brief meeting with your colonel."

The guard at the gate told him that Maritin must still be in his room. No one had logged him out. Grigg bounded up the stairs and managed to get control of his temper before he tapped on the visiting colonel's door. When there was no response, he knocked loudly. Son of a bitch could probably sleep through an artillery barrage, he thought as he went to the end of the corridor and dialed Maritin's telephone. He could hear the phone ringing through the closed door, but Maritan didn't answer. It was at that point that Grigg's anger turned to concern.

He walked quickly back to the guard gate and got the pass key for the room. He brought one of the sentries with him as he dashed back up the stairs. Inside, they found the colonel's uniform hanging neatly in his closet and his crumpled clothes in the laundry basket. But there was no sign of Maritin.

The night guard members couldn't help him. They had all marched their rounds and made all their checkpoints. "There's no way he could have gotten by us," the ranking corporal assured Colonel Grigg. Grigg ordered the visiting officers' compound searched. But a bitter taste was already pushing up into his throat. He remembered the explosion in Major Daks's driveway, and the sudden epidemic of dysentery that had swept the parade grounds. They were under attack, and he was gripped with a numbing fear that Maritin might be the latest casualty.

It was already 0600 hours. Given the obvious political consequences of an officer from a friendly nation vanishing from his post, General Wheeler should be informed immediately. There was no way he could hope to keep this under wraps. His first call would have to be to the Pentagon, and the Pentagon would immediately be in touch with the State Department. The best Grigg could do was stall until the general arrived in his office at 0800 hours. That gave him just two hours to find an explanation for Maritin's disappearance. He began calling his staff officers to an emergency meeting.

At 0630, he had his staff assembled in the school conference room. He was able to begin the meeting by informing them that Maritin had not been found in the officers' compound. "They've searched every space. Even the electrical closet. He's not there."

"He got out without being seen by any of the guards?" Major Daks asked in dismay.

"In his underwear," Grigg added. "If you believe the evidence, he undressed, brushed his teeth, and then disappeared."

"He's been kidnapped," Captain Roy concluded.

Grigg nodded. "Maybe. Let's hope you're wrong."

They were interrupted by a sound that carried even into the confines of the conference room. A voice seemed to be crying somewhere inside the building.

"What the hell is that?" Jordan asked.

"Sounds like someone moaning," Roy answered. He got up and opened the conference room door, but now the building was deathly still. They were all listening intently to the silence when the air was shattered with a piercing scream. For a moment, they were held in their chairs by the ungodly shrillness of the voice. Then they jumped up and raced out into the hallway.

The scream continued, a mindless outpouring of fear. It seemed to fill the entire building, making it difficult for the officers to decide where it was coming from. Then, as the howling broke down into uncontrolled sobbing, they could tell it was coming from the far wing of the second floor.

"One of the classrooms," Grigg said. He led the charge down the hall and up the sturdy wooden steps to the second floor.

"It's my room," Captain Jordan decided as he listened to the moaning and crying. He rushed toward his doorway, but stopped dead as a shrill new scream exploded from the room and filled the corridor. "Jesus," Captain Jordan said in his shock.

Grigg rushed past him and turned into the room, coming face-to-face with the source of the agonized voice. Then the officers pushed in behind him. They saw Colonel Maritin tied into a chair at the front of the classroom. The rubber chock that he had bitten in half was hanging out of the corner of his mouth.

Grigg rode in the ambulance with Maritin, trying to find out what had happened to him. He pushed his questions carefully and begged for answers. But the Salvadoran colonel couldn't tell him. Each time he tried, his voice cracked into sobs.

★ ★ ★

Robert Gordon knew something was wrong the instant he reached Major Topping's office. The commander of the base military police was at the center of a conference that surrounded his desk, holding his hand over the telephone while he barked orders.

"Goddamm it, I want those choppers in the air now! I want the whole perimeter searched."

One of the officers broke from the group and rushed out through the office door, nearly knocking Gordon over.

"Who's got the gate logs?" Topping yelled at the conference.

"They're on their way over," another officer answered.

"You said that before!" the major screamed. "Find out what's holding them up."

Another frantic officer rushed by Gordon.

Topping saw Gordon peeking in through his doorway, and nodded him toward the sofa. At the same time, he lifted his hand from the speaker of the telephone, and continued a conversation that had obviously been interrupted.

"Sir, we've got everyone on this . . . Yes, sir . . . Yes, sir, we're reviewing the gate logs right now . . . No, sir, at this moment we can't be sure . . . Yes, sir, the instant we know anything . . . Yes, sir . . . Thank you, sir."

He set the phone into the cradle and then looked up at his officers.

"Get on those logs. We need the names of everyone who left this post after twenty-three-hundred hours. And one of you get over to the visiting officers' compound. I want statements from everyone who was on guard . . ."

The conference broke up even before Topping had finished, sending his staff colliding with one another as they rushed out through the door.

"You heard?" the major snapped at Gordon.

Robert shrugged. "Heard what?"

"One of the Salvadorans was attacked last night. The colonel. The top guy."

Gordon's eyes widened.

"Someone took him out of the compound, brought him over to the Special Operations school, and hooked him up to an electric shock machine."

"Oh, Jesus! Is he . . . ?"

"He's alive. Half out of his head. But he'll be okay."

"Was it our guy?" Gordon asked, thinking of the attacker they were trying to track down.

"Who the fuck knows," Topping said. He pointed toward the phone. "Colonel Grigg figures it is. And he says General Wheeler is sure that it is. Wheeler is screaming at Grigg to 'find that son of a bitch, and bring him in dead or alive.' "

"What do you think?" Captain Gordon asked.

Topping took a deep breath. "I guess it figures. The grenade was a school trick. The stuff in the water came from the school. And that's where the shock machine is. Kind of looks like someone has a beef with the school."

Topping's conclusion reminded Robert of the conversation he had with Carol Roy. "There are a lot of people who have been hurt by what they teach," she had told him. It was beginning to look as if she might have been right. He thought of the cross-tabulations that they were running to locate people who had lived in one of the countries whose military had been trained at Fort Viper.

"Did you finish those personnel record reviews?" he asked.

Topping blinked as he tried to remember what Gordon was talking about. "Oh, yeah, I think we ran the stuff last night. I haven't had a chance to look at it, and now . . ."

"I'll go throught them," Robert volunteered. "It's probably the only way I can help."

He left the military police headquarters with a thick, fan-folded computer printout under his arm, and drove back to his office at the command headquarters. The chaos at Topping's office was being repeated at General Wheeler's. His staff officers were rushing in and out in what appeared to be a fire drill.

"You heard?" a young lieutenant asked Gordon as he rushed by.

"I heard," Gordon answered.

"Don't go near the general," the lieutenant advised.

Gordon closed his office door behind him, took off his jacket, and settled in front of the computer printout. On his desk was a list of everyone at Fort Francis Marion who had ever lived in or been stationed in a foreign country. His task was to match the countries against a list of nations where Special Operations had been involved.

His phone rang. Gordon decided not to answer it so that he could concentrate on the work before him, but then he picked it up on the third ring.

"Get over here!" It was Major Topping's voice.

"I was just starting on the printouts," he answered.

"Screw the printouts," Topping told him. "We've got a finger-print."

"Do we have a name?"

"Yeah, we've got a name. Corporal Miguel Cortines. He's a trainee, in the last phase of the qualification course. The son of a bitch is a student in the school."

Gordon was already tossing through the stack of folded sheets. Cortines. As he fumbled for the page, he remembered the name. The guy was in the squad that had been loose on the base when the hand grenade exploded. Now, when he reached the record, he found where Cortines was born. El Salvador. The same country as the tortured colonel.

They didn't just have a name. They had their attacker.

He paused in Topping's office just long enough to sign an arrest order. Then they jumped into a jeep with two MPs, each carrying an assault rifle, and raced across the base to the Special Operations trainee headquarters. Sergeant Major Thompson rose to attention, saluted the two officers smartly, and then looked uneasily over their shoulders at the two armed guards who were waiting just outside his door.

"We have an order to take one of your trainees into custody, Sergeant," Topping said, holding out the paperwork.

Thompson checked the document. "Cortines? What's he done?"

"Assaulted an officer," Topping answered.

Thompson seemed confused.

"He's under suspicion," Gordon corrected. "No charges have been filed yet."

"The visiting officer?" Thompson asked. "The one attacked last night?" The sergeant had already picked up his list of trainees, and was turning to Cortines's name.

Topping didn't answer. He didn't like being questioned by enlisted men, and he was annoyed that news of the incident was already common knowledge among the noncoms.

"He's out on a training exercise, Major," Thompson said, confirming his own recollection. "Isn't due in until twenty-four-hundred hours tomorrow. Although knowing Cortines, there's every chance he'll finish early. I'll send him over as soon as he reports back."

Topping's eyes narrowed. "Sergeant, this is a serious matter. I want that man now!"

Thompson set down the file, and handed the arrest order back to the major. "I'm afraid he's out in the bush, sir. He's operating on his own. There's no way we can reach him."

"Then send someone out to find him, Sergeant. That's an order."

The sergeant major wasn't impressed by the implied threat. "Sir, I already have a whole Airborne regiment out there trying to find him. The problem is that Cortines's assignment is to make damn sure he doesn't get found. And if you were a betting man, sir, I'd recommend that you put your mortgage money on Cortines. There aren't enough Airborne troops on the post to bring him in until he's ready to come back."

★ ★ ★

Mex Cortines was moving along the northern perimeter of the exercise area, climbing into the same rugged country that Dave Baldinger had traveled a few nights earlier. Like all the other members of the squad, he had decided that his best course was to stay out of the center of the zone, where the patrols would be guarding the routes between the starting areas and the finish lines. But unlike the others, Mex had no intention of holing up during the day. His plan was to keep moving, always favoring the more difficult terrain. By nightfall, he expected to be well up into the Appalachians, with the Fort Francis Marion exercise area many miles behind.

He had added to his equipment. Besides the parrish knife and the compass, he carried two canteens, each full of cold water that he had taken from the drinking fountain in the corridor of the school. In his rucksack, he carried food rations, along with several pairs of socks and a warm blanket that had been left at the foot of his bed. Over his shoulder he carried the assault rifle that the Army had issued to him and, in his belt, the eight loaded magazines that he had secretly assembled over the past weeks. His plan was to find a rail line that would carry him westward where he could lose himself in civilian life. But, if he had to, he was prepared to stay hiding in the wilds indefinitely.

There could be no turning back. He had made his decision as he stood over the slumped form of Colonel Maritin who had passed out from his first encounter with electric shock torture. Maritin had seen his face, perhaps clearly enough to identify him, even though Mex had kept in the dark shadows. And he had told the colonel exactly where their paths had crossed in El Salvador. To assure his safety and keep his identity hidden, all he had to do was make certain that Maritin could never testify against him.

It would have been simple. Unclamp one of the wires, coil it around the colonel's neck, and pull it tight until the man's labored breathing sputtered and then went silent. He had even reached for the wire. But nothing in his life, even in the ruthless Green Beret training, had prepared him for coldblooded murder. If Maritin had been attacking him, or standing guard over a military objective, Cortines could have killed him without a thought. Or if the man's death were essential to the message Mex was trying to deliver, then he might have been able to loop the wire. But Colonel Maritin was helpless, shocked into unconsciousness, and tied to a chair. And, in the agony of his eyes, Mex had seen that his message was understood. His decision to spare Maritin's life was also a decision to escape into hiding.

The sun was beginning to climb, burning off the haze that shrouded the treetops. Soon, it would bleach the color out of the sky, giving each hilltop a stark, white background. He'd be easy to see if he moved to the high ground, where he would be silhouetted against the skyline. So he'd stay at the base of the hills, battling his way through the marshy forests.

He compromised caution for speed. He should have been moving carefully, noiselessly, lifting each branch and setting it back in place. But he guessed that he was already off the exercise map, and that what patrols there were would be able to cover only the roads and pathways. As long as he stayed in the bush, there wasn't much chance of meeting the enemy force. His real safety, Mex believed, was in covering as much distance as possible before the officers at Fort Viper identified their man and began their hunt.

But the speed was taking its toll. In the heavy heat, the effort of maintaining his pace was exhausting. He had already sweated through his clothes and, in order to battle the stupor of dehydration, he had drunk more than his allotted amount of water. Mex had been moving constantly for the past twenty-four hours. His muscles were screaming for a few moments of rest.

He kept pushing ahead, even though his boots were beginning to feel like lead weights. He wasn't moving fast, but at least he was moving, opening up space from the pursuers who would soon be setting out after him, and gaining ground on his chances for freedom. His biggest problem was keeping his mind focused. Exhaustion brought drowsiness, and with the drowsiness came carelessness. He forced himself to check and recheck his compass. He studied the shadows cast by the eastern sun to ensure that he was always turning to the west.

By noon, when the shadows gave no direction, he recognized the signs of his own delirium. The compass needle had lost its meaning. He was toying with the idea of showering in the precious water he carried in the canteens. He staggered to a halt, and wrapped his arms tightly around a tree. Carefully, he poured a trickle of water into the band of his hat and set it on his head. Then he sipped carefully. When he felt his attention refocusing, he weighed his options.

Mex admitted to himself that he had reached his limits. To press ahead was to take ever-growing risks of a serious mistake or a fatal accident. His best choice was to take himself into hiding, sleep until nightfall, and then continue his flight. He decided to move north, further up the slope and into the steep hills, and find his hiding place. It was a familiar area, one he had discussed with Dave Baldinger, Willie Derry, and the others in the squad as they exchanged their plans for the walkabout.

He moved slowly, very carefully. There was a clearing to the west, bounding a pond formed by a blocked stream. He avoided it, turning into the deeper woods to the north. He reached a ledge, exactly the type of terrain that would give him his best cover. He would climb high enough to have a view of the approaches, and then back into a crevice that would protect his rear and his flanks. Mex searched for a rugged surface that would give him handholds for climbing. It was when he reached the base that he nearly stepped on the sprawled human form clad in camouflaged fatigues. Even before he saw the face, he knew it was Tom Cavitt.

He turned him over carefully and saw the blue tints in Cavitt's colorless complexion. He touched his face and found it clammy. The pulse in his neck and his wrists was faint and fast, and when Mex pressed his ear against Tom's chest, he was scarcely able to hear a heartbeat. He lifted an eyelid. The blank, staring pupil seemed to focus as the retina contracted against the light. Cavitt was alive, but just barely. He was certainly dehydrated and probably on the verge of shock.

Mex opened his canteen, and raised Tom's head. The water flowed across his lips, but Cavitt was too far gone to swallow. He opened the shirt, and ran his hands under Tom's arms. His skin was still warm, indicating that he hadn't yet gone deeply into shock. He had to get water into his body.

There was plenty of water nearby. He had just skirted around a pond because the open country was too dangerous. But, if he carried Cavitt out into the clearing, and lingered with him by the water's edge, he would be putting his escape into jeopardy. Even though he was probably outside the exercise area, and a good distance away from where most of the patrols would be searching, it was suicide to settle down in the open by the edge of a pond.

But Cavitt was close to death. He needed water. Mex never hesitated. He picked Cavitt up, and raced back toward the pond. He laid Tom in the shade, close to the water, then stripped off his own shirt and soaked it in the pond. He wrapped the wet shirt around Cavitt's neck and torso. Jesus, let this be right, he prayed silently. If his friend were already in shock, the sudden cold could kill him. Gently, he began to exercise Tom's arms, trying to stimulate his blood flow. Again and again, he poured a trickle of water across the dry, motionless lips.

"C'mon, my friend. Taste it. Taste just a drop. C'mon, Tom. Come out of it. Please. Just taste it."

Mex could have screamed in his frustration. His friend had nearly killed himself with thirst, only a few hundred yards from a stream, just to pass a stupid test. Maybe the Airbornes were camping in the clearing. Or maybe they were on his trail, with one of their choppers circling overhead. So he had pushed himself further and further into the wilderness. He had hidden for what—maybe two days—without any water. Maybe he saw the pond, but knew that he'd be caught if he stepped out into the clearing. Or maybe he was just lost, but was too determined to give himself up. And then it had been too late.. Then, when he realized his life was ebbing away, he had been too weak to move, or too delirious to choose a direction. A life wasted. A stupid, stupid waste.

"Please, my friend. Please, drink just a little."

He tested Cavitt's skin. It had cooled a bit. Jesus, was he falling into shock? Was he going to die, right here in his arms? The shirt was already dry. Mex rushed back to the stream and soaked it again. He tested the pulse. It had slowed a bit. But was it getting any stronger? He listened at Tom's chest. At least he could now hear a heartbeat. And he thought he could feel the torso moving slightly, beginning to vent air in and out.

He raised Cavitt's head higher, and poured a stream of water over his face. Tom blinked his eyes. Then Mex set the canteen top over his lower lip. He poured a trickle directly into his mouth.

"C'mon. Take a swallow. Please."

Cavitt drank the water. His eyes flickered open, but they still seemed blank. Mex coaxed another swallow over his lips.

He held him for over an hour, moving him once to keep him in the changing shade of the trees. He soaked and resoaked the shirt, and offered a hundred tiny sips from his canteen.

"Amigo . . ."

Mex was startled by the word. He looked down and found Cavitt's eyes open and focused. The blue line of his lips was trying to smile.

Gradually, Tom was able to drink. At first, just small sips that seemed to evaporate on his tongue. Then small swallows that went down with great effort.

"I'm cold, amigo . . ." Cavitt managed.

Mex pulled off the wet shirt, and wrapped his friend in the blanket he had taken from his bed. Then he squeezed him in the hug of his arms.

"You've got to drink this. C'mon."

Cavitt leaned his head toward the canteen and downed several swallows.

"You're okay, my friend," Mex told him with a broad grin. "You're going to make it."

"I fucked up," Cavitt answered. "I really fucked up."

"You're going to make it," Mex repeated.

But he knew that Tom was still in danger. They had taught him that after long periods of dehydration, water wasn't enough. His blood was screwed up and his body chemistry—whatever the hell that was—was critically out of balance. He needed medical attention just as desperately as if he were bleeding from an open wound.

It was easy. Just carry him back into the exercise area where the Airborne troops were hunting for both of them. The troops would call in a helicopter that could lift Cavitt back to the base hospital in a matter of minutes. But in the process, they'd take Mex prisoner. Even if the Airborne force didn't know he was escaping from a criminal assault, they sure in hell would know that he was one of the Special Operations troops they were hunting.

Cavitt raised his head toward the canteen. Mex had to support him while he swallowed, and then coax more water over his lips. If he left Cavitt in the clearing, they would certainly find him, probably within a few hours. But there was every chance Cavitt wouldn't last a few hours without medical attention.

"How you feeling, my friend?" Mex begged.

"Okay, amigo. Okay." Cortines could scarcely hear his whispered words. He could still make it to freedom. But Cavitt probably wouldn't make it at all.

"Hang on," he told Cavitt. "I'm taking you home."

He filled the canteen and hung it around his neck. Then he lifted his friend in his arms, leaving the extra weight of the rifle, the ammunition, and his provisions behind, and started back into the exercise area.

Mex stayed with Cavitt when he was loaded aboard the helicopter. There was no need to keep offering him water. The Airborne medic had sedated him, and connected an intravenous bottle to his arm. But Mex kept holding him in his arms even though there was a litter that they could have strapped Tom to. He kept rocking him gently.

"You're gonna make it, my friend. You're gonna make it."

Through the open door of the chopper, Mex could see the ambulance waiting at the landing pad. He could also make out the row of white helmets, worn by the military police who were waiting to arrest him.

"We're almost there," he told Cavitt. "Everything's goin' to be okay."

The MPs rushed up to the door as soon as the rotors stopped

spinning. But they backed away as Mex climbed down with his friend in his arms. He walked through their ranks directly to the ambulance and rested Tom on the waiting litter. Then he helped the medics push the litter through the open door and stood watching as the ambulance wailed off toward the hospital.

He didn't seem to notice the guards who moved up next to him.

* * *

Colonel Grigg had Captain Gordon draw up the orders that would confine Cortines to the base prison to await trial. To Grigg, it was a simple matter. The son of a bitch was dangerous, and had to be kept under lock and key. To Gordon, it was a bit more complicated. Military law, like civil law, recognized the right of habeas corpus. You couldn't jail a soldier just because he was suspected of a crime. You had to demonstrate either that he would be a danger to others if he was left free, or that there was a high probability that he would flee to escape prosecution.

"He walked back onto the post," Gordon pointed out, "so we really can't make much of a case that he's planning to escape."

"He planted a hand grenade in a family neighborhood," Grigg snapped. "How much of a danger do you want him to be?"

"I just want to be sure that we don't screw this up on a technicality," Robert responded. "And we don't really have any evidence that links him to the hand grenade."

"Well, then use the poisoned water," Grigg shot back. "We're keeping him in the stockade so he can't poison the whole damn base."

Gordon didn't dispute the point. "There's no doubt he's the one who poisoned the water. And I think we're safe locking him up on that," he said as he edited the imprisonment order. "But let's not mention the assault on Colonel Maritin. We don't have much proof on that one."

Grigg became agitated. "Goddamm it, he fits the description we got from Maritin."

"But he was off the base on a training mission. He can't possibly have been two places at once."

"We train our men to handle the impossible," Grigg reminded the captain. "I could assign any of our guys to get back from the exercise area, break into the compound, and take out one of the officers, and half of them would pull it off."

"We may have to be able to prove that," Gordon said.

"I'll do it myself, if that's what it takes!" Grigg shouted. He had reached for his telephone. "Look, Captain. I don't want this thing to get complicated. Write the order any way you have to. Just make damn sure that he stays in jail."

He dialed the stockade and ordered Cortines moved from the holding pen to a cell. "Captain Gordon's order will be right over."

General Wheeler was even more simplistic. He ordered Grigg and Gordon into his conference room and shut the door behind them. "I want this whole thing kept to the basics. No details. No explanations. We've had a soldier attack a superior officer, poison a water supply, and then attack a visiting officer from a friendly country. We brought him to court-martial, convicted him, and sentenced him. That's it. Over and out."

The general looked at Colonel Grigg, who was already nodding in agreement. "I don't think we need to make anything of the link to Special Operations."

"Hell no," Wheeler snapped. "And I don't want anything about that fucking electric shock machine. In fact, I want that goddamn thing off this base by evening colors."

They both turned to Gordon. He would be the trial counsel in the court-martial, its prosecuting attorney. "I'll try to handle it that way," he agreed.

"What do you mean, try?" Wheeler demanded.

"He'll have a defense counsel," Gordon reminded them. "And in a general court-martial there has to be a trial judge. Someone that the Judge Advocate General will send down to run the trial. They'll understand our need to get this thing over with. But not at the expense of the kid's rights."

"Damm it," Wheeler snarled. "This son of a bitch attacked my command. I don't give a rat's ass about his rights."

But the rights of the accused were Robert Gordon's most important concern. In the past, military justice had been a cat-o'-nine-tails, or in extreme cases, a firing squad. But under the modern code of military justice, the accused had the same rights as a civilian. Violate one of them, and there was every chance that Corporal Cortines would go free. They couldn't keep the corporal in prison unless they charged him with a serious crime. Gordon returned to his office and drafted the charges and the specifications. Then he went to the base stockade so that he could present the charges to the accused, and make certain that he was aware of his rights.

He was shocked when Cortines was led into the interview room. The man's arms and legs were shackled. A chain that connected his leg irons to his handcuffs was secured to a thick leather belt that was locked behind his back. The captain was about to protest, but he noticed that the prisoner seemed completely unconcerned.

Gordon read the charge that he had prepared. In addition to assault, it listed counts of kidnapping, reckless endangerment, illegal discharge of a weapon, and attempted murder. Mex's eyes never even flickered as his crimes were enumerated.

"Before I formally present you with these charges," Gordon continued, "I want to advise you that you don't have to say anything, or sign anything without your defense counsel present. Do you understand?"

Mex nodded, but he didn't seem interested.

"Corporal, these are only charges. The Army has to prove them to the satisfaction of a court. You're entitled to have someone on your side to keep the army from proving anything. Do you understand what I'm saying?"

"It's all true," Mex answered. "I don't need someone on my side."

Gordon sighed. "I didn't hear you say that, because you never said it. And don't you ever say it again. Not until you've discussed this with your legal counsel."

"I don't want a lawyer," Mex answered. "All I want is my day in court."

Robert Gordon pushed his glasses up onto his forehead and wiped his eyes wearily. "You won't get a day in court without legal advice, Corporal. You probably won't get ten minutes in court. Now, do you have a lawyer? Is there any attorney that you know and have confidence in?"

Again, Mex shook his head.

"Then I'm going to appoint counsel for you," Gordon told the prisoner. "I'm going to pick an officer with better experience than I have and appoint him as your legal counsel."

"It won't do me any good," Mex said, almost smiling. "I'm guilty."

Gordon slapped his hand down on the table. "You're not guilty of anything. You've been charged, but nothing has been proven. And until it's proven, you can't be guilty. That's the law. That's the way it works."

Mex nodded. "Okay," he said.

"Now, if you don't want to name your counsel, I'll appoint someone. And if you don't like the person I appoint, then I'll appoint someone else. Do you understand?"

Mex looked at Gordon. It was obvious that the legal officer was trying to help him. "How about you, Captain? Can you be my counsel?"

It was Gordon's turn to smile. "No, Cortines, I'm afraid not. I'm the staff judge advocate. The base legal officer. I'm going to be the trial counsel. I'll be trying to prove the Army's charges. It will have to be someone else."

Mex looked thoughtful for a moment. "Dave Baldinger," he finally said. "Corporal Dave Baldinger. He's in my unit. He's smart, and I trust him. Can I have Dave?"

"He can help you pick someone," Gordon said. "But your counsel has to be an attorney. It's for your own protection. To make sure you get every break that's coming to you."

Mex looked down at his folded fingers. "Ask Dave," he concluded. "He'll know what I need."

Gordon's first impression of Baldinger was favorable. The next day, the corporal was shown into his office at 1230 hours, exactly on time. He was in his dress greens, stopped at attention two paces short of his desk and rendered a precise salute.

"Corporal Baldinger, reporting as ordered, *sir!*"

Gordon forgot whether he was supposed to stand to return the salute, or whether he was supposed to salute at all. He did a little of each, rising a bit out of his chair and bringing his hand close to his forehead.

"At ease, Corporal." He turned the salute into a gesture toward his side chair. "Please. Make yourself comfortable."

Baldinger sat on the front inch of the chair, his back ramrod straight. Too bad he isn't a lawyer, the captain thought. He'd have one hell of a courtroom presence.

Gordon had done his homework, reviewing every entry in Baldinger's service record. Small town, Iowa upbringing. One brush with the law for joyriding in stolen car. Three months of community service completed. Graduated high school in the middle of his class, apparently majoring in football and basketball. Was put on a waiting list for college, and decided not to wait. Joined the Army at his local recruiting station. Appointed squad leader in boot camp. Applied for parachute training and graduated second in his class with promotion to corporal. Among the first on the ground in Operation Desert Shield, and in the first group to be landed behind enemy lines in Desert Storm. Returned to the States and applied immediately for Special Operations training. And now, according to his training officer, Sergeant Major Elvis Thompson, was at the top of his class. Not surprising that one of the men he served with was willing to trust Baldinger with his life.

"You know about the arrest of Corporal Miguel Cortines?" Gordon began.

"Yes, sir."

"You know the charges?"

"Just what I've heard, sir."

"What have you heard, Corporal?"

"I've heard that Mex could have been a hundred miles from here, sir, but instead, he stopped to save his buddy's life. And I've heard that he's supposed to have done things that happened when he was with me, when he couldn't have done them. Sir."

Captain Gordon liked the hint of sarcasm in the second "sir." Cortines had made a good choice. It was obvious that Baldinger would burn down the courthouse to get him off.

"Corporal, I'm the legal officer for this command. My job is to make sure that your friend gets a fair trial. I want you know that I take my job very seriously. This will be a fair trial."

Baldinger didn't respond. He wasn't sure whether he believed the captain or not.

"Corporal Cortines is entitled to a defense counsel. An experienced attorney who will help him present his case to the court. He's asked that you find him."

The stiffness in Baldinger's spine collapsed. He settled backward into the chair.

"Sir, I don't know anything about . . ." There was no sarcasm in the "sir."

"I didn't think that you would," Gordon said. "But your friend trusts your judgment. So, I thought I'd suggest a few people who I think would help him, and then let you make the choice. It can be anyone. An Army lawyer, like me. Or civilian counsel."

Baldinger raised his hands helplessly. "I wouldn't know how to make a choice."

"I'll make sure they're all qualified," Gordon promised. "You pick someone who you think Cortines would be comfortable with."

Baldinger was wide-eyed. He didn't know what to say.

Gordon filled the silence. "I've arranged for you to meet with him at the stockade. Tell him that, between the two of us, we'll make damn sure he has a defense."

Baldinger was in a daze as he slowly lifted himself out of the chair. He turned away without the formality of rendering a salute. Absently, Gordon saluted at the back of the corporal. Then he went back to work on the prosecution case that he was preparing.

Gordon left his office at the stroke of five, and drove to the officers' club where he made a straight line to the bar. He ordered a double scotch, and ran through his day's work mentally as he sipped the drink. It was pretty obvious that the kid had no idea what he was up against. First he had admitted that he was guilty. Then he had said that all he wanted was his day in court. Maybe his friend, Baldinger, could make him understand that this wasn't a visit to the principal's office, or a hearing before a juvenile officer. These were serious charges. He could spend the next thirty years in Leavenworth.

And he probably didn't deserve it. Not that Gordon approved of what Cortines seemed anxious to admit he had done. But the kid had a good record. He was a good soldier, and he had all but turned himself in rather than abandon a friend. He couldn't have had much of life, apparently running from country to country. Yet he was making something of himself. There had to be some way to satisfy the requirements of justice without locking him in a stockade for the rest of his young life.

Captain Gordon nodded for a refill as he considered the possibilities. Maybe Cortines's defense counsel would enter an insanity plea. Hell, he could claim that the kid cracked under the stress of training. And then the court could accept it. Why not? He would be the prosecuting officer. Then they could send the kid to a hospital. Maybe six months. Maybe a year. Then he'd get out of the service with an administrative discharge. It wasn't great, but it was a hell of a lot better than Leavenworth. Someone who cared more about a friend's life than his own probably deserved a break.

A hand slapped down on his shoulder, and he wheeled on the bar stool to find Colonel Grigg. The colonel smiled at him and raised a glass in toast.

"Nice work, Captain. As it turns out, you're not such a bad detective after all." Grigg tossed off his drink. Then he said, "We were just sitting down to dinner." He nodded toward a table where the staff officers and their wives were gathered. "A bit of a celebration after the stress we've been under. We saw you at the bar and hoped you might be able to join us.''

Gordon began fumbling for an excuse, and ended up with the halfhearted claim that he didn't want to intrude. Grigg took his arm and nearly lifted him off the stool. "We probably wouldn't be celebrating if it hadn't been for you. I think all of us would like to buy you a drink.''

He was greeted enthusiastically as he reached the table. "We oughta make this guy an honorary Green Beret,'' Daks roared as he slapped Gordon on the back. "You're gonna nail that son of a bitch's ass to the wall,'' O'Leary told him, punching his fist into the air. Gordon shook hands all around, smiled modestly as the men praised his achievements to their wives, and allowed himself to be pushed into a borrowed chair that was squeezed between Colonel Grigg and Carol Roy. The waiter brought a fresh round of drinks to the table and set a new scotch in front of the legal officer.

"To the brotherhood of Special Operations,'' Grigg toasted.

Gordon couldn't help thinking of the hotel manager who had identified O'Leary's wife as Captain O'Leary clinked his glass against Major Daks's. Some brotherhood, he thought to himself.

"I read the list of charges you drew up,'' Henry Roy said, his glass still raised in toast. "What do you figure the little bastard will get? A couple of hundred years?''

"All we need is twenty,'' Grigg reminded the table. "By then, we'll all be retired generals.''

"Pretty slick, nailing him for kidnapping,'' Eugene Daks told the table with an appreciative nod toward the guest of honor. "That should get him put away for life. Although, personally, I wish you could sentence him to about fifteen minutes alone with me. I owe him a hand grenade, and I know exactly where I'd plant it.''

There was a roar of laughter from the men. Marilyn Daks blushed and gave her husband a playfully censoring glance.

"Just what was the little jerk up to?'' Captain Roy asked. "What was he trying to do?''

Gordon threw up his hands. "I don't know anything yet. But, if you don't mind, we really shouldn't be talking about it.''

The joyous faces went blank.

"I don't want to spoil your party, but I'm a court officer,'' he reminded them. "I can't discus the case outside the court. If I did, there'd be grounds for a mistrial.''

The table was suddenly quiet. Then Grigg came to the rescue. "Well, we sure in hell don't want to do anything that would get him off on a technicality. So let's talk about something else."

Within a minute, the officers were chatting about the business of the school while the ladies turned toward Marilyn Daks for a topic. Gordon didn't fit with either group. He sipped his scotch and tried to look like an interested bystander to the military conversation. Then he noticed that Carol Roy was as out of place as he was. He leaned toward her in the hope that they might be able to work a mutual rescue.

"I appreciated your help, Mrs. Roy. You put me onto a line of investigation that turned out to be very valuable."

She managed a thin smile of acknowledgment. "Carol," she reminded him. Then she added, "I'm sure you would have gotten him without me."

He began telling her how valuable each bit of information was, and how cooperative everyone had been. But she didn't seem interested in the flattery. After a few seconds, he turned back to his drink. He was startled when he heard her say, "Would you like to dance?"

He hadn't even been aware of the music. The three-piece combo was playing a slow number with a faintly Latin beat, and there were several couples heading toward the floor. Gordon stood, took Carol's hand, and then told Captain Roy, "Your wife has one space left on her dance card." Roy waved his permission and warned, "Watch yourself. She throws a mean hip."

As soon as they were on the floor, Carol told him, "You looked as if you were having a miserable evening."

He started to lie, but then admitted he didn't really fit into military conversations. "I don't understand half the things they talk about. I have a pretty good idea how long twenty millimeters is, but I don't have the damndest idea of what it is they're measuring. I mean, does a twenty-millimeter gun go on top of a tank, or do you carry it in your pocket?"

"Who cares?" she said, shrugging her shoulders, and then she moved easily into the rhythm of the music. The dance ended, and as they were leaving the floor, she asked, "Did he really give himself up in order to save a friend's life?"

"That's why he came back to the base. His friend needed medical help. He brought him back to the hospital."

"It doesn't make sense," she said. "Why would someone like that risk the lives of children by poisoning the water? Or torture another person with electric shocks?"

He shook his head. "I have no idea."

"When you find out, will you try to explain it to me? I'd really like to understand."

He knew she wasn't asking out of idle curiosity. And the "someone" she was concerned with wasn't really the soldier he was about to bring to trial.

"Okay," Captain Gordon promised. "But the explanation probably won't make a lot of sense."

"Not too many things around here make a lot of sense," she said as he seated her back at the table.

Gordon was late getting to his office in the morning, and embarrassed to find Corporal Baldinger pacing in his waiting room. He started to make an excuse for his tardiness, and then realized that Baldinger didn't have an appointment to see him.

"What's the problem, Corporal?" he asked.

"Sir, we need to talk."

"Did you see Corporal Cortines?"

"Yes, sir. That's what we have to talk about."

Gordon went into his office, tossed his briefcase on the desk and began taking off his jacket. Baldinger followed him and remained standing at attention, two paces short of his desk, until the captain turned and noticed him.

"Sit down, Baldinger. We can't have a conversation while you're standing at attention." Then he asked, "Would you like some coffee?"

"Sir, I really would like a cup of coffee."

Gordon, now in his shirtsleeves, went back into the outer office and poured two cups from the coffeemaker that rested on top of the filing cabinets. He balanced them in one hand while he took the packages of sugar and cream with the other. When he returned, Baldinger was sitting, with his elbows resting on his knees and his face buried in his hands.

The captain circled his desk, reached over, and set one of the cups on the edge near the corporal. Baldinger seemed unaware that he had returned to the room.

"Are you okay, Corporal?"

The face that looked up was red-eyed.

"Sir, we've got to help him."

"We'll do all that we can, Corporal. We'll make certain that he gets a fair trial."

Baldinger shook his head. "No, you don't understand. You've got to defend him. You've got to get him off."

"My job," Gordon began to explain, "is to conduct a fair and legal court-martial. I'm not the defense attorney. I'm—"

"Damn it!" Corporal Baldinger snapped. "You don't understand."

Gordon was stunned. The soldier had been standing at attention just a moment before, showing full respect for his rank. Now he seemed on the verge of springing across the desk and grabbing him by the throat.

"Take it easy, Corporal. What is it? What don't I understand?"

"We're the ones who are guilty. We killed his whole family. And now we're going to kill him."

THE
EVIDENCE

★ ★ ★

It all started with a truck," Mex had explained to Baldinger. "An old Ford pickup full o' rust holes and missin' a fender. A real junk heap. Left a trail of oil wherever it went. I was eight years old, and I'm sittin' with my father, Eduardo, on the porch of the Pacifica, the general store in Avila. It's a little dirt town, maybe ten miles south of San Salvador. And all of a sudden this truck comes bangin' up the road and just dies, right in front of the store. So my father sets his beer down on the table and strolls out into the hot sun to see if he can be helpful."

Eduardo, Mex went on, knew something about machines and engines. He fixed most of the equipment on the Diego plantation; the tractors that were used to clear new land, the sorters that shook the dirt and debris from the coffee beans, and the trucks that carried the heavy sacks of beans down out of the mountains. He probably could have maintained the three Mercedes sedans in which Diego family members were chauffeured between the plantation and their home in San Salvador, and maybe even the Ferrari that Emilio Diego drove personally. All gasoline engines were pretty much alike. But the Diegos treated their cars like fine horses. There was only one mechanic in San Salvador, an Italian, who was ever allowed to touch them.

Eduardo tried to start the truck, but the grinding sound told him it wasn't going to turn over. He lifted the hood and then lay down on his back and pulled himself under the chassis. When he stood up, he was shaking his head like a doctor who has bad news for a patient.

"I'm afraid you're not going anywhere, my friend," he told the owner. "The oil pan is leaking, so you've probably been driving without any oil. I think a piston has seized, and you've probably broken a rod.'' As an afterthought he commented that the clutch seemed to be worn out as well. While they shared a beer in the Pacifica, Eduardo Cortines explained the amount of work that would be needed to put the truck back on the road. He tried to sound expert, hoping that the owner would decide to leave the old Ford in Avila, where Eduardo could work on it in his spare time. He thought he would like the challenge, and he knew he could use whatever money the man agreed to pay. He was stunned when the owner threw the keys on the table, and asked if Eduardo would be so kind as to junk it for him. ''Maybe you know someone who will pay you for the scrap. That will give you a little something for your efforts.''

He couldn't put much time into the Ford, even though working on it was the one thing he enjoyed. The Cortines family, like the dozen other peasant families that sharecropped the Diego plantation, couldn't spare time for enjoyment. The land was demanding, filling all the hours of the day, nearly all the days of the week. It was in exchange for their work that they were given a house, really a one-room shed that they divided into rooms by hanging split-opened coffee sacks from stretched cord lines. They were also given a small piece of land to cultivate for themselves. They could grow beans and a few green vegetables. And they could also cultivate a few coffee trees, carrying the beans down to Avila, where they could sell them below market price. That gave them the money they needed for things that they couldn't grow. The arrangement was renewed annually at the pleasure of the Diegos, a fact which made most of the families afraid to be seen not hard at work, and which prompted them to smile and take off their sombreros whenever one of the Mercedes came down the road.

Eduardo generally visited the truck on Sundays. The owner of the Pacifica let him keep it behind the building, so Eduardo Cortines could bring his family to church, visit with friends, drink a cold bottle of beer, and work on the truck, all in one visit to town.

One day, Eduardo poured his savings out of a jar. ''I helped him count the coins,'' Mex remembered. ''He put the money in his pocket and we walked to town. All along the road, he kept tellin' me about this big surprise he had for me. He said I was goin' to remember this day forever, and he was right. I remember every little thing like it all happened yesterday.''

Eduardo bought two gallons of gasoline and some engine oil from the gas station and led a crowd of his friends down the street to the Pacifica. Miguel had to stand on tiptoes to watch his father pour the gasoline and the oil into the truck, and then he waited in anticipation with the rest of the men while Eduardo climbed into the driver's seat and carefully inserted the ignition key. The engine growled, and then roared back to life. Its sound was immediately drowned out by the cheering of the crowd.

When he released the clutch he had rebuilt, the truck jumped forward, sending his friends diving for safety. Then they all piled into the back with the bottles of beer that the owner donated to the celebration.

"Seems dumb," Mex admitted to Baldinger, "but we rode up and down the street for the rest of the afternoon, just shoutin' and wavin' at people. It was like a holiday, just because we had a truck that worked. But that night, we didn't have to climb the mountain back to the plantation. We drove back, in our own truck. We were the first sharecroppers ever to own one."

The plantation foreman, Roberto, congratulated Eduardo on his accomplishment. When he looked at the wheels, he thought that there was a set of tires from one of their old trucks that might be the right size. The next day, he drove them to the Cortines home, and was broadly pleased when they fit the wheels. "No more carrying your coffee bags down the mountain, my friend. Now you can load them into your truck and drive them down."

That's exactly what Eduardo did. And, for a few colons, he carried his neighbor's coffee as well. It was a convenience that had the fundamentals of a business, because his neighbors' contribution paid for the gasoline and the oil, which meant that the Cortines coffee traveled into town free.

Mex's eyes shined as he told Baldinger how he had taken care of the truck. "It was like I owned it. I used to wash it. Just get the dirt off it. There was no way that old paint was ever goin' to look bright. But I thought it looked better than the Diego's limousines. I used to sit behind the wheel and pretend I was drivin' it. I even bounced up and down like I was goin' over bumps."

It was his older brother, Francisco, who came up with the idea of enlarging the truck. They could build a wooden platform, twice as big as the nearly rusted-through truck bed. It could stretch out an extra three feet on each side, and overhang the back by a full six feet. The coffee was already in bags, so there was no danger of it spilling over the edges. With the doubled capacity, they could serve twice as many of the sharecroppers. And they could take the larger cargo all the way to the markets in San Salvador, where the prices were higher than those they could beg from the small merchants who came to Avila. Eduardo was able to pay the peasants more than they had ever gotten before for their produce, and still pay himself for his efforts. And he was getting more for his own produce as well.

He and Miguel were washing the truck one night, following their trip to the market, when the foreman pulled up in his jeep. Eduardo knew that something was wrong. He and Roberto had been friends for several years. In fact, he had been the one to walk Roberto through the sheds and explain the equipment when the younger man was first hired by the Diegos. Now Roberto was standing uneasily, shifting from foot to foot as he struggled to make small talk. He seemed unwilling to look Miguel's father in the eye.

"Señor Diego asks that you stop hauling coffee to the market," he finally managed to say. "Your own goods present no problem. But he asks that you stop carrying anyone else's goods."

Eduardo was stunned. He gestured dumbly toward the large deck that he had built over the truck bed. He could never hope to fill it with the small crop he was able to raise on his allotted patch of land. "But why?" he asked. "I have so much room."

"It's the other planters," Roberto explained. "They say you're running a cooperative."

"What's a cooperative?" Eduardo asked.

"A company," Roberto explained. "An organization that supplies coffee to the market. The families are the only ones who bring coffee to the market. The merchant who bought your coffee didn't buy from one of the other families. They complained to Señor Diego."

"But," Eduardo stammered, looking at the truck which now seemed ridiculously small, "we sell so little. How can it make any difference?"

Roberto threw up his hands. "I don't know. But it does. They meet, and when one of the planters has a problem, all the others agree to help him. Señor Diego had to agree that there would be no cooperative. He gave his word. That's why he has to ask you to stop. He told me that he didn't want you to get in trouble with the National Guard."

"The guard?" Miguel's father was stunned. The National Guard was a private Army, paid and equipped by the families who ran the government. They funded an Army to protect the country, and the National Guard to protect their estates. He remembered when labor leaders from San Salvador had come up into the mountains to organize the workers. The guard had stopped their car and arrested them. The burned-out shell of the car was found in a ravine. The labor organizers were never seen again.

"I told Señor Diego that you would understand. Once you knew that he had given his word . . ." Roberto waited for Eduardo to signal his answer.

"Of course," Eduardo said. "Whatever Señor Diego wants."

When he told his neighbors, they begged him to make one more trip. They had harvested much more than they could ever hope to carry on their backs. He repeated Emilio Diego's wish, which they all knew was law. But perhaps he could take their coffee and vegetables into La Libertad. It was much further away, to the southeast on the coastal plain. And the prices wouldn't be as good. But if he drove down there at night, he could be the first to unload in the morning. None of the planters would even suspect what he had done.

Eduardo weighed the wishes of the patrone against the plight of his neighbors, and made the risky decision. He arranged for sacks of coffee and baskets of vegetables to be carried to collection points near each of the plantations. Then, with Francisco and Miguel in the truck, he drove the dark, nighttime paths through the mountains until the truck was loaded.

"It was after midnight when we started down the mountains toward the coast. The road wasn't really a road. More like a path with a lot of sharp switchbacks. My father was driving in low gear, so we were makin' a lot of noise. He was worried about attractin' attention, but he didn't trust the brakes."

Mex had been looking down toward his folded hands as he told the story to Baldinger. But his eyes were focused back into the past. Dave realized that his friend was no longer seated across the table. He was bouncing in the worn-out seat of the truck, trying to see the road in the yellow glow of the single headlight.

"Francisco kept his head out of the window so that he could watch the edge of the road on the side with the headlight. We were comin' around a tight turn, and I saw a light up ahead, dim, almost like a flashlight. My brother says, 'Do you see it, Papa?'

"My father wipes the windshield with his hand. 'I can't make it out. What is it?'

"It was a truck, parked on the road. All of a sudden, there's these beams of light, so bright we had to turn our eyes away.

"'Soldiers,' my brother whispers.

"I was scared. 'Stop, Popa,' I begged my father. 'Turn around.'

"But the road wasn't wide enough to make a turn. And my father didn't think we were doin' anything wrong. 'They're looking for bandits,' he told us. 'Don't worry. There won't be any trouble.'"

He didn't mean bandits, Mex explained, suddenly looking up at Baldinger. There were revolutionaries in the eastern mountains. Peasants and laborers who had taken up arms against the landowners and the government they controlled. Communists, according to the official government pronouncements. Liberators, according to the crackling radio broadcasts and hand-printed leaflets that the revolutionaries distributed. The Army was reported to be searching the countryside for them.

They rolled to a stop near the parked truck, and only when they were out of the glare of its headlights did they see the line of soldiers stretched across the road, their rifles aimed at the windshield. An officer strolled up to the window of the cab.

"Whose truck is this?" he demanded.

"Mine, sir," Eduardo Cortines answered.

"Let me see your ownership papers."

"There are no papers. It was abandoned. I fixed it."

The officer looked back at the cargo. "Does all this belong to you?"

"To me. And to some others. I'm taking it to the market."

"Let me see your trucking license."

"License?"

Three of the soldiers walked up and stood behind the officer. Several other soldiers were moving up to the passenger door. Francisco pulled his head back in through the window and sat staring straight ahead.

"You need a license to truck other people's produce. Do you have one?"

Eduardo gestured helplessly. "I never heard of a license."

"Get out," the officer ordered.

Eduardo opened the door carefully and started to step out. The officer grabbed him by the shirt collar, and threw him into the arms of the soldiers.

Mex was once again looking vacantly down at his hands. "Other soldiers pulled open the passenger door and dragged my brother out onto the road. Two of them took his arms and bent them behind his back. Then this one son of a bitch took his rifle and drove the butt into Francisco's stomach. My brother was a big kid, but still just a kid. The way he fell, I thought he was dead.

"My father tried to break free from the goons who were holdin' him. The officer took his pistol like a hammer and smashed it across Poppa's jaw.

"I started screamin'. I guess I was cryin'. I was so scared. Then one of the soldiers reached in through the other door and grabbed me by the hair. He tossed me out onto the road, and another guy started kicking me in the stomach.

"The officer ordered the soldiers to get back, and then he took a hand grenade from his belt, pulled the pin, and dropped it into the cab. It was the loudest noise I think I ever heard. I mean, it was just a grenade, and I've stood right next to howitzers. But I'll never forget that blast. The cab blew apart. The roof flew into the air and the doors blew off to the sides. The frame snapped and the truck broke completely in half. Christ, it was nothin' but a pile of rust to begin with."

Mex looked up at Baldinger and smiled. "Funny what you remember when you're a kid. I remember the heat, like I got too close to the stove. And then it started to rain. Only it wasn't rain. It was a shower of glass from the windshield and the windows. Little pieces that made a tinkling sound when they landed. Anyway, what was left of the truck was burnin'. All the coffee sacks were on fire. There was nothin' to save."

Eduardo staggered around the truck to find his sons. Francisco was sitting by the roadside, holding Miguel in his arms. Eduardo had lifted Miguel onto his shoulders, and helped Francisco to his feet. They began walking back up the hill. They had a long way to go, and all of them had to be back in the fields by morning.

They reached the plantation just as the sun was coming over the eastern mountains, and staggered the last few hundred yards toward the shed.

"When I saw the house, I started runnin'. I just wanted to be with my mother. But then I stopped. Everything we owned was out in front—the two beds, the table and benches, pots and pans, and sacks of clothes—were piled up on the road. My mother and my sister were sittin' on the benches. I didn't know what was wrong. But then I heard my father talkin' to my mother, and I figured it out. While the soldiers were takin' care of us, Roberto and his men had kicked my family out of the house. We didn't work for the Diegos anymore, and we didn't have a place to live. My father had made a big mistake. He forgot that Señor Diego always kept his word."

*　*　*

"So what are you telling me?" Robert Gordon challenged Baldinger when the corporal had finished repeating his conversation with the prisoner. "Just because we gave the Salvadoran Army the hand grenades we're responsible for everything they did with them?"

Baldinger wasn't interested in logic. All he could think about was what had happened to his friend. "There's a lot more, Captain. Things Mex doesn't even want to talk about. If you could just meet with him, and hear him out you'd understand why we have to help him."

Gordon got up and refilled the coffee cups. Patiently, he explained his own role as the trial counsel. Cortines should be talking to his defense attorney, not the prosecutor.

"I already feel for him, Baldinger. He's a good soldier, and I don't know a lot of men who would have given themselves up to save a friend. I want to help him. When he picks a defense lawyer, I'll work with the man. Maybe we'll drop some of the major charges and let him plead guilty to the less important stuff. There are lots of ways we can try to get him a fair deal. I know he's your friend. But nothing you've told me gives him the right to poison the drinking water, or plant hand grenades in people's driveways."

"You have to listen to him, sir," Baldinger kept repeating. He was begging more than asking.

Gordon sighed. "Okay, I'll go over to the stockade with you, and I'll listen. But then you have to do something for me."

"Anything," Baldinger agreed eagerly.

"You have to get your friend to agree to meet with the defense attorneys I'll be sending over. And then you have to help him pick one."

They settled into the chairs across the table from the prisoner. Mex sat silently, rubbing his wrists where the guards had removed his handcuffs, and Gordon and Baldinger waited for him to finish.

"Mex, tell Captain Gordon what happened to your parents," Baldinger tried.

"They're dead," Mex answered, and then there was another tense silence. Baldinger looked toward Gordon for help.

"How did your mother die?" Robert asked.

"An accident."

"Can you tell me about it?"

"Just an accident. She was in the wrong place at the wrong time."

"A traffic accident?"

Mex's response was a thoughtful nod. "I suppose that's what it was."

But Gordon was patient. The man didn't want to talk about his parents. He took another tack. "Tell me about your sister. Baldinger says you were very close to your older sister."

"She was very beautiful," Mex remembered. Then he added, "To me, anyway. Maybe not to some guys. But she smiled a lot at me."

Gordon nodded. "I know what you mean. My older sister took care of me a lot. I knew she was beautiful before any of the guys in the neighborhood caught on."

Mex smiled. He wanted to talk about Maria.

* * *

They were living near San Salvador, in a shantytown that was tolerated by the authorities because it was far enough away from the business center and the wealthy residence districts to be completely out of sight. Again, it was one room, divided by woven curtains that afforded a bit of privacy but still let the air circulate. It had a single faucet for running water, and an electrical line that lit a string of light bulbs when the power plant was working.

The Cortines family was better off than many of its neighbors. Eduardo's skill with machinery had proven valuable to some of the American companies that had moved light-assembly plants into the area. The wages were a fraction of what they paid in the States. There were no taxes, other than the share of ownership they gave to the ruling families. And there were no labor problems. The Guardsmen made sure of that.

Eduardo worked for one of these companies, maintaining the motors, pumps, and compressors that were used in manufacturing, and the vans that shuttled between the plant and the airport. His work took him throughout the factory, and he got to know most of the workers and the supervisors. It was because he was well known, and well liked, that he found himself in the middle of a petty labor dispute that was, in truth, of little consequence. With hat in hand, he went to the supervisor to plead the workers' case.

"If I tell them that this is a temporary situation, there will be no problem," he assured the manager. "And if it is permanent, then all they need to know is that they will be paid for the additional time. We mean no disrespect. We are all grateful for the work."

The supervisor promised to talk with the owners. "We all want to keep the production line running," he agreed cheerfully. "I'll find out what the situation is, and I'll tell you in the morning."

The guards looked up as Mex stood up from the table. He began pacing in a small circle across the interview room, glancing from the floor to the ceiling as he spoke.

"That night, four men kicked down the door of our house. They weren't soldiers. Just a bunch of ORDEN goons, dressed in sport shirts and baseball caps."

"ORDEN?" Robert Gordon asked.

Mex tried to explain. "Street thugs. They sucked up to the army for favors, and did the dirty work that the officers didn't want to do themselves."

Gordon scribbled a note on his legal pad.

"I was sittin' up in my bed. It was in the big room, so I was only a couple of feet away from 'em. They pulled my father and mother out from behind their curtain.

"The leader grabbed my father, and screamed at him. 'You want to be a labor leader, Cortines?' My father didn't know what he was talkin' about. I didn't know either. I was just scared.

" 'I'll show you what happens to labor leaders,' the guy started yellin'. He looked around, and then he grabbed Maria, I guess because she was lookin' right at him and didn't seem as scared as the rest of us.

" 'They pay for the trouble they cause.'

"He grabbed Maria's hair and twisted it into a knot. It must have hurt like hell, but she didn't cry or anything. He pushed her down to her knees, and bent her head back. Then he took his pistol . . ."

Mex stopped talking. He blinked, and his eyes glistened in the glare of the fluorescent tubes that were recessed into the ceiling.

"He took his pistol . . ." Mex tried again.

Gordon looked away and waited to hear the gunshot.

"He took his pistol and he jammed the muzzle into her mouth. Her teeth just broke, and her lips split wide open. Then he pulled back the hammer of the weapon with his thumb, and let it catch in the cocked position. I wanted to help her. I wanted to stop him," Mex whispered to his memories. "But I was too scared.

" 'This is how they pay,' he said. And then he pulled the trigger."

Mex sank slowly into the chair. His eyes dropped to his hands which he was once again rubbing to bring the blood back into his wrists. "I squeezed my eyes shut, but all I heard was a click. It was the hammer hittin' against the empty chamber. The son of bitch wasn't going to kill us. He was just playing with us. It was only a second before I opened my eyes, but it seemed a lot longer. I saw the guy pull the bloody muzzle out of her mouth and then throw her on the floor. Then they all started laughing. The leader waved the gun in front of my father so he could see Maria's blood, and then he said. 'No more labor trouble. Next time I won't forget to load my gun.'"

Gordon lifted his glasses and wiped his eyes. Baldinger buried his face in his hands.

"I shoulda been glad that they didn't kill her. But when I looked at her, she had no more smile. I remember thinkin' that killin' her smile was worse than killin' her. Dumb, the things you think when you're only a kid."

He looked up at his two visitors, and went on with his story.

"My father didn't go back to the factory, In the morning he went to the church. The priests were trying to help the people. It was dangerous for them. The government was killing priests the same way it was killing labor leaders. A lot of them were stripped and beaten and thrown off the cliff at Puerta del Diablo. The only way you knew who they were was by the white collars left around their necks. The priest gave us the name of a family in Mazote, out in the eastern mountains. It was about as far as you could get from San Salvador. We hid in the basement of the church until night. Then we were taken away in a truck."

The visitor's room in the prison went silent. Mex had said all that he wanted to say.

"Your sister was all right?" Gordon asked with genuine concern.

"Yeah. Fine," Mex said. "She couldn't smile anymore. So maybe she wasn't beautiful to other people. But I always remember her smiling." There was a tremor in his voice as he finished the thought.

* * *

The legal officer was shaken by the tragedy that had been the young soldier's life. There were many things that could be brought up in a pre-sentencing hearing that might well move the court toward leniency. But none of it was evidence. He explained the difference to Baldinger when they were back in his office.

"He lived in a terrible country at a terrible time. But none of that has any bearing on the fact that he planted a hand grenade in Major Daks's driveway. Or on his poisoning the water. And we'd be reaching too far to claim that the sight of a Salvadoran officer drove him insane. There really is no defense case.''

Baldinger tried to interrupt him, but the captain silenced him with a gesture.

"I'm giving you the best advice I can. Get him a defense lawyer. A good lawyer will bring up his background during the investigation. I'll support a recommendation for leniency.''

"We owe him better than that,'' the corporal said.

"Why do we owe him?'' Gordon demanded. ''Because the grenade they stuck in his father's truck was made in the U.S.? Because the goon's pistol was probably bought with American military aid dollars? Be serious, Corporal. It was an ugly war. Both sides were commiting atrocities, and there were lots of victims. He was one of them. But that doesn't give him the right to start killing anyone who wears a uniform. You wear an American Army uniform, Baldinger. Does Mex have the right to plant a hand grenade under you?''

"Maybe he does!'' Dave shouted back, with no hint of the respect due an officer. Then he caught himself, and shook his head in a gesture of apology. "I don't know, Captain. I guess I'm just mixed up. We were helping these bastards. Our guys were working side by side with scum who could push a pistol into a girl's mouth. Don't we have to answer for that? Because if we don't, then why am I wearing this uniform. Why are you wearing one?''

Gordon understood that it was a serious question. He gave it the only honest answer he could think of. "We won the war, Baldinger. We don't have to answer to anyone.''

But he wanted a better answer for himself. Like the young corporal, Gordon was beginning to feel indicted by what had happened to Miguel Cortines and his family. Many of the officers and men at Fort Viper had been part of the military assistance group in El Salvador. Many of them had trained the Salvadoran officers in anti-insurgent tactics. Gordon needed to know more about how those tactics had been used. Not because it had anything to do with the case he was prosecuting. But because he wanted to be able to show Baldinger that leniency was all that Cortines had any right to expect.

He went back to the prison the next day, this time by himself.

"You said your mother was killed in an accident,'' he said, after they had exchanged a few awkward words of greeting. Mex's eyes narrowed defensively. He didn't answer.

"Baldinger thinks that maybe the American Army caused the accident."

Mex turned away from the table. "I don't want to talk about my mother," he said.

"How? How are we responsible for your mother's death?"

"I don't want to talk about it."

The captain began pushing his notes back into his briefcase. "Baldinger told me that you wanted me to defend you," he said as he snapped the latches.

"I do," Mex answered, turning back to face him.

"I don't see any reason why I should. But it's important to your friend, so I'm willing to think about it. No promises. Just think about it. But if you want me to help you, you have to help me. So I'll ask you once more, and that's it. How are we responsible for your mother's death?"

Cortines nodded his agreement with the bargain, and Gordon pulled his notes back out of his briefcase. "We were livin' in the hills, with the revolution," Mex began. "That was when the Americans had come back into the war, and things were gettin' pretty rough. The hills were the only place where we were safe." Slowly, he began to explain what was happening.

In 1980, the United States resumed military assistance to the government of El Salvador. The insurgents had established ties with the Cuban communists, and boatloads of Russian weapons and ammunition were being put ashore in the Gulf of Fonseca, at the country's eastern edge. The Martí revolutionaries controlled half the country, everything east of San Vicente, and all the mountains to the north. At night they moved freely into San Salvador, itself, forcing the landed families to surround their estates in the wealthy Escalon and San Benito districts with coils of razor wire. The Army and the National Guard were in full retreat.

But the Americans, still smarting over the loss of Saigon to the communists, couldn't allow a communist-supported people's front to gain a foothold on their own continent. They had stopped sending aid during the Carter Administration, which had demanded civil reform. Now they forgot about civil reform, and poured in money, arms, and military advisers. It didn't take the Americans long to get the Salvadoran military back into the field.

The officers were given counterinsurgency training at a Special Operations school set up in the Canal Zone. Special Operations units fanned out through the ranks and taught the techniques for tracking insurgents into the jungles. Small jet fighters, affectionately named "Dragonflies" appeared in the skies with teardrop-shaped tanks of napalm strapped to their wings.

Slowly, the military began to roll back the people's front. With great patience, they shut down all the insurgents' sources of supply, information, and new recruits. They burned down all their safe havens. They forced them out of the jungles into open confrontations. And then they annihilated them with the mortars, recoilless rifles, helicopters, and planes that the Americans provided.

Eduardo Cortines had taken his family into the mountains of Morazán where they lived under the protection of the Martí revolutionaries. He did what he could to pay for his keep. He maintained the few trucks that they had to bring supplies up from the coast into the mountains, and built pumps that would lift water up from the streams to the meager farms they were able to plant. Using the knowledge he had gained in the electronics factory, he was able to fix an electrical generator that fleeing Army troops had abandoned. At times, he was even able to assemble the guns and rocket launchers that were delivered in pieces from Cuba and Nicaragua.

"My brother joined the Martí army. He trained in Morazán, but his unit was fightin' in Cuscatlán, near the capital. My father used to say that when the revolution marched into the city, Francisco would be in the front ranks where he would hear the cheers of the people."

Miguel worked with his mother and sisters on the small farm they had planted together with several other families. "I didn't like working with the women." Mex smiled toward Gordon. "I wanted to be a soldier, like my brother. But it wouldn't be for long. I was twelve. In another year, I'd be old enough."

Their lives changed abruptly once the Americans came into the war. There were no longer any safe havens. Soldiers attacked into the mountains, and probed into the folds of the valleys. Helicopters came in over treetops, and fired down on anything that looked like a military column or a supply line. One day a helicopter landed a squad of Salvadoran soldiers, who went from house to house searching for insurgents. They pushed the women and children about, and dragged the few old men out into the woods for questioning.

"Where are the young men?" they demanded. "Where are the soldiers you have been supplying?" They were enraged when they didn't get the answers they wanted. They slapped the old men around, then came back into the settlement and beat some of the women. Before they climbed back into the helicopter, they machine-gunned the three pigs that the community had been raising. A few hours later, an airplane flew over and sprayed chemicals onto the farmland, killing the vegetables, and sending the women and children screaming into the hills.

They had to move constantly. It seemed that as soon as they were settled, the soldiers would come and tear down the houses. And moving became more difficult. Even the narrowest paths were bombed into ditches. Bridges were blown. Whenever a truck set out on a roadway, the Dragonflies would appear overhead, and blast it into a smoldering frame.

"We set up camp on the northern edge of San Miguel and built huts on a small stream. We thought we were safe from attack because the country was dense and rugged, and because the few paths coming in were easy to guard. We even had an answer for the Dragonflies and the helicopters. The Cubans had sent in Russian antiaircraft missiles. Small, shoulder-fired heat-seekers. I couldn't believe it, the first time I saw one. A couple of American choppers appeared, and one of the soldiers fired at 'em. The pilots saw 'em, and started maneuverin' down under the tree line. But the missile locked onto one of 'em and flew right into the rotors. We all cheered. It was like we weren't chickenshit anymore. We could stand up and fight."

But the Americans had given the Salvadorans other weapons, as the Cortines family learned when the whole community was suddenly taken sick. "In the middle of the night, I woke up sick," Mex told Gordon. My stomach was on fire and I kept throwin' up. All the little kids were cryin', and then, in the morning, the women began gettin' sick. Pretty soon, the soldiers were throwin' up. They couldn't even stand at their guard posts. No one knew what the hell was happenin' to us. Everyone was sick, and no one was gettin' any better. Pretty soon, no one was strong enough to take care of the kids. It was damn scary.

"There was this priest who used to come and say mass for us. A Jesuit who was on the run, just like we were. When he came to the village, he figured out that the problem was the water. For some reason that he couldn't explain, the water had gone bad. Drinkin' more of it was makin' the sickness worse. We had to move, he told us, and find new water supplies.

"My father and the other older men packed the supplies. The

women gathered up the children. We tried to march out of the mountains.''

But now, as Cortines explained, the narrow, easily guarded roads that had been their protection became their death trap. The Army was in position, with armored personnel carriers sitting on the roads, their heavy-caliber machine guns raised and waiting. The guerrilla leaders saw that they couldn't fight their way through, and so they led the procession onto the small, serpentine trails that were hundreds of years older than the roads.

Miguel was with the men, carrying supplies. His mother and his sister were walking ahead, each carrying one of the sick, younger children in their arms.

"I didn't see what happened," he told Gordon. "I heard an explosion. Loud, but nothin' like the one when the truck exploded. I looked ahead, and I saw smoke. Then, when the smoke cleared, my mother was spread out on the ground, still holdin' onto the baby she was carryin'. The kid was cryin' but my mother wasn't sayin' anything. My father started runnin' to her, and I ran right behind him. I remember my father stopped, and then he turned and tried to catch me so I wouldn't get closer. But I ran by him. Then I saw it was only half of my mother. She had no legs.

"My father lifted her head off the ground, and started brushin' the dirt out of her eyes. I wanted to help him . . . I mean, I shoulda gone to her. But I couldn't. It wasn't her anymore. It was somebody ugly and I couldn't even look at her.''

Mex turned his face and looked directly into Gordon's eyes. "You know what I mean, sir. She was my mother, so it woulda been wrong to look at her when she was all messed up like that, wouldn't it?''

Robert nodded slowly. "I know what you mean," he whispered. "You did the right thing.''

Mex smiled in gratitude that the captain understood why he had turned his back on his mother. "I guess that's why I don't like talkin' about it. Or even thinkin' about it. I shoulda done something.''

The priest ran back. He looked briefly at Miguel's mother. There was nothing he could do except encourage Eduardo back to his feet, and then say a brief prayer. There was no time for a proper burial. The procession had to keep moving.

Seconds later, there was another explosion. One of the children, who had been walking by himself, flew into the air. And moments later, another blast divided a woman and a young girl who had been traveling hand in hand.

"All the paths had been mined," Mex continued. "We started back through the woods. It was almost impossible without the pathways; a straight climb through rough country. I think some of the older people just sat down and died. But by morning, most of us had worked our way back to the river. We started across. It wasn't deep, only up to our knees. But it was open. So when the Dragonflies came over, we had no protection. They made one pass, firin' their machine guns, and people disappeared into the water. I remember the streaks of red flowin' downstream from where people had gone under. The planes banked and swung around for another pass. We thought we were all gonners. My father wrapped his arms around me and turned me away from the planes. I guess he didn't know that the machine-gun rounds would go right through both of us. But on the second pass, they didn't fire. Maybe they got a better look at us and saw we weren't soldiers. Or maybe they were out of ammunition. They just roared by, only a few feet higher than the trees, and then turned away. Those that were still alive crossed and kept going higher into the mountains."

His voice had been winding down, becoming softer and weaker. And then there was no sound at all.

Gordon's voice was only a whisper when he asked, "Who made it? Maria, and you, and your father?"

Mex nodded. "Yeah. We made it."

"So you poisoned our water because we poisoned your water?" Gordon had regained his composure, and he sounded more as if he were interrogating a witness.

Mex looked up at him. "The Salvadoran Army didn't figure out how to drive us out of the mountains. The American military advisers taught 'em."

"And you planted the mine because they planted mines. They didn't care who stepped on them, so you didn't care."

"I cared," Mex said firmly. "I'm glad no one stepped on it. But they put 'em in my backyard. All I did was pick 'em up and toss 'em back over the fence."

Gordon took a moment to consider Mex's answer. Then he asked, "Why did you tell me your mother died in an accident?"

Mex shrugged his shoulders. "It *was* an accident. I don't think they wanted to kill her. They didn't care who they killed, just as long as they kept us from controllin' the countryside. They planted mines to keep us from movin'. There's probably a couple of thousand of 'em still buried in open fields and on mountain paths, still waitin' for someone to step on 'em. And when someone does, it will just be another accident."

They sat for a few more moments, quietly staring at one another. Then Gordon asked, "When did you decide to . . . throw the mines back over the fence? Is that why you joined the Army?"

Cortines seemed startled by the suggestion. "No. I was just tryin' to get by. The Army was just a job. It didn't mean nothin'. But then I came here to Viper. I started trainin', and I saw all the things that happened to us. Me and my family. They were still teachin' people to do the same things. And I figured I had to put a stop to it. I didn't know how, but then they trained me how."

Gordon nodded that he understood. He began pushing his papers back into the briefcase.

"Do you still want me to defend you?"

"I'd like that," Mex said.

"Can I ask you just one more question?"

The corporal told him that he could.

"Why did you torture the Salvadoran officer?"

"Because he was a Salvadoran officer."

"But you didn't kill him. You broke into the officers' compound; you carried him out past a parade of sentries, and then took him into the school past another row of guards. You could have killed him easily, right in his bedroom, with far less risk to yourself. Why did you have to torture him with the electric shock?"

"No special reason," Mex said. He rose on his side of the table, nodded to Gordon, and then turned back to the guards who were waiting to return him to his cell.

Gordon didn't believe him. There had been a particular reason for planting the grenade and poisoning the water supply. There had to be a reason why he would go to such lengths just to connect the Salvadoran to the torture machine.

When he got back to his office, he called the trainee barracks and asked for Corporal Baldinger.

"This is Captain Gordon." And then, without waiting for an acknowledgment: "Did Cortines ever say anything to you about an electric shock machine?"

"I don't think so, sir."

"Did he mention that anyone in his family might have been tortured? His father? Or maybe his sister?"

"No, sir. He never said anything like that."

Gordon mumbled his thanks and was about to hang up.

"Sir," Baldinger asked, "are you going to try and help him?"

Gordon thought about his answer. "You're right, Corporal. Some-one has to answer. And it sure as hell shouldn't be your friend. I'm going to do everything I can for him. As a matter of fact, I'm going to pay him another visit tomorrow. It might be a tough conversation. Maybe you ought to come along."

In the morning, Baldinger and Gordon met at the stockade, and then waited while Cortines was brought into the conference room and his shackles were removed. Dave greeted his friend enthusiastically, and Mex responded with a laugh. Gordon busied himself arranging his pad and pen on the table while the two friends talked. Then he began his interview, not as a friendly, sympathetic listener, but more as an attorney preparing his case.

"How did you get into the United States?" he asked as soon as he had Cortines's attention. Mex explained that they had fled through the mountains into Nicaragua, and then by boat, along the Pacific coast to Mexico. They had crossed into the United States with the usual tide of illegal immigrants.

"Who besides you? Your father and your sister?"

"Just Maria," Mex answered. And then, after a pause: "My father was already dead."

"Can your sister tell about any of the incidents you mentioned? From her own knowledge."

"No," Mex answered.

"Why not?"

"I don't know where to find her."

Gordon looked confused.

"When we came into the country, we both went into hidin'. The government was tryin' to send us back to El Salvador, and there were a few families . . . members of a church in California . . . who were hidin' us. The Immigration guys found Maria. They sent her back."

"Back to El Salvador?" Baldinger asked.

Mex nodded sadly.

"Jesus Christ," Baldinger said. He turned his eyes on Gordon, almost as if he thought the captain was responsible.

Gordon pressed on with his questions. "Which one of you was tortured with electric shock?"

Mex recoiled in horror. "We weren't tortured."

"Someone was," Gordon insisted. "Who was it?"

Mex turned away from the table. "I don't wanna talk about it."

"You want me to help you," Gordon challenged.

Baldinger reached out, grabbed Mex's shirt, and pulled him back toward the attorney. "For God's sake, Mex. Tell him."

Mex looked pleadingly at Dave.

"Tell him. Please," Baldinger begged his friend.

Cortines's shoulders sagged. "My brother was killed in combat during the fight for San Salvador," he began.

In March of 1983, the Martí rebels launched a Tet offensive of their own into the very heart of the capital city. To many in America, the attack was a cause of great alarm. The common wisdom held that the Salvadoran guerrillas were an arm of the international communist conspiracy, which was advancing from across the Pacific as part of a global pincer movement, poised to attack across the Rio Grande. "If El Salvador goes, Mexico will be next," government spokesmen threatened. And it looked as if El Salvador were going. The communists were already in the streets of the capital city.

But as the American military advisers understood, the attack was a death rattle for the revolution. The whole purpose of the strategy they had brought to the country was to deny the guerrillas sanctuary. Scatter their support communities. Mine their lines of supply. Keep on them. Never let them go back into the jungle to regroup. Sooner or later, you'll back them into a corner where they'll have to stand and fight. And then, the superior firepower of a modern Army, useless in the bush against roaming bands of insurgents, will turn the tide.

The strategy was working. The insurgents were driven out of one district after another. The communities that supported them were methodically destroyed. With each defeat, it became harder for them to recruit new soldiers. They were forced to conscript young men from the fields. Food and supplies that had been freely offered to them now had to be stolen from intimidated peasants. They were being turned into enemies of the people instead of their protectors. To survive, they needed to show that they were winning.

They began attacking Army strongholds, and at first, probably because the attacks were not expected, they found some success. Francisco's unit hit an Army barracks in Santa Tecla, only a few miles southwest of the city. The government forces ran, leaving behind an armory filled with American-supplied weapons. They swung to the east and attacked a garrison in La Paz. In San Vicente, they took control of the radio station for an entire day, broadcasting their demand that the government dissolve itself in favor of national elections. They fled when a major military force moved toward them, but then looped around and hit the flank of the unit, causing heavy casualties.

Encouraged by their success, and sensing that they were regaining popular loyalty, they infiltrated one of the poorer districts of the capital. But the American intelligence forces learned of their plans, and set up the counterattack. The Martí guerrillas enjoyed several hours of success, when they were able to strike into the heart of the city. But the government encircled them in one district, and then pounded the district to dust with air attacks and heavy artillery. The civilians begged the guerrillas to leave, but the rebels had no path of escape. Most of them died fighting. Those who were captured were immediately executed.

The extent of the civilian casualties caused a world outcry. Hundreds of women and children, with no connection to the revolution, were killed in the cross fire. At American urging, the government declared an armistice. In the calm of the cease-fire, the rebels were told to come and bury their dead.

Eduardo learned, through church relief organizations, that his son had been killed. He spent a day of mourning, and then he and young Miguel went to the morgues that had been set up in San Salvador, to search for Francisco's body.

The Army arrested the two of them as soon as they made their first inquiry. It may have been that they overestimated Eduardo's role in the revolution, or just that they felt anyone with a relative in the guerrilla Army must know other people connected with the movement. But Eduardo and Miguel were thrown into the back of a canvas-covered Army truck, along with a dozen other men and women. They were taken to an old abandoned schoolhouse on the outskirts of the city.

The interrogations were a model of efficiency. One by one, the prisoners were taken into a small basement room and questioned by an officer. For some, the simple fact of being alone with the soldiers in a dark, cold basement was sufficient persuasion to name every name they could think of. The Army had never made any secret of its brutality, and Salvadorans who had been disloyal in any way had good reason to fear its representatives. Others tried to buy their freedom by offering insignificant bits of information that they knew were of no consequence. But then they would hear the screams of pain echoing from other parts of the cellar, and understand that they toyed with their inquisitor at terrible risk.

"I was in an empty classroom, sittin' on the floor with a lot of other people. There were women and a few kids, but mostly men. We could hear the screams comin' from the basement. I thought I heard my father, but you couldn't be sure. People sound the same when they're screamin'."

Eduardo's background told the soldiers that they had stumbled on a gold mine. They had his name on a list that one of their earlier prisoners had provided under torture. It indicated that he had served the revolution by assembling their weapons and maintaining their radios and vehicles. Certainly, he must have high-level contacts with the revolutionary forces. The interrogating officer sneered at his claims that he was just a rural farmer, come to claim the body of his misguided son. He passed Eduardo on to the next level, where the questioning became more determined.

"They beat him with hoses and riding crops. When I finally saw him, he was cut up a lot. But I guess he never told them nothin'," Mex said proudly, "because they dragged him upstairs to the room where they kept the machine. I saw him when he went by the door. He looked . . ."

Mex bit down on his lip. He didn't want to remember how his father had looked.

"They hooked him up to the shock machine," Gordon offered.

Mex nodded. And then they sat silently. They could all visualize what it had been like.

"I didn't hear anything," Cortines finally went on. "There were no screams, because they stuffed your mouth with somethin' to keep you from bitin' off your tongue. It seemed like he was in there a long time. I guess they figured he had taken everything they could do to him. And then someone figured maybe he wouldn't be able to take what they could do to his kid. So they came and got me, and took me to the room."

Gordon had set his pen down. He was staring down at the blank lines across his pad of paper. He couldn't look at the young soldier while he was reliving the worst moment of his life. Baldinger reached his hand across the table until the tip of his finger was just touching the edge of Mex's hand. He wanted Mex to know that he was there.

"They had to send out and get a new chair. I guess my father had kicked so hard that he had torn the legs off the old one. I didn't see him at first. I saw the machine, and I saw the clamps. They stung when they hooked them on me. I was so scared that I started to cry. Like a baby. I was thirteen years old, and I was crying like a baby. And then I heard my father scream. He was sittin' on the floor in the corner. His eyes were like fires, and he was screamin' to them, beggin' them not to hurt me. And then he started tellin' them everything. I didn't understand what he was sayin', but they did, and they were writing down everything. He kept talkin' and they kept writin', and I began to understand what was happenin'. He was sellin' out so they wouldn't have to shock me."

Mex turned away from the table so that his friend wouldn't see his shame. "And I was glad he was sellin' out, because I was afraid of being' hurt. I wasn't thinkin' about him. I was just scared for me."

He fell so silent that Gordon and Baldinger could hear his breathing. And then his choked sob.

"Anyway," Mex continued, "they got what they wanted. And they called this captain who I guess was in charge. He came in and read the paper. He never looked at my father, and he never looked at me. He just told the soldiers to get rid of us. They took me out in the street and just let me go. I never saw my father again. But I heard that they took him to Puerta del Diablo. I guess they shot him and pushed him off."

"Okay, Cortines," Gordon said softly. "That's enough. That's all I need."

But Mex wasn't finished. A door on his past had been flung wide open and he couldn't close it. "I always figured that if I was a man—if I hadn't been cryin'—that my father wouldn't have had to tell 'em. And if he didn't tell 'em everything they wanted to know, maybe they wouldn't have killed him. I don't know. Sometimes I think they probably would have killed him anyway. They didn't care. But then, I think that maybe . . ."

His thoughts trailed off.

"You couldn't have helped him," Baldinger said. "Jesus, Mex, you were just a kid."

Cortines nodded that he understood.

"I'm sorry, Corporal," Gordon whispered. "I just had to get it all down. I understood everything else. I needed to know why you . . . went after the colonel. Why you hooked him up to the machine? I guess it was the uniform, and what it reminded you of."

"It was Maritin," Mex said. "He was a captain then. The officer who was in charge . . . the one they called into the room . . . was Colonel Maritin."

★ ★ ★

Baldinger and Gordon walked silently out into the sunlight. There was an unanswered question between them. Was Gordon going to defend Cortines? Baldinger didn't want to ask it again, and Gordon wasn't sure of the answer he should give.

"Corporal, your friend has already paid enough for what he did here at Fort Viper. I don't want to see him go to jail."

Baldinger nodded. "I swear I won't let him go to jail."

"We'll do the best we can," Gordon promised. "Give me a bit of time, Corporal. I'm not sure how to handle this, but there's been a wrong, and I guess I have to try to set it right."

Baldinger saluted, and Gordon returned the salute. Then they took separate routes away from the stockade.

His best chance of saving Mex from prison would be if he could keep the case from ever going to trial. The military didn't make it a policy to prosecute patently unsuitable soldiers and sailors who had managed to hide their deficiencies from recruiting officers. Where possible, they simply gave the person an administrative discharge from the service, and dumped him and his problems back into the arms of civilian authorities. Technically, they could prosecute malingerers and military personnel who had gone AWOL. They could try them for dereliction of duty and send them to military prisons. But why burden the service with the problem of maintaining a prisoner for five or ten years. It was easier and more practical to simply face the fact that he didn't belong in a uniform, and process him out.

True, Mex was not simply a malingerer. Every word in the charge sheet that Gordon had drawn up was accurate. He had planted a grenade, he had assaulted the entire base by poisoning its water, and he had physically assaulted an officer. But there were reasons why, despite his crimes, it might be to the Army's benefit to turn Mex loose. There was information about Army activities that would certainly be introduced in his defense. Information that the Army wouldn't want to share with all the attendees of an open court.

Captain Gordon began promoting his idea the next day, at a picnic that Colonel Grigg threw for his officers and their wives. It was a typical summer outing, organized around the wooden benches in Fort Marion's recreation field. A keg was tapped. Hot dogs and hamburgers were tossed on fiery grills. There were horseshoes, softball, and sack races for the children.

Gordon was welcomed heartily by the school staff. Marilyn Daks brought him a paper plate with a singed hamburger and potato salad. Colonel Grigg stepped out of the batting cage to lead him to the keg and pour a paper cup of beer. "We've got to do something to get you in shape," the colonel said, with a feigned poke into Gordon's soft midsection. "Maybe you'd like to try our obstacle course."

He found the inevitable officers' conference at a picnic bench that was at a safe distance from where the women were spreading out the food. The military conversation faltered as soon as he joined them.

"Hey, Bob, you ready for seven innings of softball?" O'Leary asked.

He looked hesitant. "It's been a long time since I've swung a bat."

"That makes it easier," Henry Roy laughed. "If you don't hit the ball, you don't have to run the bases."

The trial was the only thing they had in common. Just as Gordon guessed, it soon became the conversation topic.

"So how's our Mexican marauder doing?" Daks asked. "Getting his things packed for Leavenworth?"

Jordan laughed at the joke, and Henry Roy added, "I hope he's packing for a long trip."

Gordon shook his head morosely. "I can't talk about the legal aspects. But let me tell you. I wish to hell we could just move the guy out. This trial is really going to hurt us. All of us."

Jordan stopped laughing. Daks lowered the paper cup from his lips. The legal officer tried to look surprised by their obvious interest.

"You know this guy's story, don't you?"

The training officers looked at each other. "What story?" Henry Roy asked for all of them.

Gordon tried to sound casual. He told them about the truck, and then about the ORDEN goons stuffing the pistol down Maria's throat.

"I remember those fuckers," Daks said knowingly. "Scum of the earth. We used to beg the officers to take them out and shoot them. There was no way the Army was ever going to win the respect of the people as long as they were buddy-buddy with ORDEN. One of the officers—I think he was a captain—said they kept them around so they could kick the shit out of people without getting shit on their shoes. I told him, 'You're getting shit all over your uniform and everything it's supposed to stand for.' He couldn't understand what I was talking about."

Gordon went on with the story, following the Cortines family up into the hills. He tried not to look at Captain Roy when he got to the part about the water being poisoned. That's why he didn't notice Carol Roy, who brought a hot dog for her husband, and stayed to hear the story.

"Did we use bacteria in El Salvador?" Major Jordan asked Captain Roy. Roy's head bobbed thoughtfully. "We showed them how to use it. Very precise doses calculated according to the water flow. They didn't bother to calculate. They'd just get far enough upstream so they weren't in any danger, and then dump a week's supply into the river. Sometimes they used so much of it, the water turned white."

While Roy was lamenting the misuse of chemical agents, Gordon hit Daks with the hand grenade. He was purposefully graphic in describing how the mine had blown Cortines's mother in half, and how the children who wandered into the minefield were thrown about like smoking projectiles. The major immediately became defensive.

"They were living with guerrillas. They knew the chance they were taking. How many innocent people do you think got blown in half every time the damn guerillas ambushed a truck? Or fired mortar rounds into a police station?"

Colonel Grigg sidled up behind the row of officers and ladies that encircled Gordon. Robert tried not to look at him, even though his next comment was aimed directly at the colonel. He fixed his eyes on Major Daks.

"You see what I mean, Gene? We're just having a conversation. But you start talking about things like this and, right away, we're on the defensive. Imagine what's going to happen when his lawyer brings all this up in court. 'Did you teach them how to plant mines so that they could blow up women and children?' There's no way Special Operations doesn't come off like a bunch of bloodthirsty killers. And then the tabloids pick up the story. Poison, booby traps, torture . . ."

Major Jordan's eyes snapped into focus. "Torture?"

"That's what it's going to sound like," Gordon answered. "That machine in the classroom! The one he hooked the Salvadoran officer up to! It turns out one of our students hooked Cortines's father up to the same kind of electrodes. And then he clamped them on to Cortines. He was thirteen at the time. Imagine when the television news guys get ahold of that."

"We shouldn't be talking about things like this," Carol Roy suddenly said from just behind her husband. "My God, we're supposed to be having a picnic with the children."

Gordon apologized. "You're right, Mrs. Roy. I started this by saying it was exactly the kind of talk we don't want to hear. I wish this case never had to come to trial."

The group fell into silence. The distant voices of the children lining up for a potato race was the only sound. Gordon listened. He guessed his message was sinking in.

"Let's play some softball," Colonel Grigg shouted like a cheerleader. He tossed a bat to Major Daks so they could use it to choose sides. The men jumped up and moved to the batting cage. Son of a bitch, Gordon thought. He'd taken his best shot, and all the colonel could think about was softball.

But after the game, Grigg managed to get him alone at one of the distant tables where they sat with their cups of beer.

"I've been thinking about what you said earlier, Bob."

Gordon tried to look puzzled.

Grigg moved to his point. "Before, when you said this trail would hurt our reputation. You're probably right. A lot of what we do in counterinsurgency is really great. Do you know that in El Salvador, we inoculated more kids against typhus than all the doctors in all the hospitals?"

Gordon knew that Special Operations put great stress on winning over the people. Providing medical aid was one of the ways they showed that the government forces had the interests of the people at heart.

"But some of the other things are a lot harder to explain. We have to fight very close to the enemy—meet him on his own ground with his own weapons. Sure, when you plant a mine, there's a chance some kid is going to step on it. But what do you think happens when a B–52 drops a bellyful of bombs over a city? The Air Force guys don't know who they kill. But we know we killed Corporal Cortines's mother. And there's nothing we can say that doesn't make us look worse than the damn communists we were fighting."

Gordon agreed. "It's a no-win situation," he said.

"Can't we keep this sort of thing out of the trial?" Grigg was plainly concerned.

The captain looked thoughtful. "It will be tough, Colonel. Cortines's best defense is to put the whole Army on trial. I know that's what I'd do, if I were defending him, and I'm not even an experienced defense lawyer. In effect, he says, 'I didn't do anything to you that you didn't already do to me.' You charge him with putting a hand grenade in Major Daks's driveway, and he says that you put a hand grenade on his mother's footpath. And all of a sudden, you're on the defensive, trying to explain why mining a valley in El Salvador is okay, but mining a driveway in Fort Marion is a prison offense."

Grigg nodded solemnly.

"It's a bitch, Colonel. There's no doubt in my mind that the Army will win its case. Cortines will get twenty years at hard labor. And with the public outcry, Special Operations will get rolled right back into the main Army where the brass can keep tabs on its little idiosyncrasies. To my mind, Special Operations is going to be the big loser."

"What do you suggest?" Grigg asked.

Gordon took a deep breath. "This will probably rub you the wrong way, but I'd declare the guy a psycho, write him up an administrative discharge, and put him on the next bus back to Texas, or California, or wherever the hell he came from. You don't need twenty years of this kid's life. But you sure as hell need to keep Special Operations intact."

Grigg drained his beer, which by this time was flat and warm. He didn't seem to notice. "General Wheeler would never buy it. He likes to keep law and order on his post."

"I suppose so," Robert Gordon agreed. "But you might ask the general how he's going to feel when the whole country knows he keeps an electric shock torture machine on his post."

*　*　*

Dave Baldinger wasn't up for a party. He had missed two training exercises because of his involvement with Mex, and Sergeant Major Thompson had been less than sympathetic.

"What do you want to be, Baldinger?" he had snapped. "A Green Beret, or a goddamn clerk on the general's staff?" There was no doubt which he considered to be the higher calling.

"A Green Beret, Sergeant Major," Dave answered without hesitation.

"Okay, then. You'll have to make up the exercises you cut."

Thompson hadn't meant sometime before Dave graduated. He meant right now.

One of the exercises was a fifteen-mile trek, up into the mountains, with an eighty-pound rucksack. It shouldn't have been difficult after the constant training on the obstacle course. But Baldinger had begun to feel the effects of his layoff by the third mile. He was panting, shuffling rather than walking, and falling behind the time allotted for completion.

"You'll get a second wind," Dickie Morgan had promised him, explaining his own experience of a few days earlier. "About halfway, I thought I was goin' to die. Then, all of a sudden, I started to feel good again."

"Bullshit," Willie Derry argued. "By the halfway mark I thought I was carryin' a piano. Thompson must have stuffed an extra couple of bricks in my bag just to bust my hump."

By the halfway point, Baldinger had sided with Derry. His shoulders were numb from the cut of the rucksack straps, and his boots were rubbing his feet raw. He collapsed by a stream, off-loaded the sack, and stretched his bare feet into the cold water. He could have quit right there. His time with Mex had cost him more than the fine edge of his conditioning. It had eroded his enthusiasm for the mission. The physical challenge seemed pointless if he couldn't believe in the results. And how could he believe in the justice of helping the landowners destroy Mex's family?

But it would be his decision. If he left, it would be after marching into Sergeant Major Thompson's office and handing in his papers. He wouldn't let them wash him out for flunking one of their damn tests.

He had dried his feet, put on fresh socks, and squatted down under the sack. Suddenly, his mental drive was more than a match for Willie's piano.

He hadn't come close to the record, but he reached the finish line before his time ran out. Then he made camp, found a meal around the roots of the trees, and started back. When he staggered into the barracks, Derry told him about the party.

"Art Walters is back. Would you believe the dumb jerks who run this man's Army? They send him down to Benning so the medics there can assign him back to the hospital here. As a taxpayer, this kinda waste makes me damn mad."

Dave managed a smile. "That's great. Tell him I'll see him in the morning."

"No way," Derry said. "We're goin' out tonight. Cavitt's out of the hospital. Art Walter's back. We're gonna do some celebratin'."

Derry followed Baldinger into the showers to make sure he didn't fall asleep, and kept talking to him while he got dressed. They picked up Luther Brown at his room and went over to the hospital for the reunion with Art Walters. Dickie Morgan, Tom Cavitt, Jim Ray Talbert, and Bobby Long were waiting at the gate. Twenty minutes later, they were sitting at the bar in a club called the Special Force. Baldinger found his bottle of beer almost too heavy to lift.

"Tough about Mex," Art Walters said when he had finished telling them how good it was to be back. They all nodded sympathetically. Art asked Dave, "What are they going to do to him?"

Baldinger shrugged. "I don't know. I guess it depends on how badly they feel about what they already did to him. Maybe they'll decide he's already been punished enough."

"We didn't do nothin' to him," Dickie Morgan said. "It was a war. People get killed."

"Not innocent people," Brown cut in. "At least they shouldn't get killed."

Derry sided with Morgan. "Who's innocent? For chrissake, his family was helping the communists. I like Mex, and I hope he gets off. But he says himself that his father was packin' ammunition for the rebels. His family was at war with us."

"They weren't at war with us, Willie," Baldinger said. "They were fighting the people who controlled all the money."

"That's what I'm sayin'," Derry argued. "When you attack money, you attack the good old U. S. of A. That's what we're all about. What do you think we were fightin' for over in the desert? You think we spent a zillion bucks just so the Emir could stay in his harem with all that squeeze?"

"Willie's right," Bobby Long agreed. "If we didn't kick the commies' butts in El Salvador, they'd be kickin' our butts in Texas. Mex was just on the wrong side of the war."

Art Walters sided with Dave and Luther. "So what are you saying, Bobby? You think Mex ought to go to jail?"

Bobby Long wouldn't go that far, but Willie Derry was more pragmatic. "Personally, I hope Mex beats the rap. But, hell, look at what he did. Hand grenades in an officer's driveway. Diarrhea juice in the water supply. And then he hooks the visiting colonel's balls up to a car battery and gives him a thrill he'll never forget. What are they supposed to do? Give 'im ten demerits and take away his good conduct badge?"

No one could dispute the point Willie was making. As the bartender set up the next round of beers, there was loud agreement that Mex had gone too far. Then Baldinger asked, "Did you know that they had Mex hooked up to an electric shock machine?"

They didn't. "He never said anything about it," Dickie Morgan recalled.

"I think he was thirteen at the time," Baldinger continued. "They tortured his father, but the old man wouldn't tell them anything. So they hooked Mex up and made his father watch."

"Jesus," Luther Brown said. "What kind of bastards were we helpin'?"

Baldinger answered, "Murdering bastards. After Mex's father told them everything he knew in order to keep them from burning his kid, they put a bullet in the old man's head."

"Nice fellas!" Willie admitted. "I'd like to get my hands on the guy who made that call."

"Mex did get his hands on him," Baldinger told them. "The guy was Colonel Maritin."

A half dozen Airborne noncoms came through the door and paused while they looked over the ladies at the tables. "Tiffany," one of them called enthusiastically, and a girl in a painted-on silver dress rose to greet them. Then one of the paratroopers recognized Art Walters, and walked over to the bar.

"For chrissake, Art. What are you doin' slummin' with these jungle rats?"

"He's improvin' his mind," Derry answered for Walters. "You jumpers have landed on your heads too many times."

The Airborne soldier squinted at Willie. Then he looked carefully down the line at the bar. "Hey, guys," he called to his friends over his shoulder. "Don't we know these creeps from somewhere?" His friends crowded up behind him.

"These the guys that torched Marty's car out at the Oaks?" one of them asked. The paratroopers began studying the faces suspiciously, and the Special Operations troops, who decided they didn't like being stared at, eased up off the stools. The bartender moved toward the telephone. It was Tiffany who saw that an evening's worth of business was about to be hauled off to jail, and diffused the situation.

"C'mon fellas," she oozed as she slid between the hostile camps. "Make love, not war!"

The Airborne leader broke eye contact with the enemy, and then his hard face softened into a smile. He draped his arm around Tiffany's shoulder. "Naa! These ain't the ones," he told his friends.

"Yeah," Derry agreed as he turned back toward his beer. "We're peace-lovin', friendly types."

It would have ended right there, except one of the Airborne soldiers was determined to have the last word. "Peaceful, my ass," he said toward Derry. Then he told his comrades, "They're all like that stupid fuckin' Mexican that's been runnin' around tryin' to kill people."

The squad might discuss Mex among themselves. But he was off-limits to anyone else. As soon as he heard "Mexican," Luther Brown was on his feet. The instant the paratrooper finished saying "people," Luther's fist crashed against the side of his jaw. Then one of the Airbornes blindsided Luther with a right cross while he was standing over his fallen mate, and nearly instantly, Willie's beer bottle shattered over Luther's attacker's head. A second later, and there were two parallel lines of men standing shoulder to shoulder, with fists flying in between. Behind the bar, the bartender was already on the phone screaming at a police officer on the other end.

Luther and the man he had punched were locked in a bear hug, rolling across the floor. They hit a nearby table like a bowling ball, and shattered it off its legs. Willie and the one he had hit with the bottle were toe to toe, until Willie brought a crisp knee up into his groin. Baldinger held one of the paratroopers by the throat and was banging his head against the bar, while directly next to him, a paratrooper held Jim Ray Talbert by the throat and was banging his head against the bar. Dickie Morgan was getting the best of a slugging match with the tallest of the Airborne soldiers, while another of the Airbornes was using Bobby Long for a punching bag. One of the paratroopers was raising Tom Cavitt high over his head, prior to throwing him at the rows of liquor bottles on the other side of the bar. Art Walters lowered his head and charged like a billy goat. He hit the paratrooper right on the belt buckle, carrying him out from under Cavitt and all the way to the dance floor.

Two of the town policemen charged through the front door swinging their night sticks. Two more came right behind them. The instant the soldiers saw the police, they began to back off. It was automatic that if the locals arrested you, you did the night in jail. And then there was double jeopardy, because the officers back at the fort threw the book at you just to kiss up to the local magistrate. The fighting stopped before the police had to arrest anyone.

"What happened here?" the police sergeant demanded.

"No problem. Just a misunderstanding," Baldinger answered. "It's all over."

"Yeah," one of the paratroopers said. "A couple of guys got in an argument. We were just breakin' it up."

The sergeant looked at the bartender, while the soldiers were brushing themselves off. "Who started this?" he demanded. The police knew that the nightclub owners didn't want all their customers hauled off to jail. But they had answered a call. They had to arrest someone.

"Those two," the bartender said. He pointed at Willie Derry and his Airborne adversary who were trying to get untangled from under a table. The paratrooper's legs were locked around Willie's waist in a scissors hold. Willie was leaning on his elbow trying to get up, but the elbow was resting on the other man's throat.

"Hold those two," the sergeant ordered two of his officers. "Go get the car and bring it around back," he said to another.

Baldinger tried to intercede for Willie. "Hey, there's no problem. Why don't we just take him back to the base."

The police officer pressed the tip of his night stick under Dave's chin. "You're not takin' him anywhere, son, because I'm takin' him in. And if you don't keep your mouth shut, you'll be goin' with him."

Derry and the paratrooper were handcuffed. Two of the policemen began leading them toward the back door of the Special Force.

Tom Cavitt eased up next to Baldinger. "We got to do something," he whispered out of the corner of his mouth. "Willie will wash out."

Baldinger nodded. He had been thinking the same thing. Willie was right on the edge of going over his demerit limit. He could handle the extra duty he'd get when they brought him back to the fort. But the demerits they would slap on him would wash him right out of Special Operations.

"We can't attack the police," he reminded Cavitt.

"Well we can't just stand here," Tom answered.

Baldinger was grasping for a plan. He reached into his pocket and handed the keys to the station wagon to Art Walters. "Bring the car around front. Fast." Art left without even asking him why, which was exactly what Dave wanted because he didn't yet have an answer. Then he noticed that the sergeant was leaving the club reluctantly. He was ogling each of the provocatively dressed women as he worked his way toward the entrance.

"Hey, Tiffany," Baldinger said.

She swung everything as she walked over to him.

"You want to make a hundred bucks."

Her eyes narrowed suspiciously.

"Half an hour's work. That's all."

"Half an hour is longer than most of you guys need," Tiffany said. "What's for half an hour?"

"Nothing like that," Baldinger told her. "C'mon, yes or no. I need you right now."

She smiled. "What do you need me for?"

"To keep my buddy out of jail. Please. It's easy. It'll only take a couple of minutes."

She seemed agreeable, so Baldinger grabbed her hand and started rushing her toward the front door. Tom Cavitt, and then Luther Brown ran after them. Art was making a U-turn in front of the club when they reached the street. They all piled into the wagon, Dave pushing the girl in, and then sliding in next to her.

"Where to?" Walters asked, already pulling away from the curb.

"The state road. Any isolated spot between here and town. And step on it. We gotta find a place before the cops bring Willie in."

They drove for nearly a minute in silence before Luther Brown asked, "What are we doin'?"

Dave turned to the girl. "What's your name?" He had completely forgotten.

"Amber," she answered.

"Okay, Amber, here's what we need you to do."

"I thought you were Tiffany." Luther said.

"Tiffany, Amber, what the hell difference does it make," she snapped. "If you really want to know, it's Louise. Now what am I supposed to do for the hundred bucks."

"Stop a police car," Baldinger told her.

"Louise?" Luther said incredulously. "Who the hell is named Louise?"

Walters turned his eyes from the road. "Luther, will you shut the hell up?" Then he asked Baldinger, "How's she supposed to stop a police car?"

"Stand on the road and show a little leg," Dave said.

Tom Cavitt looked at Baldinger as if he were crazy. "No way. The cops aren't going to pull over for a hitchhiker. Not when they got a car full of prisoners."

"You got a better idea?" Baldinger argued.

Luther shook his head. "I think we're gonna need a better idea. Tom's right. They ain't gonna stop for a hitchhiker even if she does look like . . . ." He couldn't call her Louise, so he just nodded toward her.

"I can stop them," the young woman answered. Then with a smile, she added, "Hell, I can stop a freight train."

"How?" Cavitt demanded.

"Well," she said easily, "not for a lousy hundred bucks."

They all looked at her. "How much?" Baldinger asked.

"A hundred for trying, and another hundred if I get them to stop."

Luther gasped. "Two hundred bucks. You're outta your mind."

Louise leaned back into the seat. "Hey, he's your friend. I don't care if they lock him up." She looked professionally unconcerned.

Baldinger polled his friends. "How much have we got?" They opened their wallets and searched their pockets. Together, they were able to meet Louise's fee.

"How about here?" Art Walters asked. It was a deserted stretch, with heavy trees up to both sides of the road.

"Anywhere you can pull off," Dave said.

Art slowed and found a narrow turnoff. The station wagon bounced over the shoulder and disappeared into the brush.

"Okay, Louise. We're counting on you," Baldinger said as he opened the door and turned to help her out.

In response, she extended her hand, palm upward. "Could we handle the finances in advance. That way it won't interfere with our party."

They handed her the hundred for trying.

"Where do you want them stopped?" she asked. She sounded as if it were a science, and she could bring the police car to a halt within inches of any point they specified.

Baldinger thought for a second. "About fifty yards up the road. And you have to get both cops away from the car. You have to keep them occupied while we get our friend."

Louise nodded. "Okay. Just have the other hundred ready." She stepped out on the highway, and her silver dress began swaying as she started walking along the edge of the pavement.

Luther Brown watched the swing of her hips. "She might just do it," he allowed.

Baldinger posted his attack force. Luther and Tom crossed the highway and took positions in the bush, fifty yards ahead, where Louise would be standing. He and Art Walters set up in the cover of the woods, directly across the road from them. Between them, Louise stood on the white divider stripe, shifting casually from one foot to the other.

"I don't know," Luther whispered to Tom. "She looked better walking than she does standing."

Cavitt sighed with exasperation. "So why don't you go out there and show her how to stand?"

Headlights appeared in the distance, coming toward them from the nightclub strip. As soon as she saw the lights, Louise reached around behind herself, and unzipped the silver dress. Slowly, she began to wiggle it down over her hips.

"Holy shit," Brown said.

On the other side of the road, Art Walters elbowed Dave. "I think this thing has a chance."

She stepped out of the dress and tossed it to one side. She was wearing a black bra and bikini panties. A garter belt held up her stockings.

The headlights grew clearer, and they could all hear the sound of the engine and the tires whistling in the distance. Louise reached behind her back again, and this time her hands came away with her bra. She tossed it without even looking, and it landed right on the center of her dress.

"No way her name's Louise," Brown told Cavitt.

Baldinger was smiling as he watched her undress. "I think she probably could stop a freight train," he said to Art.

The glare of the headlights was approaching quickly. In the still night air, the tires sounded as if they were screaming. Louise unsnapped the bikini pants and pulled them through her legs. All she was wearing were the garter belt, the stockings, and her silver, high-heeled shoes. When the light hit the shoes, she put one hand on her hip and then shifted her weight to one leg. Her figure, pleasing enough as it was, suddenly became a centerfold. She turned her upper body to put her breasts in profile, and then turned her head up the road, tucking her chin into her shoulder.

"Unbelievable," Luther Brown said, more in a breath than in his voice.

Cavitt nodded. "You still want to go out there and show her how to stand?"

The light beam rose slowly up her legs. When it illuminated the garter belt, they heard the scream of brakes. It rose to a pitch of agony as the police car's wheels locked up and the tail end began to break free. By now, Louise was bathed in the headlights, like the star of a show taking the key light on centerstage.

The police car was almost out of control, rocking from side to side as it slid along the pavement.

"Jesus, it's going to hit her," Baldinger said out loud.

Even with the two tons of iron rushing toward her, Louise managed to look unconcerned. She smiled seductively toward the two faces pressed up against the windshield, and at the moment when she should have been leaping out of the car's path, she pursed her lips and blew a kiss. The car skidded to a stop twenty feet from where she was standing. The instant it stopped, she turned casually, strolled over to her clothes, and bent to pick them up. She swung the bra by its strap around one finger, and tossed the dress over her shoulder. Then, with the police officers still staring out through the windshield, she sauntered into the woods, pausing for one lingering glance back toward them as she disappeared behind the trees.

Doors opened simultaneously on both sides of the police car and the two officers flew out. They ran into one another as they rushed down the road toward the spot where Louise had vanished.

Baldinger and Walters darted out of the trees and ran to the car. Dave pulled open the back door, and Art dragged Willie Derry out by his shirt collar. His hands were cuffed in front of him. From across the highway, Luther Brown and Tom Cavitt reached the car. Tom saw the keys hanging from the ignition, snatched them out and flung them into the woods. Luther pulled open the back door. When he saw the Airborne soldier, he quietly eased it closed.

"Hey, what about me?" the paratrooper called after Willie.

Willie stuck his head back into the car. "Sorry, but we're short one parachute."

Baldinger started to close the back door, but then he thought better of it. "You got fifty bucks?" he asked.

"Yeah, sure."

Dave reached inside and pulled the paratrooper across the backseat.

They glanced down the road. The police were still in the woods trying to find Louise. They dashed up to the turnoff where the station wagon was hidden and clambered aboard, stuffing the two handcuffed soldiers over the tailgate.

"Let's get outta here," Derry called from the backseat.

"We're not leaving without Louise," Baldinger said. He started through the thicket toward the point down the road where she had vanished.

"Who the fuck is Louise?" Derry asked.

"Tiffany," Luther Brown said.

"Amber," Tom Cavitt answered simultaneously.

The paratrooper looked at Willie. "You live with these guys?"

Baldinger opened the side door and pushed Louise into the backseat, which was already crowded with four. She had gotten her bra and panties back on but she was carrying the silver dress.

"I got mud all over my shoes," she complained.

Art Walters started the engine and immediately backed out onto the highway, without turning on the lights. The two police officers broke from the bushes, saw the station wagon, and began running toward their patrol car.

"Take your time," Luther told Art. "They ain't goin' nowhere."

Walters shifted gears and started leisurely back up the road toward the strip.

Baldinger twisted in his seat and called back to the deck where Derry and the paratrooper were still handcuffed. "We owe the lady some money," he said. "Your share is fifty bucks apiece."

"Fifty bucks!" Willie Derry was outraged.

"That's the fare," Luther told Willie. "You ain't got fifty bucks, you can get off here."

The paratrooper volunteered enthusiastically. "I got fifty. Here. Right here." He began tossing about on the back deck as he tried to find his pockets.

"Do you take plastic?" Derry asked Louise.

They stopped on a side street, a block away from the Special Force. They figured the police were probably looking for them, so they sent the girl to get Bobby, Jim Ray, and Dickie.

"So, where we going?" Derry wanted to know. The fact that he was wearing handcuffs didn't seem to lessen his need for a night on the town.

"Nowhere," Baldinger said. "The cops will be all over our places."

The paratrooper piped up. "We could go to the Garter. The cops don't dare go into that place."

"Sure," Derry said sarcastically. "Green Berets in the Garter with all you airheads. We'd last longer in downtown Tehran."

"No problem," the paratrooper said. "I'll tell the guys that you sprung me. You won't be able to buy a beer. I swear."

They sat silently considered the offer. Then Cavitt said, "I wouldn't mind drinking free beer. Especially since Louise has all my money."

"I'm game," Brown added.

A car pulled up beside them. They were about to duck down out of sight when Baldinger noticed that Louise was driving. Two of her girlfriends were in the front seat. Dickie, Jim Ray, and Bobby were squeezed into the back.

"Where are we going?" one of the ladies called out to them.

Baldinger shrugged his shoulders. "The Garter, I guess."

Louise smiled. "This ought to be one hell of a night," she told her friends, and then she stepped on the gas. The procession moved out onto the strip and headed toward the Garter.

The paratroopers owned the place. Airborne unit patches were displayed as artwork behind the bar, and an open parachute was hung across the ceiling rafters. It was crowded and noisy, but the conversations seemed to soften when they appeared in the doorway, and every eye followed them as they snaked around tables and found a booth in a far corner.

"Friendly bunch," Willie Derry whispered to Luther Brown. "About the kind of open-armed greeting we'd get in Hanoi."

Luther took in the hostile faces. "I hope your friend from the police car knows some of these guys. If he don't speak up for us, we're dead meat."

They had nothing to worry about. A waitress in net stockings carried a dozen cold bottles to their table, compliments of a group of jumpers who were standing by the bar. Tom Cavitt went over to them to say thanks, and brought six of them back with him. One of them saw Derry's handcuffs and assured him that they had already sent out to the parking lot for a hacksaw.

"You guys really sprung Danny right outta the backseat of a cruiser?" one of the men asked in awe.

"Routine," Jim Ray Talbert assured him. "It's one of our practice exercises. Any of you guys get caught behind the lines, just call our eight-hundred number."

When they heard about Louise's role in the rescue they insisted that she join them. When she came to the table, they coaxed her into a repeat of the strip act that had stopped the police car. "Right out in the middle of the highway?" they asked, shaking their heads. "Or in your bedroom," she answered with her mischievous wink. They listened to her version as well as the several variations of the story that came from the Special Operations unit.

"You guys are all right," an Airborne spokesman concluded. He semaphored toward the bar and ordered another round of beers.

Then someone asked about Mex. "That son of a bitch nearly killed me. I got sick during the parade, and had two days of the worst case of the shits I've ever had in my life."

"I'd like to get my hands on that little bastard," another added. "What kind of guy puts poison in the drinkin' water? Jesus, even the little kids were sick as dogs."

"That's a damn good question," Dave Baldinger interrupted. "Let me tell you exactly what kind of guy puts poison in the drinking water." He began telling them Mex's story, just the way Captain Gordon and he had heard it. The merriment began to subside and the group grew quiet. More and more of the Airborne soldiers wandered up to the booth and stood listening at the back of the crowd. Before long, Dave's voice was the only sound. That, and the scratching noise of the hacksaw that was being used to cut off Derry's handcuffs.

"So we used it, and then we taught our friends in El Salvador how to use it. And that's how Mex learned about it. His mother was carrying one of the sick kids when she stepped on the mine that had been planted on the trail." No one commented, so Dave added, "By the way, we taught them how to plant the mines, too."

They shuffled uneasily. The saw sound continued and there was an occasional clank of beer bottles. "So, what are ya sayin'?" a paratrooper asked. "Ya sayin' it's our fault that this guy is crazy?"

"Naah," Baldinger answered, fondling the neck of an empty bottle. "I'm not saying anything. I'm just asking. And I'm asking because I don't know the answer. Maybe you can tell me. Why is it okay when we do it to them, but coldblooded murder when they do it to us? Why does a guy get a medal for planting mines in someone's front yard in El Salvador, but gets twenty years to life for doing the same damn thing in someone's front yard at Marion?"

"It ain't the same thing," an Airborne solider answered instantly. "Marion ain't a battlefield. It's where we live. No one's got any business comin' into my home and plantin' mines or poisonin' the water. Nobody, no matter what the fuck he thinks we done to him."

There were grunts of agreement, and then silence as they waited for Baldinger to say something. But he didn't answer. Instead, he nodded in agreement and raised a bottle for another swallow of beer.

"That's the same answer Mex would give," Art Walters finally said. "That dirt village was his home. And he could say no one's got any business coming into his home and planting mines or poisoning the water. Nobody. Not even us."

"Yaa-hoo!" Willie Derry jumped up and waved the sawed-open handcuffs over his head. "Now I can get my arms around somebody." He scooped up Louise, spun her around, and carried her toward the dance floor. There was a roar of approval from the soldiers, and they carried their beers toward the center of the room where Willie and Louise were beginning to shake to the beat of the music.

The sun was up when they staggered back through the gate of Fort Marion. Art Walters took his leave and headed back toward the hospital. The others took the road to the trainee barracks. When they reached their building, they saw Sergeant Major Thompson waiting in his jeep.

"I hope you been getting plenty of rest, Baldinger."

Dave fell out of the meandering rank and came to attention. "Yes, Sergeant Major," he snapped.

"That's good," Elvis Thompson answered with a hint of a grin under his sunglasses. "Because you've still got an exercise to make up." He shifted the jeep into gear. "Be at my office, oh-eight-hundred. Full battle gear."

               ★   ★   ★

Colonel Grigg had been right in his assessment of General Wheeler. When he had suggested that the Cortines trial might not help the Army's image, and that perhaps they should find an administrative solution rather than a legal one, the general had reddened with rage. He had pounded his desk so hard that the water pitcher had toppled, spilling water across his papers. "That little son of a bitch is going to the stockade, and he's going to stay there until you and me are both retired, Grigg. There's no way in hell I'm going to let him off with an administrative discharge."

Grigg had repeated Captain Robert Gordon's arguments. "The kid was victimized by his own government. A government we were helping. Everything that happened here at Marion had already happened to him in El Salvador. I think the publicity could put the Army in a very bad light."

"We're not going to try anything that happened in El Salvador," Wheeler had snapped. "We're going to try what happened here at Fort Francis Marion. And if Captain Gordon doesn't see it that way, I'll get a staff judge advocate officer who does."

All Grigg succeeded in doing was getting Gordon summoned to the general's office. Gordon tried to remember the procedure for saluting Wheeler at his desk. He recalled that Baldinger had marched across his own office, stopped two paces from his desk, come to attention, and rendered a salute. It seemed simple, but when he stepped into the general's office, his plan came apart. Colonel Grigg was standing next to Wheeler's desk, and he didn't know whether he was supposed to salute both of them, or simply ignore Grigg and follow Corporal Baldinger's example. He was already at the desk before he made up his mind.

"Good morning, sir," he said to the general as he rendered the salute.

Wheeler had a simpler procedure. "Sit down, Captain," he ordered, without attempting to return the greeting. He folded his hands on the edge of his desk. "Colonel Grigg tells me that you think this Cortines crap might embarrass the Army. I called you here so that there won't be any misunderstanding about exactly what I want to have happen."

"Sir," Robert Gordon tried, hoping he would be able to repeat his argument. But General Wheeler hadn't paused to listen. He had paused only to take a breath, and continued right over the interruption.

"What I want is to get this piss-ant case closed and off my desk." He tapped a file folder that rested on his desk blotter. "What I have here are reports of three separate incidents of criminal activity. And I have your investigation report that says this Miguel Cortines is the criminal. Now what I need is a court-martial record and a paper clip. Then I can send the file to Washington, and put this whole damn incident behind me." He paused to give the brevity of his message the instant it should take to sink in. "You have any problem with that, Captain?"

"General, what I'm trying to do is to keep you from having any problem with it. As I said to Colonel Grigg—"

"I heard what you said to Colonel Grigg," Wheeler interrupted. "But I don't want any mention about El Salvador, or any of the details of Corporal Cortines's deprived youth coming anywhere near the courthouse. I want an open-and-shut case."

Gordon drew a deep breath. "General, this isn't a military ceremony that we can arrange. It's a legal trial. The accused has a right to a defense. If we violate any part of that right, the case will never pass review. You'll find it back on your desk before Cortines leaves for Leavenworth."

Colonel Grigg sensed that Wheeler was close to his flash point. He spoke to save Gordon the sting of Wheeler's anger.

"The general doesn't want anything violated," he told the captain. "I think he wants things expedited."

But it was too late for splitting words. There was anger in his voice as General Wheeler squeezed out, "What I want, Captain, is loyalty. Loyalty to me personally. And loyalty to this command." He glared across the desk, but his voice softened a bit as he continued. "I know you're not a field officer, Captain. I know that your first report is to the lawyers in Washington. So maybe you don't get my meaning. Loyalty is what this Army is all about. Loyalty to one another. Loyalty to the mission. That's what builds a winning command. And winning commands win wars."

Grigg tried again. "I think we can count on Captain Gordon's loyalty, General." The two senior officers locked onto the legal officer and waited for his answer.

Gordon had no room for escape. "General, if we bring this man to trial, it's my responsibility to assure that he has a proper defense. I beg you to find some other way."

Wheeler's eyes lingered on the man across his desk. Then he said, "Captain, I'm going to bring in a more experienced judge advocate officer to handle this case. Hold yourself available in case he needs your help." His eyes fell from Gordon back to the papers on his desk. "You're dismissed, Captain."

Robert was stunned by the abruptness of the decision. Even Grigg registered his surprise. Gordon stood unsteadily, backed a pace further away from the desk and saluted. He didn't expect any acknowledgment from Wheeler, and he wasn't disappointed.

General Wheeler didn't look up until he heard his office door close. Then he shook his head slowly, more toward the empty chair where the captain had been sitting than toward the colonel. "I don't know why we let bastards like him into the Army," he said softly. "We pay his college, put the son of a bitch through law school, give him a commission and a post, and then he turns on us. How in God's name are we supposed to protect this country with people like that in the ranks?"

Grigg understood his commanding officer. It was okay for junior officers to express an opinion and, within their specialty, even to give advice. But Gordon had overstepped himself. Once his commanding officer decided, his clear duty was to get with the program.

"Don't worry about it, Colonel," General Wheeler told him. "I'll talk to a couple of friends, and we'll have a new staff JAG down here tomorrow. One who knows what loyalty is all about. And while I'm at it, I'll see what I can do to help Captain Gordon earn his tuition.''

The general was true to his word. Late the next afternoon, Major Cletus O'Brien, Army counsel on the staff of the judge advocate general, was delivered by executive jet to the airstrip at Fort Francis Marion to take up the prosecution of Corporal Miguel Cortines. O'Brien was a big man with a round, pleasant face and a shock of red hair that he had difficulty keeping in place. He had a weight problem that kept him moving up and down the scales between two hundred and two hundred fifty pounds, and his waistline gyrating between forty-five and fifty inches. When he arrived at the post, he was close to the high end of his specifications. No one would mistake him for a battlefield commander.

He was long removed from prosecuting court-martials, having spent the past two years consulting on the legal aspects of Army supply and real estate contracts. But he did have a three-year background as a public prosecutor. He had graduated from West Point, put in his obligatory years of service, and then opted for civilian life where he became a lawyer. But he had undergone a change of heart. He was single, with no romantic interests, and unhappy living alone. He missed the comradery of his fellow officers, and the patriotic overtones of military life that seemed to give the most routine duties a higher purpose. He had been readmitted to the army as a reserve officer and had been assigned to General Wheeler's staff during one of the general's earlier stints at the Pentagon. Wheeler had been instrumental in helping him transfer from the reserves back into the regular Army. In his own mind, he was a solider who happened to be practicing law, just the opposite of Captain Gordon, who considered himself a lawyer who happened to be wearing a uniform.

He greeted the general as an old friend, and then joined him and Colonel Grigg at the officers' club for dinner, where he was briefed on the problem at Fort Francis Marion. He listened attentively while he enjoyed a rare steak and a bottle of claret, asked a few questions, and then put the paperwork on the case into his well-traveled briefcase. ''I'll study this carefully,'' he promised the two officers, ''but from what you tell me, I don't see that we have any real problem. The rules of evidence in a military court are pretty much the same as in criminal courts. Generally speaking, anything that isn't connected with the indictment is irrelevant and inadmissible. We simply won't allow any testimony or evidence about the soldier's problems in El Salvador.

And we're certainly not going to allow any testimony connected with past Army activities. None of that would have anything to do with the case at hand.''

Wheeler leaned back from the table with a sigh of relief. ''Good to have you here, Clete,'' he told his new staff judge advocate.

Grigg's eyes were still narrow with concern. ''Gordon indicated that a defense lawyer might plead insanity, and claim that the kid was unbalanced by what happened to him and his family. That's how all this stuff could get into the trial.''

O'Brien shook his head. ''If the kid's crazy, we can't even try him. But from what you tell me, it would seem this guy was very much aware of exactly what he was doing.'' He paused for a moment of thought. ''I suppose he could try an insanity defense, and then have some shrink introduce his past problems with the military as part of his diagnosis. But that would all be pretrial stuff. It wouldn't be something that would come out in an open court.''

He finished off his drink, and tossed his napkin onto the table. ''First thing we have to do is get this guy a defense counsel. From what you say about the evidence, I don't think it should be too hard to get agreement on a guilty plea. From then on, it's just a matter of paperwork.''

Wheeler and Grigg were in good spirits as they left the club. Major O'Brien obviously had the professional skills to protect the interests of the command. And he seemed to know the meaning of the word *loyalty.*

O'Brien dug into his assignment early the next morning, reading the reports on each of the incidents and the details of Captain Gordon's investigation very carefully. Then he turned to the charges that Gordon had prepared, and compared them chapter and verse with the requirements of the Uniform Code of Military Justice. He was impressed. Gordon had pulled the noose of circumstantial and hard evidence tight around the neck of the accused, and had expertly avoided every conceivable legal loophole in drawing up his indictment. From all appearances, it was exactly what General Wheeler wanted: an open-and-shut case.

The only thing that O'Brien found puzzling was Gordon's failure to move the case promptly to a court-martial. He still hadn't appointed a defense counsel, something that O'Brien would have done the moment the charges were prepared. Now a delay in getting the matter off General Wheeler's desk was inevitable. The defense counsel would have to be given reasonable time to review the charges and prepare a defense. He wondered why Gordon's efforts seemed to have ground to a halt, and couldn't understand why the captain had hesitated to prosecute an issue that seemed so simple, especially when he was getting pressure from the base commanding officer. O'Brien picked up the phone and called Gordon's office with an invitation for the captain to join him for lunch.

He liked Gordon immediately when they met on the steps of the club, and was impressed by the credentials that the captain presented. Inexperienced, to be sure, but well educated, highly motivated, and obviously sincere. Idealism was an attractive characteristic of young lawyers, and it was probably what impressed him most about the captain. The reality, of course, was that it was a professional handicap. He guessed quickly that it was probably the cause of his falling out with General Wheeler. The general, he knew from his past assignment, was oriented toward results, which was probably the most important character trait for a successful military career. How the results were achieved was of secondary importance, a battlefield philosophy that he had carried over into all his military responsibilities.

Gordon explained the delay quite simply. By the time he had drafted the charges, he had learned a great deal about the man who was being charged. He had come to the conclusion that Corporal Cortines had already been victimized enough, and that further punishment really wasn't called for. And, he had seen how a public airing of the Cortines case might prove embarrassing to the Army in general, and to Special Forces in particular.

"I was kind of caught in the middle, Major," he summarized. "Serving the interests of the Army meant limiting the possibilities of the kid's legal defense. I guess I was still trying to make up my mind where my duty was."

O'Brien pretended to be sympathetic to the young officer's problem, but actually he was marveling at the man's naivety. For a soldier, there was no possibility of a dilemma. Your duty was to serve the will of your commanding officer.

The major was genuinely touched by the details of Corporal Cortines's story. He winced in real pain when Cortines's mother stepped on the mine, and he had to wave away the detailed description of torture that the soldier's father had undergone.

"Awful. Christ, that's awful. How can people do things like that to one another." Then he added, "I can see your point, Bob. The corporal hasn't gotten a very fair deal out of life."

"I keep thinking," Gordon said, "that he wasn't trying to kill anyone. He's told me as much. I think he was trying to show us just what we were doing. And, in a sense, he got his message across. Every officer I interviewed was sick at the thought that Cortines had planted a mine where it could kill or maim innocent women and children. Major Daks told me that he wouldn't have been offended if the guy had confronted him directly, or taken a shot at him, but he was outraged that the corporal had left a grenade where it might kill the paperboy. Yet that was exactly what the major had done in El Salvador. It was exactly what he was teaching to the Special Operations trainees."

O'Brien saw the point. But he reminded Gordon, "He could, of course, have used less dangerous ways to make his point. He could write an article, or get himself on one of those junk television shows."

"Cortines has never been in a school," Gordon reminded the major. "The only time he sat in a classroom, the curriculum was on planting hand grenades and poisoning water holes. I think his actions were based on the only training he's ever had."

Gordon then explained his efforts to get Cortines out of the Army on an administrative discharge. "Who would it hurt?" he asked O'Brien. "The Army would be spared any potential embarrassment, and the kid might be able to salvage the rest of what's been a pretty miserable life.

"Certainly a reasonable approach," O'Brien agreed. Then, after a thoughtful pause, he added, "But it's all academic now. You've drawn the charges, and General Wheeler has ordered that they be presented to a court-martial. I guess the thing we have to do right now is get the boy representation. Did you have anyone in mind?"

"He asked me to defend him," Gordon said. "I'm not sure how to respond."

"A simple 'no,'" the major suggested. "You can't defend him. You drew up the charges. Besides, you're about to be transferred."

"Oddly, enough, I could defend him," Gordon contradicted O'Brien. "If the accused asks me to defend him, I'm allowed to accept no matter what role I've played in the investigation. And I don't think the Army could transfer a defense counsel out from under his client. Not if they hope to get the verdict past a review board."

O'Brien had to search his memory of the Uniform Code of Military Justice. Gordon, he realized, was right. He could defend a man against charges that he himself had drawn up. "Maybe it's legal, but it wouldn't be very smart. He has no case."

"I think I might be able to make a case out of his story. Everything he did had already been done to him. By people our Army trained. I think if General Wheeler and Colonel Grigg know that's the case Cortines is presenting, they might not be so anxious for a trial."

The major smiled mischievously. "You're talking about putting the Army on trial."

"It's the corporal's best defense," Robert answered.

"You know what you'd be doing to yourself?" Cletus O'Brien suggested. "You know what a stunt like that could mean to your future in the service?"

Gordon nearly laughed. "I don't think it's much of a future."

The major stared at him for several seconds, taking the measure of the young officer. He had to admit to himself that he liked what he saw. "Do yourself a favor, Bob. Don't even think about getting involved. Jesus, General Wheeler would have you drawn and quartered. Colonel Grigg would lean all over you. Believe me, you don't need the grief."

Gordon nodded through the entire litany. "You're right. It would be a dumb move, and I'll probably turn Cortines down. I wish they'd just give the kid his walking papers."

"You take on the defense, and they'll go easier on the kid than they will on you. In it's simplest form, you'd be a traitor, betraying the Army's trust. No wonder the general wants you out of here. Hell, you're dangerous."

Gordon bristled under the word *traitor*.

"You're an attorney, Major. What would you do," he asked, "if you found yourself prosecuting an innocent person?"

O'Brien answered without a second's hesitation. "As you say, Bob, I am an attorney. So I don't concern myself with issues of guilt and innocence, or right and wrong. What I do is apply the law as carefully and skillfully as I can in the interest of my client. Your client was General Wheeler. If you don't mind my saying so, I think you've fucked yourself royally. And all out of sympathy for a guy who can't win."

He saw that Gordon was confused by his answer. "You do understand that there's no way in hell you could win this case by putting the Army on trial? Oh, you might be able to muddy the water. Maybe you could even introduce a few bits of information about vitally necessary military operations that will embarrass the Army in the minds of a few simpletons who don't understand the reality of war.

But when it's all over, Corporal Cortines is going down, and if you're his attorney, you'll be going with him."

"You're that confident," Gordon challenged.

O'Brien realized that their confrontation was about to become personal, and that wasn't what he intended. "Not confident in myself, Bobby. I'm not for a moment suggesting that I'd prove to be a better litigator than you are, or that I'd whip you in the courtroom. But I am confident in the system. Your jury wouldn't be a sympathetic public. It would be a panel of Army officers who think their careers count for something and who are very bit as committed to the service as General Wheeler and Colonel Grigg. They wouldn't be very patient with suggestions that they are somehow responsible for this man's troubles. They don't think they hurt anyone in El Salvador. Christ, Bobby, El Salvador is one of their triumphs. If you tried to make it sound like a tragedy, all you'd do is get them real mad at you, and real mad at your client. You'd get the poor kid hung instead of just imprisoned."

He waited for Captain Gordon to fight back. When there was no response, he switched to a more matter-of-fact tone. "Take my advice and stay out of it, Bobby. The court will judge the evidence. Did or did not Corporal Miguel Cortines plant a hand grenade in a private residence with the total disregard for the safety of the inhabitants? Did he or did he not introduce a potentially deadly bacteria into a public water supply, injuring hundreds of women and children with God knows what terrible future repercussions? Did he or did he not assault, kidnap, and inflict cruel and unusual punishment on a foreign officer who was a guest of the United States Army? And, as you have so skillfully documented, they will answer 'yes' to every one of those questions. Jesus, Bobby, you're not jousting with windmills. You're beating your own heart out on a stone fortress."

"You're right," Gordon admitted. "It's just that Cortines has already been through hell."

"So let's get him a good lawyer who will plead the kid guilty, explain his impoverished background, and beg the court for leniency." He smiled at Gordon. "Someone who won't even suggest that the Army is anything but the noble defender of all our freedoms. It doesn't make sense to insult the people whom you're about to beg for mercy." He lifted his glass to his lips. "Lousy strategy," he allowed as he took a sip.

"He'll go to jail," Gordon said.

"He's already in jail," O'Brien countered. "All we're arguing about is for how long."

Gordon weighed what he had just been told. And he measured the oversized man with the pleasant face who had just given him the advice. He didn't agree with O'Brien's cynical separation of justice from the law. But he respected the experience that stood behind his opinion. The man was probably right, and his advice was probably on target.

"Thanks," he said with a nod. "I guess you're right. You've probably just saved my ass." He reached for the check.

O'Brien beat him to it. "No, if you were going defend Cortines, General Wheeler would be all over me. You may have just saved my ass."

Gordon went straight from the club to the base stockade, and asked to see Corporal Cortines. As he waited in the visitors' room, he rehearsed the grim speech he was about to make. There wasn't anything terribly hopeful that he could offer the corporal. Just good legal advice.

He heard the sound of the shackles dragging on the floor even before Mex was brought into the room. He watched as the guards began removing the handcuffs and leg irons, but he turned his face away before they started to unbuckle the thick leather belt. He couldn't watch the corporal's humiliation. The chains seemed more fitted for a wild animal than for a human being. They belonged on the torturers more than on the tortured.

"Cortines, I've just met with the attorney who's going to prosecute you. The Army's lawyer."

Mex's eyes lit up. "Then you're going to defend me."

Gordon hated his own words. "I'd like to . . . but I can't. It wouldn't be in your best interest."

He saw the confusion roll like a cloud across Mex's face, and then the disappointment when his words registered. He kept talking so that he wouldn't have time to visualize a Roman magistrate washing his fingers in a basin of water. "I was trying to get the Army to drop the charges against you. I hoped to get you an administrative discharge so that—"

"I don't want 'em to drop no charges," Cortines interrupted. "I want to tell 'em what they did."

"Corporal," he was pleading more than lecturing, "what they did to you will never be discussed in a trial. The only thing that anyone will be allowed to talk about is what you did to them." He repeated parts of his conversation with O'Brien, pointing out that the officers of the court wouldn't take kindly to having the conduct of their operations in El Salvador called into question. "We'll get you a good lawyer, Cortines. The best one available. I think he'll advise you to admit what you did, and help you put together a plea for mercy."

"I ain't goin' to beg anyone for mercy," Mex said. "All my life I been beggin'. Not no more."

Gordon didn't know why, but he reached across the table and took the young soldier's calloused hand. "Believe me, this is the best way. It could cut your sentence in half."

Mex pulled his hand away. "Why won't you defend me? Don't you believe me?"

"Of course I believe you. But if I start defending you, the officers on the court are going to get mad. First, at me. And then at you. They'll come down on you harder."

"It don't matter," Mex said. "I ain't gonna spend time in prison no matter what they say. What matters is makin' 'em know what they did to us."

"They won't listen. They don't want to listen."

"Please," Mex said. "You can make 'em listen."

He knew what Major O'Brien would say. "You gave him your best advice and he turned it down. Let a different attorney try. You don't have to saddle yourself with his stupid opinions of how the law ought to work. You'd be a fool to climb on board a sinking ship."

Gordon stood up slowly. "I can't do it, Corporal." He watched Cortines's shoulders sag. "I'll get you a lawyer. A damn good lawyer."

As he walked away, he heard the rattle of the chains that the guards were bringing toward the prisoner.

He dug for the bottle of scotch that he kept in back of his lower desk drawer. It had been there for a couple of months, and he was surprised that he hadn't yet broken the seal. He filled a paper cup from the water cooler and then nearly choked himself as he tried to toss it down. He was sipping it slowly when Corporal Baldinger tapped on his door.

Baldinger looked close to death. He was in dirty, sweat-soaked fatigues, his face pale, and red-eyed from an obvious lack of sleep. He made no pretense of rendering a military salute, but simply touched his forehead as he collapsed into a chair.

"You all right?" Gordon asked.

The young corporal nodded. "Yes, sir. Just beat."

"What the hell happened to you?"

"Just making up some of the training I missed. Sergeant Major

Thompson is trying to tell me that he has a low opinion of lawyers. I don't think he likes me being involved with Mex."

"They hassling you?" Gordon demanded.

Baldinger shook his head. "No. I don't think so. Thompson just doesn't want me to get distracted." Then he asked, "How's Mex doing?"

"Fine," the captain said. But then he overruled himself. "No, he's not fine. He's all fucked up." Gordon briefed Dave on his being replaced as the staff legal officer, and told him about the gunslinger that Washington had sent down to prosecute the case.

"Your friend wants his day in court, but there's no way he'll get to tell his story. And he wants me to defend him. But if I do, all I'm going to do is get him screwed to the wall."

The attorney explained his dilemma to the corporal in full detail, pacing back and forth behind his desk. "So the best thing we can do for Mex is get him a lawyer who will plead him guilty. But that's the one thing Mex doesn't want to do."

Captain Gordon noticed the drink he was holding in his hand. "Why don't you close the door, Corporal, so I can pour you one of these. Right now, I could use a drinking buddy."

Baldinger stayed in the chair. "Sir," he asked, "do you think Mex is guilty?"

Gordon couldn't think of a way to soften his answer. "Yeah, legally, he's guilty as hell."

"I don't mean 'legally.' I mean, does he deserve to go to the stockade. Because it seems that if he belongs in prison, then there's a lot of guys wearing Salvadoran Army uniforms who ought to be in there with him. And maybe a few guys wearing our uniform, too. Do you see what I mean, sir?"

Robert Gordon saw exactly what he meant. "No, I don't think he deserves to be in prison," he agreed as he paced behind his desk. "And yes, if he should be in prison, then there are a lot of top ranks who ought to get to share his cell."

"That's what I think, Captain. Most of the guys don't agree with me, but I just can't shake it. I think about everything that's happened to him, and about what he did, and I just don't think he should be in the stockade for the next ten years."

Gordon nodded in agreement as he walked back and forth, sipping from the paper cup.

"I don't really know why I joined the Army," Baldinger continued.

"I guess I was just bored. But once I got into it, I liked it. I liked the idea that I was working damn hard to be one of the good guys. I think that's why I signed up for Special Operations. I didn't just want to be a good guy. I wanted to be the best."

Gordon smiled. "I know what you mean. I think that's why I went to law school. I wanted to be a good guy." There was bitterness in his voice.

"Then shouldn't we be using our training to keep Mex out of prison?" Baldinger asked.

Gordon stopped and put down the drink. The corporal's simplicity was disarming. "Yeah, that's what we should be doing. Only we can't. This is one time that the good guys can't win."

Baldinger looked at him, unwilling to accept his decision. Gordon finished the drink and then crushed the cup in his fingers. "Why don't you get some sleep, Corporal. You look beat."

Dave lifted himself wearily out of the chair. "Good night, Captain." He started for the door, but then he stopped, leaning against the door frame. "You know, sir, most of these training exercises are stacked against us. We can't win. But we keep fighting. And every once in a while we come out on top." He turned through the doorway. "Good night, Captain," he repeated.

Gordon slumped into his chair. They were crazy. Mex who wanted his day in court. Baldinger who wanted to keep fighting. What was the matter with them? Didn't they understand what he was telling them? Didn't they know that they couldn't beat the system? What was he supposed to do, risk the rest of Cortines's life and bring the whole command down on his own head? Why? Just because it was right?

"Yeah," he mumbled to himself. "That's what I'm supposed to do."

He pushed the bottle back into the corner of the lower drawer. "Crazy," he told himself. "Dumb, stupid, crazy."

Gordon paid a call on Major Cletus O'Brien the next morning. Before he sat down, he told the new staff judge advocate, "I'm going to defend the kid, Major. And I'm going to plead him not guilty."

O'Brien studied the captain. "What changed your mind?"

"A pair of dumb corporals," Gordon answered. "They're not big on quitting."

"They're not big on common sense, either," O'Brien said. "I think you're making a mistake."

"You ever see a man in chains, Major?"

Cletus O'Brien didn't understand the question.

"Or a guy who just wanted to be the best?"

"What do you mean?" O'Brien asked.

"I mean that I'm not making a mistake," Robert Gordon said.

"Your funeral," the major sighed. He handed Gordon the list of charges, which he proclaimed "properly served," and the names of the witnesses he planned to call. "I'll need a chance to interview your witnesses," he added.

"I haven't got any yet," Robert admitted sheepishly. "I'm going to need a few days."

O'Brien looked at him skeptically. Then his face softened into a grin. "Tell you what," he said. "Why don't I get you off the hook. I've been thinking about offering you a deal."

Gordon's interest was unprofessionally obvious, so the major outlined what he had in mind.

"This kid has already paid for his crimes. No one wants to see him spend the rest of his life in Leavenworth."

"Except General Wheeler," Robert interrupted.

"Naah. General Wheeler doesn't give a damn about Corporal Miguel Cortines. He's got a crime. He needs appropriate punishment so he can get the mess off his desk. The simpler the better. He'll be satisfied when a report showing that he's a hard-assed commanding officer hits the mailroom in the Pentagon."

"So what do we do?" Gordon asked.

O'Brien reached across the desk and took back the charges he had just given to the captain. "Suppose I toss two of these out. Forget the grenade. There's nothing solid that ties it to your client. And forget the shock torture. Your boy fits Colonel Maritin's description, but so do lots of people. I'll charge him with poisoning the water because that's the one where I've got physical evidence. I've got the bottle with his fingerprints. You plead him guilty, and I'll recommend a sentence of, oh say, five years. That's not that bad for attempted mass murder."

"Five years is a long time," Gordon contradicted.

O'Brien smiled. "You're a fast learner. Okay, say I recommend three just in case the court doesn't agree and wants to add a couple of years. Your client will be out while he still has most of his life ahead of him. General Wheeler will be satisfied that justice has been done. Colonel Grigg will be delighted that we won't have to haggle over the past sins of Special Operations. You'll be back in the good graces of your commanding officer because I'll tell him how helpful you were.

And, most important, I'll be able to get out of this snake pit. Do you know there isn't a decent French restaurant for a hundred miles?'' He paused to let the opportunity sink in. Then he asked, ''What do you think?''

''I think I'll discuss it with my client,'' Gordon said.

''I think you should recommend it to your client,'' the major added.

''How much time does he have?''

Cletus O'Brien pursed his lips. ''He shouldn't need more than a second. I'm giving away the case. But let's say by the end of the day. Oh, hell, why don't we make it ten-hundred tomorrow morning. I was hoping I might get in nine holes this afternoon. In fact, if you can convince him in the next hour, you could join me. You do play golf, don't you?''

Gordon was ecstatic. He had been staring at twenty years of hard labor, and now it was down to three. If Mex kept his nose clean in the stockade, he would probably be out in two. But he could already see the corporal shaking his head, and hear him insisting that he wanted vindication, not mercy. There was every chance that Mex would turn him down.

Of course, Mex was right. It was the officer who had dropped the grenade into his father's truck, and the ones who had poisoned the village water and salted the ground with explosives who should be on trial. The officer who had attached his father to the shock device, and then put a bullet in the back of his head probably didn't deserve a trial at all. He should be taken straight up to the cliff at Puerta del Diablo. But the fact that he might be right didn't count for much. What Gordon had to make him understand was that the people who had beaten the insurgents in El Salvador didn't have to answer to anyone. They were the winners. He, on the other hand, was a loser. He had been caught in a criminal act, and had to answer to a court of military officers. Like it or not, that was the fact. And then he had to make Mex look at the cold reality of spending his life in the stockade.

He brought Dave Baldinger with him when he went to the prison.

''We can win this one, Corporal,'' he told Dave. ''We can get him off with a slap on the wrist.''

Baldinger wasn't as enthused as Captain Gordon. ''I don't think he'll like it, sir. He wants the Army to hear him out. And he probably won't think that three years in Fort Leavenworth is just a slap on the wrist.''

Gordon thought of some of the exercises that had been described in the Special Operations school catalog. "Look, Baldinger. When you go to rescue a downed flyer from an enemy prison, you win if you bring him home alive, right?"

"Yes, sir."

"Maybe it isn't perfect. Maybe he's wounded. Or maybe he's exhausted from the ordeal. But if you get him back alive, you've done your job."

Baldinger nodded. "I suppose so, sir."

"Okay," the captain said. "This morning I signed onto your mission. I agreed to help you bring your friend back alive. I can't make it perfect, Corporal. I can't guarantee that he won't be bruised or maybe even wounded. But the prosecutor is giving us a damn good deal. We can get our man back alive. That's what I want you to explain to Corporal Cortines."

Gordon sat back and listened as Dave explained the alternatives to his friend. "I know it's a bitch," Dave sympathized. "But you've made your point. That's why they're dropping most of the charges. They know you don't deserve to be in prison. They know you're right."

"Then let them say so," Mex interrupted without looking up from his hands that were resting on the table. "Let them admit what they did, and go find the people who did it."

"Mex, that isn't ever going to happen. You know it won't. When was the last time you ever heard an officer admit he was wrong about anything?"

"I didn't do anything to them that they didn't already do to me," the prisoner answered. "I wanna tell them that to their faces."

Baldinger sighed and leaned back from the conversation. "Okay, Mex. If that's the way you want it. You know I'm with you. All the guys are with you."

Gordon saw O'Brien's deal slipping through his fingers. "No you're not," he snapped at Baldinger. "Nobody's with him. There won't be anyone with him in the courtroom, and there won't be anyone with him in the stockade." He turned pleadingly to Cortines. "You asked me to defend you, Corporal. And that's what I've done. I've gotten the rest of your life in prison cut down to three years. Maybe even less. You'll be out of the stockade before you would have been out of the Army. You want to tell them what they did to you. Let me tell you something. They won't even listen. And if they happen to hear what you say, they won't even care. You want to know why? Because

246

they don't want to know. Now maybe that's not the way you think the world ought to work. But listen to what I'm telling you. That's the way it works. Do you understand me? That's the way it works."

Mex was still looking down at his hands. Nothing that Baldinger had said or that Gordon had said had caused him to stir.

"Look, Cortines," Robert Gordon tried in calm, measured tones. "It comes down to this. You can shout your case to the wind, because that's the only one who will hear it. And you'll pay for the privilege with twenty years of hard labor. Or, you can say that you did what everyone already knows you did, and walk out in three years. I'm not asking you to admit that you were wrong, or to agree that what they did was right. Right and wrong aren't the issues. All I'm asking you to do is admit that you poured a chemical in the water system. Hell, you don't even have to say it. I'll say it for you. Now, those are your only choices. And to my mind, it's no contest. I'm telling you to take the three years. Why can't I get that across to you?"

Mex raised his eyes. "Maybe because you didn't see your mother get blown in half."

Gordon could only stare at him in disbelief. For an instant, he was angry. So angry that he wanted to grab Cortines by the neck and pound his head against the wall until he beat some sense into him. But slowly in dawned on him that they weren't talking about what was practical, or what made sense. They were talking about having your mother blown up, your sister disfigured, and your father shot through the head by someone who probably didn't even know whom he was shooting. Maybe, when all that has happened to you, where you spend the rest of your life isn't the issue. Maybe the important thing—the only important thing—is to try to do something so that it never happens again.

"What do you want me to do, Corporal?" the captain asked.

Mex shrugged as if the answer were obvious. "Get me my day in court."

Gordon called Cletus O'Brien and turned down the deal. The trial officer seemed surprised. "I think you're letting things get away from you, Bobby. You're supposed to be directing the defense, not running errands for your client."

He told Robert to stop by and pick up the charges, and added, "All three of them," just to show that there would be no further consideration for Corporal Cortines.

In the morning, Gordon got another hint at what he was up against.

When he reached his office, there was a staff officer already sitting behind his desk. A different corporal was guarding the reception area. "I understand that you're being transferred, sir," the corporal said apologetically. "Lieutenant Mills has been assigned to your space."

Gordon charged into Major O'Brien's office with his protest seething on his lips. But O'Brien was already holding up a soothing hand. "Your transfer has been delayed," he announced before Robert could say a word. "I told the general that you couldn't be transferred during a court-martial to the disadvantage of your client. He understands, and nothing is going to happen until after the court-martial."

"I'll need an office, damn it."

"Hey, be reasonable," the major said. "You got the general damn mad at you, and you can't expect him to be worried about finding you new office space. It's probably going to take a couple of days."

Captain Gordon searched around town, and found an empty office at the firm of Amos Granger, Esq. "Hell, half our practice is suing the Army," Amos explained as he introduced his two associate attorneys and the one legal secretary that they shared. He showed Robert into the back office that overlooked a yard, where a continuously barking dog was leashed to fence. "Grace will give you hand with the typing when she's not doing our work, and I suppose you can keep track of your long-distance calls."

The long-distance calls started immediately as he tried to find eyewitnesses to any of the incidents that had destroyed Mex's family. He could bring them in as character witnesses, and maybe bring the corporal's ordeal into the record through the back door.

He reached the minister who had run the underground railway that smuggled Mex and his sister out of El Salvador.

"I remember the Cortines family very well," the minister told him. "Fine young people. We were able to place Miguel with one of our parish families, and Maria—was it Maria?—yes, yes, Maria . . . with another family."

"You processed them through Immigration?" Gordon asked.

The line went silent for a few seconds. Then the minister's voice said, "Captain, I'm not sure how much you know about what was going on at the time. We weren't working with Immigration. We were hiding the Salvadorans from Immigration. The Immigration people were trying to find them to send them back."

"Back? To El Salvador?"

The reverend sighed at painful memories. "You have to remember that we were allied with the Salvadoran government against the Salvadoran people. It was assumed, as a nicety of diplomacy I guess, that anyone the Salvadoran government was attacking had to be on the communist side. They weren't allowed to claim status as political refugees. And that was the only way they could stay in the country. So the Immigration people had to round them up and send them back.''

"And you were hiding them? From the authorities?

"We were. It got very difficult because my parishoners are law-abiding citizens. We really weren't very good at disobeying the law. But, we're also God-fearing people, and we simply couldn't obey a law that required us to turn these people over. So we hid them. In our garages. Our basements. I had two families living in the rectory while I was sleeping on a cot over in the church. All in all, I suppose we were harboring over a hundred fugitives.''

Gordon was stunned. "Here? In the United States?'' He was thinking of the families in Holland, and the churches in Italy, that hid Jews from the Gestapo. "In California?''

"Maria was discovered,'' the minister continued. "The family that hid her is still being prosecuted in court. I think Miguel stayed in hiding until the government declared an amnesty.''

"Do you know how I can reach her?'' Gordon asked. "Miguel says she was sent back, and he doesn't know what happened to her.''

"We know that she was arrested as soon as the plane landed. Personally, I doubt whether she's alive. I think she would have contacted the family that was hiding her if she could. They grew very close. The family was taking her to a doctor here to see if something could be done for her mouth. A plastic surgeon.''

"Reverend, can you help me find anyone who might have firsthand knowledge of what happened to Miguel and his family?''

There was nothing about the activities of the Salvadoran government and its military that the minister knew firsthand. But he was able to supply the names of two people who had escaped with Mex, and the name of the Jesuit priest who had been living in the hills with Mex and his family. Neither of the people were known to anyone at their last addresses. It figured. They were fugitives, and they had probably been careful to cover their tracks. It took him five more calls to find out that the Jesuit priest was dead. He had been captured and executed by the Salvadoran Army. It was beginning to look as if Mex was the only living witness to his family's tragedy.

He would ask Baldinger to line up some of the trainees as character witnesses, and get Mex's training records from Sergeant Major Thompson. Anything that would indicate that Mex wasn't a wild-eyed fanatic, but rather a good soldier. He wrote his thoughts out in longhand. He could certainly use a secretary, but he could hear Grace's typewriter laboring over the affairs of Amos Granger, Esq.

He was still writing when Granger stuck his head in to tell him that they were finished for the day. While he was giving Gordon a key, Amos looked over his shoulder and saw what he was working on. "Does the defense ever win one of those court-martials?"

"Not often," Robert admitted.

Granger shooks his head. "Funny. When we sue the Army for money, we win every time."

It was growing dark by the time he had finished his preparatory notes and turned to the charges and the witness lists that Cletus O'Brien had given him. He would start by drafting petitions for dismissal. All the evidence on the hand grenade and on the electric shock torture was circumstantial. As O'Brien had reminded him, the only charge that was supported by physical evidence was the one relating to the water supply. If he could have two of them thrown out, then the sentence that Mex was certain to receive would at least be a lighter one.

He heard a knock on the building's front door, knew it couldn't be for him, and ignored it in the hope that the person would go away. But when the knocking turned into pounding, he let himself out of the law offices and went down the stairs to the front door. Dave Baldinger was there with two other uniformed soldiers.

"This is Willie Derry," Baldinger said, pointing to the boyish looking redhead, who responded to the introduction by firing a shot at Gordon with his thumb and forefinger. "And Luther Brown," he said of the muscular black soldier who gave no acknowledgment at all. Gordon led them back up the stairs and pushed Grace's desk chair into the small office for an additional seat.

Derry opened a brown paper bag and produced two six-packs of cold beer. "We figured you might be able to use one of these," he said.

Gordon pulled the tab and joined the soldiers in a lengthy gulp. "How did you know where to find me?" he asked Dave as he blotted his lips with the cuff of his shirt.

Baldinger gave him the rundown on the noncoms' grapevine. "The corporals always know before the generals," he said proudly. Then he pulled a thick roll of cash out of his pocket, set it on the edge of Gordon's desk, and carefully pushed it toward him. "Something else you can probably use," he explained.

"What's that for?" Gordon demanded.

"Expenses," Baldinger answered. "We don't want you paying out of your own pocket."

Gordon hesitated so Willie Derry added, "All the guys wanted a piece of this. Hell, even a couple of Airbornes kicked in." The defense attorney looked suspiciously at the stack of bills. There was a twenty on the top and a fifty on the bottom. He guessed it was over five hundred dollars.

"Thanks," he said, "but I can't." He started to push the money back toward Dave. Luther Brown's huge hand landed on top of his.

"We insist," Luther said, and he moved the pile back toward Gordon. The argument ended right there.

"What else do you need?" Baldinger asked.

Gordon gestured at the scattered sheets of yellow paper. "Some office help, if any of you know how to type."

Derry nodded. "We'll round up a couple of company clerks and have them here in the morning." He glanced around. "Looks like you could use a computer and a printer. Probably a copier, too. We'll see if the Army can lend them to you."

"The Army can," Luther assured.

Robert enjoyed the beer and then raised the subject of witnesses. Everyone in the squad, he was assured, would want to put in a good word for Mex.

They finished the two six-packs and then walked down the stairs together. It was the best moment of Robert Gordon's day. He realized that he wasn't the only person trying to save Corporal Miguel Cortines.

Willie's recruits arrived the next morning, even before Gordon did. When he stepped through the door into the law office, Amos Granger, both his associates, and Grace were all standing at the entrance to the back office, looking in with awe. Robert peeked over their shoulders. There was a long table that hadn't been there the night before. On the table were two personal computers and a laser printer. There was a young man seated in front of each of the computers trying to make sense out of the scribblings he had left behind. A huge copier took up the whole back wall under the window. It was like the one in base headquarters that could turn out a hundred copies a minute.

"Just who in hell are you defending?" Amos Granger asked in nearly reverential tones.

"Amos, I really didn't know about this," Gordon started to apologize.

"It's okay. Okay," Amos nearly sung as he herded his assistants and Grace away from the doorway. "The boys said they'd start on our work as soon as they finished yours."

The two clerks snapped to attention as the captain entered the room. He reached out and shook their hands. "Thanks, fellas. I really appreciate this. I'm Bob Gordon." They introduced themselves and immediately went back to work.

"Oh," one of the soldiers suddenly remembered, "that dog out back wasn't yours, was it, sir?"

Gordon realized that the backyard was deathly silent. "No," he answered suspiciously. "I just heard him barking yesterday."

"Well, you won't hear him today," the other soldier said without looking away from the words on his screen.

Gordon had a terrible image of what had probably happened to the mutt. The clerk nearest to him read his anxiety.

"Nothing serious, sir. The dog wanted off the leash, so we let the dog off the leash. Then the guys who brought the copier took him for a ride in their truck." He turned to his friend. "Where the hell was it they were heading?"

"Someplace in Ohio," his friend remembered.

Late in the morning, he was back in Cletus O'Brien's office to present him with his petitions for dismissal of the charges and the lists of witnesses he had been able to gather. The major thumbed through the material. "I don't think this stuff will fly," he said. "Courts generally like to hear the evidence before they decide whether or not it proves anything." He stopped when he saw the witness list. "You got to have more than character witnesses," he said in surprise.

"I need a few more days," Robert answered. "People who escaped from El Salvador aren't on a mailing list. I'm having trouble finding anyone."

"I still think I can get that deal for you," O'Brien mentioned casually. "The sooner we can wrap this up, the better we'll look to General Wheeler."

"I think we're past that," Gordon said, almost sadly. "My client has been trying to deliver a message. He wants to make sure he gets it across, even if it's going to cost him the rest of his life."

"Crazy," O'Brien said, wagging his head.

Gordon drove back to the law office, planning an evening of phone calls to some of the other pastors on the Salvadoran underground railway. He met Amos Granger, charging out of the front door with one of his associates in tow. "You've got a visitor," Granger warned him. "A very attractive young woman. She's in the waiting room." He was puzzled until he opened the office door and saw Carol Roy seated on the uncomfortable leather sofa. She was wearing a plain dress decorated with a colorful scarf.

"I was in town," she said, looking up from the magazine. He settled into the chair opposite her, and felt Grace's eyes peeking up from over her keyboard.

"I guess you're pretty busy," Carol continued. "I just thought I'd stop in and see how you were doing."

Gordon admitted that things were hectic, and gave her a polite rundown of what was involved in preparing for a trial. But while he was talking, he was wondering why she was there. Certainly she understood that this was the enemy camp.

"I thought you might need some help," she told him, "although I guess there's not much I can do. I type a little. And I know how to do research."

He tried to end the small talk. "You really shouldn't be here. I'm a pariah back at the fort. You'll let yourself in for a lot of grief, and it certainly won't help the captain."

She nodded that she had already thought about it. "You're a dirty word at the officers' club, all right. Corporal Cortines would beat you hands down in a popularity contest. I think they're more interested in seeing you get your butt kicked than they are in sending the guy to jail. I told Henry that all you were doing was defending him. That's what lawyers are supposed to do. Henry said maybe that made you a good lawyer, but it also made you . . ." She smiled as she tried to recall her husband's actual words: "a backstabbing mother something or other."

"If it wasn't me, they would have appointed another officer to represent Cortines. The man has to have a fair trial."

"They know that," Carol said. "But they don't think another officer would come at them so hard. Henry's really afraid that you're going to make him sound like a mass murderer for the kind of work that he does. And Colonel Grigg is frightened stiff that you're going to make Special Operations look like a bloody band of bandits in front of the regular Army officers on the court."

For an instant he wondered whether Captain Roy knew she was here. Could he be hoping that she might be able to coax him into going easy on Special Operations? "I didn't want any of this to happen. I warned the colonel, and I think the colonel agreed with me. But General Wheeler isn't concerned with the reputation of Special Operations."

"The wives won't even talk about it," Carol went on. "Marilyn Daks had us in for coffee this morning. Planning a flower show. We talked about everything except the court-martial. You know that's what everyone is thinking about, but no one says a word. It's like a crazy conspiracy. We have a problem, but if no one mentions it, then maybe it will go away. We know what our husbands do for a living, but if we don't think about it, then we don't have to come to grips with it."

"I'm sorry—" Gordon started, but Carol cut off his apology.

"Don't be. The fact is I'm hoping the trial will bring it all out into the open. Because that's what we need. That's what Henry and I need, anyway. Someone has to get Henry away from all the macho talk. Take him out of Army for just one minute and say, 'Look what you're doing. This isn't a mark-two, antipersonnel hand grenade. It's a terrible explosive that can cut people in half. This isn't an anti-insurgent bacterial agent. It's a poison that can rip a child's stomach open and leave him to bleed to death.' And then Henry has to decide whether that's what he wants to be involved with. And then, maybe, Henry and I can decide what we want to do for the rest our lives."

Gordon raised his hands in a gesture of helplessness. "I'm sorry, Carol. I don't want to confront anybody. I just want to stop this kid from disappearing into a stockade."

But she wasn't thinking about Cortines. She was thinking about herself. "The wives won't do anything that might break the scabs on top of their wounds. The sores aren't as ugly if they don't look at them. But honest to God, I can't live that way. I can't keep hiding from the truth. At the end of our flower show meeting, when all the wives were leaving, I asked Marilyn if it didn't bother her. 'What doesn't bother me?' she asked, as if she didn't know what I was talking about. And then she said, 'Don't let it bother you either. Don't even think about it.' So she knew damn well what I was talking about."

She realized that her monologue was beginning to ramble. The captain's expression was more confused than sympathetic. "I'm sorry," she apologized. "I just needed to talk about it. I couldn't think of anyone else I could talk with."

She gathered up her purse. "But you must be busy. I really shouldn't take up your time. Good luck at the court-martial. I hope you can help the corporal."

He walked her to the stairs. Then he warned her, "Carol, there aren't going to be any winners in this trial. Corporal Cortines will lose, and the Army will lose, and I've already lost. Do yourself a favor. Do me a favor too, because I really care about you. Don't let yourself get involved. Just stay on the sidelines with the other wives. I'd hate to see you become one of the losers."

He smiled toward Grace when he returned to the office, but she pretended not to notice that he had ever left, or even that Carol Roy had ever been there. In the back room, he found the stack of work that the renegade company clerks had prepared for him and went through it carefully. Then he began preparing his cross-examinations. He didn't have much time left. The court-martial was scheduled to convene at 1400 hours the following afternoon.

The
Trial

★   ★   ★

The court-martial convened.

Five commissioned officers and two noncoms, all in their best dress greens, filed into a bare classroom that had been stripped of the teacher's furniture and students' desks. They paused for an instant behind the seven microphones that had been positioned on a long table covered with gray felt. Then they sat between the American flag and the command colors, which flanked the table.

To their left, Miguel Cortines, in full dress, replete with his campaign and achievement ribbons, sat at a bare wooden table with his counsel, Captain Gordon. They ignored each other, Gordon lifting files of papers out of his briefcase while Mex glanced curiously at the proceedings, almost like a child on a visit to the zoo. Directly behind them, standing at rigid parade rest, were the two military police sergeants who had brought Cortines from the stockade. They wore helmets and white belts that held side arms and billy clubs, indicating that they didn't buy into the presumption of innocence.

To the right of the court, directly across from the defense table, Major Cletus O'Brien settled down beside a woman first lieutenant who was serving as his assistant. The lieutenant disguised an attractive face with a short, efficient hairstyle, and she busied herself with O'Brien's papers. The major leaned back in his chair, avoiding eye contact with either the court or the accused, pretending to find the ceiling fascinating.

Two enlisted clerks were at a pair of desks that filled the space between O'Brien's table and the court. One was loading a fresh cassette into the recorder to capture the record of the trial.

In the center of the room, surrounded by the three parties to the trial, was a single, straight-backed, wooden armchair. It was placed in the intersection of the sight lines between the trial counsel, the defendant, and the court, and would be the only comfort offered to the witnesses.

When everyone was settled, the room fell completely silent. The only sound was the distant hum of the air conditioner that was obviously unaware of the gravity of the moment.

The president of the court, Colonel Fred Elder, slipped wire-rimmed glasses over a weather-hardened face, cleared his throat, and announced, "The court will come to order." He then began reading the order of General Wheeler, which established the proceeding and appointed all its members. Elder, a regimental commander with the Airborne division based at Marion, had been a classmate of Wheeler's, a full sixty numbers below the general in class standing. He had eschewed prestigious staff posts, preferring the more physical challenges of leading his men in the field. His choice had made him a favorite with his troops, who had learned to appreciate his decisiveness, but to avoid his moments of lightning temper. Both O'Brien and Gordon had guessed that he would run a fair, no-nonsense court.

Elder's gravelly voice and an East Texas drawl made the document sound as routine as the recitation of the breakfast menu at a roadside diner. The officers whose appointments he read, included two majors who commanded Airborne battalions, and a captain from the Supply Corps. The Airborne officers wore sculptured jackets over athletic shoulders. The Supply captain looked completely comfortable behind the desk. None were particularly anxious to be sitting in judgment. The fifth officer, Major Drew Brinkman, was the staff judge advocated at Fort Hamilton, rushed down from New York to serve as trial judge, the court's nonvoting legal authority. He was an attorney with twelve years' legal experience, admitted to the federal bar as well as the New York State bar. His pale complexion and delicate frame announced that he didn't throw hand grenades or jump out of airplanes.

The noncoms, who were at the opposite ends of the gray table, were both sergeant majors wearing paratrooper wings and jump boots. Both were broad-chested enough to display arrays of campaign ribbons that covered twenty years of America's foreign excursions. Both seemed annoyed at the prospect of being kept indoors for the rest of the day.

Colonel Elder, following a typewritten script, asked if the defendent were present. Gordon stood to affirm that he was. Elder dropped to the next line of his text and asked if the defendant had been served with the charges being brought against him. Gordon answered that he had.

Elder then turned to the trial counsel for a reading of the charges. The first lieutenant, whom O'Brien introduced as Lieutenant Monica Nugent, read each charge clearly in a loud, firm voice.

The court's president then turned back to Cortines and asked him to affirm that he had heard and understood all the charges. It was at this point that Robert Gordon rose to present his petitions. Colonel Elder, his prepared script thrown out of order, looked toward Major Brinkman for help. The legal officer dipped his chin, advising the president that it was all right for the court to receive the documents.

Gordon stood behind his table as he gave a brief summary of each of the petitions. First, he asked that two of the charges, pertaining to the hand grenade and the kidnapping of the Salvadoran officer, be withdrawn.

"As the court will see from the Army's list of intended witnesses and exhibits of evidence, there is no testimony or physical evidence that directly links the accused to either of these acts. Rather, the Army assumes that all three acts were committed by the same individual. Because this assumption is unsubstantiated, we petition the court to withdraw these charges from further consideration."

Gordon handed the document to Sergeant Robinson, one of the clerks, who, after noting it, handed it to Colonel Elder. The colonel, without even glancing at it, passed it to Major Brinkman. Cletus O'Brien received his copy and set it down in front of Lieutenant Nugent.

"The defense further petitions the court for an adjournment and reasonable postponement of these proceedings," Gordon continued. Mex looked up at his attorney in surprise. Postponement? He didn't want a postponement. He had waited long enough.

Gordon cited several precedents from the Court of Military Review, which upheld the accused's right to counsel from the moment an investigation begins to focus on him. Because of his own reassignment, Gordon said, there was a delay of several days in assigning defense counsel. Then he added that since his assignment, he had had less than a week for discovery.

"The accused is faced with charges that, if substantiated, could cost him many years of his life. Certainly, the Army can spare him a few months in which to prepare his defense."

Again, Brinkman signaled to Elder that he should accept the documents, and copies were recorded and passed to all parties.

Gordon's last document was a petition for change in venue. It was risky, because questioning the ability of jurors to render a fair verdict wasn't a good way to win their sympathy. But he reasoned that there wasn't a great deal of sympathy for his client to begin with.

He explained that the crimes specified in the charges involved incidents occurring at Fort Francis Marion. "All members of this court have been directly involved in at least one of the incidents charged. In some cases, members of their families have been personally involved. Further, on a closed military base, none could have avoided hearing rumors of the progress of the investigation, and none could have been unaware that the accused was arrested as the suspected perpetrator. It would be unreasonable to assume that none of the members has formed any opinion about this case. Convening this court at another post, under the jurisdiction of a different commanding officer, would eliminate the strong potential for bias that exists here at Fort Francis Marion."

While this last petition was being received and recorded, Major Brinkman suggested to Colonel Elder that the court adjourn until the next morning to consider the petitions. The colonel cleared his throat and repeated Brinkman's words for the record. Then he ordered the prisoner returned to his cell.

"Why are we stalling?" Mex asked quietly while the MPs were fastening his handcuffs. "I want to tell 'em what happened."

"We're not stalling," Gordon whispered back to him. "We're trying to get you set free."

"I want to tell 'em," Mex repeated as the guards turned him toward the door.

As soon as the court filed out, Cletus O'Brien crossed past the witness chair. "What are you pulling?" he asked. "You could have brought all this up in pretrial. You know none of that stuff is going to fly."

Gordon looked up from his papers. "What pretrial? This is all happening too fast. The general is trying to stampede this kid, and if you rush it through, I'm going to have a case for the review board."

"So, what do you want? A couple of extra days? What's that going to buy you?"

Gordon was ready with his answer. "I want a couple of months. And I want this tried somewhere else. Maybe in New York, or Washington, where someone will care about the kid's story."

"Never happen," O'Brien said.

The captain looked at his opponent long and hard. "Do you really think officers who report to General Wheeler can be objective about this? Do you think Airborne officers and a pair of paratroopers are going to take a liking to a Green Beret?''

O'Brien broke the confrontation. ''Let me buy you a drink? I'll stop by that hole-in-the-wall office of yours in an hour.''

Gordon smiled. ''Bring ice. The refrigerator is broken.''

One hour later, O'Brien struggled up the stairs from the street to the offices of Amos Granger, Esq. He could see Gordon through the open door to the back office, so he strolled straight in and closed the door behind him. He set a bottle of gin and two quarts of tonic on Gordon's desk, two plastic picnic glasses, and a small bag of ice cubes. Then he collapsed in a chair and watched the captain fix them each a drink.

''I heard about these computers,'' he mentioned, waving toward the table with the word processing equipment. ''You have a bigger staff than I do.''

Gordon studied him for an instant. ''I don't want these guys to get into any trouble.''

O'Brien waved away the suggestion. ''Naah! They're just trying to help a buddy. What do you think? That I'm going to tell the general that he's missing half his office equipment?''

The major sipped a bit, and then eased into his subject. ''I chatted with Drew Brinkman, our trial judge. Nice guy. I think I may have met him before.''

Gordon drew on is drink. It was O'Brien's meeting. Obviously, there was something he wanted to discuss.

''He made the same suggestion that I made to you. He wondered why we were making such a damn fuss over something that was open and shut. So I told him the kid's story. He was really touched.''

''What suggestion?'' Robert asked.

''That we cut a deal. I told him I'd recommend three years for a guilty plea on the water thing. He said recommend one year, and he'd talk the court into accepting no more than two.''

''Sounds generous,'' Gordon agreed without showing any traces of enthusiasm.

''Christ, Bobby, on some posts you can get two years for missing the urinal. He's practically letting your kid off free.''

''My kid wants his day in court,'' Gordon shrugged.

''And your job is talk him out of it. Look, we go in tomorrow and we tell the court we've got a deal. They throw out the charges on the hand grenade and on plugging the Salvadoran into the light socket.

You plead the kid guilty on putting the shit in the water. Brinkman will negotiate the sentence and we'll all be on the golf course before lunch.''

"I don't think my client has his clubs with him," Gordon said.

"You're right. I'm sorry," O'Brien answered sincerely. "It was a dumb, insensitive remark, and I apologize. But how in hell can you take him to trial at a minimum of ten years, even if you do get two of the charges thrown out? You ought to be able to teach him to count. One to two isn't as long as ten to twenty.''

Gordon nodded in agreement over the top of his drink. "I've told him, Major. And his best friend has told him. When we got done telling him then he told us. He wants the Army to understand what it did in El Salvador.''

"Jesus," O'Brien sighed. He finished the drink and began fixing himself another. "Well, it isn't my ass. Why should I give a damn?'' He tasted his efforts and nodded his appreciation. "It's just that I feel sorry for him. He shouldn't have to rot in the stockade just because he's stupid. Somebody has to help him.''

"I'm trying," Gordon answered.

"Not hard enough," the trial counsel corrected. "You're not getting through to him. Who in hell would risk twenty years when he can walk away free in less than two?''

Gordon smiled, remembering it was exactly the same question he had put to Cortines. He gave O'Brien Cortines's answer. "I guess somebody who's seen his mother blown in half.''

The major's expression froze, his lips squeezing into a thin, colorless line. "Yeah, maybe so," he allowed. "Jesus, it must have been awful.''

He downed his drink. "I'll leave the gin with you. I think you're going to need it.'' He picked up his cap, buttoned his jacket. "See you in court," he said with a sigh of disappointment.

As soon as he was gone, Amos Granger tapped on the office door and sauntered in. The bottles and plastic glasses were still on the table.

"Can I fix you a drink?" Robert offered.

"Never touch the stuff," Amos answered, and settled into the chair that O'Brien had just vacated. "Been to too many tent meetings, I suppose. Too many preachers calling it the devil's brew. But you go right ahead.'' Gordon capped the bottles and put them in his desk drawer.

"I couldn't help overhearing your guest. What is he? The prosecutor.''

Gordon nodded. "We call him the trial counsel. He's the Army's prosecutor."

"Sounds like a man in trouble," Amos said.

The thought made Robert chuckle. "I should have his troubles, Amos. He's got an airtight case."

The attorney pursed his lips. "I wouldn't be too sure about that. He was practically begging you to take a deal. People with airtight cases don't need deals."

Gordon explained that there was potential testimony that the Army didn't want on the record. "The defendant wants to say some things that the Army doesn't want to talk about. The problem is that most of the things he wants to say are inadmissible. They're irrelevant. The court will stop him before he gets to say two words, and I can't seem to get that across to him."

Granger's eyes lit up. "So you bring it in during cross-examination. You get their witnesses to say what you want said."

Gordon was obviously interested, so Amos launched into a folksy explanation. He had defended a farmer named Billy against an assault charge. The man had beaten up a neighbor who was stealing his chickens. He knew the guy was a thief but he couldn't catch him in the act, and he couldn't prove it, so he had taken the law into his own hands. "Now, there was no jury in the county that was going to convict my client for settling the score with a chicken thief. Around here, a chicken thief is the lowest form of humanity. But, hell, I couldn't just say the guy was stealing chickens. I had no proof. And what my client thought wasn't evidence. The prosecutor would never let him say it on the stand. So, anyway, the doctor gets up and tells the jury how badly this guy was beaten up. Cuts, bruises, an awful description. I can see the jury looking at my client like he's a bloodthirsty brute. He's as good as in jail. And I'm half-afraid to cross-examine the doctor. The last thing I want is more gore being poured out in front of the jury."

Amos began to smile at the memory. Gordon waited for him to go on.

"Just to kill time, I ask the doctor if the victim was in good health before the incident. 'Sure,' he says, and then to drive the nail into my client, he adds, 'and I oughta know, because I'm his doctor.' I was foundering, but I had to say something, so I asked, 'Have you seen him recently?' Damned if he doesn't answer, 'Yep. About six months ago when he got all cut up in the barbed wire around Billy's chicken coop.' "

Gordon began to laugh.

"Just like that," Amos said. "The state's witness tells the jury that the guy is a chicken thief, and all of a sudden my client is a hero. The whole jury is wishing he'd hit the son of a bitch a lot harder."

"You got an acquittal?" Robert asked.

Amos answered, "Just as good. I got a hung jury. And the prosecutor wasn't about to start a new trial over a chicken thief."

Gordon opened the file that listed the Army's witnesses. "I don't think there are any chicken thieves in here," he said.

Amos reached into his pocket and took out his glasses. "You never know. Why don't we just take a look."

The court-martial reconvened at 0900 hours the next morning. Cletus O'Brien rose immediately to argue against the defense motions.

"There is no cause to withdraw any of the charges or specifications," he claimed. "These charges were drawn up by the same officer of the court who now argues against them. At the time, he decided that the court had every right to hear the evidence, to dismiss charges for which no case is made, and to find the accused innocent of any charges on which there was reasonable doubt. I agree with that decision.

"And there was no undue delay in appointing defense counsel," he continued, addressing the second of the petitions as he sauntered across the room toward the defense table. He stood next to Gordon as he pointed him out. "Captain Robert Gordon, then serving as staff judge advocate, was in consultation with the accused from the very first moment, days before a trial counsel had been appointed. When he decided to defend the accused he was already completely familiar with the case." He slipped his hands into his pockets and gave Gordon his most pleasant smile. "If anyone should be asking for more time, Captain, it's probably me."

Finally, he addressed the petition on a change in venue. He walked directly up to the felt-covered table and spoke intimately to each of the officers. "Court-martials are specified in the Uniform Code precisely to allow commands to conduct trials of their own personnel. The underlying assumption is that the officers and men of the United States Army have the intelligence and the integrity to provide a fair trial for one of their fellow soldiers. The defense motion—unintentionally, I'm sure—seems to call that intelligence and integrity into question."

As he watched O'Brien walk quietly back to his table, Gordon could feel the eyes of the court boring into him. The major had just defined the characters in the drama, and had cast him in the role of the villain.

It was theater, not law, and he realized that his opponent was a master actor. Gordon was reciting legal precedent to a jury of fighting men. O'Brien was giving them meat to chew on. Why offer them a poor immigrant corporal who might arouse their sympathy, when he could give them a backstabbing, turncoat officer, who had no regard for their intelligence and integrity? The first act, Gordon realized, had gone against him.

The court recessed for only a few minutes, scarcely a polite interval, before returning with its decision. The petitions were denied. Lieutenant Nugent stood and read the charges once again. Gordon rose to acknowledge that Corporal Cortines had heard them and understood them.

Then Colonel Elder read the charges one at a time. After each charge and specification, he looked up from his notes, peered over his glasses at Corporal Cortines, and asked, "How do you plead?"

Each time, Gordon responded, "Not guilty."

The Army's opening statement was a model of brevity, demonstrating that there was nothing complicated about the case.

"The government will show a direct linkage among the three events charged," O'Brien promised the court, standing directly in front of Colonel Elder. "We will show similarities in missions and technique that will demonstrate that all three were the work of the same assailant. Further, we will show that Miguel Cortines had the training, the knowledge, and the skill to be that assailant. And finally, we will link the accused to one of the events with irrefutable physical evidence."

He nodded confidently. What could be simpler? What could be more straightforward? Then he turned and called his first witness.

Captain Martin Johnson was the ordnance expert from Major Daks's staff who headed the investigation of the grenade explosion. O'Brien led him through a recitation of his experience and impressive credentials, and then through the analysis that had determined the location and type of the explosive.

"You say it was a grenade mine, Captain?"

"Yes. On ordinary hand grenade that had been partially armed by removal of the safety pin. It was placed in the driveway so that the arming handle was held in position by the terrain. The handle was released by the impact of Major Daks's car, and the grenade detonated."

"Is that the normal use of hand grenades, taught to infantry combat personnel?" the trial counsel asked.

"No, sir," the witness said.

"Which Army forces are taught this technique?"

"Special Operations Forces," the captain answered.

O'Brien emphasized his point. "Would anyone trained for Special Operations be able to set a grenade, like a mine, in this manner?"

"Yes, sir. It's a requirement for completing the weapons course."

"Thank you, Captain," Cletus O'Brien said cordially. "You've been most helpful."

Colonel Elder turned to the defense counsel and offered him the opportunity for cross-examination. As Gordon rose, Mex tugged at his sleeve. "That's the way they set mines around our villages. Make him tell about that."

Gordon nodded reassuringly toward his client. But he wasn't nearly as confident as he tried to appear. "Get their witnesses to bring in your arguments," Amos Granger had coached him. The problem was that he didn't have Amos Granger's courtroom experience, and judging from the morning's performance, he wasn't in the same league with Cletus O'Brien. He began the cross-examination from behind his table.

"Captain, forgive me, but I'm confused. Did you say this explosion was caused by a mine or a hand grenade?"

"By a hand grenade used as a mine. The pin was removed and the arming handle served as the trigger."

It's theater, Gordon reminded himself, as he put on his most baffled expression. "What determines when the grenade explodes?"

One of the noncoms on the court chuckled, and Captain Johnson smiled at the innocence of the question. "When someone steps on it, or near it, and disturbs the terrain, the arming handle springs free."

"Forgive me, Captain, but I'm still not quite sure I understand. How does the grenade determine that the person who steps on it, or near it, is an enemy soldier?"

O'Brien's chin snapped up. He suddenly saw exactly where Gordon was going. But he had no reason for objection. He had plainly set the groundwork for questions on the use of grenade mines in his direct examination. The defense counsel had an open door and a wide open playing field.

"It doesn't sir," the witness answered, having a hard time keeping his composure in the face of such asinine questions. But then he decided to strike a serious note. "That's what makes placing the mine in a driveway so rotten . . . so cowardly. Anyone could have been killed by it. A woman. A child."

Gordon got up slowly and circled around the table. "I recall you testifying, Captain, that using a hand grenade as a mine is something taught just to Special Operations Forces. Why is that?"

The witness answered precisely. "Because Special Operations troops are usually operating in counterinsurgency situations, among indigenous populations, and outside of normal supply channels. They have to carry what they need on their backs. So they learn to make multiple uses out of everything they carry. The grenade serves as both a thrown weapon, or as a planted mine. We also teach them to make flares and fuses out of the black powder in their rifle rounds."

Robert was still trying to appear unthreatening, his questions leading no place in particular. The captain was still involved in the dialogue, but the members of the court were clearly losing interest. They didn't need a lesson on the art of mining. But Cletus O'Brien, who understood exactly what was happening, was squirming on the edge of his chair.

"I see," Gordon allowed. "And they might need to mine a route or a path used by the insurgents and the indigenous populations."

"That's correct, sir." There was a hint of sarcasm in the "sir." The witness was showing his annoyance at being questioned on his specialty by someone who didn't understand the first thing about the use of military weapons. The defense counsel was wearing a uniform, but he might as well be a damn civilian.

"And, as you have explained, Captain, the mine has no way of deciding whether it kills an insurgent soldier, or a woman or child. Just as the mine that was placed in Major Daks's driveway might just as easily have killed a woman or a child?"

The court was suddenly awake, the captain suddenly cautious.

"I'm not sure I understand the question, sir."

O'Brien started to rise. Gordon rushed his next question.

"And I don't understand the difference. Why is it rotten and cowardly to place a grenade mine in Major Daks's driveway, but approved Army policy to teach our people how to set the same mine on a pathway used by Corporal Cortines's mother in El Salvador? Those mines did, in fact, kill women and children."

"Objection," O'Brien said, bounding out of his chair. "There is no basis in evidence to support charges about mines causing deaths anywhere. And how mines can and might be used in various combat zones goes well beyond the scope of my direct examination. It's completely irrelevant to the court's deliberations."

Gordon went back to his table and checked his notes before he countered. "I believe the trial counsel's exact question was 'Which Army forces are taught this technique?' and the witness answered, 'Special Operations Forces.' I'm entitled to explore the accuracy of that answer."

Colonel Elder turned towards his legal officer. Major Brinkman struck Gordon's statement that mines had been placed on a particular footpath in El Salvador and had killed women and children. But he allowed the original question. When Gordon turned back toward the witness, he no longer appeared confused. He seemed terribly menacing. In a strong voice, clipping his words as if they left a bad taste in his mouth, he asked, "What's the difference, Captain, between placing a mine in Major Daks's driveway, here at Fort Marion, and placing a mine on a footpath in a foreign country?"

"Sir, I don't know the difference. My field is weapons technology."

"Not whether it's right or wrong to risk women and children?" Gordon challenged.

"Objection!" This time O'Brien was shouting. "Absolutely no foundation for either the question or the comment in direct examination. And I repeat, the line of questioning is completely irrelevant."

This time Brinkman acknowledged the court president's questioning glance with a nod.

"The Court agrees with the trial counsel. The question, the answer, and Captain Gordon's comment will be deleted from the trial record."

O'Brien sat. Gordon turned back to his witness, who no longer had a sarcastic smile to suppress. "You answered, Captain, that Army Special Operations Forces were the ones who were taught this particular mining technique. But haven't you also instructed foreign military personnel in these methods?"

O'Brien deflated. The question was completely proper for the defense. Gordon could simply be demonstrating to the court how many people, besides a Special Operations trainee named Miguel Cortines, were trained to set grenade mines. But the major knew perfectly well that Gordon didn't give a damn about other explanations for the mine in Daks's driveway. Gordon was interested in opening the door on El Salvador much wider.

"Yes, sir," the captain answered.

"From what countries?"

"Many, sir."

The defense counsel sauntered back to his notes. "You indicated that you taught this technique in a Special Operations training center in the Canal Zone. What countries were your students from?"

"Panama."

"Anywhere else?"

"El Salvador."

"Were there many students from El Salvador?"

"Yes, sir."

Mex leaned forward in his chair, staring directly into the witness. There were many indeed. He had met quite a few of them.

"And all of them learned how to plant grenade mines," Gordon continued.

"Yes, sir."

"On footpaths, where the grenades wouldn't know the difference between insurgent soldiers and civilians?"

O'Brien bolted to his feet. "Objection. Where or how they might have used the training they received is absolutely irrelevant."

Gordon struck instantly. "Is the Army's representative suggesting that the Army doesn't care whether it's training is used to kill soldiers or civilians? That the difference is irrelevant?"

Every face on the court turned toward Cletus O'Brien. "I'm suggesting nothing of the sort," he assured them. "I'm stating that this issue is irrelevant to the deliberations of this court, in this case."

Colonel Elder waited for the trial judge. Brinkman leaned toward his microphone and said, "The court agrees with the objection. How many people know this technique has a bearing on how many people could have set the mine. But, in the context of this proceeding, it doesn't matter how else they might have used the knowledge." Elder had the clerk read back the last exchange between the defense counsel and the witness. He struck Gordon's statement that the mines could have killed innocent civilians.

"No more questions," Robert told the court. On his way back to this table he whispered a silent "thank you" to Amos Granger. Mex looked up and flashed a thin-lipped smile. The Army was beginning to listen.

O'Brien's next witnesses established the facts surrounding the contamination of the water supply. First, Colonel Richard Liggett, the fort's chief surgeon, documented the number of cases of dysentery that had been brought into the hospital in a one-day period. He told how he had been called by Captain Henry Roy, who had advised him that the water was tainted, and how a laboratory analysis had confirmed Roy's suspicions. Next, a civilian chemist from an outside laboratory in Atlanta provided the name, shigella shigae, for the contaminant found in the water. O'Brien established that the laboratory had also analyzed a bacterial agent provided by the fort's military police. "And was this chemical material delivered by the military police the same as the agent you were able to separate from the fort's water samples?" he asked.

"Chemically identical," the witness said.

O'Brien then called Major Franklin Topping, who testified that he had taken samples of a bacterial agent from Captain Roy's classroom and sent them to the outside laboratory. The link between Roy's classroom and the water aerating plant was forged. Next, he established the unbroken chain of possession for the plastic container that held the contaminant. He asked Topping, "Where did you first find this container?" He held up the clear plastic bag with the bottle inside.

The officer answered, "We found it jammed into one of the aeration panels at the water purification facility."

"And you retrieved it and delivered it directly to Captain Gordon, who was then serving as the command's staff judge advocate?"

"I did."

"And did Captain Gordon take steps to establish the origin of the container?"

Topping told the court that it had been identified by Captain Roy as one he had used in his classroom.

"Did you then send that container for fingerprint analysis?"

The military police officer explained how he had marked and sealed the container, and sent it to the FBI fingerprint laboratories. All that remained was for the FBI fingerprint expert to show that he had found prints on the bottle that matched those of Miguel Cortines.

"You have no doubt that the last person to touch this bottle, before it was put into the aeration tank was Corporal Miguel Cortines?" Cletus O'Brien asked Special Agent Thomas Sellers.

"No doubt whatsoever," the fingerprint expert stated.

Gordon hoped to raise some doubts.

"Agent Sellers," he addressed the witness, "how long would a fingerprint remain on a plastic surface, such as the bottle that was offered in evidence?"

"Indefinitely," the agent answered.

"So Corporal Cortines's fingerprint could have been placed on the bottle when he handled it during his training at the school."

"It could."

"Might not that account for the fact that his fingerprint was on the bottle when it was retrieved from the water system?"

"Not really," Sellers explained. "It probably would have been obliterated by the prints of other students. Certainly by the person who carried it from the school to the water aerator."

Gordon pressed on. "Suppose that no one in the school handled the bottle after Corporal Cortines. And suppose, further, that the person who carried it from the school to the water aerator was wearing gloves."

"Then the gloves would have wiped away the corporal's fingerprint," Sellers answered.

"Maybe not," the defense counsel said. He lifted the plastic bag that held the bottle so that it was clearly visible to the members of the court. "Suppose the accused, during a classroom training session, held the bottle like this." He grabbed it through the protective bag and held it by its sides. "And suppose the person who took it from the school, while wearing gloves, held it like this." He shifted his grip so that his fingers were on the top of the bottle, and his thumb on the bottom.

The fingerprint expert smiled. "Then Corporal Cortines's print would remain on the bottle."

"So if this particular bottle wasn't circulated in the classroom after the corporal handled it, it's possible that the accused was not the last person to touch it."

Sellers nodded. "Under the circumstances you describe, it's possible."

"Thank you, Agent Sellers," Gordon said as he returned to the defense table.

Mex leaned close to Gordon. "What's it matter? They know I did it."

Gordon squeezed Mex's arm to silence him. His attention was riveted on O'Brien who was hesitating over his notes before announcing his next witness. Gordon thought he knew why. To eliminate the doubt that his cross-examination had raised in the FBI agent's testimony, he should call Captain Roy. The captain could certainly testify that countless students had handled the bottle in his laboratory after Cortines. But O'Brien would have to be very careful of the questions he asked. He would have to avoid any mention of why Special Operations trainees were being taught to use chemical agents. Otherwise, Gordon would be able to do with the poison exactly what he had done with grenade mines. What was most important to the Army? To remove all doubt and lock up the case? Or to keep a discussion on the use of chemical agents out of the record?

"Major O'Brien?" It was Colonel Elder trying to keep things moving.

"Sir, we're close to noon," O'Brien answered. "It might be more convenient if we recessed for lunch before I call my next witness."

Elder was apparently hungry. "The court will reconvene at fourteen hundred hours," he said.

Major O'Brien and Lieutenant Nugent left the room quickly. Gordon waited while the two military police officers snapped handcuffs back onto Cortines's wrists.

"Thanks," Mex told him as the guards were taking his arms.

"We've got a long way to go," Gordon answered.

He was the first one back in the classroom, and he waited nervously while the participants filed back into the court. Major O'Brien's expression gave no hint of the decision he had reached. Colonel Elder was chatting with his trial judge as he drifted toward his place in the center of the table. The two sergeant majors marched back in together.

The two MPs took Mex's handcuffs off, and he slid into the table next to Gordon. "I don't get it. What's goin' on?" he asked, picking up the question that had been interrupted.

Gordon nodded toward the trial counsel's table. "They're trying to decide whether they want to talk about poisoning the water."

"I wanna talk about it," Mex said.

Elder called the court back into session, and O'Brien announced his decision. Instead of calling Captain Roy, he moved directly to the witnesses concerned with the next charge: the kidnapping and torture of Colonel Pedro Maritin.

Maritin's story was presented in a deposition which the colonel had dictated, sworn, and signed before he returned to his country. Gordon had been the attorney who took the deposition, so he had no grounds for objecting to it. But even if the document were flawed, he would have welcomed it. Maritin, in describing his ordeal, had specifically referred to "an electric shock machine."

The trial counsel presented the captain of the guard that had been patrolling the visiting officers' compound. He identified the logs that checked Maritin into his building, and confirmed that the visiting officer could not be found the next morning. Robert Gordon had no questions for cross-examination. Major Victor Jordan was sworn in and recalled finding Maritin tied to a wooden chair, with electrodes still clamped to his body. Gordon was on his feet the instant O'Brien finished with his perfunctory questions.

"Major, you mentioned that electrodes were connected to Colonel Maritin. Were the other ends of those electrodes connected to an electrical device of some sort?" Jordan said that they were.

"Was that device," Robert read from Maritin's deposition, "'an electric shock machine'?" The witness acknowledged that it was. Gordon asked him to describe the function of the device, and Major Jordan told the court how it increased the voltage of an electrical source to a high level in order to produce local electric shocks.

"Extremely painful electric shocks?" Gordon asked.

"Yes."

"Painful, but not deadly?"

"No, not deadly. There isn't enough current to be fatal. Or even dangerous."

"So this isn't a humane method of executing a person, like an electric chair. This is a very inhumane way of torturing a person, isn't that so?"

"All torture is inhumane," Victor Jordan answered, speaking clinically rather than emotionally.

"Then why would such a machine be in a classroom on a post of the United States Army? A classroom where our young men are taught techniques for fighting war?"

The officers of the court locked their attention on Major Jordan. The major never wavered. He looked directly back at them and answered in a strong voice. "We teach our men how to survive capture and imprisonment. If captured, they may face terrible methods of interrogation. Some far worse than electric shock. We want them to be ready to cope with such situations, and to survive them."

"And in teaching them to 'cope' and 'survive,' do you also teach them how to use this machine?"

The answer was instant. "We teach them how such a device might be used against their person. We do not teach them how to use it against someone else. Basically, we want them to recognize the device, understand that they will not be able to remain silent if it is used on them, and to reveal any noncritical information they know that may save them the ordeal."

Jordan glanced toward Cletus O'Brien. They had rehearsed his answers carefully, and he was hoping for some gesture of approval. O'Brien did his best to look totally disinterested.

"Major, when a soldier enters your class, the supposition is that he does not know anything about electric shock torture, is that right?"

"We assume complete unawareness."

"And when he leaves your class, he knows how such a machine works, and how it might be applied, isn't that also so?"

"Yes, but—"

Gordon cut him off. "Now I want to ask you, Major, isn't that same information presented to the officers and soldiers of foreign countries who attend the school?"

"Yes, it is."

"Would it be presented to Salvadoran officers, such as Colonel Maritin?"

"Most likely."

"So if he were a good student, the Colonel would take that information with him, back to his country—"

"Objection," O'Brien bellowed, and strode from behind his table. "What might happen with that information, in another country, is completely irrelevant to these proceedings."

"To the contrary," Gordon fired back. "It leads directly to how many people in how many countries may have ultimately learned how to use electric shock torture, thanks to Major Jordan's scholarly lectures."

O'Brien looked pleadingly toward the trial judge, Major Drew Brinkman. "This is cross-examination of a witness, and none of the witness's direct testimony concerned anything that happened outside his classroom. There is no basis whatsoever for questions about what might have happened in El Salvador, or anywhere else. The direct testimony concerned events that occurred here at Fort Francis Marion."

Colonel Elder and his trial judge leaned into a huddle. It was Brinkman who announced, "The question goes to the issue of how many people other than the accused would have the knowledge to have used the machine against Colonel Maritin. The court will allow it."

But Gordon wasn't really looking for numbers. He was trying to show the court what Jordan's training had done to his client.

"Major Jordan, in teaching this inhumane method of interrogation, did you ever consider, for even one moment, that your foreign students might use it against civilians in their own countries?"

"Objection," O'Brien said with an edge of anger.

Colonel Elder didn't need to wait for the advice of his trial judge.

He had no love for the peculiar skills of Special Operations. But he was an Army officer, and he saw clearly that the Army was becoming the accused in the trial. "Objection sustained." Then he told Gordon, "As the trial counsel has pointed out, we're not concerned with what might have happened somewhere else. Our interest is in what did happen here at Fort Marion." His eyes stayed fixed on Gordon, to make sure that he understood. The captain returned to his chair.

Sergeant Major Elvis Thompson was called. He referred to his duty logs and indicated that Cortines had been on the base when the first two incidents occurred. At the time of the third incident, Thompson said, he was out on a field exercise in an area adjacent to the base.

"Could he have returned from the exercise area to the base undetected?" O'Brien asked.

"Yes, it was within the range in which he is trained to operate," Thompson answered.

"And could he then return to the exercise area, again undetected?"

The sergeant nodded. "Yes, that would be within the scope of his training."

In his cross-examination, Gordon focused on the whereabouts of Corporal Cortines when Maritin was abducted.

"How far from the base perimeter was Corporal Cortines when he was released from the helicopter?"

"About nine miles," Thompson said.

"What kind of roads could he have used in returning to the base?"

Thompson showed a smile. "There are no roads. We picked the training area because it is extremely difficult terrain. It isn't easy getting around in there."

Gordon continued, "Did Corporal Cortines know what routes were available to him when you dropped him from the helicopter?"

"No, sir," Thompson replied. Then he explained the reasons why the men were blindfolded and why the helicopter took deceptive routes to their drop sites.

Gordon then went through the difficulties of entering the base, the guarded wire fence that surrounded the visiting officers' quarters, the distance between the quarters and the school, and finally the fact that the school was guarded as well. Sergeant Thompson acknowledged that he was aware of every one of the difficulties posed.

"So, to recap," Gordon said, "Corporal Cortines would have to establish his position and pick a course back to the base, cover nine miles of difficult country, enter a guarded post of the United States

Army undetected, get to the visiting officers' quarters, again undetected, break into Colonel Maritin's room, subdue the colonel, carry him from the officer's quarters to the school, again avoiding detection by two different sentry patrols, break back out of the school, and back out of the base, and then retrace his steps through the nine miles of difficult terrain. Is that about it, Sergeant?''

Thompson beamed with pride. ''That's what it would take, sir.''

Gordon turned to the court. ''Quite an evening's work,'' he allowed.

Colonel Elder and one of his majors smiled. One of the noncoms shook his head slowly as if to say to Thompson, ''Who do you think you're shittin'?'' They had all heard Special Operations troops brag about their exploits. They weren't prepared to take Thompson's version of Cortines's exploits at face value.

''Where was the corporal when he completed his exercise?'' the defense counsel said, turning back to the witness.

''He didn't complete it,'' the sergeant major answered.

''Why not?''

''Because he found another trainee in great distress. He carried him back to a landing area and flew with him back to the base.''

''You mean during the same exercise when he supposedly returned to the base to attack a visiting colonel, he also found time to rescue another soldier?''

Thompson was smiling broadly. ''He sure did, sir. At least, I know he rescued the soldier. I don't know about the other stuff.''

Gordon was able to join in Thompson's obvious satisfaction with his answer. ''I agree with you, Sergeant Major. I don't know about the other stuff either.''

As soon as Sergeant Major Thompson left the witness chair, O'Brien announced that the prosecution had completed its presentation. Colonel Elder nodded and then ordered a fifteen-minute recess before the defense would begin its presentation. Sergeant Robinson called the participants to attention as the members of the court filed out of the room. Cletus O'Brien and Lieutenant Nugent followed right on their heels, and a second later the two clerks left, already in process of lighting their cigarettes. Gordon remained at the table beside his client. They had a decision to make.

''Mex, I want you to listen carefully. This is important.''

Mex was looking straight at him. He nodded that he was listening.

''They didn't call Captain Roy. That means we won't be able to bring in information about poisoning the water in your village.''

"Then you call him," Mex said. "You can do that, can't you?"

"Yes, I can do that. But I don't want to, and I want you to understand why."

Mex looked disappointed.

"We've got a chance to beat this thing," Gordon began. "The only hard evidence they have to link you with anything is the fingerprint on the bottle. And we've raised some doubts about it. Maybe—just maybe—some of the judges think it's possible that none of the students touched the bottle after you touched it in class."

"Everyone used it," Mex contradicted.

"Maybe," Gordon snapped impatiently, "but no one told that to the court. And no one will, unless I call Captain Roy to testify. But if I put him on the stand, then they get to cross-examine him. And the first question Major O'Brien is going to ask him is, "Did other students handle the bottle after Corporal Cortines?""

"So?" Mex asked.

"So, he'll say yes, and then our argument goes up in smoke. And you go to prison. For God's sake, Mex, I'm trying to keep you out of jail."

"Don't worry," Mex answered confidently. "I won't stay in the stockade."

"Jesus, Mex, will you stop trying to sound so hard-assed. If they find you guilty, you'll go to prison. That can't be what you want."

"I want him to talk about poisonin' the water," the corporal answered.

Gordon stared at him for several seconds. "I'm trying to save you."

"Don't worry," Mex assured him. "I'll be okay."

Robert still hadn't made up his mind when Colonel Elder reconvened the court and called it to order. But then the row of brass-laden Army uniforms forced his decision. His client wanted to talk to the men who had trained the murderers in his country. He wanted it so badly that he was willing to trade years of his life for the opportunity. And they were sitting across the front of the room, ready to listen.

"Sir," he said to Elder, "I think we might want to recess until tomorrow morning. With the court's permission, I then intend to call as a defense witness a person whose name and area of testimony I have not submitted to the court."

O'Brien was up instantly with his protest, arguing that he was entitled to disclosure of any witness that the defense planned to call. "The name and area of testimony should have been made available before this court was called into session," he said.

"It was," Gordon answered. "He was listed as an Army witness, and I expected to have access to him during cross-examination. Since the trial counsel chose not to call him, I was denied essential access. That's why I need to present his testimony."

O'Brien was plainly annoyed. "Who are we talking about, Captain?"

"Captain Henry Roy," Robert Gordon answered.

★   ★   ★

Dave, Willie, and Luther were waiting in the office when Gordon climbed to the top of the stairs. They had already pulled the tabs on their beers and offered one to the captain as soon as he came through the door.

"Hear you really kicked butt in there today, Captain," Willie Derry greeted him.

Robert looked surprised. It was a closed courtroom.

"Sergeant Robinson was duly impressed," Willie explained, naming one of the noncoms serving as a court clerk.

"Says you're turning the Army's witnesses into Mex's witnesses," Luther added.

Gordon shook his head. "I wish Sergeant Robinson was on the court. We could use his vote."

Baldinger saw that Mex's lawyer wasn't as optimistic as the court clerk. "How do you think it's going?" he asked.

Robert settled into one of the chairs and opened his beer. Then he tried to explain what was going on in the classroom that had been converted into a courthouse. It had been a good day. Better than he had any right to expect. The Army's contention was that all the acts had to be the work of someone trained for Special Operations. He had shown that there were many people who could have set the grenade. And because the evidence had opened the door for the mention of atrocities in El Salvador, the trial counsel had been careful to avoid any link between the poisoned water and the Special Operations trainees. "I don't think they're going to be able to link the charges," he thought out loud. "And without linking them, they won't be able to prove the grenade, or the kidnapping charge."

"Like I said, you kicked butt," Willie applauded as he reached for another beer.

Gordon was also pleased with the information he had suggested to the court about El Salvador. The court members had heard that Mex's mother had been killed by a grenade mine. And they certainly understood that electric shock torture had been used by the Salvadoran officers trained at the Special Operations school. Bit by bit, he was telling Mex's story.

But, he reminded his small audience, the linchpin of the Army case was the fingerprint on the bottle. He explained his dilemma in calling Captain Roy to the witness stand.

"You'll kick his ass," Luther Brown laughed, trying to offer encouragement.

"Yeah." Robert Gordon nodded. "The problem is that I could sink any chance Mex has of going free. Without Roy's testimony, the Army hasn't proven anything."

Baldinger frowned. "Mex already made that call."

Derry agreed. "He wants the brass to know what they done to his family."

"Damn it," the captain snapped. "There was a good chance that I could have gotten him off."

Luther looked confused. "If that's what he wanted, he'd've taken the deal they offered."

★　★　★

Henry Roy sat across the desk from Cletus O'Brien. It was already a half-hour later than he had promised Carol he would be home for dinner, and the trial counsel was only halfway through his yellow pages of handwritten notes.

"Why are we training our men to use chemical and biological agents?" O'Brien asked.

"So that if they should ever have to use them, they'll know how to set the proper dosage," Roy monotoned.

"Should *ever* have to use them? Aren't they considered a standard weapon? Aren't your trainees expected to use them?"

"They're expected to know how to use them. They're intended only for extreme situations when they could force an enemy to give up terrain without the heavy loss of life that would result from a firefight."

O'Brien nodded. Just the kind of answer he wanted. It made the bacteria sound almost humane. "But don't these agents cause terrible suffering?" he went on. "Aren't they sometimes deadly?"

"When used properly," Captain Roy answered, "they aren't deadly. That's why we train our men carefully. And as for suffering, their effects are less painful, and much less permanent than, say, a thirty-caliber round through the head."

O'Brien smiled. "Good. Very good." He turned to his next page of practice questions.

"The only problem," Henry Roy said, "is that it's all bullshit."

Cletus O'Brien set his notes aside. "Captain, all that's required is that you give a specifically true answer to a specific question. Was there anything untrue in what you just told me?"

"No, I suppose not," Henry admitted.

"Then it isn't bullshit," O'Brien corrected. "You may know that your trainees aren't always as careful as you'd like them to be. But the witness stand isn't the place for debating all the possible answers to a question. It's a place for giving a simple, direct answer to the exact question that's asked."

Roy nodded. He had been duly chastised.

O'Brien returned to his notes. "Captain, isn't it true that in some countries these bacterial agents have caused hundreds of deaths?"

Roy said nothing.

"Right," Major O'Brien complimented. "Any question that goes outside your classroom, just pause. Give me time to object. We're not going to let them ask about anything beyond the training in your classroom."

Roy paced in his living room while Carol reheated the dinner that had been ready two hours earlier. He was still practicing his responses when he sat down at the table.

"I wanted to testify," he snapped at Carol. "Then the goddamn lawyer says he isn't going to call me. Doesn't want to give Gordon a chance to talk about El Salvador and Panama. Then, just as I'm leaving my office, he tells me I am going to testify. The guy is out of his mind."

He paused to compliment her on the fish she had fixed for his dinner. "I'm supposed to make it sound like we're teaching a neighborly new way to fight wars. Hell, who does he think he's kidding. That stuff is designed to knock out a whole city."

Carol set down her fork. "He's not telling you to lie?"

"He might as well be," Henry answered. "I spent the last two hours learning how not to say anything."

She listened while he repeated the lessons that O'Brien had taught him. "But that's not true," Carol interrupted.

Henry shook his head despairingly. "Oh, it's probably true, as far as it goes. But it sure in hell doesn't answer the question."

He finished his fish and reached across his plate to spear his salad. "Half the time, I won't even have to answer. Major O'Brien wants me to count to three before I give any answer. He wants enough time to raise objections if he doesn't like the questions."

He fell morosely quiet, and stayed hunched over the table while Carol cleared the dishes. He was almost startled when she set a dish of sherbet in front of him.

"Sorry," he apologized. "I haven't been very good company."

She sat next to him. "What have you been thinking about?"

"That I'm the one who's on trial," he answered. "That I'm the one who has to be careful what he says." He took a spoonful of the dessert, but then dropped it back into the dish. "And I've been thinking about what you've been saying. We're not really honest about what we do. In a way, the medals, the uniforms, the evening colors—all of this—they're a disguise. The truth is that we're afraid to stand up and say what we really do. 'We destroy the enemy. We destroy his home, his fields, his job. We destroy the roads he uses to get to his job.' It isn't pleasant. But that's what he's trying to do to us. Whoever does it best, wins. And, damn it, we're finally beginning to win. So why are we afraid to talk about it?"

"Maybe because we've been pretending for so long that we're all afraid of the truth," she offered. "Maybe you should just tell them exactly what you do."

"I can't," Captain Roy said. "The truth is that I've known exactly what we were doing. I knew what Jordan's students were doing with his goddamn shock machine. I knew what my students were doing with chemicals. Christ, I even wrote a paper on capturing guerrillas when they brought their sick children for medical help. I knew exactly what that stuff does to a kid's stomach. The truth is that I've been lying to myself—to both of us I guess—for the last seven years."

She was surprised at the sympathy she suddenly felt for him. "You did what you thought was right."

Henry nodded. "I really did. We looked for ways to beat guerrilla armies, and we found ways that worked. Damn it! That's what we were supposed to do, wasn't it?"

Carol couldn't answer. It was only half the question. The other half was, at what price? Were they supposed to win if it meant supporting governments that murdered their own people? If it meant teaching them how to poison and torture, and then looking the other way when they put their lessons to work?

"We did what we had to do," Captain Roy concluded. "So why should one man who happened to be on the wrong side be able to put us on trial? Why in hell should I have to squirm on the damn witness stand like I'm some sort of criminal?"

"You shouldn't have to," Carol agreed.

* * *

General Wheeler was close to rage. He had been greeted at the officers' club with the first reports of the open-and-shut trial he had ordered. "A difficult day, sir?" the uniformed waiter had consoled as he placed a dry martini on his table, along with a dish of salted peanuts. Wheeler had been confused by the comment until an Airborne colonel had paused briefly to pay his respects. "Electric shock torture," he had mentioned, shaking his head in disgust. "Those guys in Special Operations are out of control." Wheeler had downed his drink, and sent an aide to find Colonel Griggs and Major O'Brien. Then he had listened with mounting anger as Cletus O'Brien explained what was happening in the courtroom. Now he was pacing back and forth behind his desk while the two officers endured his wrath.

"You told me you could handle this, Clete," he reminded his new staff judge advocate. "You said it would be just paperwork."

"It's not nearly as bad as you've heard, General," O'Brien said in his own defense. "Half the stuff has been stricken from the record. Most of it will never make the transcript."

Grigg was solemn. "But people have heard it, and they're talking about it. You said there would be no mention of . . ." He couldn't finish the sentence.

O'Brien threw up his hands. "I can't prosecute without showing the court what the kid did. And everything he's charged with is something that we teach in the school. It comes up in the cross-examination. I object to it. The court strikes most of it. But I can't keep Gordon from asking the questions."

"But it's all out of context," Grigg said. "It makes us sound like savages. Damn it, counterinsurgency warfare may not be pretty. But it wins wars."

General Wheeler sagged, and leaned against his desk. "I should have taken that bastard Gordon's advice and processed the kid out as a psycho."

"That might not have worked," Cletus told his mentor. "I offered Gordon a deal to let the kid off easy and wrap everything up in a hurry. The kid wouldn't go along with it. He wants his day in court."

"He wants our asses," the general snapped in response.

Griggs shook his head in bewilderment. "Why in God's name is he doing this to us?"

Wheeler sunk into his chair. For a second, he stared morosely at the file that was still waiting on his desk. Then he looked up at Cletus O'Brien. "I want this controlled," he ordered. "No more mention of mines"—his fiery gaze swung slowly toward Griggs—"or bacteria, or electric shock machines." Then back toward O'Brien. "Do you understand me, Major?"

"Yes, sir," the staff judge advocate answered. "There's only one more witness who could give us a problem, and he understands what we're up against. I think he'll do fine."

"He better," General Wheeler growled.

★　★　★

Captain Roy marched into the courtroom early the next morning, saluted, repeated the oath, and then sat uncomfortably on the edge of the witness chair. The members of the court leaned forward as Robert Gordon bent over his notes for a few moments, and then stepped around his desk.

"Captain Roy, you teach a course at the Special Operations school called 'Chemical Weapons,' is that correct?"

"Yes."

"Is that course taught in classroom Bravo Three?"

"In part, yes. The course combines classroom sessions as well as field training."

Gordon asked him to describe the classroom sessions, and Roy explained that it was primarily laboratory work. Each of the chemicals and agents dispersed in water. Their effectiveness depended on evaluating water quantities and flow rates so that accurate concentrations could be achieved. O'Brien was pleased. The captain was making his work sound as dull as an undergraduate course in chemistry.

"Is one of the materials you use in your classroom the bacterial agent, shigella shigae, described in Army Exhibit Six, a copy of which I am now handing to you?"

Roy took the laboratory analysis of the Fort Francis Marion drinking water, and skimmed through it quickly. "Yes, it is," he said.

"Do you agree with the effects and consequences of ingesting this agent, as described in the exhibit?" Roy read the list of symptoms and nodded as he reached the end of the paragraph. "Yes, those are the symptoms it's intended to produce."

"And you agree, as this report states, that if ingested in sufficient quantities, this agent can cause death?"

"Yes," he said. "That's why we teach our men to use it properly. It's not intended to kill people, but rather to disable them."

So far, so good, Cletus O'Brien thought.

"But it has the potential to kill?" Gordon asked.

O'Brien started to his feet, but Roy answered before he could voice his objection.

"Yes, it has that potential."

The trial counsel was settling back into his chair when Gordon asked, "Why are we teaching our men to use crippling and potentially deadly poisons? Aren't such things outlawed—"

"Objection!" O'Brien screamed. "Matters of military tactics are completely irrelevant to this proceeding."

Elder caught Brinkman's eye, and then the trial judge ruled the question improper. Gordon took an instant to regroup and then tried another approach. He asked if all Army personnel were taught to use bacterial agents, and Roy told him that only Special Operations trainees were. He said that all Special Operations recruits were given at least cursory training, and that some were selected for in-depth training.

"Why just Special Operations trainees?" Gordon pressed. O'Brien immediately objected, but the defense counsel countered that the number of people who had been trained indicated the number of people other than Cortines who would have been able to use the chemical. "The Army is linking the charges by attempting to show that the accused was specially trained in the events involved in the charges and specifications. The defense certainly has the right to show that many people, other than the accused, were similarly trained." Elder huddled with his legal expert, and then agreed with Gordon. The objection was overruled. Gordon repeated the question.

"Because of the nature of Special Operations missions," Roy said in a strong, defiant voice. "One soldier can easily carry enough of this material to disable an entire guerrilla brigade and its support structure.

And that's one of the prime missions of Special Operations. Fighting guerrillas.''

Cletus O'Brien winced. Captain Roy was departing from his rehearsed text. The trial counsel didn't want the door opened on disabling "support structures," which was nothing more than jargon for civilian populations. But Henry Roy was leaning forward in his chair, anxious for the next question. He didn't want to avoid the issue. He wanted to tell the truth.

"Support structures?" Gordon continued.

"Objection," O'Brien insisted. "The defense counsel is simply using different words to ask questions that the court has already ruled irrelevant."

Elder glared toward Gordon. "The objection is sustained," he said.

Gordon tried again. "Captain Roy, by support structures, do you mean the noncombat personnel who might be the wives, children, and neighbors of the troops in a guerrilla army?"

"Objection."

"Sustained," Elder snapped.

Gordon was stymied. He stepped toward the gray-covered table at which the court was seated. "Sir, the Army's charge and specification mentions specifically that the material was introduced into a water supply that serves not only Army personnel here at Fort Francis Marion, but also their wives and children. I am attempting to show that any number of men, other than the accused, were trained to do exactly that."

Elder didn't wait for advice from his trial judge. "I know exactly what you're trying to do, Captain. You're trying to bring issues that have nothing to do with the charges into this court. Your point is that everyone in Special Operations received the same training as Corporal Cortines. And you've made that point. I don't want to hear anything more about how that training might have been used against civilian populations."

Gordon turned back to the witness. He asked if any others, besides Special Operations trainees, were taught the chemical weapons curriculum.

"Yes," Roy said. "We teach the same course to the military personnel of friendly countries that are confronted with guerrilla military operations."

Gordon decided to risk one more tongue-lashing from Elder. "And would those soldiers have the skill to poison a water supply serving women and children, such as the water supply here at Fort Marion?"

Major O'Brien was ready to object, but Colonel Elder did it for him. "Strike that question," he ordered the clerk. Then he turned toward the defense counsel. "Captain Gordon, I'm not going to tell you this again. Your questions about support structures, and women and children, have nothing to do with this case. If you want to ask how many soldiers of friendly nations received this kind of training, fine. But who the targets for these weapons might be is irrelevant. You know, and I know, it doesn't make a damn bit of difference who might end up drinking the water."

"Sir, the Army's charge specifically mentions the danger to women and children at Fort Francis Marion."

"And I've specifically told you that I don't want you using that phrase to bring in irrelevant material about the possible use of this training. Do you understand me?"

"Yes, sir," Robert said. He walked humbly back to his table and raised his next question while he tossed through his papers.

"Captain Roy, did you once author a paper on the use of shigella shigae in counterinsurgency warfare?"

"I did," Henry answered defiantly.

"And would that paper have been made available to military personnel from friendly nations who were interested in the subject?"

"It could have been."

"How many people might have read it?" Gordon looked directly at Elder and stressed "how many" so that the colonel would see the question was within the guidelines the court had just promulgated.

"I don't know," Roy answered. "Anyone who studied here, or in Panama."

"Hundreds, then?"

"I suppose so."

He walked toward Roy, carrying a blue manuscript folder.

"Is this the paper you authored, Captain?"

Roy tossed quickly through the pages and confirmed that it was.

"Would you please read it to the court."

O'Brien jumped to his feet. "Irrelevant," he snapped.

Gordon turned to Elder. "Sir, the kind of information on the precise bacterial agent in question, that was available to hundreds of foreign military officers, bears directly on the number of people other than the accused who might have used that agent here at Fort Francis Marion."

He was right, as Elder immediately recognized. Brinkman overruled the objection and Henry Roy began a monotone reading of the eight pages of advice he had written for the students at the Special Operations schools.

The scholarship was impressive. Roy read authoritatively as he described the life cycle of the bacteria, the conditions under which it multiplied and its rate of dispersion in fresh water. Major O'Brien stole glances at the faces in the court. They seemed bewildered by half of what they heard and plainly uninterested in the rest. No problem, he thought to himself. All Gordon was succeeding in doing was documenting that foreign students were probably given more information than they could handle.

"When properly deployed," Roy read on as he turned to a new page, "shigella shigae will have devastating effects not only on the enemy's ability to fight, but also on his will to fight. It causes acute symptoms of dysentery and dehydration, which grow more painful and debilitating as greater quantities are ingested. Since water seems to provide momentary relief from the symptoms, poorly educated soldiers and their dependents, will drink increasing quantities of water, which will only aggravate their symptoms, making their suffering ever more intense . . ."

Roy's voice began to fade as he read his own words of admiration for a weapon that was designed to cause suffering that was "ever more intense." The disinterested eyes of the soldiers on the court were suddenly focused toward the witness chair.

"Victims will suffer great fatigue from internal bleeding, loss of muscle tone—" he stopped momentarily to clear his throat—"and loss of mental capabilities. There will be dizziness, loss of balance and motor coordination, and even delirium."

The court was deathly silent. The droning of the air conditioner seemed to be growing louder. Captain Roy set the paper aside as he searched his pockets for a handkerchief and dabbed at the shiny beads that were forming on his forehead. Shigella shigae was beginning to sound worse to him than the large-caliber bullet. He squared his shoulders and turned the page. The ripple of the paper sounded like a whip snapping.

"Particularly dramatic are the symptoms that the material causes in—" he paused, and his voice fell to a whisper—"causes in, eh, children."

"Could you speak up, Captain," Gordon coaxed. "The court may be having difficulty in hearing you."

Roy nodded. "Symptoms that the material causes in children," he repeated, his voice still much fainter than when he had begun reading. "The children are generally the first stricken, and their symptoms are more"—he cleared his throat again—"more immediately apparent.

He lifted his eyes from the paper, and saw Mex's face looking directly into his own. How old was Cortines? Maybe twenty? How old was he wen Roy was training the Salvadoran Guardsmen at the school in Panama? Fourteen? Maybe thirteen?

"They will exhibit explosive vomiting and diarrhea, frequently . . . passing blood." They were his words, written to encourage the proper use of shigella shigae. Now, for the first time, he was reading them not in the presence of potential users, but in the presence of an actual victim. "Skin will become pale, even taking on a blue cast. Stomach irritation and intestinal cramping will cause"—he stopped, rereading his work as if he were suddenly unfamiliar with it—"will cause . . ." He looked up hopelessly as if the word was incomprehensible.

Colonel Elder and his court waited.

"Will cause . . ." Robert Gordon coaxed.

Roy looked back down at the paper, read the word, and then repeated it as if it were too ridiculous to be true.

"Will cause crying."

He found the soldiers on the court gasping in disbelief. He could hardly believe it himself. Children crying? Why had he even thought of such a thing, much less written it?

"These are symptoms highly visible to parents and other adults in the insurgent families," he whispered. He stole another glance at Mex as he turned a page. The corporal was still staring at him, biting down on his lip. Did he remember this? Had he seen it? Jesus, had he felt it?

"Please continue," Captain Gordon asked politely.

Henry Roy nodded. Then he heard the rush of the air conditioner. The court was absolutely still, waiting to hear more from his training manual.

"For this reason, it is strongly recommended that, whenever the material is deployed, military personnel be stationed at area hospitals and clinics. Insurgent guerrillas, who would not leave the protection of their inaccessible communities under other circumstances, will rush to medical resources to obtain help for their children. They may surrender their weapons and even themselves in order to have their children treated."

"Treated?" It was Mex's voice, whispered through his hands, not loud enough to reach the court. But Henry Roy heard it. His paper said nothing about treatment. He had never considered what might await the children brought to the medical centers. And he had never written what might happen to the parents, although he certainly knew. Hell, it was war. Not pretty, but not his fault. A tough break for people like Mex, who happened to be on the wrong side. That's what he should say to Corporal Cortines, and to anyone on the court who wanted to listen. But he had a question of his own. What side was he on when he used the cries of children to capture their parents?

Roy finished the paper and handed it back to the defense counsel.

"Thank you, Captain," Gordon concluded. "I have no further questions." Maybe calling Captain Roy hadn't helped his client win an acquittal. But if the glances that the officers and the two enlisted men were aiming at Henry Roy were any indication, he had helped Mex tell his story.

Cletus O'Brien was on his feet before Gordon got back to his table. He ignored the recitation he had just heard as if it had never happened, and went right to the fingerprints on the plastic container.

"Captain, the issue that concerns the court at this point is how the accused's fingerprint came to be on the container that held the bacterial agent."

The court stirred, suddenly remembering that they hadn't gathered to pass judgment on a training paper. It was Corporal Cortines who was on trial. Quickly, O'Brien led Captain Roy through his classroom procedures, establishing that all the students, did, in fact, handle all the bottles of chemical and bacterial agents. He enumerated the numbers of students who had been in Roy's class after Corporal Cortines.

"Is it possible that one bottle, handled by the accused, could have gone unused subsequently?"

"No," Roy said, without any great enthusiasm. There was only one bottle of each material.

"Then that bottle," O'Brien hammered home, "would have to be passed from hand to hand." He lifted the exhibit, and moved it from one hand to the other, wrapping his thick fingers all around it.

"Yes," Henry managed.

"You yourself would have handled it, long after Corporal Cortines was a student in your class."

"Yes."

"So if the bottle were found with Corporal Cortines's fingerprints on it, it could only be because Corporal Cortines was the last one to handle it?''

Gordon could have objected to the form of the question. But there was no point. He had presented the information that Mex wanted the court to hear. The sooner Henry Roy left the stand, the better it would be for his client.

''I suppose so,'' the witness mumbled.

O'Brien turned to the court and nodded just as he had done in his opening statement. What could be simpler?

Dave Baldinger was Captain Gordon's next witness. The defense counsel directed him to the date on which the grenade had exploded in Major Daks's driveway, and asked, ''From your own knowledge, Corporal, can you account for the whereabouts of Corporal Cortines during the day in question?''

''Yes, sir. Cortines was in the training area, as a member of a squad under my command, conducting an escape-and-evasion exercise.''

''He had no opportunity to leave the exercise, and return later?''

''No, sir. He was in my line of sight for the entire day.''

It was obvious that the court believed Baldinger. He was an ideal soldier, athletic, bright, neatly turned out, and with an obvious respect for authority. Gordon tried to milk his testimony.

''What about during the evening, after the exercise was completed? Was Corporal Cortines with you then?''

''Yes, sir. We had an assignment to bury a rucksack full of rocks that we had carried back from the training area. Cortines and I worked side by side. We didn't finish until about twenty-one-hundred hours.''

''And after that?''

''We were pretty beat, sir. He turned in right away.''

O'Brien recognized that the court liked the witness, so he treated him gently in his cross-examination.

''Corporal Baldinger, was there any extended time during the prior few days when you were not with Corporal Cortines?''

''Yes, sir.''

''So, then, if he had been in Major Daks's driveway the day before the explosion, or two days before, you would have no way of knowing?''

''No, sir.''

''Or if he had slipped out of his bedroom window after you thought he had turned in, you wouldn't know that either.''

Dave admitted that he wouldn't.

O'Brien applied the same logic to the poisoning of the fort's water supply. No one was sure when the plastic bottle had been thrown into the aerator. It could have tossed around for a few days before it caught between the paddles and was broken open. No one could account for all of Mex's time.

"Thank you, Corporal," O'Brien said when he was finished. He hadn't destroyed the import of Dave's testimony. But at least he had raised the possibility that Mex could have acted without even his closest friends knowing where he was and what he was up to.

Gordon called Luther and Art as his character witnesses. Both carried military bearing, and answered respectfully. Willie Derry had protested the choice. "Why ain't you calling me? I could really set those assholes straight about Mex!"

"Because calling the court members assholes," Robert had told him, "probably wouldn't help Mex's case."

Finally, he introduced Mex's service record, reading his fitness scores, comments of his commanding officers, and his standing in the classes he had attended. The record described a first-rate soldier.

There was one more decision Gordon had to make. The best one to tell Mex's story was the corporal himself. And he knew Mex wanted to take the stand. But he had already tested the limits of the court's patience. There wasn't a chance they would let Mex wander away from the case at hand, and into the darkness of the war in El Salvador. Since he couldn't testify to the horrors worked against his family, there was no reason to call him.

By his calculation, the Army hadn't come close to proving that Mex had ever set a grenade mine, nor that he was the one who had attacked Colonel Maritin. He had even been able to raise some doubts as to the validity of Mex's prints on the bacteria container. But if he exposed him to cross-examination, O'Brien could simply ask him, "Did you set a live mine in Major Daks's driveway? Did you attack Colonel Maritin?" He knew Mex wouldn't hesitate to take full credit.

Gordon rose behind his table. "The defense rests," he said.

He tried not to look at his client as he settled back into his chair.

"Whatta ya doin'?" Mex hissed into his ear.

Robert kept staring straight ahead, his attention fixed on Colonel Elder.

"I gotta tell 'em," the corporal said. His grip tightened like a vise around the lawyer's wrist. "You said I would tell 'em."

Gordon turned and looked into raging eyes. "They know, Mex. They already know."

"But I was supposed to tell 'em. They gotta listen."

"They already listened."

The grip relaxed. Mex stared at Gordon in disbelief, looking as if he had been betrayed. Then he turned his face away.

Cletus O'Brien rose and walked directly to the court table for his closing argument. "This court," he began in a calm, conversational tone, "was perfectly correct in ruling the work of Special Operations and the training provided by the Special Operations school to be irrelevant to the facts of this case. The Army, and its activities, are not the subject of the charges. The only one on trial here is Corporal Miguel Cortines. The only facts we are empowered to consider are those pertaining to the crimes with which he has been legally charged." He then recited the facts, anchoring his argument with the fingerprints on the plastic bottle. "Those prints are the signature of the man who terrorized this base, injuring and endangering all its personnel and their families. At no time during this trial was there any testimony that would deny the accused's responsibility for these actions." He then recited the charges and specifications, and asked for a verdict of guilty on each of them.

"I, personally, have great sympathy for the accused," O'Brien said. "A sympathy that I'm sure you, as soldiers in the finest Army this world has ever seen, share with me. We know that Corporal Cortines hasn't had the kind of life we would wish for our young people. And if we were gods, free to right all wrongs, we would undoubtedly try to help him. But, at this moment, we have a clear and important duty. That duty is to pass judgment based solely on the facts that have been presented in evidence and in testimony."

O'Brien lifted the bag with the plastic bottle, and walked it slowly in front of each member of the court.

"This is the undisputable fact that demands we find him guilty as charged."

Gordon began his argument by reminding the court that the corporal was under no obligation to deny anything. Rather, it was the Army's obligation to prove each charge and every specification. And, he argued, there was no evidence, no witness, nothing at all that linked the accused to the grenade in Major Daks's driveway, or to the kidnapping of the visiting military officer.

"The prosecution assumes that these events were the work of one man. They make that assumption even in the face of evidence that puts the accused on a training exercise with his squad on the day that the grenade exploded, and miles away, in a dense, pathless forest, at the time of Colonel Maritin's kidnapping. At the time when the trial counsel would have you believe that Corporal Cortines was escaping, he was, in fact, returning to his post to save the life of a fellow soldier." He asked for a finding of innocence on these charges and their specifications.

He then attacked the evidence of the fingerprint, repeating his theory that the print could have been left by Cortines when he handled the plastic bottle in class.

"One fingerprint, for which there is a perfectly logical and plausible explanation, is hardly enough to convict a man of a serious crime and deprive him of his freedom." He suggested that the case could be concluded at this point. The Army, he said, has simply not proven beyond a reasonable doubt that Corporal Cortines did any of the things in the charges and specifications.

"But there is one further consideration: the quality of the soldier." He reviewed Cortines's record and the glowing reports of his superiors. "Corporal Cortines has earned the trust and confidence of his commanders and his fellow soldiers. Isn't he also entitled to the trust of this court? Where there is great room for reasonable doubt, shouldn't we resolve the doubt in his favor?" He asked that Cortines be found innocent, and returned to his duties.

The court filed out to deliberate on its verdict, taking the two clerks and documents and exhibits with them. Major O'Brien and Lieutenant Nugent remained on their side of the room. Gordon and Mex stayed at their table, with the two military police guards standing at rest behind them. Between them was the empty witness chair.

O'Brien caught Gordon's eye, and nodded toward the door at the back of the room. When they were both outside, O'Brien produced a pack of cigarettes and tapped one out for himself. "You use these things?" he offered his adversary.

"No, thanks," Gordon said.

"Neither do I," O'Brien mumbled as he struck a match, "except when I'm waiting for a jury."

"Sounds like a good idea." Robert smiled. He took a cigarette and lit it as carefully as if he were lighting a fuse.

"You did a fine job in there," O'Brien said. "Good law, with enough suggestions of reasons why they ought to give your guy a break. Having Captain Roy read that paper was genius. They knew your client was one of the children he was writing about."

"You think they might let him off?"

"I don't know," the major answered, fanning the smoke away from his face. "He's in trouble on the fingerprint. But I think you probably got him off on the other two charges."

Robert Gordon nodded. He had come to the same conclusion when he was delivering his summation. He had killed his client's chances of freedom when he had called Henry Roy.

"I screwed up when I called the captain," he acknowledged.

Cletus O'Brien shrugged. "Maybe not. You won sympathy for the kid. You showed the court how he got screwed by our operations in El Salvador."

"You think that will help him?"

"Sure," the major allowed. "You took all their anger on yourself. If they could get it past the review board, they'd let the kid go free and they'd send you away for twenty years."

Gordon drew on the cigarette. "That wasn't what I had in mind," he told the major.

"Well, hell, you showed them what the Army has been up to. You showed them the part of themselves that they don't like to think about. You can't expect them to appreciate having their noses rubbed in the dark side of their personalities. You know what happens to the messenger who brings bad news."

The court adjourned for the evening, which gave Gordon a moment of hope. The judges were obviously laboring over their verdict, which might mean that some members of the court were ignoring the evidence of the fingerprint. That evidence was damning, but the jury could bring back any verdict it wanted. Maybe they wanted to set Mex free.

Early the next morning, Colonel Elder called the court back into session. They all waited in silence until the MPs brought Mex in from the stockade and snapped off his handcuffs. He didn't even look at Gordon as he slipped into his chair.

Elder ordered Mex to approach the court. He stood quickly, marched to the center of the room and saluted the officers. Then he stood at military attention.

Elder adjusted his glasses, cleared his throat, and began monotoning.

"With regard to charge number one, of attempted murder, in that the accused did knowingly set an explosive charge . . ." He reread all the charges and the detailed specifications connected with the explosion in Major Daks's driveway, and then, still without looking up at Cortines, read, "This court, in closed session, two-thirds of its members consenting, finds you not guilty."

Mex's expression never changed. Gordon felt his gut tightening.

"With regard to charge number two, of reckless endangerment, in that the accused did knowingly introduce a disabling and potentially deadly substance into the public water supply of Fort Francis Marion . . . " He droned on through the specifications, and concluded, "In closed session, two-thirds of its members consenting, finds you guilty."

Gordon sunk in his chair. His hands came up over his eyes. Elder didn't miss a beat as he launched into this reading of the charges pertaining to Colonel Maritin, but Gordon didn't hear a word. It was over. Mex was going to prison because he had allowed O'Brien to cross-examine Captain Roy. He should have let Roy alone no matter how much his client wanted the Army to hear about the poisoned rivers of El Salvador.

"Two-thirds of its members consenting, finds you not guilty."

Elder set the papers down on the table, but never raised his eyes toward the man he had just convicted. Mex saluted, turned smartly, and marched back to his place. He still hadn't looked at Captain Gordon.

Robert leaned toward him. "Okay, Mex. Now it's your turn to tell them what happened."

Mex's head snapped up just as Elder offered, "Before this court passes sentence, the accused has the right to make a statement in mitigation of punishment." He was reading from a prepared form. "This may be an unsworn statement, which cannot be challenged by any member of this court, nor will any member form any conclusion on the basis of the accused's decision not to offer sworn testimony. Or the accused may offer sworn testimony, in which case the trial counsel, and any member of this court, may ask questions in cross-examination. In either case, the statement will not be included in the record."

For the first time, Elder looked directly at Cortines. "Do you understand your choices, son?"

Gordon whispered to his client. Mex nodded. "The accused understands his options," Gordon said. "The accused chooses to make a sworn statement."

Mex stood and walked to the center of the room. Sergeant Robinson read the oath, and then pointed the corporal toward the witness chair. For a moment, Mex sat silently, the lone criminal in the center of a gathering dedicated to justice. Then, while staring down at his folded fingers, he began.

"My father had a truck. It was a battered old wreck that you had to shift all the way to first just to get up a hill. But it was the only thing he owned. It made him free. It sort of reminded him that he was a man. That he was in charge of somethin'."

His voice was soft, but steady. He spoke unemotionally, like an impartial observer. Even when he related the ORDEN visit to his house, when the leader had smashed the gun into his sister's mouth and clicked the hammer against the empty chamber, his voice never wavered.

"She was kinda skinny. Kinda plain. But she had this smile that just sorta warmed you up. That made everything okay."

He wasn't there. He had left the court, and was a barefoot child in short pants, and she was in front of him.

They weren't there either. The court had gone with him to the shed of a house on the rubbled edge of San Salvador. They were looking at a young girl's smile, more inspiring than stained glass. And right before their eyes, the glorious glass was shattered, broken into shards that could never be reassembled. They felt her pain, and they felt his.

He told about the poisoned water, and the sickness that had swept through his village. The flight through the woods and then about the mine that had blown his mother in half. Through it all, he did nothing to embellish the details. But as he disappeared from his own story, like a voice heard over a radio, the story itself took over the room. The members of the court, all of whom had seen the devastation of a mine, and the effect of a large-caliber bullet on a human skull, were able to fill in the descriptions he omitted.

"He was a small man. Strong, I guess, because he worked all his life. Yeah! Strong! He used to lift me with one hand, while he was carryin' a sack of beans with the other. But still small. When they shocked him, they had him tied to this chair. A heavy wooden chair. It hurt him so much that he tore the chair apart. It was just a bunch of broken sticks when they threw it out."

They were with him again. Not in the courtroom, but now in a shabby schoolhouse that had been turned into a torture chamber.

"But he never told 'em nothin'. Not one word. Until he saw that they were goin' to do it to me. Then he told 'em. I think he was ashamed, because he couldn't look at me while he was tellin' 'em. I wanted to say that it was okay. I knew he was doin' it for me. But I never saw him again.''

They were able to see the execution at Puerta del Diablo, and fill in the parts that they had played. They knew who had provided the Dragonflies that strafed the fleeing villagers when they tried to cross the river. They knew who had taught the Salvadoran soldiers to plant the mines and to poison the rivers. They were able to guess where the interrogators had learned how to hook electrodes to the eyes, the tongues, and the genitals of their witnesses. When they heard the pistol fire through the back of his father's head, they knew who had supplied the bullet.

They were still listening for a full minute after Mex had finished and the room had gone so silent that the hum of the air conditioner had built into a deafening roar.

Mex looked up, surprised to find himself sitting alone in the center of the room. He turned toward Gordon, as if to ask what he should do next. But Gordon didn't see him. His face was hidden in his hands.

"Does the trial counsel have any questions?" Colonel Elder finally asked.

"No . . . no, sir . . . no questions," O'Brien said.

Elder looked up and down the table. None of the court looked back at him.

He glanced carefully at the prisoner. "Is that why you . . . ?" He was trying to ask a question, but he couldn't find the words. "Is that why you attacked us?" he finally managed. "To pay us back?"

Mex raised his eyes directly to the Colonel. "I wasn't tryin' to get even, sir. And I'm glad I didn't hurt nobody. I just wanted you to know what the soldiers in my country did with the things you taught 'em. I wanted you to know what it feels like when your family gets caught in the middle of somethin' they don't know nothin' about. I figured if you knew, you'd make sure that it don't ever happen again."

He looked back down at his hands.

The court recessed, leaving Cletus O'Brien staring across the empty room at Corporal Miguel Cortines. He realized that the young soldier was not so much the perpetrator of a small crime on an Army base, as he was a victim of a much larger crime that reached into the dark corners of the world. He hoped that the court understood it as well.

Colonel Elder clearly didn't enjoy pronouncing the sentence. Although Mex was standing at attention, two paces in front of him, he kept his eyes on the paper he was holding. He mumbled the charges and specifications of which the accused had been judged guilty. Then he said, "This court sentences you to spend two years at hard labor at the United States Army correctional facility in Fort Leavenworth, Kansas." He ordered Mex returned to the Francis Marion stockade until he could be transferred to Leavenworth. Then he stood, declared the court-martial dismissed, and hurried away from the table.

General Wheeler now had the trial record to paper-clip to the investigation report. His desk was clean, and his reputation as a tough, effective commanding officer intact. Colonel Grigg had gotten the quick, quiet trial that he wanted. True, there were references and statements in the transcript that could tarnish the medallion he wore on his green beret. But, all things considered, the trial had attracted less attention than he had feared. Those references and statements would soon be buried out of sight in the mounds of Army archives. O'Brien had pretty much delivered on his promise. And Mex had gotten his say in court, without paying too great a price. It was a light sentence, which may have meant that somebody had listened to what he had to say. Somebody, for at least a few moments, may have even cared.

Now the case was closed.

THE
VERDICT

★ ★ ★

Sergeant Major Thompson had been pleased. Not that he had admitted it. His critique had been as biting as usual.

"How in hell am I going to keep you dumb bastards from killing yourselves?" He had looked up toward heaven as if hoping for a miracle. "The idea is to build a defense that keeps the enemy out, not one that keeps you in. Didn't even one of you lamebrains figure you might need an escape route if the fortification got overrun?" He was looking directly at Willie Derry, who had been unit leader for the exercise.

"We were planning on fighting to the last man, Sergeant Major," Derry had answered.

Thompson had stared at him, then shook his head in disgust. "Jesus, I might as well be talking to a bunch of Marines. Marines are big on dying to the last man." He had thrown his hands in the air. "I've always thought it was better if the enemy died to the last man. But I'm not a Marine. I'm just a poor soldier who tries to get back home alive, and in one piece if possible."

The exercise had been called "Seize and Hold." They were to circle behind an enemy force, construct a defensive position, and then hold that position as a landing point for a counterattacking army. The notion had been developed along the southern end of the line that separated NATO forces from East Germans. The assumption had been that the Warsaw Pact troops would advance almost at will. Special Operations planned to get behind that advance and organize pockets of resistance that would divert reinforcements from the front.

Derry had lead the squad up the side of a rocky ridge to nearly inaccessible high ground. They had dug into bunkers that were invisible from the air, but that afforded open shooting lanes down the slope of the cliff. An enemy force of paratroopers had failed in three attempts to dislodge them. And while they had the jumpers pinned down, their own friendly forces had landed on a nearby riverbed.

"Textbook," Thompson had finally complimented. "Great use of terrain. They'd have had to turn a whole division around to get you idiots out of that place." A hint of a smile had broken across his lips. "But when that division arrived, you'd want to be leaving. And without an escape route, the only way you assholes would have gotten out would have been in body bags."

They had started down out of the exercise area, prepared for a five-hour forced march back to the fort. But Thompson had ordered them toward the riverbed, where two helicopters were waiting.

"If you were Marines, you'd want to walk back," he said.

They rushed through the door and laughed giddily as the copters lifted over the trees. The sergeant major stared straight ahead so that they wouldn't see the smile that was ruining his carefully cultivated expression of disappointment.

Art Walters was waiting for them when they charged up the steps to their barracks rec room. Baldinger pulled up short as soon as he saw him, and the others piled up behind Dave in the doorway.

"Guilty?" Baldinger said, reading the expression on Walter's face.

Walters nodded. "Yeah. On one charge."

"How bad?" Baldinger asked.

Walters told them, "Two years. At Leavenworth."

They walked quietly into the room, unslinging their weapons as they sprawled onto the sofa and chairs.

"Captain Gordon did one hell of a job," Walters continued, repeating what he had heard from the court clerks. "Robinson says he thought Mex might even beat the rap. They found him innocent on two charges, but they nailed him on the other. The goddamn fingerprint on the bottle."

"Two years ain't so bad," Luther Brown said. "Shit, I got a cousin who did two years waitin' for his trial."

"He coulda got ten," Willie Derry added, agreeing with Brown.

Jim Ray Talbert nodded. He had figured they would throw the book at Mex. Two years was better than he could have hoped for.

"It might as well be ten," Baldinger commented absently. He was surprised when every face turned toward him. "Mex isn't going to sit still for two years earning points for good behavior," he explained.

"He's going to try to bust out of the place. Remember what he said about the flyer in the escape-and-evasion exercise. We were pissed, because we killed the guy. Mex said we did him a favor. He said he'd rather be dead than locked in a cell."

Tom Cavitt sneered. "Nobody busts out of Leavenworth." It was a moment later before he realized that was exactly the point that Baldinger had been making. Mex would try, and he would fail, adding more years to his sentence. Two years would quickly turn into life.

"He told me that it didn't matter how much time they gave him," Baldinger went on. "He said he wasn't going to serve it anyway." Then he went back over the conversation he had with Mex in the stockade visitors' room. Mex hadn't been interested in any deal that would reduce his sentence because he had no intention of serving a sentence. As far as he was concerned, he'd done nothing wrong. Just picked up the grenade that someone threw into his backyard and tossed it back over the fence. So why should he stay in the stockade? The guys who blew up his mother and his sister were the ones who should be in prison.

"So why ain't they in prison?" Jim Ray Talbert asked.

Derry laughed. "They own the fuckin' country, Jim Ray. Who do you think's gonna put them in jail?"

"Us!" Talbert snapped. "Americans. Damn it, we know what they did. We oughta make 'em pay for it."

"Jesus, Jim Ray," Dickie Morgan sighed impatiently. "We taught 'em to do what they did. We helped 'em. So how are we supposed to make 'em pay for it?"

"It ain't right," Talbert argued.

Luther Brown stood and picked up his rifle. "It ain't right," he repeated, mocking Talbert's drawl. Then he shook his head as he started out of the room. "Where the hell you been livin' all your life?"

"We oughta do somethin' about it," Talbert yelled after him.

Brown wheeled, the anger flashing in his eyes. "Like what? People like Mex are gettin' fucked over every day, and no one does nothin' about it. What makes this different?"

"He's our friend!" Talbert shouted back.

"I got lots of dead friends," Brown countered. "And the people who killed 'em ain't in prison."

Art Walters could see that Luther Brown and Jim Ray Talbert were edging toward each other. He jumped up in front of Brown. "Let's take it easy guys." Willie Derry moved in front of Talbert. "No sense in fightin' each other," he said. "We're the good guys."

Talbert's head darted from side to side and he tried to look past Derry. "I'm just sayin' that we oughta make it right."

Brown's voice boomed back. "And I'm tellin' you that you can't. People get screwed and there ain't nothin they can do about it. The ones who do the screwin' get away with it every time."

"Let's get a beer," Derry offered as a solution to the argument. "We had a great day today. We oughta be celebratin'."

Talbert looked at Brown. "Sounds good to me."

"Yeah, a couple of beers would go down nice and easy," Brown admitted. He poked Baldinger. "You comin', Dave?"

"Not tonight," Baldinger answered. "I'm going to see if I can find Captain Gordon. Someone ought to thank him for trying."

Gordon came down to the lobby of the bachelor officers' quarters and met Baldinger at the guard desk. He returned the corporal's salute, then took his elbow and steered him back toward the front door. "Let's take a walk. I feel like a leper in this place."

His orders had been delivered as soon as the trial was over. He would serve out the last six months of his military obligation at an arsenal in central New Jersey, where the command stood guard over stores of obsolete weapons. The place was a dead end to his short military career.

"I'm leaving in the morning," he told Baldinger. "Not that I'm anxious to get there, but I sure in hell want out of here."

The word had circulated that Captain Robert Gordon had fallen out of favor with the brass at Fort Francis Marion. Other officers, afraid that their buttons might tarnish if they got too close to him, had backed off to a safe distance. He could feel disapproving eyes burning holes into his back.

Baldinger mumbled his word of thanks as soon as they had cleared the building. "The guys know you stuck your neck out, sir. A lot of officers wouldn't have done that for an enlisted man." Robert Gordon answered with a shrug, "It just didn't seem right for him to go to jail. Not after all he's been through." But even as he was saying it, he remembered Cletus O'Brien's comment. What was right has nothing to do with the law. Gordon realized that if he didn't change his attitude, he wasn't going to be any more successful as an attorney than he had been as an army officer.

They followed the path that circled the officers' housing complex, then took a narrow street between administrative buildings. Gordon reviewed the highlights of the trial, explaining why he couldn't just put

Mex on the stand and let him tell the court exactly what had happened to him. Mex didn't get to speak until after he had already been found guilty.

"But if they just heard his story," Baldinger protested.

"They heard his story," Gordon assured him. "They knew exactly why he had done it. I think some of them even wanted to let him off. But, in the end, they had to pretend not to hear, and not to know."

"Why?"

"I guess once they decide what they have to do, they don't want to hear why they shouldn't be doing it."

"You think they had to send Mex to the stockade?"

Gordon shook his head. "Mex wasn't the issue. He was just an inconvenience. Mex showed them what happens when they help some of their friends stay in power. He made them look at what the presidents and generals do with the money and the training that we give them. They didn't want to look. They didn't want to change. They want these bastards as allies. So the sensible thing to do was to pretend not to listen."

They came out onto the parade grounds, the summer-scorched lawn that filled the center of the Fort Francis Marion complex. Even though it was after sunset, there was enough light in the sky so that they could see the ceremonial artillery pieces and the bare flagpoles.

"But they did listen," Captain Gordon went on. "That's why they handed down a light sentence. With good behavior, Mex should be out in a year. Considering what they could have given him, they just about let him off."

"No, sir," Baldinger contradicted. "They didn't let him off. What they did was sentence him to death." He told the captain about Mex's reaction when they had screwed up an exercise, and killed the flyer they were supposed to rescue. He and the men in the squad knew that Mex would try to escape. He'd keep trying until they killed him. As they circled the parade grounds, Baldinger repeated the argument that Luther Brown had with Jim Ray Talbert a few moments earlier. Mex was a victim, being punished for striking back at a system that had destroyed his family. Talbert had argued that someone had to make it right.

"You tried to make it right, Captain. You took on the whole Army."

"I didn't get very far," Gordon reminded him.

"But you tried. And Mex wasn't even your friend. He's my friend, and I ought to be doing something. I shouldn't just be standing by and watching them take him off to the stockade.''

"What can you do?'' Gordon asked. He watched Baldinger's fists tighten in frustration. "Just try to talk to him. See if you can convince him that two years isn't forever. It isn't his whole life.''

"He won't make it,'' Baldinger answered.

"He has to make it,'' the captain said. "There's nothing you can do to save him from the stockade. Maybe you can save him from himself.''

★   ★   ★

Henry and Carol Roy were a few minutes late getting to the club. The officers were already gathered at one end of the bar, and the wives, after a few words of conversation with the men, had retreated to the table at the edge of the dance floor. Henry led his wife to the ladies' table, exchanged pleasantries, and then took Carol's order for a glass of white wine back to the bar.

Colonel Grigg was all smiles as he watched Major Daks flex his wrist through the lightweight, plastic cast. The heavy plaster that had encased his arm had been cut off that afternoon, and the new cast was hardly visible under his shirtsleeve. The last piece of evidence of Corporal Cortines's attack on the Special Warfare school was hidden out of sight.

It had been a difficult ordeal for Grigg. The Special Operations mission, which he had rebuilt and nurtured from its darkest days following the Vietnam War, had been threatened. For a few days it had looked as if the glare of public exposure might raise difficult questions. Questions about the alliances his men formed with tin-pot dictators and police state bullies. Questions about the methods he taught them for keeping their own people away from the palace gates. Not that he was embarrassed with the role he played. In counterinsurgency warfare, the people were often indistinguishable from the enemy. Victory often demanded that the wheat be cut down with the chaff. But it wasn't always easy to explain the necessities of battle with communist-supported insurgents. Americans cherished fair play, and often they couldn't understand why you had to fight fire with fire, or barbarism with even more barbarism. It was better for the country if some of the details of his operations weren't brought up for public discussion.

But the ordeal was over. The court-martial had been quick and orderly. The record, sanitized by O'Brien's objections, had been basically routine and generally unspectacular. Cortines's presentencing statement, which was the most damaging part of the trial, wouldn't appear in the transcript. There was no reason why anyone in the higher ranks should become concerned, and more important, why any of the congressional friends of Special Operations would be forced to reconsider their positions. Instead of a retreat to safer ground, he could now lead his forces in a new attack.

He turned away from Daks's mending arm to welcome Captain Roy to the group. "Good to see you, Henry. Where have you been keeping yourself?" He laid a friendly hand on the captain's shoulder. "I know you had a rough time in the courtroom. That prick, Gordon, ought to get his ass kicked for making you read that paper to a bunch of guys who have no idea what we're up against." And then, with a broad smile, "But, hell, you told it like it is. We're not playing games out there. We're fighting a dangerous enemy."

Roy flashed his own smile. His comment that one Green Beret, carrying a vial of his chemical agents, could hit the enemy harder than a whole division, had been repeated among the officers. His stock had gone up. But the smile faded as he reached across the bar to take his drinks. "What made it so hard to read the paper," he told the colonel, "was that I wrote it."

Grigg stepped back in confusion as the captain turned away from the gathering and walked back toward the ladies. Carol rolled her eyes in despair when she accepted the drink. The wives were discussing a bake sale for the base grade school, and she was already tired of pretending to be interested. "Can we leave early?" she whispered to her husband.

He nodded. "The sooner the better. I'll think of something to tell Grigg."

They made it through the dinner, but left before the cordials, Henry telling Grigg that he wasn't feeling well. The colonel looked suspicious, but Henry didn't really care. His mind was churning, and he couldn't keep feigning enthusiasm for the conversation that was celebrating another Special Forces victory. They drove down the hill from the club, and circled around the parade grounds. Henry braked the car alongside the antique artillery pieces that were used to fire the evening salute.

Carol sat quietly beside him, remembering evenings when they had stood together at the edge of the Plains at West Point. Then, they had been filled with enthusiasm for the life they were planning together. Now that life was in crisis. For Henry, because the honor of the service that was so important to him had been called into question. For Carol, because the man she loved had wandered away from her, and seemed to be pausing for one last look back.

"I'm sorry," he said suddenly, breaking the silence that each of them had been holding for themselves. "I know none of this—these past few years—has been easy for you."

She started to answer, but settled for a simple nod of her chin. He wanted to talk, and she wanted him to know that she was desperate to listen.

"I didn't hear what you were trying to tell me," he continued. "Or maybe I just didn't want to hear. I wanted to believe in what I was doing. I wanted to believe that it was important. We were losing. All over the world, we were losing. And then we found a way to win. Grigg, and a couple of men like him, figured out how we could win the damn wars. I was part of it, and I thought that was important."

"It was," she agreed with him. "It is."

"Yeah. But now I've got to figure out what's more important. What happens to us. Or what happens to a guy like Corporal Cortines."

"Isn't it the same thing?" Carol asked.

He didn't understand her question, so she tried it a different way.

"What are we saving, if we don't save him, and his family, and people like him? That's what I couldn't understand. What happens to us if we pretend we don't see when a town is poisoned, or when a little girl has a pistol pushed into her mouth."

"Jesus," he growled. "Do you think I didn't care?"

"I think you were afraid to let yourself care. Afraid that if you cared, you couldn't be a soldier."

"But we were fighting for everything we believe in. We had to win."

Carol nodded slowly. She understood exactly what he meant. "I'm as confused as you are, Henry. What is it that we believe in?"

He couldn't answer. It was a simple statement of the question that was now tearing at him. On the parade ground, it was an easy question to answer. Country. Honor. Duty. That was his officer's creed. In the real world, it was more complicated. Corporal Cortines had made him look away from the parade grounds and into the dark corners of the real world. He was beginning to understand what he saw.

"I don't think I can find the answer here," Carol continued.

Henry was stunned. What was she saying? That she was leaving him?

She gestured toward the parade grounds. "Here, everyone already has the answer. No one asks any questions."

He was almost afraid to ask, "Where are you going?"

"I thought I might visit my sister. We used to talk by the hour when we were growing up. I think I need to talk with her." She paused, and then reached over and put her hand on his arm. "Just a visit. I haven't seen her in two years."

"And then you'll come back?" He was begging more than asking.

"Of course I'll come back. It will give you some time to think things out for yourself."

"Stick with me, Carol. Please. Just for a little longer. I'm trying to get this right. Honest to God I am."

She leaned over and rested her head on his shoulder, just as she had often done when their whole lives were ahead of them.

"I love you, Henry. I want to stick with you."

*   *   *

Baldinger was waiting in the rec room when the troops stumbled back into the barracks. They were in a boisterous mood, still winding down from their evening of celebrating in town.

"We got it knocked," Willie Derry was saying as he bounced up the stairs. "We're all gonna get flashed."

"Yeah, but I'm gonna miss you guys," Dickie Morgan interrupted. "They really ought to keep us together."

"Boy, wouldn't that be great. The squad from hell," Bobby Long added from the bottom of the steps. "We'd really kick ass around this man's army."

Seize and hold had been their final exercise. And judging by the privilege of a helicopter ride home, they'd come through with flying colors. Even Derry had managed to stay under the demerit limit. And they hadn't washed Tom Cavitt out, even though he had gotten lost in the forest. Unless one of them screwed up in a major way before their final grades were posted, it looked as if they were all going to be ordered into the Green Berets.

Derry's broad grin tightened a bit when he saw Baldinger. He remembered that his friend had gone to see Captain Gordon, and that reminded him that one of their squad members was sitting in a prison cell. The laughter died as they poured into the room.

"You see him?" Luther Brown asked. His expression was still as grim as it had been when they started out. It was obvious that he hadn't enjoyed the evening.

"Yeah," Baldinger answered. "Great guy. He really put his ass on the line for Mex. Now he's getting the silent treatment from the other officers."

Derry sneered. "Bastards. Too bad we can't take the captain into town with us. We could show him someone appreciates what he's done."

"He knows, Willie," Baldinger said. "I told him. And I don't think he was planning on doing another tour anyway."

Brown, his frown hardening, asked, "What'd he say about Mex?"

"That we ought to talk to him. Try to make him understand that he can make it for two years so he doesn't do something stupid."

"He don't know Mex," Tom Cavitt said, almost to himself.

Dickie Morgan agreed. "Mex ain't gonna sit still for no two years." He was thinking about the bag of rocks they had buried, and what Mex had said about the guy being better off buried in the ground than in a prison cell.

A morbid silence settled like fog over the gaiety of a few seconds earlier. Jim Ray Talbert broke it by repeating what he had said before they had gone out. "We gotta do something." He glanced over at Brown, hoping that his dark, brooding rage wouldn't explode again. But Brown seemed more discouraged than angry.

"Something," he said morosely. "Like what?"

"Like busting him out," Dave Baldinger answered.

Brown's dim eyes brightened. Derry's head snapped toward Dave.

"Out of the stockade?" Tom Cavitt gasped.

"You been smokin' somethin'?" Derry said.

Baldinger scanned the suddenly wide-awake faces. "Captain Gordon did what he was trained to do. Maybe we ought to do what we're trained to do."

Dickie Morgan jumped to his feet. "That's crazy. It's impossible."

"We're trained to do the impossible," Baldinger reminded him. "That's what we've been doing for the last four months."

"Jee-suss," Luther Brown breathed.

"Hey, you ain't serious," Talbert told Baldinger.

Baldinger didn't answer. He just stared back at Jim Ray.

"You are serious," Derry realized out loud.

They looked curiously at one another. The idea was preposterous.

"No way," Dickie Morgan finally said. "It can't be done. It's a fuckin' stone building with bars on the windows. There's a wire fence all around and the place is filled with guards."

Derry suddenly laughed. "You gotta remember, Dave. When we rescued that flyer, we got to bury him the next morning. Gettin' Mex killed ain't exactly the answer to his problems." But his laughter ended with his words. Mex, he remembered, had already decided that the dead flyer was better off.

"Gettin' *us* killed!" Dickie Morgan shouted. His height towered over Baldinger. "If we attack the stockade, they won't be shootin' blanks. You won't get a bad score if you fuck up. You'll get a couple o' holes in your head."

"Even if you don't get dead, you could get caught," Derry reminded the men. "Our trials could keep Captain Gordon in court for the rest of his life."

"And us in the stockade," Bobby Long said. "Christ, Mex would be comin' to visit us on Sundays."

Luther Brown had stayed apart from the exchange, just staring at Baldinger. "You got somethin' in mind, Dave?" he asked when there was an instant of silence.

"They can't take him to Leavenworth without bringing him out of the stockade," Baldinger told Brown. Then he asked, "How many guys are they going to send down from Leavenworth to bring Mex back? Two? Maybe three?"

Brown nodded. "So we hit 'em someplace between the stockade and the airfield."

Willie Derry screamed, "What in hell are you two idiots talkin' about? Two guys. Three guys. Hit 'em here. Hit who? These guys are Americans. They're on our side. We can't pick a fight with our own Army."

"You're outta your minds," Dickie Morgan chimed in. "No way I'm gonna attack our own guys."

There were grunts of approval. The sentiment was nearly unanimous.

Then Brown said, "Mex don't deserve to rot in prison."

Derry jumped all over him. "Christ, Luther. That's what Jim Ray said before, and you were ready to punch him out. You said yourself you had friends in the slammer, and there wasn't nothin' anyone could do about it."

"Yeah," Brown admitted, "only maybe this time it don't have to be. Maybe, just for once, we can do somethin' about it."

"It won't work," Dickie Morgan repeated.

Derry climbed up from his seat on the sofa. "I'm goin' to bed before I start likin' this idea."

"It's worth talkin' about," Brown called after him.

Derry turned and looked patiently at Brown. "Take a guess, Luther. How many demerits you figure they give you for attackin' your own stockade?"

Dickie Morgan followed Derry out of the room. Bobby Long left. Jim Ray looked around and decided that he didn't want to join the conspiracy. "I wish there was somethin' we could do," he said apologetically. He raised his hands in a gesture of helplessness and shook his head as he walked through the door. Tom Cavitt hesitated. "You guys know how much I owe Mex. He saved my life. If I thought we had a chance . . ." His voice trailed off as if to say that they had no chance at all.

Baldinger nodded, but didn't answer. Luther Brown didn't even spare Cavitt a glance.

"How many guys you figure we need?" Brown asked when he realized he was alone with Baldinger.

"Three. Maybe four. And some outside help."

"What kinda help?"

Baldinger stood up and began pacing. "We'd need some communications gear. We'd have to set up on our own frequency so we could coordinate things. But I can handle that. And we'd need a way to get Mex off the base. That's the tough part."

"Someplace on the perimeter," Brown suggested.

Baldinger bit his lip. "That's risky. There's the patrols. And even in the woods, they have the place bugged with electronic sensors. I've been trying to think of some way we could take him out right through the front gate."

Brown shook his head. "No way. Once they know that Mex is sprung, they'll close this place down like a cathouse."

"Yeah," Baldinger agreed. "But I was trying to think of a way where they wouldn't know. What we have to do is kidnap him without anyone knowing he's been kidnapped, and then get him out without anyone knowing he's gone."

Luther Brown whistled.

Baldinger nodded, acknowledging that he was asking a lot. Then he

314

added, "What we really need is intelligence. We have to know when they're coming for him. We have to know when they land and when they leave the airfield, right down to the second. And we have to know how many of them there are."

"Won't be easy," Brown said.

Baldinger slumped back down into a chair. "It may not even be possible," he told his friend.

He stretched out on top of his bed, still wearing the fatigues he had worn to his meeting with Captain Gordon. A confusion of ideas raced through his mind as he tried to put together a plan. He had ways of intercepting the car that would bring the Fort Leavenworth guards from the airport to the stockade. But that wouldn't do him any good. There was no way he could he get into the stockade without the Leavenworth troops. So, he'd have to let them go in and bring Mex out, and then try to take Mex away from them. But Mex might run the second he realized that his escort was under attack. Dealing with the Leavenworth guys would be tough enough without then having to go and hunt down Mex. So Mex would have to understand and be part of the plan. And what would he do with the Leavenworth guys after he took Mex away from them? If he left them behind, they'd sound the alarm before he could ever get Mex off the base. But how could he take them with him? He'd need a truck, and he couldn't requisition a truck without identifying himself and signing a half-dozen forms. That would be as good as handing himself over to the MPs once they figured out what the truck had been used for.

Maybe they ought to hijack the plane. If they could take it over and make the pilot put down on some unmarked dirt field . . . Dumb, he told himself. He didn't know anything about aircraft operations, but he was pretty sure that ground controllers would know exactly what was happening in the air. Besides, if he wasn't going to get caught, he'd have to be back on the base when they realized that Mex was gone. It could take him all day to drive back from where a plane could fly in half an hour.

He kept trying ideas and then discarding them. Some just didn't work. Others required a good deal of luck, and if there was one thing that Special Operations training had drummed into his head it was that you never counted on luck. You made your own. Some of his ideas seemed to work very nicely. But then they didn't mesh with other parts of the plan. As he tried to assemble the pieces of the escape-and-evasion mission, they spilled together to form an unfathomable maze.

He tossed and turned, unable to remember which ideas had seemed plausible and which had seemed ridiculous.

Willie Derry pushed his door open. "I figured you'd be awake," he said. He sauntered in, wearing only his underwear, his shower clogs slapping on the bare wood floor. He straddled a straight-backed chair, resting his arms on the chair back.

"You know you're nuts," he said.

Baldinger sat up on the edge of his bed. "I guess so. I don't see how it can be done."

"That's because it can't," Derry agreed. "At least not without everyone knowin' who done it. If we set Mex free, we'd have to start runnin' with him. There's no way we could just walk back into ol' Fort Viper."

Baldinger smiled. "You've been thinking about this."

"Yeah," Derry admitted with a grin. "It would be some way to finish up the course. Show these fuckers just how much we learned. I'd give my ass if we could pull it off."

"They'd never know," Baldinger reminded him. "If we did this right, no one would ever know what happened to them."

"We'd know." Derry giggled. "For the rest of our lives, no matter how much shit they dumped on us, we'd know we made 'em look like idiots."

Baldinger joined in the joke. Then he asked, "You have any ideas?"

"Not a one," the redhead answered without any hint of embarrassment. "Plannin' has never been my strong suit. I was countin' on you."

"I don't have anything either, Willie. I'm stymied. I keep thinking about what Sergeant Major Thompson is always telling us. 'Do the unexpected. Expect the unexpected.' That, and 'Keep it simple.' Somehow I just can't put the two of them together."

"How much time we got?" Derry asked.

"I don't know. Maybe a couple of days. Mex belongs to Leavenworth now. They'll probably want to bring him in as soon as they can."

"Plenty of time," Derry said as he swung his leg over the chair and started for the door. "You'll come up with somethin'."

In the morning, Baldinger took the shuttle bus back to the bachelor officers' quarters. He didn't need to check in at the guard desk. Captain Gordon was in the parking lot, loading his duffle bag into the trunk of his car. Again, he thanked the captain for all he had done for Mex.

"Try to talk to him," Gordon repeated. "I swear, if he keeps his nose clean, he'll be out in a year."

"I will," Baldinger promised. Then he asked, "Exactly when is Mex being transferred to Leavenworth?"

"Tomorrow, I think."

"Could you find out definitely, sir?"

Gordon's expression registered his confusion.

A plan was beginning to come together in Baldinger's mind, but he wasn't going to get the captain involved. "The guys are trying to put a little traveling gift together," he lied. "We were wondering how much time we have."

"He can't take anything into Leavenworth with him," the captain said. He slammed his trunk lid and dusted his hands together to indicate that he was all finished.

"We know that, sir," Dave answered.

Gordon eyed the young corporal suspiciously over the back deck of his car.

"If you could just find out exactly when he's being taken out, we'd really appreciate it," Baldinger repeated.

Gordon kept his focus fixed on Dave as he circled around the car. "Corporal, I sure as hell hope you're not thinking of doing something that could make this a lot worse."

"No, sir," Baldinger answered.

"Then what's this all about?"

"Sir, you've done all you can possibly do. You're going to be driving out of here today, and I don't think you plan on ever coming back."

Robert Gordon nodded.

"Then what happens from now on isn't your problem, sir. You've already done more than anyone could ask. The last thing I'd want to do, Captain, is tell you things that might cause you a problem."

"Baldinger, for chrissake, don't do something stupid."

"No, sir."

"I mean it." Gordon turned toward his car and suddenly pounded his fists down on the roof. "Please. You're the best, Baldinger. The very best this Army has going for it. It's God-awful that one of you is going to prison. It would be a dumb, fucking waste if the rest of the squad went with him."

"We'll be okay, Captain. But we'd certainly appreciate it if you could find out when they're moving him."

"Please," Captain Gordon repeated.

Baldinger looked straight into Gordon's eyes. "We're going to miss you, sir. The Army is going to miss you."

The captain's expression acknowledged the compliment. "Wait here, Corporal. I'll make a couple of telephone calls."

Baldinger's next step was at the base hospital. In his plan, which was still only a vague outline, the hospital was the pivot point on which everything swung. He stood in the doorway of the pharmacy, watching Art Walters count pills out of bottles into small paper cups.

"When's Tony going out?" he asked. Their former squad buddy, Tony LaRocca, was recovering from the surgery that had repaired his torn knee. He was scheduled for transfer to the hospital at Fort Bragg for post-surgical therapy.

"Sometime this week," Walters answered. "Whenever he's ready. It's an open ticket."

Dave walked up next to him. "Can it be tomorrow? Late in the afternoon?"

Walters stopped making up the medication trays. "Whatever Tony says. Why? What's up?"

Dave explained the plan that was beginning to take shape. He admitted he didn't yet have all the pieces, but Art Walter's help would be essential. "If something goes wrong, Art, they'll never hear your name from me. But I have to warn you. If you help in any way, and we get caught, they can hang you just as high as the rest of us."

"Yeah, I know," Walters acknowledged. "But how much do I have to tell Tony? Maybe we can keep him clean. He doesn't have to know what we're trying to do."

Baldinger thought about it. Then he said, "Better tell him everything and give him the chance to stay out. He'll be right in the middle of things. If we get caught, no one would believe he didn't know what was going on."

From the hospital, Dave walked to the school and signed in at the guard station. He went to the library, pulled down two field manuals on communications procedures and checked them out with the librarian. Before leaving the building, he let himself into the vacant communications classroom and picked up three hand-held radios and a battery charger. They were in the baggy pockets of his fatigues when he signed back out through the guard station.

Willie Derry and Luther Brown were waiting in the rec room when Baldinger returned to the barracks. They started to question him, but he motioned them into his room and left them waiting while he plugged in the battery charger and connected the radios. Then, quietly, he took them step by step through his plan to rescue Mex.

There were four phases. First, they had to get Mex away from the guards without the escorts from Leavenworth knowing that they had lost him. "We have to take control of their operations," he explained. Baldinger pointed toward the radios he had just borrowed. "That's why we'll need our own communications network."

Next, they had to get him off the base. That would be the most difficult part, because Mex's picture had been in the Fort Francis Marion paper in connection with the trial. The guards at the gates would recognize him instantly. "So we have to exchange him for someone else," Baldinger said. "Someone who can go through the front gate with no questions asked. Like the patient in an ambulance."

Willie Derry was already smiling. "This is great," he told Baldinger. "Jesus, Dave, you oughta be teachin' a course at this place."

But then, they would have to pull the exchange all over again in order to get Mex back. That meant they'd have to hijack the ambulance.

"No sweat," Luther Brown interrupted. Hadn't they stopped Sergeant Campbell's jeep during the exercise he lead?

"The problem," Baldinger continued, "is that the ambulance driver can't even know he's been hijacked. That's why we need Cavitt and Morgan." He explained how Cavitt's training in using remote-control detonators and Morgan's mechanical skills would fit into the scheme.

"And finally, we have to get Mex on a plane and out of here before anyone even suspects that he's gone." He put all the pieces together for his spellbound listeners so that they could see how, if everything fell into place, Mex would never be missed.

Derry's face turned to joy when everything registered. "Jesus, that's beautiful," he sighed as soon as Dave finished. "You're a genius, Baldinger."

"It's beautiful as long as everything runs like clockwork," Dave Baldinger said. "But if anything slips, then I'm not a genius. I'm a prisoner, doing twenty years in the stockade." He looked straight at Derry. "And so are you. Think about that, Willie, before you join up."

Brown had been thinking about it. "Is Art in with us?" he asked.

"Nobody's in anything," Baldinger said firmly. "As of this moment, there's nothing to be in. It's going to take seven of us to pull this off. One at the airstrip. One at the stockade. Two at the garage. One in the car inside, and two more when it comes outside. Then there's Art and Tony. Unless everyone wants to put his ass on the line to free Mex, this isn't going to work. So unless everyone's in, no one is in."

"I'm in," Derry said immediately. "I wouldn't miss this for the world. I tell ya, Baldinger, you're gonna be famous. When word gets around what you done, the Green Berets are gonna be makin' up songs about ya."

"The word isn't going to get around, Willie. If we do this right, no one will know anything happened."

Derry was disappointed. "We gotta tell someone. We'll be the most famous class that ever made it through this place."

"If someone knows," Dave insisted, "it will be because we're in prison."

Brown wasn't nearly as enthusiastic as Willie. "When do you hear from Walters?" he asked.

"This afternoon, and he'll have Tony's answer by then."

"And?" Brown pressed.

"If they both want to help Mex, then I'll explain it to everyone before we leave for dinner. Those that want to help can meet me back here after dinner. Those that don't probably ought to take in a movie. Just go somewhere where they'll be seen, so no one can accuse them of being involved."

"I thought we needed everyone?" Luther persisted.

"We can get by with one no-show," Baldinger answered. "But I don't want to announce it." He smiled. "I don't want everyone thinking he's the one no-show who doesn't matter."

"I'm in," Derry repeated. He slapped Baldinger on the back. "I mean it, Dave. Pure genius! You oughta be a general."

Luther Brown hesitated. He still wasn't sure it was workable. Baldinger gave him a temporary reprieve by saying, "Nobody is in anything until I hear from Walters."

They didn't have to wait long. An hour later, Art Walters called the pay phone that hung on the rec room wall. "Tony is ready to travel to Bragg," he said. "Ambulance that takes him up there will be leaving about sixteen-hundred. I thought the guys would want to know."

"I'll tell them," Baldinger answered.

Walters continued, "And I'll be there to help put him in the ambulance. I've got the medication he's going to need."

"Thanks, Art," Dave said. "I'll be over in the morning to fill you in and pick up the pills." He was about to hang up when he remembered something Art Walters had told him. "Hey, I guess you're still human, Walters. You didn't learn to forget."

"Neither did you, Baldinger," Art answered. "It could get you into a heck of a lot of trouble."

He had the whole unit together in the rec room an hour before dinner. Tom Cavitt and Jim Ray Talbert were in field gear. They had been making up missed runs on the obstacle course. Bobby Long and Dickie Morgan were in dress greens, just back from assignment as color guards for a local civic ceremony.

"Guys, I asked you stick around for a minute because I think I figured out a way to help Mex," Baldinger began.

"Help him?" Morgan asked. He seemed pleased with the opportunity.

"Rescue him," Baldinger said. "A standard escape-and-evasion operation. Free him from the enemy and help him avoid recapture."

Morgan fell back against the back of the sofa. "Christ, here we go again," he said.

Baldinger scanned their faces. "Anybody who doesn't want to hear about it?"

No one protested, so he started into his explanation. His voice was soft and confidential, but it sounded clearly in the silent room. They listened carefully. Their eyes followed his every gesture. The silence continued for several seconds after he had stopped speaking.

"You sure did your homework," Tom Cavitt finally said. He turned to Luther Brown and added, "I think it'll work."

Brown nodded. "I heard it before. It gets better each time you hear it."

Bobby Long was quick to jump on the plan's major weakness. "It's like a fuckin' train schedule, Dave. You get one train late and the whole line stops. I mean, if just one little thing doesn't happen when it should . . ."

"Absolutely right," Baldinger admitted for the benefit of all. "We get a little behind, and we miss the ambulance, and we find ourselves sitting in the middle of a military base with an escaped prisoner on our hands. It would be damn hard to explain."

"Nobody gets hurt," Jim Ray Talbert said in surprise. "No one gets shot. No one even gets hit."

"They're all our guys, Jim Ray. We don't want anyone getting hurt."

"This is crazy," Dickie Morgan announced, jumping to his feet. "We'd all be riskin' prison. I mean, I like Mex as much as any of you. But let's face it. What he did was fuckin' nuts. And what they done to him wasn't all that bad. Two years ain't much more than a slap on the wrist. I think we should leave it alone."

"Mex may not want us messin' around in this," Bobby Long added. "If he gets caught escapin' he'll do a lot more time."

Baldinger agreed vigorously. "Absolutely. I'll be talking to Mex tomorrow morning. If he says no, then the whole thing is off. But I want to tell him that we're ready to try."

"When do you need to know?" Jim Ray asked.

"Right after dinner. If it's a go, we have a lot of work to get done by tomorrow.

"I'll tell you right now. I'm in." It was Tom Cavitt who stayed seated while the others were standing to leave for dinner.

Baldinger answered, "Take your time. Think about it. Be damn sure."

But Cavitt shot right back, "There's nothing to think about. I'm damn sure." He was suddenly the center of attention. He looked up at the startled expressions that surrounded him. "You guys remember how Mex got caught, don't you? He carried me back to the base when he could've been runnin'. If it wasn't for Mex, I'd still be out there. Christ, the buzzards would be fightin' over me."

Cavitt jumped up to follow the others to the mess hall, but he was blocked by Luther turning back into the room. "I'm in too," Brown said.

"You can think about it, Luther," Dave reminded him.

Brown answered. "That's all I have been thinkin' about. Mex was fightin' back. That's what I should've been doin'. Fightin' back. So that's what I'm gonna do now."

Brown turned and followed the others. Willie Derry gave Dave a thumbs-up signal as he fell in beside him for the walk to the mess hall.

Jim Ray Talbert was the first one to return from dinner. "I was the one who said we ought to be doin' somethin'," he told Baldinger. "So I guess I'm in."

Dave reminded him that what he said couldn't get him into any trouble. "We'd all like to do something, Jim Ray. But this is different. You'll be putting your ass on the line."

Talbert swallowed hard. "I thought about that. Up to now, everything here was just an exercise. This time, it's real. But this is what I been trainin' for. So I guess I'm ready."

Bobby Long wandered in a few minutes later and settled into a chair across from Baldinger. For a few minutes, he didn't say anything. Then he looked at Dave and asked, "What's my assignment?"

Dickie Morgan was the last one to return. They were all sitting silently in the rec room when he slammed the screen door and started up the stairs. Dickie stood in the doorway and glanced around at the other members of the squad.

"All you guys in on this?"

Baldinger answered before anyone had a chance to comment. "That's not important, Dickie. No one's going to decide for you. Everyone has to decide for himself."

"It's a good plan," Morgan said.

"It's a dangerous plan," Dave corrected.

"Yeah," Morgan agreed. "I been thinkin' about all the things that could go wrong. Nothin' ever runs exactly like it's supposed to."

Dave nodded. "Nothing is certain."

"The only thing I'm sure of," Morgan continued, "is that Mex isn't goin' to make it through a prison sentence. He'll die in Leavenworth."

No one answered. The room was deathly quiet.

"So I guess I'm in," he concluded.

"Attaway!" Willie Derry screamed, breaking the tension, and suddenly everyone was laughing.

"Let's kick some ass," Jim Ray Talbert chimed in.

Tom Cavitt punched his fist into the air. "This is going to be one Special Operations raid they'll never forget."

"We've got a lot of work to do," Baldinger said seriously. "The first thing we have to do is figure out how to get Tom and Dickie into the garage at the hospital."

* * *

Carol Roy had finished packing. Henry lifted the heavy suitcase down from the bed and set it into the closet. She had a few things in a small bag that she would carry on the plane with her when they left the next day. The suitcase would be checked through to Denver, where her sister would meet the flight.

"It's always been me who was packing to go away," Henry said sadly. "I don't remember you ever going off by yourself."

"It's only for a week," she reminded him. She had helped Henry pack for tours of duty when he was going to be away for a year. "I'll be back before you know it."

He forced a smile, even though he wasn't sure that she would be coming back. Fort Francis Marion held nothing for Carol. He knew she had never been happy here. For the past day, while she had been on the phone, making arrangements with her sister, and then making her plane reservations, there had been an enthusiasm in her voice that he hardly remembered. He had a sinking feeling that this might be the beginning of the end. Only a few days before, he had accused her of forcing him to choose between her and the Army. Perhaps that was what she was doing right now.

Henry had never thought of a life outside the Army. From the day he had arrived at West Point, and traded the high school sports jacket he had outgrown for the cadet uniform, military life seemed to fit. Even the plebe hazing, with its demeaning ordeals and its shouted mantras of military trivia made sense to him. He had willingly given up his individuality to become part of the corps, and surrendered his personal possibilities to join the great work of defending freedom.

At graduation, he had been welcomed into a brotherhood of honor where he was assured of always being on the side of righteousness. The Army and its allies were good and just, fighting for human freedom and individual dignity. Their enemies were the dark forces of evil. His companions were flesh and blood, men with names and voices, carrying photographs of their wives and children. The enemy was distant and faceless, like the devils in hell.

Special Operations had increased his sense of purpose. The enemy, stymied in the battlefield, had taken the war into villages, hamlets, and homes. Outgunned in tanks and fieldpieces, they had made it a battle of knives and punji sticks. Then, when the regular Army had faltered in confusion, he had rushed to the rescue. He had joined hand in hand with the allies, and gone out to meet the enemy face-to-face.

And that was when it had all begun to unravel. The allies, he had found, weren't always defenders of freedom and dignity. And the enemy weren't always the dark forces of evil. Sometimes the allies were in jackboots. Sometimes the enemy were in monks' robes. Then came the trial, when the enemy sat across from him, and he saw that it had a name and a face. He heard its voice. For the first time in his adult life, he was confused in his purpose.

Neither had he ever imagined a future without Carol. He loved her deeply, and had never doubted her love for him. She had seemed to share his devotion to the Army, and had been a good soldier, accepting the difficulties of camp life with humor and good grace. Certainly, she had been disappointed when his overseas tours forced them to live apart. But she had used the time well, devoting her energies to furthering her education and filling the time with worthwhile social work. She had written almost daily, short chatty notes filled with humor, restating her devotion. And always she had been waiting to welcome him back.

His assignment to Fort Marion had seemed to be her reward as well as his. His faculty position was the closest thing to a nine-to-five job that military life offered, guaranteeing that they would be together every day. Just as important, it confirmed that his career was secure. He would be working in the temple of Special Operations technology, side by side with Colonel Grigg and the other apostles of the Army's most important service. His promotion to major was a given, with the promise of more prestigious housing and with the pay increase that would ease her financial worries. There was no reason to suspect that their life together wasn't completely secure.

But Fort Marion had given Carol her first intimate look at the true nature of his work, and she had been repulsed by what she saw. As she sat at the edges of conversations that were filled with knives, and mines, and chemicals she had understood the horror of hand-to-hand killing. The ceremonial cannons on the parade ground had ceased to be symbols of gallantry and honor, and had become instruments of cruel and painful death. And she had begun to understand Henry's companions in uniform. The officers seemed indifferent to the victims of their art. The allied officers who came to the school for their training seemed disdainful of their own people.

Henry had tried to cover over her misgivings. "Don't look!" he had tried to tell her. "Don't listen!" he had advised. But Carol did look, and did listen. Gradually, the Army they had shared had become a barrier between them.

Corporal Cortines had forced her decision. He brought to Fort Marion the same danger and fear that Henry and his companions had brought to his country. He gave her growing misgivings a name and a face. And Corporal Cortines would force the captain's decision. Before Henry could secure his life with Carol, he had to decide who was responsible for the horror that had been visited on the young man and his family. And, if any of the responsibility was his own, he had to decide what he was going to do about it.

"I'll miss you, Carol," he told her as he slipped into bed beside her. "This week is going to seem longer than all the years when I was away."

★　★　★

Tom Cavitt and Dickie Morgan circled around the edge of the field behind the base hospital. They were wearing their forest greens and dress shoes, not the ideal uniform for a trek through the woods. But they would be crossing open ground to the back of the hospital garage, and then walking down a corridor where they might encounter someone from the medical staff. Combat gear, with greasepaint to darken their faces, would attract a lot more attention than normal dress uniforms.

Cavitt was keeping up a stream of commentary, first about the brightness of the moon, which he swore made them visible from every house on the base. "Thompson will flunk us right into the supply corps for bein' so stupid," he complained to Morgan. "General Wheeler will get up to take a leak, and he'll wonder who in hell is trampin' through his backyard." And then, about the density of the woods they were moving through. "This place is worse than Sector Foxtrot. There's probably more snakes in here than out in the exercise area."

Morgan wasn't answering. His hands were clammy and his mouth was dry. This mission counted. On all their previous exercises, failure meant a tongue-lashing and a dozen demerits. This time it probably meant a jail sentence. "Christ," he cursed as the cloth travel bag smashed against his knee. He had figured that the small overnight bag would be less conspicuous than a toolbox. But it was harder to carry. The wrenches and pliers inside were jingling as they bounced together. "You sound like an ice-cream truck," Cavitt had told him.

Morgan pulled up short. They were opposite the back door of the hospital, where the building joined the garage. Before them was a small lawn, and then a parking space where the night shift's cars were scattered. "Try and look like we belong," Cavitt advised as he stepped out of the woods and brushed the leaves from his shoulders.

They crossed the lawn and stepped over the curb barrier into the lot. "Nice and easy," Cavitt said. "We're not in any hurry." The advice was as much for himself as for Morgan. He could hear his heart pounding in the still night air.

The back door of the hospital building opened, and two nurses stepped out. "Damn it," Dickie whispered. He stopped dead, standing like a statue in the middle of the parking lot.

"Keep moving," Cavitt answered. Everything depended on their looking so normal that they would become invisible. The surest way to attract attention would be to get out of the flow of the fort's numbing normality.

One of the nurses was an officer. Cavitt snapped a salute and held it so that his hand was covering his face. Dickie did the same.

"Evenin', ma'am," Cavitt barked.

The officer shifted her briefcase and returned the salute. "Evening, Corporal." She wasn't at all interested in his face.

Cavitt caught the door and held it open for Dickie Morgan. They walked down a basement corridor, passing two medics who didn't even seem to see them, and reached the door to the garage. Then they stepped through and locked the door behind them.

There were two sedans with Army markings in the back of the area. The base ambulances were parked at the front, their bumpers nearly touching the overhead doors. One was a converted combat vehicle, painted khaki, with heavy tires holding it high off the ground. The other was a white civilian ambulance with the base insignia painted on the doors.

"This one," Cavitt whispered, walking around one side of the civilian vehicle. He opened the door carefully, reached in and pulled the hood release. Morgan went straight to the front of the ambulance, and raised the hood as soon as it popped free. Cavitt stepped up next to him to hold the flashlight.

"Strange setup," Morgan mumbled, examining the tangle of machinery that was packed into the small space. Cavitt's eyes rolled. Someone could walk in on them at any second. They didn't have time to admire the details of the engine.

Morgan, with the mechanical skills gathered in his training, got to work. He found the fuel line and traced it down under the frame until it led him to the fuel pump. Then he cut the electric line that carried power from the alternator to the pump. Carefully, he spliced a radio-controlled detonator switch, which Cavitt had rigged, into the electrical circuit. It should have taken him only a few seconds, but his hands were trembling and he was having trouble twisting the small wires.

"What's wrong?" Cavitt's voice begged in a whisper.

"Try it," Morgan hissed as he finished taping the wire ends.

Cavitt backed across the garage, holding the battery-powered detonator in his hand. In his training, he had used the same kind of device to set off dangerous explosive charges. Now, when there were no explosives, he was more frightened than he had ever been before. He closed his eyes as he pressed the key. The only response was a faint click under the car as the relay snapped open, breaking the electrical connection to the pump. Dickie reached out from under the car and held a thumb up. Cavitt smiled and touched the button again. He heard the relay click closed. Then he stuffed the detonator back into his pocket and carefully closed the engine hood.

They eased the door open a crack and peered out into the corridor. It was empty. A few moments later, they were back in the woods, making their way around the periphery of the hospital grounds.

Back in the barracks, Bobby Long slipped the white cover over his helmet and then stood up to model his attire. In addition to the helmet, he was wearing a white webbed belt and white spats that he had lifted from the unit's color guard parade gear.

"Whatta ya think?" he asked Jim Ray Talbert.

Jim Ray whistled. "Ya coulda fooled me." Then he asked, "Shouldn't you be carryin' a club, or somethin'?"

"Too risky," Long answered. "Only place you can get a white stick is from the MPs, and I ain't gonna ask."

Talbert looked him up and down. "I don't think anyone's gonna notice."

"I hope to hell nobody's gonna notice," Bobby Long said. "I'm gonna be directin' traffic right in front of the stockade. If someone figures out that I'm a phony, they won't have far to take me."

They heard footsteps on the stairs. Bobby Long hurried out of the MP trappings. Talbert sauntered into the rec room in time to meet Dave Baldinger. Baldinger gave him two battery-powered, hand-held radios.

"They work?" Talbert asked.

Dave nodded. "They work."

Jim Ray looked over the two devices. "They look okay."

"They're on their own frequency," Baldinger explained. "The only radios they can talk to are each other. And no one can listen in."

Bobby Long, back in his fatigues, came into the rec room. "We oughta hang on to them," he said. "They could come in handy when we're tryin' to get back into the base after hours. It'd be like havin' our own network."

Baldinger smiled. "Afraid not, Bobby. One of them, we're never going to get back. The other one gets fixed and then put back in the communications shed. We don't want some radioman asking questions."

"Whatta ya worryin' about?" Talbert laughed. "Nobody is goin' to figure this out."

"Just try them in the morning," Baldinger advised. "You take one of them out on the road," he told Bobby Long, and to Jim Ray Talbert he said, "and you take the other out by the airstrip. Make damn sure you guys can talk to one another."

Jim Ray raised one of the radios to his mouth and began mimicking the impersonal voice of a base station radio operator. "This is base. Take him straight to the hospital. Emergency entrance. I'll alert them, and I'll let them know at the airstrip."

Then he looked at Baldinger. "Whatta ya think?"

"I think you could have a career in broadcasting," Dave told him with a grin.

"Yeah," Talbert allowed. And then he added glumly, "The voice of Radio Leavenworth."

The screen door banged below them, and their heads turned apprehensively toward the stairs. Then they heard Cavitt's voice. "Christ, look at these pants. Mud up to the knees. I'll never get these shoes clean."

He and Dickie Morgan came into the room. There were mud stains on their trousers and the pocket of Dickie's jacket was torn.

"All set?" Baldinger asked.

In response, Cavitt tossed him the detonator. "Here! You're now the proud owner of a genuine Army ambulance."

In the morning, the squad dressed in combat gear and reported to the obstacle course. Baldinger begged off, asking Sergeant Major Thompson for permission to pay a last visit to Mex. Thompson agreed.

"Give him my best," he asked Dave. "And tell him I think he's a fine soldier. I've never trained a man who could have covered as much ground as he did that night."

"I'll tell him, Sergeant Major."

Dave turned and marched out of the office.

"Baldinger," Thompson screamed after him. Dave stopped in in the doorway. "You can make up the obstacle course tomorrow. Six-hundred hours. And I want your best time."

"Yes, Sergeant Major."

He jumped on the shuttle bus and rode it to the base stockade where he was processed into the visitors' area. Then he paced nervously for the half hour until the heavy wire door at the far end of the room rattled and swung open. Mex shuffled out in the pajamalike fatigues that were the uniform for long-term prisoners. He turned so that the guard could unfasten his handcuffs, and then massaged the blood back into his wrists as he walked to his side of the table.

"Amigo," Baldinger said. "Good to see you."

"You, too, my friend."

They paused awkwardly, until Baldinger asked, "How you feeling?" He regretted the comment instantly. How could he be feeling when he was about to be transported to a maximum security prison?

Mex shrugged and they sat through another silent pause. Then he leaned forward and told Dave, "Thanks for all you've done."

Baldinger's hands came up in a gesture of helplessness. "Sorry it wasn't more." Then he changed the mood. "Hey, all the guys send their best. Especially Sergeant Major Thompson." He repeated Thompson's sincere words of praise.

"He's a good man," Mex said. "I don't think he liked the idea of killin' anyone. I think he was tryin' to keep us all alive."

Baldinger agreed. Then he got down to the purpose of his visit. He took Mex through Captain Gordon's advice about staying out of trouble, and Mex kept nodding that he understood. "Gordon says you could be out in a year. Year and a half tops. And that's not so long, Mex. Hell, it's sooner than you'd have been getting out of the Army."

"It ain't the same as the Army," Cortines reminded him. He jerked his head toward the wire door that he had just come through. "In there, you ain't alive."

"A year," Dave said. "You can make it for one lousy year." But his words trailed off into a mumble. He'd never been in prison. He had no idea whether he could stand it for even a day.

Mex smiled across the table. "Don't worry. They'll never get me to Leavenworth, my friend. They got to take the handcuffs off before they put me on the plane. And the second they do, I start walkin'. I keep walkin' until I'm clear of Fort Viper."

"They'll shoot you Mex. The guards carry guns."

"That'll be their choice. They can let me walk, or they can shoot me in the back. I already made my choice. I ain't goin' to the stockade."

It was the same conversation they had had before. And just as before, Dave knew that he meant it. Mex didn't care that much about his life. It had been painful up until now, and the future would hold more than its share of ugly memories. He could go on, or let it stop right here. But if he was going on, it would be on his terms. He was through lifting his sombrero whenever the landlord drove past. He wasn't going to be bound by someone else's rules. He sure as hell would never stand by while a young girl was brutalized, or ever again be cowered by a bully with a pistol. They could shoot him. Kill him. But they couldn't ever again own him. By nightfall, he would either be free, or he would be dead. But he wouldn't be beginning a sentence at Leavenworth, whether it was one year or twenty years.

Baldinger leaned in close to him. "We're going to help you escape, Mex. Me and the guys in the squad. All of us. It's all worked out."

Cortines started shaking his head. "No. No, my friend. I don't want that."

"And we don't want you shot. We figured you wouldn't let them take you to prison, and we're not going to let them kill you. So, we have to get you out of here."

"No way," Mex argued back. "I don't want none of you guys gettin' in trouble."

"It's too late, Mex. It's all set. The clock is already running."

Cortines's eyes flashed and he started out of his chair toward Baldinger. Then he remembered where he was and settled back slowly. "No, I won't let you do this."

"The only way you can stop us to turn us in," Dave said. "If you aren't going to do that, then you better listen, because we don't want you screwing this up."

"No," Mex hissed once more.

Baldinger ignored the protest and began laying out the details of the plan. He took Mex through it step by step, even though Cortines wasn't involved in most of the moves they were making. Sergeant Major Thompson was always telling them to make sure that everyone involved understood the operation. "The details change," he preached over and over again, "and the plan has to change with them. To make any operation work, a lot of people have to make a lot of right decisions. And they can't do that unless they know what the hell is going on." Baldinger wanted to be sure that, if something went wrong, Mex would make the right decision.

He saw Mex's eyes brighten as he began putting the pieces together. Cortines smiled when he heard that the squad had set up its own radio frequency, and he laughed when Dave told him that they had already rigged the base ambulance.

"Sounds like a big plan just to spring one guy," he said when Baldinger was finished.

"He's an important guy," Dave answered.

"It's risky," Mex decided.

Baldinger nodded his agreement, and said, "So's turning your back on a guard and hoping that he won't shoot."

Mex sat silently for a few minutes, reconstructing the plan in his mind. He wasn't sure whether everything would come together, but he trusted Baldinger. He had never worried about any of the exercises when Dave was in charge, and if his friends weren't taking such a terrible risk, he certainly wouldn't be worried now.

Dave read his thoughts. "Trust me, Mex. We're going to get you out of here. It's going to work."

Cortines thought for a few moments longer, and then decided, "If you say so, my friend."

★　★　★

Henry Roy carried Carol's suitcase out into the driveway and lifted it into the trunk of the Mustang. He checked his watch, even though he knew there was no reason to hurry. It was only 1300, and her plane wasn't leaving the Greenville airport until 1720. The drive would take less than an hour, giving them plenty of time for a leisurely cocktail and a light supper. He strolled back into the house and found Carol in the bedroom, putting the finishing touches on her makeup.

"You look great," he told her. She smiled appreciatively as she concentrated on her eyeliner.

He wandered into the kitchen, and glanced at the list of notes she had pasted to the door of the refrigerator. Her sister's telephone number. Emergency numbers for the plumber and the electrician in case they were needed. The schedule for milk deliveries and trash pickups. Trivia he had never bothered with that would now be his concern. Suddenly, he felt lost and disoriented. His orderly world was coming apart.

"All ready," Carol announced as she emerged from the bedroom, wearing a smart cotton suit and carrying an oversized handbag over her arm. He took the handbag, and then felt foolish carrying it to the car.

They drove through the residential streets, past the administrative buildings, and then circled the parade grounds. There were uniforms hustling in every direction, and a new squad of candidates for Special Operations training was being marched by a ramrod drill sergeant toward the enlisted men's barracks. Everything around them suggested military order. He stopped at the gate and returned the salute from the guard, who took a cursory glance through the window and then waved them ahead. Within a minute, Fort Francis Marion had disappeared from the rearview mirror.

Henry scarcely listened as Carol ran through her list of household instructions, repeating the information she had left on the refrigerator. Then she went back over her travel arrangements, which they had already reviewed dozens of times. He waited patiently until, at last, she fell silent.

"Carol, while you're away, there's one thing you ought to be thinking about."

She turned toward him, but didn't answer.

"Do you want me to get out of the Army? Because if that's what you really want . . ."

"I will," she promised. "But you have to think about it too. It's the only life we've ever had together. We have to decide together. I know what it means to you."

They drove silently for another few minutes, almost to the point where the small country road joined the interstate. Then he said, "I'm not sure what it really means to me. I know I don't ever again want to feel ashamed for what I'm doing."

Carol admitted, "I guess I didn't learn enough about what you were doing, Henry. I didn't want to know. I didn't want to know the people you were training."

Henry shook his head slowly. "There were some of them that you wouldn't want to know. I guess I understood what they were doing in their own countries. I guess I just tried not to think about it. You were more honest than I was, Carol. You thought about it."

"We'll have a lot to talk about when I get home," Carol said.

"We will," he agreed. "I can't wait for you to come back."

★   ★   ★

Jim Ray Talbert crouched in the heavy brush at the end of the runway and watched the executive jet drop its landing gear. It touched down with a puff of dust, and roared as it reversed its engines. Then it taxied to the control shed where a jeep and its military police driver were waiting.

Two noncoms stepped down the ladder, sergeants in forest-green uniforms with rows of service stripes down the sleeves. They wore web belts over their jackets with leather pistol holsters hanging by their sides. One carried a briefcase. They talked briefly with the driver, and then climbed into the jeep, which backed out onto the gravel road and then started down the hill toward Fort Francis Marion.

Jim Ray switched on the radio. "Jailhouse, this is Base Station."

Bobby Long's voice crackled back. "This is Jailhouse."

"There's two of 'em. They're on their way," Jim Ray said.

Long slipped the radio into his belt, checked the white cover of his helmet, and straightened out his uniform. Then he stepped out from behind the corner of an administrative building and walked across the road to the parking area in front of the stockade.

"Act natural. Look like you belong there," he kept telling himself. It had sounded so easy when Baldinger was explaining the plan. But there was nothing natural about the way his knees were shaking. And how could he look like he belonged at a guard post where no guard had ever been posted before?

He took up his position near the entrance and stood at parade rest, hoping that none of the prison officers would drive in. A guard on duty certainly wouldn't attract any attention at a military base. But someone connected with the stockade might well remember that there usually wasn't a soldier posted in the parking area.

"Just salute, and direct them to parking spaces," Baldinger had told him. "If you act like a guard, you'll be damn near invisible."

He snapped to attention as a car turned toward him, and fired a salute at the officer behind the wheel. "Visiting, sir? Or official business?"

The officer leaned out the window. "I have a meeting with the prison commandant."

"Yes, sir," Bobby responded cheerily. He pointed toward the close-in parking spaces. "Anywhere over there, sir." Then he stepped back and rendered another smart salute. He exhaled as the car pulled away.

Great, he thought. I've probably directed him to the commandant's reserved space. He could almost hear the conversation.

"Sorry, sir. But you're not allowed to park there."

"But the guard at the gate told me to park here."

"What guard? There's no guard at the gate, sir."

"Then who's that MP standing right over there?"

"Oh, he's an imposter, sir. Part of a scheme to spring one of the prisoners. We're just about to pick him up for questioning."

Baldinger's plan didn't sound all that brilliant to Bobby Long now that he was standing out in the open no more than fifty yards from the front door of the stockade. There were just too many things that could go wrong.

Mex was sitting in the stockade office, a prison guard hovering over his shoulder. He held a glass of water in his cuffed hands and drank steadily. "I don't feel so good," he told the duty clerk. He held up the water glass. "Could I have a little more?" The clerk looked at the guard for permission. Mex had been drinking water steadily, first in his cell, and now in the office.

"It'll be a long while before you're near a head, soldier," the guard reminded him.

"I got cramps," Mex explained.

The guard nodded to the clerk, who took the glass over to the water cooler.

"Maybe you ought to see the doctor," the guard said.

Mex shook his head. "I'll be okay. Just nerves, I guess."

Baldinger had told him to drink all the water he could swallow. He was going to be deathly sick in just a few minutes, and the more he was able to throw up, the more convincing he would be. "It will just last a few minutes," Baldinger had promised. "But it has to look real."

The jeep turned into sight at a distant corner, and moved toward the stockade gate. Bobby Long braced himself. If it went according to plan, the MP driver would assume he was a prison guard, just as the stockade staff would assume he was one of the base MPs. The car turned into the gate and stopped.

"We're picking up a prisoner," the driver told Long. "For transportation to Fort Leavenworth," the sergeant in the front seat added.

"Pull right up to the front gate," Long instructed them. He was amazed at how authoritative he had managed to sound. He padded his part by pointing toward the front door. "Right over there," he ordered the driver.

The jeep parked at the stockade entrance, and the three soldiers climbed out and entered the building. As soon as they disappeared inside, Bobby marched to the open car. Now he had to try and act like a driver so that no one would be suspicious when he climbed into the jeep.

He pulled the hand-held radio out of its battery charger, and slipped his own radio into the socket. It was the identical model, and it clicked smoothly into position. He slipped the car radio onto his belt. The driver would never notice the difference. From now on, he would be taking his instructions from Jim Ray Talbert's radio instead of the one at MP headquarters.

He climbed out, and marched around the jeep to the backseat on the side farthest from the driver's seat. That was where the prisoner would be placed to make it difficult for him to interfere with the driver. Then he pushed a small, tinfoil packet down beside the seat cushion, where it would be out of sight, but still easy to find. Long paused for just a second to check his work. Then he marched back to his position at the parking lot gate, glanced around to be sure that no one was looking at him, and walked smartly away from his post and down the road. A minute later, behind the corner of the administrative building, he stripped off the white helmet cover, belt, and spats and strolled nonchalantly back to the barracks. It had worked. Just as Baldinger had promised, he had been totally invisible.

The transfer of responsibility for Corporal Cortines took place in the stockade office. One of the escorts, Sergeant Lansman, sat down at the desk, opened his briefcase, and presented his orders to take charge of the prisoner and return him to Leavenworth. A first lieutenant, the stockade duty officer, read the order, signed the acknowledgment, took one copy for his records, and handed the other back to the sergeant. Then he presented his own document, transferring custody of Miguel Cortines to Sergeant Lansman. This time the sergeant signed the acknowledgment, taking a copy for his records. He closed the case, saluted the officer, and turned to the prisoner.

"Corporal, you are now officially under my custody and will remain under my custody until I have handed you over to the commanding officer of the United States Army correctional facility at Fort Leavenworth, Kansas. Do you understand?"

"Yes," Mex mumbled.

The sergeant took his elbow and helped him to his feet. The prison guard took a key from his pocket and unlocked the handcuffs.

"You won't be shackled while you're being transported," Lansman said. "I'm advising you that both Sergeant Crimmins and myself are armed, and that we have orders to do whatever is necessary to prevent your escape. Do you understand?" Again, Mex acknowledged that he did.

He blinked his eyes when they stepped out into the sunlight. "Bright out here," he said.

Lansman climbed into the seat behind the driver, his briefcase on his lap. Sergeant Crimmins held the front passenger seat forward so that Mex could get in next to Lansman. Then he jumped in and sat next to the driver. The MP started the car, backed out of the parking space, and then swung out onto the road toward the airstrip. No one noticed that the guard who had waved them in was no longer at his post.

Mex reached down beside his seat and found the foil-wrapped capsule exactly where Baldinger had told him it would be. "I feel sick," he moaned to Sergeant Lansman.

"You'll be okay, son," the sergeant said kindly. "It isn't as bad as it seems."

Mex pretended to take the capsule from his pocket. He made no secret of tearing away the foil. "This is supposed to help," he said, almost to himself. He slipped the capsule into his mouth, and sat back while he waited for it to do its work.

The jeep had just cleared the fort's administrative area, and was approaching the narrow road to the airstrip, when Mex groaned. Lansman and Crimmins both turned in time to see him jam his fist against his mouth and lean out over the open side.

"Stop!" Crimmins ordered the driver, and the jeep skidded to a dusty halt.

Mex turned a sweat-soaked face toward Lansman. "I gotta get out. I'm gonna be sick."

The two sergeants made eye contact. Crimmins bounced down and pulled his seat forward. He gave Mex a wide berth as he staggered out.

"Just to the edge of the road," Lansman ordered. Crimmins's hand wandered down his side and opened the catch on his holster. But he didn't have to draw the pistol. Mex had only gone a few steps before he dropped down on his hands and knees. A torrent of fluid poured from his mouth. Again and again he retched, and when he looked up, his eyes were wide and unfocused. He folded his arms across his stomach and, in obvious pain, rolled over onto his back.

Sergeant Crimmins moved closer to him. "You okay, soldier? You going to be all right?" Mex grimaced but didn't answer.

"Cover me," Lansman told his companion as he jumped over the edge of the jeep and rushed up to Mex. He bent down close and winced at the foul smell of the vomit. "Are you in pain, son?"

Mex's fingers dug into his stomach. "Something exploded. In

here." He started to sit up, but then he pitched back up onto his knee, and the vomiting started all over again.

"He needs help," Lansman said to Crimmins. Sergeant Crimmins turned to the MP. "Get your headquarters on the radio. Tell them our prisoner is violently sick. We need instructions."

The MP was still staring out at the writhing form of the prisoner when he lifted his radio and keyed the power. "Base, this is Fourteen."

Out at the airstrip, Jim Ray Talbert heard the transmission. He lifted the radio to his mouth and pressed the send key. Now the whole plan depended on him.

The radio in the jeep hissed, and then a voice came back. "Fourteen, Base Station. Go ahead."

"This is Fourteen," the MP said. I've got the two escorts from Leavenworth and their prisoner. The prisoner is violently sick. The escorts think he needs a doctor. They want security instructions."

"Wait one, Fourteen. Be right back to you," Talbert's voice responded.

Talbert moved his lips as he counted. "Don't be too fast with the answers," Baldinger had suggested. "You're supposed to be checking with the officer of the watch."

When he reached twenty, he keyed his radio. "Fourteen, exactly where are you?" It didn't really matter where they were. It was just the kind of stupid question that would make the response sound more authentic.

"Eh . . . Base. This is Fourteen. I'm at the foot of the airstrip road. Just past the turnoff to the officers' club."

"Wait one," Talbert answered and then keyed off.

Mex rolled over on his back, again clutching at his stomach. "Man, I'm hurtin'," he groaned.

Lansman turned on the driver. "What the fuck is holding things up, soldier? This man is sick."

The MP pointed at the radio. "They'll be right back to us, Sergeant."

As if on cue, the radio crackled. "Fourteen, take him directly to the base hospital. Emergency entrance. We'll alert them. We'll get additional security over there right away." Mex tried not to smile when he recognized the voice that was ordering him to the hospital.

"Fourteen out," the MP answered. Then he shouted to Lansman. "Get him into the jeep. We gotta get him to the hospital."

Lansman unholstered his pistol and handed it to Crimmins. "Keep me covered," he reminded his partner. Then he bent over Cortines and lifted the prisoner's arm over his shoulder. "Try to stand up, son. We have to get you to the hospital.'' Mex turned onto his knees, and let the sergeant boost him to his feet. He stayed hunched over, his free arm folded across his midsection. Carefully, Lansman helped him back into his seat. Crimmins kept a distance, Lansman's pistol hanging loosely in his hand. It was a tribute to procedure. He felt no threat from their prisoner. Mex was clearly stricken, his face deathly pale and his breath coming in short gulps.

"Let's go,'' Lansman ordered the driver as soon as he was in beside Cortines. Crimmins jumped into the front seat of the already-moving car.

They turned back down the road they had just left, shot between two of the administrative buildings, and headed along a road toward the hospital. Mex was already feeling better, just as Baldinger had told him he would. He feigned a groan of pain. "They'll be waiting for us,'' the MP assured the two sergeants.

As they were pulling up to the hospital, the emergency room doors swung open. Two medical attendants in white outfits rushed out rolling a litter between them. One was in a surgical cap, with a white mask hanging loosely over his face.

"We'll take him, Sergeant,'' Art Walters said through the surgical mask. Lansman jumped out so that Walters could get in next to Cortines. Together with the other medic, Walters lifted Mex expertly from the car and stretched him out on the litter. Quickly, they snapped the safety harness around their patient.

"This man is a prisoner, sir,'' Lansman said. "He's in our custody.''

Walters nodded. "Come in with us, Sergeant.''

They pushed Mex up the ramp and through the swinging door. The two escorts followed right at their heels. There was a nurses' station just inside. "Sergeant, could one of you stop here and give the nurse any information you can?'' Walters asked over his shoulder. He never broke his stride as he rushed the litter through a second set of swinging doors and into the emergency treatment area. Lansman stopped at the station to answer the nurse's questions. Crimmins pulled up short as the door swung into his face. There was a large red sign: NO ADMITTANCE. MEDICAL PERSONNEL ONLY.

"I'll take it from here,'' Walters told the other medic. He pushed the litter through the doors of the trauma center. The room was empty because no one had been alerted to the arrival of an emergency patient.

"Okay, Mex,'' he whispered when he had released the restraints. Mex sat up like a body rising from the dead, and smiled as Art peeled off his mask and pulled the cap from his head.

"Goddamn! We did it!"

Walters was nearly laughing as he helped Mex into a wheelchair and began fastening the inflatable cast to his knee. They had done it. The first phase of Baldinger's plan had gone off without a hitch. They had gotten Mex away from his jailers. But the worst was yet to come. The two Leavenworth guards were prowling like cats outside a door that was only twenty feet away. There was nothing except a routine sign to keep them from bursting through the door. And they still had to get Mex off the post, past sentries who would recognize him instantly if they ever bothered to look at his face.

"Hang on, Mex," Walters said as he spun the wheelchair toward the door of the trauma room. "Here we go!"

He pushed the wheelchair out of the room, into the corridor, and turned away from the entrance area where the two sergeants were waiting. Then he took a right turn into a long hallway that ran through the basement of the hospital. He nearly collided with Tony LaRocca, who was sitting patiently in a wheelchair, his transportation orders resting in his lap.

LaRocca held out the orders, and Walter snatched them out of his hand as he rolled past. "Good luck, Mex." Tony smiled.

"Thanks, my friend," Mex answered.

Walters kept the wheelchair rolling toward the transportation dock.

LaRocca looked around. He was alone in the corridor. Calmly, he released the air from his temporary cast, took it off his knee, and stuffed it under his jacket. He winced at the ache in his knee as he raised himself out of the chair. Then, with the aid of the cane that had been leaning on the wall beside him, he slowly began to limp down the hallway in the direction that Art and Mex had just come from. His step was labored. The pain from his knee was spreading through his entire leg.

He turned past the empty trauma center, and pushed open the doors into the lobby. Sergeant Crimmins, who was pacing in the waiting room, looked up and stared directly into his face.

Normal, LaRocca warned himself. Act normal. You're just walking out of the hospital after treatment. They don't know you. They're not looking at you. They have other things to worry about. But it wouldn't be normal if he passed out and fell at their feet. That would attract a lot of attention and start people asking questions. And right now, his head was spinning. The searing pain was spreading like an electric current throughout his body.

*   *   *

Art Walters was suddenly part of a parade. The corridor had been empty when he had started pushing Mex toward the ambulance dock. But now it had come to life. An orderly had backed a patient out of the X-ray room and was rolling the chair straight toward him. Two nurses had swung another patient on a litter out of a doorway and were moving slowly directly in front of him. And two doctors had just turned toward him at the far end of the hallway.

"Don't look up," he whispered to Mex. Cortines was slumped in the chair, his military cap pulled down low over his forehead. But he couldn't cover his face. The last thing he wanted to do was look suspicious.

Walters broke into a big smile as the orderly and wheelchaired patient drew near. "How you guys doing?" he asked.

"Okay," the patient answered.

"There's a waiting line in X-ray," the orderly said.

They were both looking at Walters, and not noticing Mex.

*   *   *

Sergeant Crimmins saw Tony LaRocca struggling as he tried to juggle the cane and the heavy swinging door. He rushed forward and held the door for him.

"Thanks, Sergeant," Tony said. He smiled in gratitude, even though he wanted to scream out in his pain.

"You need a hand?" Crimmins asked.

LaRocca struggled to walk as easily as he could, without showing the crippled limp. He had to look as if he were supposed to be walking out the door on his own. "No, thanks, Sergeant. I got a friend picking me up."

He could feel the sweat on his forehead as he walked past the nurse's station, where Sergeant Lansman was still describing the sudden onslaught of his prisoner's illness. The nurse, he realized, might recognize him. Or she might find it strange that an ambulatory patient was leaving through the emergency room. Jesus, it could all end here. The whole plan could come crashing down with one question: "Hey, Corporal. Where are you going? You're not supposed to come through here."

*   *   *

Walters couldn't decide whether to speak or keep silent. The two doctors were walking right toward him. They were absorbed in a conversation, referencing a patient chart that one of them was carrying. Maybe they wouldn't even look up from their work.

He gambled on not distracting them, and kept moving quietly, over the sound of his own footsteps and the rubber wheels squeaking on the tile floor. The doctors' voices rose as they drew near, and then seemed deafening as they passed right next to him. But their eyes never lifted from the chart.

"Jesus," Walters heard Mex breathe in relief.

"Just a little further," Walters said reassuringly, although he knew that another test awaited them at the loading dock.

★   ★   ★

The nurse never saw LaRocca. She was so absorbed in writing down the information that Sergeant Lansman was giving her, that she wouldn't have noticed if LaRocca had been leading an elephant by his trunk. He pushed open the final door and stepped outside. Luther Brown was waiting, leaning casually on the fender of Baldinger's old station wagon.

Luther ran up the ramp and put a supporting arm around Tony's shoulder. "How's it goin'?" he asked.

"Hurts like a bitch," Tony said.

"Stop complainin'," Luther told him as he helped Tony into the front passenger seat of the car. "You're supposed to be exercisin' it."

★   ★   ★

The ambulance backed up to the transportation dock, and the driver, a white jacket over his uniform trousers, climbed out.

"Ya ready?" he asked.

Mex sat silently in the wheelchair, the cast visible on the the leg that was thrust out in front of him, his head bowed to hide his face beneath the peak of his cap. "All set," Art Walters answered, and he handed the driver Tony LaRocca's transportation order. The driver glanced at the document only long enough to find the copy he needed. He tore it from the folder and pushed it into his side pocket.

"Want some help?" he asked Walters.

"Just get behind him and take the chair away when I stand him up."

The driver walked around behind the chair. Walters stood in front of Mex and carefully lifted him to his feet. Then he walked him slowly away from the driver and into the ambulance. While he settled Mex onto the litter and fastened the safety belts, the driver was pushing the wheelchair off the dock and out into the outside corridor. When he returned, all he had to do was close the back door of the ambulance.

Walters pulled a blanket up over Mex's chin. "I think we got it made," he told his patient. "The guards at the gate don't usually bother to look inside."

★　★　★

Luther Brown pulled the station wagon up to the gate. "Smile," he ordered Tony LaRocca. "Look like your goin' on leave." The best LaRocca could manage was a tight-lipped wince. Brown got out of the car, walked around to the back, and opened the tailgate. The guard took a quick glance through the car windows, then stuck his head through the tailgate, and poked through the folded blanket and the empty beer cartons.

"Okay," he told Luther. Brown climbed back into the car and waved at the guard as he drove off the post. He went straight to the parking lot where the car was usually kept. Dave Baldinger and Willie Derry were waiting, and they jumped into the backseat.

"How we doing?" LaRocca asked.

"So far, so good," Baldinger answered. He held up the radio he had been listening to. "Nobody has reported anything over the MP frequency. I don't think they suspect anything yet."

"Great," Luther Brown allowed as he pulled the station wagon out of the parking lot and out into the street traffic.

"Not yet," Baldinger answered. "We don't have anything until the ambulance clears the gate."

★　★　★

Sergeant Lansman jumped to his feet as soon as the nurse reappeared from the emergency area. She was carrying the forms that Lansman had helped her fill out.

"How's he doing?" he asked.

She shook her head. "I don't know, Sergeant. They must have taken him right up to surgery. I'll call up and see if I can get some information."

343

"He's not in there?"

"No, he's not," she said. And then she allowed. "Or he may be in X-ray. I'll call around."

Lansman followed at her heels as she marched back to her desk. "Is there an MP in there with him? The guy is a prisoner."

"I'm sure I don't know," she answered.

He hesitated for an instant, unsure of exactly what he should do. Then he ran out into the parking lot where his MP driver was leaning back in his seat, his feet draped across the passenger seat.

"They have him inside," Lansman announced. "I want to be damn sure that there's an MP in there with him."

The driver lifted his radio. "Base, this is Fourteen."

"Go ahead, Fourteen," Jim Ray Talbert answered. He was beginning to feel like the military police base radio operator, even though he was still hiding in the grass near the airfield.

"This is Fourteen. I'm at the hospital. That prisoner I was takin' to the airstrip is inside. The sergeant from Leavenworth wants confirmation that we got a guard posted with him."

"Wait one, Fourteen. I'll get back to you," Talbert's voice announced. Then he clicked off.

Lansman stuffed his hands into his pockets and paced nervously beside the jeep. After a few turns, he snapped, "How long does it take to get an answer to a simple goddamn question?"

The driver shrugged.

"Fourteen, this is Base."

"Fourteen," the driver keyed.

"Fourteen," Talbert drawled, "we have two guards posted with the prisoner inside the hospital."

Lansman shouted at the driver, "Ask him where they are. Which room? The people here don't know."

The MP registered his annoyance. "Base, the sergeant wants to know where they are. Which room?"

The radio crackled. "Wait one, Fourteen," Talbert told him.

*　*　*

It was a few minutes later when the ambulance reached the front gate. The driver held his copy of Tony LaRocca's orders out the window, and the guard looked it over. Inside the ambulance, Art Walters held his breath. He had been out of touch with the outside world since the

344

ambulance pulled away from the hospital. For all he knew, Mex's escape had been discovered and the entire Airborne division had been turned out to bring him back.

"What's happening?" Mex asked in a whisper.

"Shut up," Art Walters hissed. "Just keep your head turned away and don't make a sound."

The door latch clicked, and the back door of the ambulance flew open. The military police sentry put his white-spatted boot over the tailgate, and started into the back of the ambulance.

Art Walters held up his hand. "Keep it quiet," he snapped in a stage whisper. The guard stopped with his head just inside the door. Art leaned toward him. "He just passed out. Poor son of a bitch has been in a lot of pain."

"What happened to him?" the guard asked Art, jerking his head towards the form that was strapped to the stretcher.

"Tore up his knee," Art said. "One of them crazy Green Berets. We got him all doped up."

"I thought those assholes were always doped up." The guard laughed.

"You wake one of 'em and they attack anything that's movin'," Walters laughed back.

"Get him the hell outta here," the guard agreed. He stepped out and closed the door carefully behind him. The ambulance rolled quietly through the gate.

Art Walters dug a playful punch into Mex's ribs. "Goddamn it! We made it, Mex. We're out."

Mex sat up smiling, and Walters had to push him back down onto the litter. "Just stay put, Mex. We got one more stop to make."

*　　★　　★　　★*

Luther Brown drove slowly, sticking to the far right, with two wheels bouncing on the uneven shoulder. Willie Derry was turned in his seat, looking out through the tailgate back down the road.

"I don't see nothin'," he repeated for the third time. "Maybe somethin' went wrong. Maybe they stopped 'em at the gate."

"Nothing went wrong," Baldinger said calmly. He waved the hand-held radio that was tuned to the military police frequency. "If they were on to something, we'd have heard about it."

"Yeah, well where the hell are they?" Luther demanded. "They shoulda passed us already."

"Bingo!" Derry suddenly shouted. Baldinger turned and Brown looked into his side mirror. The ambulance had appeared behind them and was overtaking them rapidly. Luther steered toward the center line and added some speed. He watched as the ambulance continued to draw near. The headlights flashed behind him. He eased back to the right and the ambulance swung across the dividing line and roared past. Baldinger pushed the button on the detonator. He looked up, expecting to see the ambulance falter. But, instead, it seemed to be gaining speed and pulling away from them.

"What the hell is wrong?" Brown demanded as Baldinger hit the detonator key again and again.

"Nothing's happening," Dave said. He felt a stab of panic deep inside his gut. The whole plan would collapse if they couldn't stop the streaking ambulance. The last thing they wanted was to have their escaped prisoner delivered to the stockade at Fort Bragg.

"Damn it!" Baldinger cursed. He hadn't turned the unit on. He threw the switch on the edge of the detonator. "Get me closer, Luther. The son of a bitch is getting away from us."

"I got it all the way to the floor," Luther Brown snapped. "This tub ain't no drag-racer."

"Jesus," Willie Derry prayed.

Baldinger rolled down the window and held his arm out into the airstream. He pushed the button again. Underneath the ambulance, right next to the fuel pump, the relay that Dickie had installed the night before clicked.

It took several seconds before the ambulance driver noticed the loss of power. He pumped the gas pedal, and for a moment, the engine seemed to be responding. But then it began sputtering, and a few seconds later it died.

"Christ," he cursed. He snapped on his flashers and steered toward the side of the road. In his mirror, he could see the car he had just passed coming up behind him. He stuck his arm out the window and waved furiously. When he came to a stop, he was relieved to see that the car was pulling in behind him.

He got out just as Luther Brown and Dave Baldinger were stepping out of the wagon. "Somethin' wrong?" Brown asked, walking toward him.

The driver threw up his hands. "Fuckin' thing just died."

"You have gas?" Baldinger speculated.

"Of course I got gas," the driver said angrily. "Whatta ya think. I'm drivin' down to Bragg without any gas?"

"I'm a mechanic," Luther told him. "Let me take a look."

The ambulance driver reached into the cab and popped the hood. Then he joined Baldinger and Brown, peering in at the silent engine.

"You got a screwdriver?" Luther said, looking knowingly.

The driver went back to the cab to get the toolkit. As soon as he was out of sight, Brown pulled the feed wire from the distributor.

"I got your problem right here," Luther told him when he returned to the front of the car. "Take a look. Down under all these wires." The driver's head disappeared under the hood.

Baldinger reached out and signaled to Willie Derry in the station wagon. Derry eased open the door and helped Tony LaRocca hobble up to the back of the ambulance. He opened the door. Mex was already on his feet and he stepped out as LaRocca climbed in. While Art Walters was helping LaRocca onto the stretcher, Willie Derry was pushing Mex through the open tailgate and onto the back deck of the wagon. He spread the blanket over his friend and closed the gate.

"All you gotta do is make sure this stays on," Brown was explaining to the driver. "I got it on nice and tight, so you shouldn't have any trouble. But if it happens again, all you gotta do is reconnect it."

"Think it'll get me to Bragg?" the driver asked.

"No sweat," Luther Brown said. "Should be as good as new. Get in and give it a try."

While they were talking, Baldinger pressed the button on the detonator that he carried in his pocket. He thought he heard the relay snap shut under the car.

The engine ground over for several seconds before it caught. Then it settled into a pleasing hum. The driver jumped back out and extended his hand to Brown. "Hey, thanks a lot, guys. I don't know what I woulda done without ya."

Luther waved away the compliment. "Nothin' to it. Just lucky we happened to be passin' by."

* * *

Back at the hospital, the radio in the jeep crackled. "Fourteen. This is Base," Jim Ray Talbert's voice announced. Sergeant Lansman nearly jumped into the jeep to hear the transmission.

The MP driver keyed his radio. "Fourteen," he answered.

Jim Ray's voice told him that the prisoner was in surgery. "It's pretty serious. You won't be hearing anything for a couple of hours.''

Lansman stormed back into the hospital where the nurse raised her hands in bewilderment. ''I still can't find him,'' she said.

''Try your goddamn operating room,'' Lansman snapped at her. ''The guy is in surgery.''

She looked surprised.

★   ★   ★

Inside the ambulance, Art Walters and Tony LaRocca were giddy with their success. The plan had worked to perfection, leaving not even the trace of a trail that could lead anyone to Mex. LaRocca had been checked out for transportation to Fort Bragg, and that's exactly where he was heading. The driver held orders to deliver Corporal Anthony LaRocca to the fort's medical center, and it was Anthony LaRocca who would be helped out the back door of the ambulance when it reached Bragg. All the pieces of paper would fit together. There would be nothing to investigate.

Sooner or later, someone was going to identify the medic who had helped Walters bring Mex into the emergency room. And eventually they would realize that the masked doctor who had rushed up to the medic and ordered him to meet an emergency arrival hadn't really been a doctor at all. But when they started questioning people about their whereabouts, the one member of the hospital staff they wouldn't bother to question would be Art. ''Waste of time,'' someone would say. ''He was off the base, bringing a patient down to Bragg for therapy.'' Which was exactly where Art was.

★   ★   ★

Dickie Morgan, Tom Cavitt, and Bobby Long were waiting in the recreation room when Jim Ray Talbert danced up the steps of the barracks. ''We done it! Goddamn, we done it.''

''They bought it?'' Cavitt asked. He was already laughing in anticipation of the answer.

''Hook, line, and sinker,'' Jim Ray said. Then he imitated his radio voice. ''Eh, Fourteen. Your prisoner is still in surgery. But don't worry. We've got guards all over the place.''

They howled at the thought that the escorts from Leavenworth were still waiting outside the emergency room. ''When do ya think they'll catch on?'' Dickie Morgan chuckled.

Talbert speculated, "Maybe when the guys out at the airstrip get tired of waiting and call the MP headquarters to find out what happened to their passengers."

"Or maybe when MP headquarters begins to wonder what happened to its jeep and driver," Cavitt offered.

They knew their hoax couldn't go on forever. The MP base station wouldn't be able to reach the jeep. And now that Talbert was off the air, the jeep wouldn't be able to reach anyone. Headquarters would insist that it had never gotten a message about a critically ill prisoner. The two sergeants would sputter that they had heard the radio exchanges. Lansman would scream that he had personally been told by the MP base station that Cortines was in surgery and under guard. And about that time, in the midst of all the finger-pointing, someone would think to check the radio. But they'd run into a dead end when they tried to figure out who had switched it. No one would remember an MP in the stockade parking lot. And they'd never know whom the driver had been talking with.

"Jesus, we really pulled it off," Talbert said jubilantly.

"Not yet," Cavitt reminded them, as he looked at his watch. "Mex ain't on the plane yet."

★   ★   ★

Luther Brown swung the station wagon up the driveway to the Greenville airport terminal building, and then made two turns around the access circle. Dave Baldinger and Willie Derry searched for any signs of military activity; a parked jeep or a posted guard. They had been monitoring the military police radio channel, and there had been no hint that Mex's escape had yet been discovered. But they weren't taking any chances.

They stopped just long enough for Derry to jump out and hurry into the terminal. He scanned the waiting lounge, the restaurant area, and the ticket counters. Then he peered across the metal detectors and security X-rays into the gate area. There was a crowd of people boarding an outgoing flight, but nothing that looked at all out of the ordinary. Finally he checked the monitors to make sure that Mex's flight was still on time. He walked back to the circular access road and got back into the car.

"Clean as whistle," he reported. "The flight leaves in twenty minutes."

Baldinger handed Mex his ticket, along with an envelope of leave papers, all in a fictitious name. "You ready, Mex?"

"Ready," he said.

Brown leaned over the seat and held out his hand. "Be seein' ya."

Mex slapped his palm. "I'm gonna miss you, my friend."

"Amigo," Luther answered.

Baldinger, Derry, and Mex got out of the car and walked into the terminal.

"Almost there," Baldinger whispered to Mex.

"Piece of cake," Derry added.

They walked confidently up a broad corridor, past the ticket counters, and toward the waiting area, their pace quickening with every step. Before they could sit down, the boarding announcement for Mex's flight echoed over the public address system.

"That's it," Baldinger said. They continued on up to the security gate, almost skipping in childlike anticipation.

"We done it, Baldinger," Willie Derry sang. "The best Special Operations mission ever, and we pulled it off."

Then they pulled up short. Twenty feet ahead, and walking straight toward them, was Captain Henry Roy.

"Oh, Jesus," Dave Baldinger prayed.

Roy hadn't yet seen them. He seemed to be involved in his own thoughts. But he was about to bump into them. They stood frozen, uncertain of what to do, leaning first in one direction and then in another. They had to hide. But there was no place to hide. A sudden rush out of his way would only attract Captain Roy's attention. They were out in an open area. There was simply no escape. Their defeat and capture was about to walk into them, the unexpected element that they had been taught over and over again to expect.

The captain looked up, at first seeing only the uniforms. His arm began to move up in the perfunctory gesture of returning a routine salute. But then his eyes cleared. His hand hesitated. He scanned the faces. And he recognized his former students.

They stood motionless, understanding that they had been caught. The joy of their escapade and the thrill of their victory drained like wine out of a suddenly shattered glass. They could read the confusion in the captain's face. Then, they saw his instant of understanding as his gaze zeroed in on Corporal Cortines.

Baldinger saluted. He wanted to say something, but his mouth had turned to glue. Derry raised an uncertain hand in salute. Mex didn't move. He and the captain simply stared at each other, just as they had stared across the courtroom a few days earlier.

Roy automatically returned the salute, but his eyes never left Mex's face. Finally, Baldinger managed to say, "Afternoon, sir."

The sound of Dave's voice broke through Henry Roy's trance. He glanced at Dave. "Good afternoon, Baldinger." Then at Willie, "Corporal Derry."

"Captain," Willie Derry acknowledged in a voice that was barely audible.

Roy turned back to Mex. "Good to see you, Cortines."

Mex was still frozen. He couldn't make a sound.

"Where are you heading?" Captain Roy asked.

Mex swallowed hard. "Home, sir." Then he mumbled, "Just home."

The captain nodded. "Have a safe trip," he told Mex.

He stepped around the three dumbstruck soldiers, and started down the corridor. But before they could catch their breath, he stopped and turned back to them.

"Corporal Cortines," he called.

Mex turned slowly to face him. "Yes, sir."

"I'm sorry," Henry Roy told him. "Truly sorry."

He didn't wait for Mex's response. He turned smartly and marched across the waiting area.

Mex, Dave, and Willie watched him until he disappeared through the terminal door. None of them made a sound.

The boarding announcement was repeated over the address system. Mex held out his hand to Baldinger.

"Thank you, my friend. I hope I'll see you again."

Dave nodded and shook his hand.

"Thank you," he repeated to Willie Derry.

Derry started to shake hands, but then he threw an arm around Mex and hugged him. "It ain't goin' to be the same without ya, amigo."

Mex broke free, nodded, and then stepped through the security checkpoint and walked toward his plane. Dave and Willie waited until the plane taxied away from the gate.

THE
GRADUATION

★   ★   ★

They marched across the parade grounds, toward a small, flag-draped reviewing stand that had been set up between the ceremonial cannons. The uniform was dress greens, trousers tucked into glistening boots, with the berets cocked slightly to the right. Sergeant Major Thompson was a step to the left of the rank, calling out the cadence in his booming baritone.

"Right col-umn, march!" They turned a sharp corner and marched parallel to the reviewing stand until Thompson commanded them to halt. "Uh-left, face!" They snapped around into a line abreast, facing the reviewing officers. Then Thompson bellowed, "Pree-sent, ahms!" In unison, the squad snapped to a salute.

Colonel Grigg, who had stood like a uniformed statue in the center of the reviewing officers, returned a firm salute. The officers who flanked him, Major Daks to his right and Captain Roy to his left, followed his example. "Or-der, ahms!" the sergeant major commanded, and squad dropped their hands to a position of attention.

"Special Operations candidates ready for inspection, sir!" Thompson announced.

Grigg stepped down and trooped the line, marching in front of the squad for a cursory inspection. "Outstanding," he complimented Thompson when he had reached the end of the row. "A great job, Sergeant." Then he climbed back up on the reviewing stand, and ordered Thompson to bring his troops to parade rest.

"It's an honor to be with you men," Grigg began, launching into his graduation speech. He didn't need any notes. He had delivered the same message dozens of times before. But it wasn't a memorized text. Rather, it was always the same because it came from his heart. Like a prophet, he had no need to rehearse the words of the one true god. "An honor, because you are truly the best that our country has to offer. Dedicated to its ideals and its traditions. Trained to defend it against the jealous, cunning, dark forces that would subvert its ideals. Ready to lay down your lives to preserve its precious freedoms."

Grigg was undistracted by the normal routine of Fort Francis Marion that was passing around the periphery of the parade grounds. Nor was he troubled by the recent events that had threatened the sanctity of the Special Operations mission. The conviction of Corporal Migual Cortines was a detail of the past, lost in the countless procedures, the mountainous files of paper forms that were the fuel of every military organization. His escape was nothing more than another notation in a record that reached back to Valley Forge.

"Corporal Cortines, while in the custody of guards from the United States Army Correctional Facility at Fort Leavenworth, Kansas, effected his escape from the grounds of Fort Francis Marion, and became a fugitive at large."

Federal authorities and local police forces had been given his description, photograph, and fingerprints, along with the request that he be apprehended on sight. Officially, the Army was pursuing him with vigor. Actually, it hoped it would be spared the annoyance of ever having to deal with him again.

"He isn't our problem," General Wheeler had smiled, nodding toward the receipt for his custody that the Fort Leavenworth guards had signed and left behind them. "They lost him. It's up to them to find him."

Grigg had nodded in agreement, hoping that no one in the Army would spend a great deal of effort searching for the corporal. He guessed that Cortines had already disappeared into Mexico, or maybe back into his native El Salvador. With his Special Operations training, he could provide a nasty surprise for military investigators from any country who were unfortunate enough to catch up with him. Worse, if someone did bring him back, then there would be a further opportunity for his story to attract the attention of the press or some television junk documentary show. The safest place for Cortines was wherever he had chosen to begin his new life. The colonel hoped that no one would disturb him.

"Your mission," Grigg's commencement address continued, "will often demand great initiative. Separated from the chain of command, undermanned, and outgunned, you will have to confound your enemies."

"Ain't that the fuckin' truth," Willie Derry whispered from the corner of his mouth.

Dave Baldinger supressed a smile. They *had* decided for themselves how to serve the cause of freedom. And they had certainly confounded their enemies. No one in the Fort Viper chain of command could understand why the escorts from Leavenworth kept insisting that their prisoner was in surgery. And no one could document the radio transmissions that the guards swore they had heard. There were no records to be found in the base radio logs. The MP driver, when he had been unable to raise his dispatcher, had assumed that his radio was broken. He had simply turned it into the repair facility and drawn a new one. In the repair facility, a technician had taken it apart, replaced its circuit board, and returned it to service. There was no longer any physical evidence that the radio had been altered.

Nor did anyone suggest a connection between Cortines's escape and the breakdown of an ambulance on its way to Fort Bragg. The driver showed the mechanic the wire that had disconnected from the distributor cap, and the mechanic pulled the ambulance out of service long enough to rip out and replace its electrical system. The ambulance was put back into service with a new electric line connecting the alternator to the fuel pump. Tom Cavitt's radio-actuated relay was discarded with the old wiring.

Captain Robert Gordon knew who had engineered Mex's escape. He had called the pay phone in the barracks recreation room and asked for Corporal Baldinger.

"I was told by the captain I'm relieving that my client escaped from the stockade," he said.

"That's what we've heard, sir," Baldinger told him.

"I didn't think that could be done," Gordon said, his voice on the edge of laughter.

"It can't," Dave answered. "The command here has no idea how he pulled it off."

"I hope he's not in any danger."

"None that we know of, sir. If I had to guess, I'd figure he's out of the country, working on a new life for himself."

"And the squad? Is everyone okay?"

"Couldn't be better, sir. We all graduate tomorrow."

"Give everyone my congratulations, Corporal. I truly admire what you've been able to accomplish. I'm glad you all made it."

"Thank you, sir. I'll tell them." Baldinger had paused for a moment, and then added, "Captain, I plan to get out after my tour and go back to school. I think I want to be an attorney."

Gordon understood what he was saying. "Thank you, Corporal. I'm flattered. I appreciate the compliment."

"See you in court, sir."

"See you in court," Captain Gordon had answered.

And Captain Henry Roy knew. In fact, he had joined the conspiracy when he looked Corporal Cortines in the eye, and wished him a safe journey. But everyone else in the command at Fort Francis Marion was completely baffled. The recruits had, indeed, confounded their enemies.

Grigg moved toward his conclusion. "You are a select group of men. A small force that might seem insignificant in the roster of the world's armies. But you have a most significant mission. You are the guardians of your country's honor, the guardians of the honor of its fighting forces. You have been specially trained to operate on your own. You will often have to decide for yourselves what course of action your mission requires. To help you make that decision, I can give you one unfailing rule. Always act to defend the honor of your country and the honor of the United States Army. When in doubt, act like a guard of honor, and you can be certain that you have chosen the right course."

Grigg stepped down onto the parade grounds and approached the squad. Major Daks and Captain Roy fell into line behind him. Sergeant Major Thompson called out the name of each candidate as the colonel reached him, and Grigg took the Green Beret medallion from Major Daks and presented it to the soldier.

"Corporal Luther Brown."

Grigg handed Luther his shield and shook his hand.

"Congratulations, Brown. You're the one who cleared the way for the Airborne, aren't you?"

"Yes, sir."

"Outstanding. An honor to be serving with you."

"Thank you, sir."

They saluted.

Colonel Grigg paused in front of Willie Derry.

"Derry, I'm glad you made it. For a while, we had our doubts, but you've proven your worth."

"Just confounding the enemy, sir," Willie Derry answered from his position of military attention.

Grigg smiled and nodded. "Keep up the good work."

"I intend to, sir," Willie assured him.

"Corporal David Baldinger," Thompson announced.

Grigg handed him his shield, complimented him on his class-leading score, and shook his hand. As Grigg moved to Tom Cavitt, Major Daks stood in front of Dave.

"Outstanding performance, Corporal. I'd be proud to have you in my command."

"Thank you, sir."

And then Captain Henry Roy stopped in front of Baldinger, their faces only a few inches apart.

"Congratulations, Baldinger."

"Thank you, sir. Thank you for your help."

Roy hesitated. "No, I should be thanking you, Corporal. We all should. You saw things clearly. And you made the right call." He tipped his head toward Colonel Grigg. "The honorable call."

"I hope so, sir."

Captain Roy continued on down the line, mouthing compliments to each of the graduates. But his attention wandered away from the parade grounds. He was thinking of Carol, who was already in the air, flying back to Fort Viper. He didn't know what she had decided. But he had already made up his mind. His life was with her and he thought she would be pleased with his choice.